COLLECTOR'S EDITION

How to Lose a Lord in Ten Days

Sophie Irwin's debut novel, *A Lady's Guide to Fortune-Hunting*, was an instant *Sunday Times* bestseller and has since published in nearly thirty countries worldwide.

Sophie grew up in Dorset before moving to south London after university. She has spent years immersed in the study of historical fiction, from a dissertation on how Georgette Heyer helped win World War Two, to time spent in dusty stacks and old tomes losing herself in Regency London for research.

Her love and passion for historical fiction bring a breath of fresh air and a contemporary energy to the genre, and Sophie hopes to transport readers to a time when ballrooms were more like battlegrounds.

@SophieHIrwin
@sophie.irwin

Also by Sophie Irwin

A Lady's Guide to Fortune-Hunting
A Lady's Guide to Scandal

SOPHIE IRWIN

How to Lose a Lord in Ten Days

HarperCollins*Publishers*

HarperCollins*Publishers* Ltd
1 London Bridge Street
London SE1 9GF

www.harpercollins.co.uk

HarperCollins*Publishers*
Macken House, 39/40 Mayor Street Upper
Dublin 1, D01 C9W8, Ireland

First published by HarperCollins*Publishers* Ltd 2025
1

Copyright © Irwin Editorial Limited 2025

Sophie Irwin asserts the moral right to
be identified as the author of this work

A catalogue record for this book
is available from the British Library

ISBN: 978-0-00-869674-0 (HB)
ISBN: 978-0-00-869675-7 (TPB)

This novel is entirely a work of fiction.
The names, characters and incidents portrayed in it are
the work of the author's imagination. Any resemblance to
actual persons, living or dead, events or localities is
entirely coincidental.

Set in Adobe Caslon Pro by HarperCollins*Publishers* India

Printed and bound in the UK using 100% Renewable
Electricity at CPI Group (UK) Ltd

All rights reserved. No part of this publication may be
reproduced, stored in a retrieval system, or transmitted,
in any form or by any means, electronic, mechanical,
photocopying, recording or otherwise, without the prior
written permission of the publishers.

Without limiting the exclusive rights of any author, contributor or the
publisher of this publication, any unauthorised use of this publication
to train generative artificial intelligence (AI) technologies is expressly
prohibited. HarperCollins also exercise their rights under Article 4(3)
of the Digital Single Market Directive 2019/790 and expressly reserve
this publication from the text and data mining exception.

This book contains FSC™ certified paper and other controlled
sources to ensure responsible forest management.

For more information visit: www.harpercollins.co.uk/green

For Lucy,
the hardest bit about writing this dedication was not discussing
it with you at great length – which, I think, says everything

1

'*Who* wishes to marry me?' Lydia demanded, looking up from her novel in some alarm.

'I can hardly believe it myself,' Aunt Agatha said, pulling vigorously at the bell to call for Lydia's maid. 'Quick, let us tidy your hair – we mustn't keep him waiting.'

Turning a deaf ear to Aunt Agatha's wittering was one of Lydia's chief policies in life – what one didn't hear couldn't upset one – but today it was clear she had missed something rather crucial.

'Keep *who* waiting?'

Aunt Agatha ignored her. In a few deft movements she had pulled the book from Lydia's hands, Lydia from her armchair, and deposited her at the dressing table, where – too impatient to wait for assistance – she began to tug at Lydia's chignon herself.

'How on earth do you dishevel so quickly?' she muttered.

Lydia submitted to the manhandling without protest, too busy cudgelling her brain for any gentlemen who might be desirous of marrying her. Not one came to mind.

'If your grandfather could only see this,' Aunt Agatha breathed. 'You to wed to such a person as this!'

Lydia reached up to still her aunt's hands.

'Of whom can you possibly be speaking?' she asked.

'Were you not listening?' Aunt Agatha demanded. She drew in a rapturous breath and declared, with the same fervour their Vicar invoked Jesus Christ Our Lord and Saviour: 'It is *Ashford*!'

Lydia stared. Had the disappointment of Lydia's second failed Season sent Aunt Agatha mad?

'Aunt . . .' she began, slowly and carefully – she did not wish to upset her fragile faculties further – 'That is utterly absurd.'

For the Marquess of Ashford, Earl of Bath and future Duke of Ancaster, one of the highest-ranking peers in England and certainly the most eligible, most certainly did not wish to marry Lydia, Miss Hanworth of Nowhere, Lady of Nothing. Why, she was barely better born than Aunt Agatha's pug and given the fastidious Ashford had already rejected several diamonds of the *ton*, Lydia did not think pug was the level at which he wished to settle.

'It is beyond anything I dared to dream.' Aunt Agatha said, pulling tightly on Lydia's hair. 'I had not thought his attentions were *serious*.'

Neither had Lydia. They were barely acquainted, their first conversation occurring only a fortnight earlier, and in their encounters since, Ashford's manner had never been the least loverlike. He was always so entirely proper, so perfectly correct.

'Is it possible he has come to the wrong house?' she wondered aloud. 'Perhaps he meant to offer for Miss Callow, across the square.'

The state of the masculine intellect meant such a mistake – though embarrassing – was not improbable.

'What nonsense,' Aunt Agatha tutted. 'Consider: this must be why Lady Phoebe invited you and Pip to her house party. Ashford must have requested she do so!'

Two days before, Lydia and her brother had received billets from Lady Phoebe Henley, Ashford's enormously wealthy and tremendously fashionable cousin. The invitation to join her house party at Hawkscroft House had been flattering but incomprehensible. Until now.

'Lawks,' Lydia breathed, stunned.

'Mind your tongue!' Aunt Agatha snapped, with an accompanying jab of a hairpin to strengthen the reprimand. 'If you dare utter such vulgarities in front of Ashford, I shall see you speedily regret it. Recollect, he could have anyone!'

'He *could* have anyone,' Lydia said, 'so why me? It is not as if *he* requires my dowry.'

It was plain that most gentlemen found Lydia's impressive dowry by far the most alluring part of her character.

'Ladies do not to speak of such things,' Aunt Agatha said, weaponizing her pin once more. 'You might try to look more pleased! A thousand women should die for such an opportunity as this!'

This was true. Alas, Lydia was not one of them.

'I decline,' she said.

'What?'

'I do not wish to marry him.'

'*Why?*'

'I care not for him.'

Aunt Agatha could not have looked more shocked than if she had been run through with a sword.

'I do not understand,' Aunt Agatha said. 'You have danced with him happily enough . . .'

'I could not exactly refuse him,' Lydia pointed out. 'Though I should have, had I been able. He is dreadfully haughty, you know.'

Aunt Agatha's hands fell from Lydia's hair to her shoulders and clenched.

'Do you mean to tell me,' she said, 'you wish to decline a proposal from a marquess, because *you* do not care for *him*?'

Lydia's heart began to quicken, but she raised her chin and forced herself to her aunt's gaze.

'If you could tell him that I am very sorry,' she said. 'But—'

'You cannot decline, Lydia,' Aunt Agatha interrupted. 'You cannot! After all this family have worked towards, all these years . . . It would ruin us.'

The Hanworth family might be passably respectable now, but it had not always been so. Lydia might be the daughter of a gentleman, but she was the granddaughter of a wool merchant. For her to refuse so lofty a member of the peerage . . . there would be talk. Unpleasant talk, and lots of it. If each step of the Hanworths' climb from the streets of Cheapside to the lofty townhouses of Berkley Square was the work of two generations, a fall from grace would be the work of a moment.

But Lydia could not live her life according to such fear. She could not.

'You promised it would be my choice,' she said.

'Ashford will one day be a *duke*,' Aunt Agatha said. 'You ought to be falling over yourself to choose him.'

'I do not want him!' Lydia interrupted. 'Does that not signify?'

'I have introduced you to every eligible gentleman I could place my hands on,' Aunt Agatha's cheeks were turning blotchy with emotion, 'and you have not wanted any of them!'

'You and I have wildly different definitions of eligible,' Lydia muttered.

Indeed, judging by the specimens Aunt Agatha could 'place her hands on', the whole breed of man was in a state of emergency.

'At times, I should even suspect you of purposefully driving them away!' her aunt accused.

Lydia worked to keep her expression clear. For Lydia *had* developed certain strategies for repulsing unwanted suitors out of Aunt Agatha's sight and earshot. It was not difficult. Gentlemen of quality had high standards, and while they might be willing to overlook Lydia's birth for a chance at the Hanworth fortune, they were less willing to endure poor behaviour. Thus, Lydia had found most marital inclinations could be cured by the liberal application of her foot upon theirs during the waltz, or, failing that, a single lecture on her Views on Shakespeare.

'You are impossible,' Aunt Agatha raged on, pressing a hand to her forehead. 'You and your brother, both. What is wrong with you? You with your romantic turns, Philip with his—'

'There is nothing wrong with Pip,' Lydia said fiercely.

They glared at each other for a long moment, as bristling and hackled as a pair of alley cats.

'If you do wish to reject Ashford's suit, then on your head be it,' Aunt Agatha said, in a voice both calmer and colder and no less intimidating for it. 'But I will not ease your way. *You* shall have to tell him.'

She turned to the wardrobe, selected a fuchsia pink sash from within and motioned for Lydia to stand and turn. Lydia obeyed, reluctantly.

'Of course, such a choice will not be without consequence,' Aunt Agatha said. She held Lydia's eyes. 'If you refuse such an offer, your uncle will send you to Aunt Mildred.'

Lydia's breath caught, and not just because her aunt was tightening the sash around her waist to mythical proportions. The threat of living in rural isolation with Aunt Mildred – severe, austere, and only marginally more animated than a slug – had for years served as Lydia's very own sword of Damocles.

'You must prevent him,' Lydia said. 'Persuade him . . .'

'He is my husband,' Aunt Agatha said. 'I must obey his wishes.'

Lydia's chest was constricting. If only she had a moment to catch her breath, but there was none, for Aunt Agatha was giving each of her cheeks a pinch and pulling her from the room.

'Recollect everything I have taught you,' she said, speaking low and fast. 'Smile, but without teeth. Speak quietly and briefly and only when spoken to, laugh at his jests, *without* teeth.'

Lydia followed blindly.

She could not become engaged, now, not to someone for whom she did not care a fig. Yet could she truly face such consequences as these? Her reputation tarnished, sent far away from everything and everyone she knew?

There had to be a way out. If only she could *think*, but it was impossible with Aunt Agatha still hissing in her ear.

'Speak only of ladylike subjects: no talk of dowries, your grandparents, or any financial matters. You will utter no vulgarities, use no cant. You will not sing.'

'Why on earth would I sing?' Lydia protested.

'No singing!'

They were downstairs, now, and nearing the library, and in the next moment, Aunt Agatha was pushing open the door and thrusting Lydia inside. Lydia blinked into the gloom. The two men standing before the unlit fireplace turned at the sound of the door: Uncle Edmund, face beaming, and . . . Ashford.

Lydia's stomach sank into her shoes. Until that very moment, there had still been a part of her sure this was all some grand misunderstanding, but it really was him, dark hair and light eyes, handsome in face and frame and looking so terribly elegant, his coat and boots bearing the unmistakeable signs of the kind of expert craftmanship of which Uncle Edmund only dreamt. In appearance, he was the sort of person one might be very pleased to be in love with, if one had the inclination. Unfortunately, to Lydia, he had all the romantic allure of a tree stump.

'Good morning, Miss Hanworth,' Ashford said, making a very proper leg.

'Good morning,' she said, her voice a little hoarse. Aunt Agatha gave her a little press in the back. 'My lord,' she added hastily.

'No doubt your aunt has informed you, my dear,' Uncle Edmund said, bouncing on the balls of his feet, 'that I have just received a *very* distinguishing a proposal for your hand.'

'Yes,' Lydia said, her voice small, her courage depleting with every moment that passed. She had been raised to consider the peerage as akin to gods and disliking Ashford did not render him any less intimidating.

'It is a tremendous honour . . .' she began.

What on earth was she going to say? What words could she find to make such a rejection acceptable in his eyes? She could not anger him. One word from him, in the right ears, could destroy her reputation forever.

'I . . .'

Uncle Edmund's face darkened as Lydia hesitated. Aunt Agatha had not been making idle threats. Lydia would not be allowed to remain in this house, once she rejected Ashford.

'Do you require some time to consider the matter?' Ashford asked, and for the first time that morning, he was smiling, as if the thought of Lydia considering his proposal had amused him. There was no part of him that thought she would decline, then. Such arrogance!

'Mere shyness!' Uncle Edmund insisted, shooting Lydia a glare.

'She is a little surprised,' Aunt Agatha agreed. 'We all are, my lord.'

'I know that our acquaintance is not of a long duration,' Ashford conceded, 'and I could not show too particular an interest until I received my father's blessing.'

Aunt Agatha nodded her fervent understanding. 'No amount of time, however,' he continued, 'could make me any more certain of your niece.'

He turned to regard Lydia, more directly and for longer than he ever had done before . . . but as Lydia stared back at him, she felt no warmth. No excitement.

'Truly?' Lydia checked and felt Aunt Agatha's warning hand upon her back again.

'Yes,' Ashford said, smiling again as if her disbelief were charming. 'I knew it from our very first meeting.'

Their first meeting?

'Love at first sight!' Aunt Agatha cooed her approval.

Ashford inclined his head. Lydia felt as if she were trapped in some peculiar dream.

'Well, tell his lordship how you answer, my girl,' Uncle Edmund instructed Lydia.

'He has not asked me anything yet!' Lydia said, stung out of her silence.

Aunt Agatha pressed her back again, but Ashford did not appear to take heed of her rudeness, drawing out an enamelled snuffbox from his pocket and, unconcerned and unhurried, flicking it open.

'I am here, today, to ask if you would do me the very great honour,' he said, 'of becoming my wife.'

In novels and plays, a proposal was usually accompanied by excess of emotion: tears, choked voice, shining eyes at the very least. It had never, to Lydia's knowledge, been followed by a gentleman taking a pinch of snuff to each nostril. This was wrong. This was all *so* wrong, but Lydia did not know what to do, how to fix this, and everyone was looking at her. Ashford, brows faintly raised in question, Uncle Edmund frowning meaningfully – she could even feel Aunt Agatha's glare upon her back.

Lydia took in a deep breath. She just had to say it. Just had to say the words – and be sent to Aunt Mildred, and sentenced to a miserable life until she could find some means of escape.

'Miss Hanworth?' Ashford prompted.

'Um, I-I—' she stammered.

She had spent her whole life exerting effort to curb her tongue and yet now, when she needed words most, they were gone from her.

'A-a great honour,' she managed, with difficulty. 'And I – yes, I . . .'

She had not finished the sentence. How it was to end, she did not know, but when Uncle Edmund heard 'yes', he began clapping his hands.

'No! I—' Lydia began.

'I think this calls for a tipple,' Aunt Agatha said, reaching for the bell, and then Ashford was approaching.

Lydia took in another sharp breath. *Decline, now*, she told herself. *You can still decline, now.*

'You have made me very happy,' he said, bending his head briefly over her hand. She had seen men display more emotion over purchasing a horse!

Say something, anything, a voice in her mind was clamouring at her. *Stop this now, before it is too late.*

'I . . .'

Nothing came. Whatever magic words could have averted this horror, she could not muster them. For the next half hour, she was silent, watching as Aunt Agatha and Uncle Edmund, eager as puppies, swarmed around Ashford, almost beside themselves with nervous joy, assailing him with a flurry of flattery and questions and trivialities. Ashford, in turn, was civil and calm. He gave responses that were courteous but not encouraging, behaving toward them, in short, with the polite tolerance of one who considers himself superior. He stood to take his leave at the earliest opportunity, explaining that he was bound for Kent that afternoon.

'Before I go,' he told them, 'I must ask that news of the engagement be kept between us.'

'We . . . cannot send a notice to the journals?' Uncle Edmund asked, smile fading. He had no doubt planned to write to every journal, every single member of their acquaintance just as soon as Ashford left the room.

'My father wishes to announce the betrothal himself,' Ashford said. 'At Lady Phoebe's masquerade ball. His Grace has . . . a strong sense of occasion.'

An edge of fond exasperation entered his voice as he spoke about his father. It was the most emotion he had shown all morning.

'I will depend upon your discretion, until then.'

His tone brooked no argument.

'Of course, of course,' Uncle Edmund said. 'I should rather *die* than—'

'It is to be kept secret?' Lydia interrupted, her voice returning at last.

'Such disappointment,' Uncle Edmund said archly. '*Someone* is eager to spread the news!'

It was not disappointment rising in Lydia's chest. It was hope.

'For ten days, only,' Ashford told her. 'The duke's request.'

'And you shall be at Hawkscroft, together!' Aunt Agatha said.

'Yes, of course.' Ashford sent another smile in Lydia's direction. She did not return it. 'I thought her house party would make a fine opportunity to introduce Miss Hanworth into our circles – before the news of our engagement is made public.'

'So kind,' Aunt Agatha enthused. 'Lydia was so excited to receive the invitation!'

She had not been.

'And kept asking me what she should expect and pack, the dear thing.'

She had not.

'It will be an intimate affair,' Ashford said. 'Ten of Lady Phoebe's nearest and dearest, with all the usual fare: riding, dining, and, on the final night, the masquerade ball.'

'And none of them will know,' Lydia said, 'of our – our engagement?'

Aunt Agatha and Uncle Edmund threw twin glares her, but Ashford was unruffled.

'I imagine they will suspect us of courting,' he said, 'but otherwise, it shall be our secret.'

And with a final bow, he bade them farewell. They remained entirely silent in the library until the sound of the front door was heard closing firmly behind him. Then, Uncle Edmund let out a whoop of joy and Aunt Agatha began chattering excitedly at the top of her voice. Neither of them acknowledged Lydia and she remained entirely silent.

It was not a devastated silence this time, however, but rather a thoughtful one. Matters were not so dark as they had first appeared. She would not be getting married to Ashford, of that she was certain – and neither would she be banished to Aunt Mildred. How, she did not yet know, but she would think of something.

A great deal could be achieved in ten days, after all.

2

Monday – Ten days remaining

'You oughtn't marry a fellow you don't like,' Pip said firmly. 'Fact is: nonsense.'

As soon as Lydia could quit her aunt and uncle's company, she had sent for her brother with utmost urgency. Pip had come at once, without question, as Lydia had known he would. Ever since a bout of influenza had felled both their parents and grandparents the year she turned ten and six, it had been she and Pip against the rest. While Pip, in his gentlemen's lodgings might not be quite as ruled as Lydia was by Aunt Agatha and Uncle Edmund, he was still beholden to their guardianship.

Not half an hour after she had sent her missive to Duke Street, Pip appeared upon the doorstep and together they had crossed the cobbles of Piccadilly, eschewing Hyde Park – at this hour always thronging with barouches, curricles and strolling dandies – in favour of the quieter Green Park.

'Although, Grandfather would have been pleased,' Pip acknowledged.

Lydia's stomach twinged. Grandfather would likely have cried with happiness to think of his granddaughter as a future duchess, and his instructions would certainly have aligned with Aunt Agatha's. On this matter, however, Lydia preferred to think of what her grandmother might have advised. As romantic as Grandfather was ambitious, it was Grandmother who had regaled Lydia with stories of their own courtship, a Love at First Sight Affair followed by a madcap dash to the altar. Caring little for the family fortune, she had valued kindness above all else and had – to her very last day – refused to allow status to alter one ounce of her character.

'I will not marry someone I do not love,' Lydia said, raising her chin resolutely, 'not for anyone.'

The chilly, practical alliances made by her aunt and mother – trading independence for social advancement – did not in any way appeal to her. Since Lydia had sufficient wealth and standing to be comfortable, the advantages of marriage, to her mind, lay solely in the heart. Since girlhood she had clung to the dream of romance shown to her by her grandparents and thereafter in stories, novels, theatre. If that was not to be fulfilled . . . Well, she was not foolish enough to believe a loveless arrangement would be any sort of consolation. She would, by far, rather remain unwed.

'Might come to care for him,' Pip said. 'That's what they say happens, anyway.'

'How could I make such a gamble?' Lydia said. 'I hardly know him, and he certainly does not know me.'

Yet, somehow, Ashford had decided that she was the one for him. Had felt 'certain' of it from their very first meeting. Lydia shook her head to think of it. For far from Love at First Sight, for her, it had been Dislike at First Conversation.

It had occurred at the Alcot ball, just three weeks previous. With Aunt Agatha distracted by their illustrious surroundings, Lydia had been able to escape her chaperonage for a moment. She had heard their hosts kept a most magnificent library and was determined upon finding it. For Lydia was just about *sick* of the Season, so bitterly disappointed had she been by almost every gentleman to whom she had been introduced. Their flaws might be diverse, but each one displayed an identical condescension when speaking with her, acting as if their conversation alone were a grand favour. Worse, beyond a cursory investigation of Lydia's key attributes – dowry, family history, accomplishments – they appeared to be medically incapable of asking her a single question. Perusing bookshelves was far more appealing than attempting to jostle a conversation out of whatever Mr Lacklustre Aunt Agatha might conjure up.

Lydia had taken a wrong turning, however, opening a door to find not the library, but a long, darkened corridor. She had taken only a few hesitant steps inside when the door at the other end opened, and two gentlemen began strolling towards her. Lydia froze.

'His Grace did not approve the match?' said one gentleman.

'Another refusal,' the other confirmed. 'My father's standards are quite ridiculous.'

It took Lydia only a moment to identify who was speaking. The Hanworths might not receive vouchers to Almack's, but they were invited to enough high society parties to make these voices recognizable: the Honourable Mr Brandon, who could be depended upon to cajole even the shyest young debutantes into conversation, and Lord Ashford, whose determined appearance at every ball in town had the *ton* twittering that he intended to take a wife.

Carefully, Lydia took a few steps backwards. To eavesdrop on a private conversation, between such persons as these, would not be wise. She could only hope that the dim light would prevent their noticing her and then exclaiming all over town that Miss Hanworth was a rotten lurker.

'Such hypocrisy, Ashford,' Mr Brandon said, amused. 'Were you not the gentleman who deemed Miss Mablethorpe "hen-witted"?'

Lydia's back was at the door now, her hand groping for the doorknob, but at this she paused, ears pricking. Miss Mablethorpe was widely considered a diamond of the first water, and the gossip rags frequently identified her as the perfect match for Ashford. Thus far, however, Ashford had kept them all guessing, spreading his attentions so impartially amongst the young ladies of the *ton* that no one of them was elevated above her contemporaries.

'She didn't know the name of our Prime Minister,' Ashford said. 'I hardly think that a high bar.'

Lydia's hand fell away from the door, listening agog. She would not leave her post now for a hundred pounds.

'Then what is wrong with Miss Callow?' Brandon said. 'She speaks three languages!'

'Oh, I know,' Ashford said. 'She peppers conversation with enough "*Sacre bleu*"s to make everybody perfectly aware of that.'

'Lady Evelina?'

'Her family is deplorably eccentric.'

Lydia did not know what to think. On the one hand, such peremptory dismissal of ladies widely considered paragons, as if they were all Ashford's to evaluate and find wanting . . . Did it not display rather shocking superiority? Yet on the other, was this not the same pickiness Aunt Agatha regularly berated Lydia for?

'You must have thought Miss Spalding perfect, then, if you were considering courting her in seriousness.'

'I did,' Ashford said. 'And Miss Dudley *and* – well. My father seems determined to reject any young lady of the *ton* I suggest.'

Brandon laughed.

'Half of London's ladies deemed unworthy by you,' he said, 'and the other half, by your father! There's some irony in that predicament, isn't there?'

'You may well laugh,' Ashford said. 'But what am I to do? I cannot marry without his approval.'

'Perhaps you ought to look outside the *ton*,' Brandon said. 'Is it so important that she be high-born and accomplished and all that rot?'

Ashford was apparently so surprised by this suggestion that he halted his footsteps. 'You propose I engage myself to some Cit's daughter?'

Mr Brandon drew to a stop with him.

'They are not all title-hunters hoping for a leg up in the world,' he reasoned, as if this was some grand humanitarian concession. 'You might consider it.'

'Perhaps I would,' Ashford said haughtily, 'if such a person could conduct themselves properly. Do you truly think any woman from that class could make a serviceable duchess?'

Serviceable? Whatever kinship Lydia had felt rising within her towards him halted abruptly. It was all rather less fascinating when *she* was one of the ladies being peremptorily deemed wanting – a title-hunter, hoping for a leg up in the world? Ashford and Mr Brandon were just the same as the rest of them, then. Arrogance in the aristocracy was plainly as universal as their all-too-often enormous chins.

Wrapped up in her indignation, Lydia did not immediately notice that Ashford had turned away from Mr Brandon again, but when he began to continue along the corridor, she came back to herself with a start. He was no longer strolling and his long gait was eating up the distance between them. There was no time to flee without detection. Thinking fast, Lydia gave the doorknob a wrench, threw it open, and took two hasty strides into the room, for all the world as if she had only just walked through it.

The plan worked in one sense. There was no sign, in Ashford's face, that he suspected her of eavesdropping and yet, because Lydia had misjudged the length and speed of her steps versus his, she only narrowly avoided colliding directly into him and made an instinctive grab for his arm to prevent herself from toppling over.

'Steady!' Ashford barked, alarmed.

'I am so sorry!' Lydia gasped, flushing hard and withdrawing her hand. 'I did not mean to . . .'

In hasty recollection of her manners, she dipped into a mortified curtsey.

'I don't believe we've met,' Mr Brandon said, drawing level with them. 'My name's Brandon.'

'Oh – I'm Miss Hanworth?' Lydia said.

'Sounds awfully familiar,' Mr Brandon said. 'Perhaps I know a brother?'

'Hanworth Wool,' Ashford put in.

'Oh!' Mr Brandon said. 'Oh – yes, of course.'

Lydia raised her chin, fighting against a wave of embarrassment. Why ought she be embarrassed? They all wore wool, didn't they?

'I'm sorry, I was just looking for – for . . .' she said, tripping over her words and hating herself for it.

'The ballroom, I should think?' Mr Brandon said helpfully, seeming as cheery as Ashford was chilly, as fair as he was dark. 'Perfect! Ashford, weren't you just saying you need a partner for the waltz?'

'Was I?' Ashford said. 'My wretched memory, but I do not recollect . . .'

He and Mr Brandon stared at one another for a beat, embroiled in a silent argument that ignored Lydia entirely. She stood there, pink-faced and awkward, wishing, desperately that she had left the corridor when she'd had the chance, until Ashford turned back, extending a hand to Lydia in unenthusiastic invitation.

Indignation warred with humiliation in her chest. How she wished she might decline the offer! But she could not, could she? It could very well ruin her whole Season. Besides, she had heard what he had said. A hot-headed rejection would be just the mannerless behaviour he would expect from a Cit's daughter, wouldn't it? No, she would not give him the satisfaction.

'I should be delighted,' she said primly, placing her hand upon his arm and smiling at him – without teeth – just as she had been taught. Indeed, for that dance, and every interaction that followed, she made sure to follow every single directive Aunt Agatha had ever taught her: speaking quietly and briefly and only of ladylike subjects, professed a fascination in every one of his opinions while having none of her own and laughing at all his jests (such as they were).

'I just wanted to prove him wrong,' she bemoaned now. 'I had no *notion* of where it would lead.'

'You think that's why he fell in love with you?' Pip asked.

'Can he have fallen in love with me? That seemed to be what he was suggesting, with the proposal.'

'A good first clue,' Pip agreed.

'But he has given no other sign of it!'

She had noticed – of course she had, Aunt Agatha had been tickled pink – that he had begun asking her to dance, whenever they were both at the same ball, had begun spending a few minutes in her company whenever they crossed paths, but she had not thought much of it. He did, after all, still dance and speak with every other young lady presented to him, in just the same manner.

'He's a very starched-up fellow,' Pip observed, 'but his affections *must* be engaged. Stands to reason. Why else would he stoop so low?'

'Stoop?!'

'What I mean is,' Pip corrected himself hastily. 'He has no dearth of options, does he?'

'Apparently there *is* a dearth,' she said. 'No lady thus far has been able to meet his impossible standards.'

Was it possible that her perfect behaviour had not only encouraged him, but also somehow made her attain every item on his – and the duke's – implausible specifications? Or was Pip correct, and did Ashford's tepid warmth mask a deeper attachment?

'It doesn't signify, anyway,' she reminded. '*I* don't love *him*.'

'Only one thing for it,' Pip said. 'Have to cry off. Pay a visit to him today, before this house party nonsense.'

His expression darkened at this fresh reminder of their impending departure from London.

'I don't mind telling you, it's come at a very inconvenient time,' he added. 'What if there is a case, while I am away?'

A month previous, Pip had – by utter happenstance – aided

the Bow Street Runners in apprehending a thief, accidentally tripping the fellow as he fled the scene of the crime. The experience had captured his imagination: overnight, he had taken to smoking a pipe, wearing a quizzing glass and haunting their offices to 'assist' in investigations.

'Mr Simmons has just begun tutoring me on my investigation skills,' Pip said, aggrieved.

Mr Simmons was a Senior Officer at Bow Street. Lydia did not know the *exact* nature of their relationship, but the fellow was certainly the idol to which Pip currently worshipped. Not an hour went by that he was not quoted, imitated, or otherwise referenced.

'It was not my idea!' she said. 'Besides, Ashford has already left for the country.'

'Suspicious,' Pip said darkly. '*Very* suspicious.'

Since he had begun working with the Runners, Pip declared a great many things to be suspicious.

'You'll have to do it in Kent, then,' he said. 'Can't promise he'll take it well, and then you could still set your cap at Captain von Pratt.'

'Von *Prett*,' Lydia corrected, kicking at a stone.

Ah, the noble captain! She had met Captain von Prett, the celebrated explorer, at his lecture a week earlier, and it had been – for her at least – a *coup de foudre*. Her heartstrings had been pulled by his moving tribute to his late wife, and a few brief moments of eye contact had sent her heart to thumping for hours afterwards. Understandably, she was desirous of pursuing the acquaintance. But first she needed to get out of this cursed engagement. Ladies were, technically, permitted to call off engagements – if they accepted the accompanying shame – and Ashford's insistence on secrecy should make that all the easier, but there was still Uncle Edmund and Aunt Agatha to consider.

'I'd be sent to Aunt Mildred, as quick as a flash,' she said.

'I'd fetch you back,' Pip said, 'as soon as I come of age, and then we might live independently, at last.'

Lydia and Pip had been plotting to leave their aunt and uncle's guardianship ever since it had begun. Once Pip turned one and twenty, he would be in full possession of his fortune, and no one could stop them from setting up house together. Technically, it was less than a year away, but . . . Lydia cast Pip a quick, evaluating glance. As a man, he was less beholden than she to the diktats of their aunt and uncle, but not by much. He was expected to marry well, also, and more than once over the past years, they'd had to work together to avoid Pip's marriage, too. And Pip . . . Without her here to defend him, to keep his secrets and prevent the worst of his scrapes – would he be all right? Or would Uncle Edmund bully him into marrying some horrid young lady who would make his life miserable, just as soon as Lydia was out of sight? Lydia kicked moodily at another stone. At this rate, Ashford would be responsible for ruining two lives, rather than just one.

'If he only knew what an abominable choice I am,' Lydia said. 'Far worse than those other ladies. Without Aunt Agatha constantly in my ear, I would forever be forgetting people's names and curtseying the wrong way and – and . . .'

'Using vulgar expressions,' Pip supplied.

'Yes, and I can't sing—'

'At *all*.'

'I'm terrible at embroidery, my French is awful—'

'Your Italian is worse!'

'If Ashford knew all that, he'd soon regret his choice,' Lydia said. 'And everything would be solved.'

She stopped walking. It took several moments for Pip to realize she was no longer beside him, looking back enquiringly.

'I cannot cry off,' she said. 'But *he* could.'

'Wouldn't do that,' Pip objected. 'Not when he's only just proposed. Fact is, dishonourable.'

This was true. While ladies could call off engagements – if they were willing to bear the social consequences – most gentlemen viewed such dishonour as utterly impossible. Except . . .

'The engagement *is* to be a secret for ten days,' she said. 'He could call it off within that time and nobody should know except Aunt Agatha and Uncle Edmund – and they'll not likely broadcast such shameful news.'

They began walking again, faster now, their disconsolate drift turned purposeful march.

'If he could be made to see that he had made the most terrible, ghastly mistake,' she said, 'then he might do something drastic.'

'How would you do such a thing?' Pip said. 'Not certain telling him all about Shakespeare will cut the mustard this time.'

That was also true. Ashford did not seem the type to risk his honour without extreme provocation. Lydia remembered the way he had said 'Cit's daughter', that night at the Alcot ball, as if such people were more beneath him than worms in the soil. Aunt Agatha's rules had plainly worked magic on him, glossing over her woolly roots – but what if she ceased to behave by them? Or, indeed, what if she did the opposite? The vulgar, social-climbing, mercenary merchant class the *ton* feared was a largely fictional creation, but it need not be.

'If I wear the wrong things,' she said thoughtfully, 'and say the wrong things, and behave the wrong way . . .'

'Would it be sufficient?' Pip said dubiously. 'Fact is, I don't know the fellow.'

'Nor I,' Lydia said. All she knew was that he thought himself so above the most accomplished, most beautiful, most wealthy young ladies of the *ton*, that he had rejected each of them for the most frivolous set of flaws she had ever . . .

'He rejected Miss Mablethorpe for being hen-witted,' she recalled aloud, 'and Miss Callow for saying French words, and Lady Evelina for her eccentric family and for being capricious.'

She could not believe she had not realized it earlier. Lydia took in a deep, decisive breath. 'If I act vulgarly and foolishly and pompously . . .'

'Oh ho!' Pip said, catching on. 'Wouldn't Aunt Agatha smell a rat?'

'As foolishly and pompously and vulgarly as I can,' Lydia corrected, 'without Aunt Agatha suspecting a thing.'

If word of her behaviour reached her aunt and uncle, they would certainly consign her to Aunt Mildred.

'What of the eccentric family?' Pip said. 'Perhaps I can help on that front.' He raised his quizzing glass to his eye and squinted thoughtfully through it.

'Might be difficult though,' he said. 'Fact is, not really the eccentric type.'

Lydia's mind, so full of sludge this morning, was alive again and whirring.

'If you wish to practise your investigation skills,' she said, 'why not practise them at Hawkscroft?'

'Aunt Agatha doesn't like me to investigate things at parties,' Pip said. 'Says people don't like it.'

'Yes,' Lydia said. '*Exactly*, Pip.'

'Oh *ho*,' Pip said in sudden understanding. 'Yes, with all those fancy coves in one house together, there's bound to be a secret or two to uncover,' he mused. 'Stands to reason. *That* would impress Simmons, wouldn't it?'

His chest puffed up at the mere thought and a sudden shard of guilt cut through Lydia's enthusiasm.

'This doesn't have to involve you,' she said. 'I could make your excuses, find a reason for you to stay in London.'

'If you're in it,' Pip said, 'I am, too. Stands to reason.'

Lydia's mood lifted in a great rush. All at once, everything that was dark and worrying became bright and hopeful once more, as if the sun had abruptly risen and rendered the world light again. She had been foolish to think, even for a moment, that today was the day Ashford ruined her life. Today was, as every day had been, simply another chance for her and Pip to eschew Uncle Edmund's diktats, to dance around this pitfall as they had every other.

'First,' she said, 'we need to visit Pantheon's Bazaar today so I may purchase a new wardrobe.'

'Tick!' Pip asserted.

'Then tomorrow we go to Kent, where I shall wear the wrong thing, and say the wrong thing, and do the wrong thing.'

'Tick!'

'And you shall investigate things.'

Pip gave a triumphant clap of his hands.

'Tick!'

Lydia took in a rapturous breath of sweet, summer air. What a beautiful park. What a wonderful day.

'If we can do all that,' she said, 'I shan't need ten days to get rid of him. I shall do it in two!'

3

Tuesday – Nine days remaining

Ashford did not make mistakes. He may have been born to a great position and greater privileges, but the freedom to err was not amongst them. While gentlemen his age blundered for a pastime, Ashford did not. There was simply no need. For if one thought through every decision with reason and rationality, as he always did, then one's life would always proceed on the proper and correct course, as his always had. There was no reason to believe his marriage would be any different.

Certainly, the process had not been without difficulties. From the outset, a great deal of carefulness was required, for he did not wish to raise in any maidenly heart expectations he could not fulfil. Then, there was the fact that so very many people were so very irritating: scores of the pompous, witless and eccentric littered the ballrooms of London and, as much as Ashford needed to marry, he would not do so at the cost of his sanity. One must have standards. Finally, the *pièce de résistance*: once he had waded through this trap-laden battleground to find several ladies he could imagine courting, his father had rejected every single one of them.

He had almost been driven mad with the frustration of it all. Then he had met Miss Hanworth.

'She took me entirely by surprise,' Ashford told his cousin in the East Drawing Room of Hawkscroft House, accepting a cup of tea from her butler with a smile of gratitude.

'Oh, how *wonderful*,' Lady Phoebe enthused, clapping her hands in approval. 'You must tell me everything – quickly, before Waldo returns.'

Quitting London directly after proposing, Ashford had arrived at Hawkscroft House, the country home of his cousin, Lady Phoebe, and her adoring husband, yesterday evening. It was only now, however, the following afternoon, that he and his cousin had been able to speak properly for Sir Waldo clung to Phoebe's side with the commitment of a lovelorn barnacle.

'I saw quickly that she was exactly what I was looking for,' Ashford said.

'Love at first sight!' Lady Phoebe interpolated breathlessly.

Ashford took a sip of tea rather than answer. One did not wish to lie, of course, but to correct the assumption felt unwise, too.

'I'm not sure that's how I would describe it,' he said. This was at least true.

'Have I embarrassed you?' Lady Phoebe asked gleefully.

'You needn't be so delighted.'

'I *am*, though,' Lady Phoebe said. 'Truly. I was beginning to think, after everything, that you might never allow yourself such happiness.'

Again, Ashford took a draught of tea rather than answer.

'It was not so many years ago that you were declaring you would *never* marry for love,' Lady Phoebe said, still smiling. 'I thought, then, that you had become so frightfully dour that you should never be happy!'

Ashford raised his eyebrows. '*Frightfully* dour?'

'Oh, the hours I have spent worrying about you,' she said. 'Wondering what happened to the boy who used to swap my sugar for salt at breakfast and tie my shoe strings together at dinner?'

'I grew up,' Ashford said. 'I should think if I were still tying people's ribbons together you might have something to say about it.'

'But look at you now! So head over heels that you are willing to marry a merchant's daughter!'

'Granddaughter,' Ashford corrected.

'His Grace has approved, I take it?' Lady Phoebe asked. 'Or will it be a runaway match?'

Ashford shook his head. 'My father sent his approval by letter – he left for Scotland two weeks ago.'

It was more than mere duty that required Ashford to seek such approval from his father: family law stipulated that the heir could not marry without the permission of the incumbent duke, a clause created generations before to protect the family from scandal. In his father's hands, however, this power was being used to different purpose. His own marriage having been a famous love match, the duke had always believed his son would find happiness by this means, too, no matter Ashford's own views on the subject.

'Oh, His Grace could not possibly resist such a story.' She let out a rapturous sigh. 'Love overcoming rank!'

This was rather the point. For while Ashford had known that his father wished him to marry for love, he had not thought the duke would actually insist upon it. And yet that was exactly what his father had done, rejecting every suitable lady Ashford had suggested to him.

'It is quite plain that you do not feel a single thing for her!' he had accused, at their last meeting. 'For any of them!'

'Father, there are other considerations that weigh more with me,' Ashford had tried to explain, but to no avail.

His father could not be made to understand how seriously encumbered their Norfolk lands had become. A decade of harsh winters and severe flooding had taken their toll, despite Ashford's best efforts. Now, if they did not wish to lose estates that had belonged to their family since the Norman conquest, they needed substantial investment. A suitable marriage to a woman of fortune was the simplest means of averting disaster.

'I wish for your heart to be taken, not your head, my boy,' the duke had said, hands gripping Ashford's shoulders as if he should like to shake him. 'You will not receive my approval for anything less. The next time you wish to engage yourself, I must know it to be different. I must know it to be love.'

It had been an unwanted complication. Ashford was determined to marry this year, and marry well – but how on earth could he appease his father's wishes?

It had been Brandon who had given him the idea, though he had scoffed at it initially. The future Duke of Ancaster, marrying beneath his own class? It was absurd. But then – as if by fate – in the next moment he had met Miss Hanworth, of Hanworth Wool. Miss Hanworth, who had been so perfectly behaved that he had immediately begun to reconsider the whole idea: well-mannered, well-deported, *very* well-dowered, and obviously dangling after a title . . . It was perfect. And if Miss Hanworth's family line was not one his family would traditionally greet with approval, then that was all to the good – who would doubt, that Ashford's heart had been caught when his bride was so far beneath him?

His father had fallen for it through and through.

'Are you certain you do not mind his announcing the engagement at your ball?' Ashford asked his cousin now.

His Grace had landed upon the idea with a characteristic lack of consideration for the preferences of others – who was to say Lady Phoebe wished her party to be commandeered in such a way? – though, on this occasion, it rather played into Ashford's hands. To have this week with Miss Hanworth, ahead of the announcement, to introduce their courtship to the *ton*, easing Miss Hanworth into the world that would soon be her everyday . . . It was a sensible strategy.

'Not in the least. I only wish he could join us earlier,' Phoebe said. 'Oh, Ashford, I am thrilled for you!'

Ashford held her gaze with some difficulty. He did not enjoy lying, and to his cousin least of all, but it was a necessary evil. She was of the same ilk as his father, romantic to their very bones. They would not understand, not believe him, if he told them that a marriage of convenience was no great sacrifice. For him, it had always been about duty.

'My only concern – a mere trifling question,' Lady Phoebe went on, adjusting her skirts, 'is whether she will know how to conduct herself, this week?'

'Rather uppish of you, Phoebe,' Ashford said.

Lady Phoebe flushed guiltily. 'All I mean to say is that if she has never even been to Almack's, are you not worried such an environment might be overwhelming?'

'That is entirely the purpose of the invitation,' he said. 'When the engagement is announced, all eyes in England will be upon her so better she begins her education in relative anonymity.'

By the end of the week, he was confident he could give a solid enough performance that his father would have no qualms that this was a love match. He did not intend to debase himself – or embarrass Miss Hanworth – with lavish displays of affection for it would be entirely out of character. No, that would be quite unnecessary. From his observation of the sentiment, some people expressed love through subtler means: liberal smiles, solicitous behaviour, and a desire to spend time with one's lady would suit well enough.

'I do not mean to be churlish,' Lady Phoebe rushed to assure him. 'It is just . . . I have not been to a single party all spring; this week is important.'

Lady Phoebe had not joined this year's Season – the first she had missed since her own debut – electing instead to remain at Hawkscroft with only her husband for company.

'That was your choice,' Ashford reminded her. 'Due to your "social *ennui*".'

Lady Phoebe paid him no heed. 'I have *plans*. I wish for us to laugh, play games, have intelligent conversations, exchange witty repartee . . .'

A tiny frown crumpled her expression.

'She will not ruin your party,' Ashford said. 'She is the most perfectly behaved creature, I assure you.'

Lady Phoebe visibly softened at the warmth in his voice. It was genuine warmth. Ashford placed great value on good conduct.

'I shall not say another word on the matter,' she promised. Then, as the clock behind her struck two, Lady Phoebe rose from her seat.

'Come, it shall not be long before the guests arrive,' she said. 'Let us take a turn.'

Hawkscroft was a vast building, built more to impress than invite, with towering gothic gates, a tall sweep of front steps flanked either side by stone gargoyles. It was not Sir Waldo's ancestral home. The second son of a Baron, Sir Waldo had instead gained his title and his fortune through employment in the East India Company, and then he had purchased Hawkscroft from Lord Cavendish, whose debilitating financial troubles had forced him to part from his ancestral seat. Even the oldest families could find themselves crumbling. Despite the warm summer air, Ashford felt himself shiver.

'Come along!' Lady Phoebe said with a chivvying noise. Her definition of taking a turn constituted less of a relaxed stroll and more of a brisk patrol of Hawkscroft's acres of intricately designed gardens, as she cast a critical eye over each tree, shrub and window, searching for any tiny flaw.

'If I am to be on show in front of the busiest gossips in Society,' she explained, 'then every single thing and every single moment will be absolutely perfect.'

'Keeping expectations manageable, I see,' Ashford said. 'Can I do anything to assist matters?'

'No! You might run yourself ragged year-round,' Lady Phoebe said in reprimanding tones, as she plucked a tiny wilting bloom from a nearby hydrangea bush 'but this week, I am determined that you will *rest*.'

'Ho there!'

The bellowed greeting had them turning, rather startled, to see Sir Waldo approaching, a wide smile upon his face. He was older than Lady Phoebe, a gentleman of five and thirty years, and quite as generously proportioned as his home: very tall, very broad and possessing the thickest side whiskers Ashford had ever seen.

'Has anyone arrived yet?' Sir Waldo boomed, no less quietly for being with touching distance. Volume modulation did not come naturally to him.

'Not yet,' Lady Phoebe trilled, beaming at her husband, all worry gone from her face. Sir Waldo always did seem to bring out the sunshine and rainbows in Lady Phoebe, her impatience and sharpness vanishing in his company.

'Usually Dacre is so prompt,' Sir Waldo said, reaching out to clasp his wife's hand, quite as if they had been parted for a year rather than an hour. 'Though *why* you insisted upon inviting him, I cannot understand!'

'He *is* your brother,' Lady Phoebe pointed out, as they resumed their walk at a more sedate pace.

'He's a bore,' Sir Waldo said. 'He'll bore our guests to death, mark my words.'

'Not with Brandon and Lady Morton attending,' Lady Phoebe said. 'They can be counted on to keep things lively.'

'A famous collection of persons,' Sir Waldo said with renewed enthusiasm.

'And,' she said, with the air of a circus magician revealing their final trick, 'the Hesses are to join us – all three of them!'

Ashford frowned at his cousin.

'You did not tell me that,' he said.

Lady Hesse had spent the better part of the Season trying to matchmake him with her daughter, Miss Cynthia Hesse. She would certainly use this week as an opportunity to promote her suit once more.

'Did I not?' Lady Phoebe said. 'It is a coup, indeed. You know,

Lady Hesse has just been appointed the new Lady Patroness of Almack's and I mean to make a friend of her if it is the last thing I do.'

'Such an ambitious little thing,' Sir Waldo said indulgently. 'Well, I for one am most looking forward to meeting your lady-love, my lord!'

He threw a jocular elbow into Ashford's side. Ashford forced a smile but, once Waldo had turned, directed a fierce frown at his cousin, who gave a blithe, unrepentant shrug. He had asked Lady Phoebe not to tell Sir Waldo of his engagement – what was the point of it being a secret if it wasn't one?

'I would thank you not to refer to her as such,' he said. 'Remember, no one can know we are engaged until . . .'

'Yes, yes we remember, very *very* secret,' Lady Phoebe said.

'We shall be the souls of discretion, dear boy,' Sir Waldo promised.

Sir Waldo had taken to affectionately calling him 'dear boy' since his marriage to Phoebe, as if there were twenty years between them rather than ten.

The sound of a throat clearing had them all turning.

'Excuse me, Sir Waldo, my lady, my lord,' Reeves informed them. 'The first guest has arrived.'

Lady Phoebe smoothed a hand down the front of her dress. 'How do I look?'

'Very well,' Ashford said.

'A vision,' Sir Waldo enthused. 'Though why do you not wear your diamond necklace?'

Ashford raised his eyes to the heavens. Any fool could see that Sir Waldo's engagement gift to Lady Phoebe – the most ostentatious string of diamonds anyone had ever clapped eyes upon – would be utterly unsuitable for to wear with a morning dress of jaconet muslin.

'What is the point of it,' Sir Waldo said in a stage whisper louder than most people's shouts, 'if one does not show it off?'

'Tonight, I promise,' Lady Phoebe said, chivvying him back towards the house.

They made their way back to the front steps where the doors were being thrown open and a fleet of shiny-buckled footmen were filing out to flank the stone balustrade and greet the first carriage as it drew up. The sound of more hooves had them all turning again, to see another gleaming carriage turn in at the gate, closely followed by another, then another, each one grander the last, as guests began arriving thick and fast. Soon the front steps were overrun as ladies arrayed in elegant carriage dresses of dark blue, delicate fawn and pristine cream, and gentleman, their buckskins pressed, their boots shining, not to mention two dozen maids and manservants, countless trunks and hat boxes, and even one small yapping Pekinese descended from the carriages.

'You must all be parched,' Lady Phoebe declared, once she had greeted everyone personally. 'We will serve refreshments on—'

She was interrupted by a very loud, very unpleasant screech. A last carriage was turning into the gates at some speed, evidently having to press hard upon the brakes to make the turn in time. It careened up the drive, causing them all to flinch backwards, though whether that was purely because of the unwise speed was unclear. For the carriage was also painted in the most bizarre fashion Ashford had ever seen: a violent, garish pattern of yellow and pink stripes.

'Someone is clearly lost.' But Lady Phoebe's tinkling laugh was abruptly caught short as, with an unpleasant creak, the chaise door opened and Mr Philip Hanworth poked his head out. At first sight, he was dressed very properly, in buckskins and a frock coat, but at second glance Ashford noticed that a quizzing glass was clutched in his hand.

'Who on *earth* . . .?' Lady Hesse began in a stage whisper.

'The Hanworths!' Lady Phoebe declared, changing tack at lightning speed. 'Of course – new friends of ours, you know. Very eccentric, but we think them divine!'

Mr Hanworth did not wait for the carriage steps to be released, leaping down to the ground himself, before turning to hand out the most violently purple woman Ashford had ever seen in his life.

'Dear lord,' Lady Morton murmured, clutching her dog to her bosom in alarm.

Despite the damning contextual evidence, it was a moment before Ashford was ready to admit to himself that the purple woman was none other than his bride-to-be. The Miss Hanworth he had last encountered in London had been arranged becomingly in a gown of simple pale muslin, entirely befitting that of a young, unmarried woman; now, in a garish travelling robe of vivid puce, she resembled nothing less than a giant, walking beetroot.

'I have never seen a habit of such a colour, all my life,' Miss Hesse whispered, naïve wonder in her voice.

'Waldo, I wonder if you might take our guests to the drawing room,' Lady Phoebe interjected, 'so that they might partake of refreshment.'

The rest of the party were shepherded inside, throwing intrigued glances over their shoulders and whispering amongst themselves.

'You said,' Lady Phoebe whispered, 'that she was impeccably deported.'

'She was!' Ashford said.

'If she gives me any cause to blush in front of Lady Hesse . . .' Lady Phoebe began from between clenched teeth, before breaking off and taking in a deep, calming breath. 'I'm sorry, I did not mean to . . .'

A sunny smile swept all negativity from her expression. 'I am so looking forward to meeting her!' She began gliding towards the couple, arms outstretched in welcome. 'Welcome, Mr and Miss Hanworth!'

'Good afternoon,' Miss Hanworth said, once she had risen from her curtsey. 'Thank you so very much for inviting us, Lady Henley.'

Lady Phoebe's smile became rather fixed. The daughter of an earl, she had retained her previous title rather than take Sir Waldo's. Ashford would have thought everyone in the Polite World would know such a thing but . . .

Taking a leaf from his cousin's book, Ashford took in his own slow breath. One could forgive a momentary lapse of etiquette, and after all, she would not be the first lady to wear an unusual dress. Once they were married, he could advise her against such vegetal outfits.

'I'm so glad you could come,' Lady Phoebe said. 'Now, you must be tired from your journey.'

'La, not in the slightest,' Miss Hanworth said. 'Have all the other lords and ladies arrived? I am all of a-tremble to meet them. My knees are quite knocking together.'

Lady Phoebe cut quick, significant eyes to Ashford.

'There is not the least reason to be nervous,' Ashford said, swallowing a flicker of vexation. Young ladies did not habitually refer to knees in mixed company. Nor did they use such cant expressions as 'la', for that matter.

'You have a great many footmen, Lady Phoebe,' Mr Hanworth piped up, gazing around.

'Yes, I suppose we do,' Lady Phoebe said.

'Almost – almost a . . . suspicious amount,' Mr Hanworth added, brow furrowing.

Lady Phoebe stared at him for a moment, nonplussed.

'Come, I shall show you all to your rooms,' she said, after a beat, 'so that you might rest before dinner.'

They were not to be invited to partake in refreshment with the others, thank goodness – Ashford should rather Miss Hanworth change her dress before introductions, too. Lady Phoebe led the way, tucking Miss Hanworth's arm into her own, with Mr Hanworth following behind and Ashford bringing the rear, smiling as benignly as he could.

A strange beginning, to be sure. Had he committed a misjudgement, by inviting her here? It had not escaped his notice that while her family had been in transports of delight over his proposal, she had appeared more timorous – but this had only convinced him further that this would be the kindest way of way of introducing Miss Hanworth to the *milieu* she would soon be occupying every day. Perhaps he had been wrong.

No matter. A small misjudgement he could easily address. As soon as they had settled in, they would undoubtedly resume normal behaviour, too. There was no cause to worry; everything would proceed entirely to plan. Smile liberally, he reminded himself, be solicitous, spend time with her. It was a foolproof strategy.

'I am so glad you have joined us,' Lady Phoebe was saying to Miss Hanworth. 'I believe this is to be the most memorable week.'

'I could not agree more,' Miss Hanworth said, and she sent Ashford a smile over her shoulder.

It was not a smile she had ever given him before. And perhaps it was the great width of it, almost a baring of the teeth, or perhaps it was merely the puce dress adding a strange quality to the exchange . . . but Ashford felt it was not a nice smile.

And somewhere, deep inside, he had the smallest inkling that he might very well have made the first and greatest mistake of his life.

4

'Are you certain this is what you wish to wear? It is not one your aunt selected.'

Jane, Lydia's lady's maid, looked Lydia over with visible concern, but Lydia gazed into the looking glass with nothing but satisfaction. Tonight's dress was certainly not one Aunt Agatha had approved: a striped gown of grass-green and white, excessively festooned with pink lace at the hem and each sleeve and ornamented with a medley of brooches on her bodice.

'Don't I look awful?' she asked Pip gleefully upon his entering the room.

It was not even the worst dress in her arsenal. At Pantheon's Bazaar, an astonishing mart not commonly the shopping destination for young, unmarried ladies of fashion, Lydia had used a whole month's worth of pin money to purchase a wardrobe of such wild ostentation that Marie Antoinette herself might well have deemed it a Bit Much.

'Hideous,' Pip confirmed supportively.

'You might still change,' Jane said. 'But we must hurry, you are already late—'

'No, no,' Lydia interrupted. 'It is perfect.'

If Ashford had not visibly recoiled at her puce travelling cloak – nor the gaudy post-chaise Pip had sourced at great difficulty – then this certainly would do the trick.

Jane looked from Pip to Lydia with narrowed eyes. 'What scheme is afoot, Miss Lydia?'

Lydia hesitated. In ordinary times, there was little about Lydia's life that Jane did not know. Jane's grandmother having been a close friend of Lydia's grandmother, the two girls had known each other all their lives. Behind closed doors, they never stood on ceremony – indeed, Jane was quite Lydia's closest friend – but on this matter, would it be better for Lydia to remain silent? She did not wish to put Jane in the position of having to lie to Aunt Agatha, if questioned.

'My apologies, I have overstepped . . .' The hurt in Jane's voice made up Lydia's mind instantly.

'Later,' she promised, 'later I will explain everything.'

She tarried a little longer in front of the mirror, for she did not wish to ruin her poor first impression with punctuality, but she needn't have worried. Traversing Hawkscroft's halls to the East Drawing Room, where the guests had been instructed to gather for dinner, took them several minutes. Together, she and Pip walked along the long first-floor corridor, flanked on either side with gleaming suits of armour, down the great winged staircase, and were just hesitating in the grand hallway, when Reeves, Hawkscroft's butler, materialized to escort them to the East Drawing Room.

They halted in the doorway for a moment, somewhat awestruck. Lydia and Pip were not strangers to finery, but even so, the sight within was most impressive. The room was decadently proportioned, with lofty ceilings overhead, and high sash windows whose curtains had been left open. The last rays of sunshine poured in to cast a golden glow over the people within, murmuring and laughing and sipping from sparkling champagne flutes.

Lydia's breath caught. For the first time since the walk with Pip in Green Park, she was abruptly aware of the absurdity of their scheme. Of its impossibility. Surely, *surely*, she could not follow through with what she had planned in front of such persons as this?

'Mr Hanworth, Miss Hanworth,' Reeves announced quietly, but in a voice of such assurance that the hum of voices instantly quietened, and eight heads turned in their direction.

'Good evening,' Pip said, braver than she, for Lydia could not speak. From the widening eyes and smirks that were blurring together in front of her, she had not erred in her choice of outfit. An instinctive sting of humiliation, to be noted as so immediately and clearly out of place, sprang to Lydia's cheeks. *This is the whole point, you fool*, she told herself fiercely. *This is what you intended.* But shame did not respond to logic and instinctively, Lydia found herself searching out the friendliest face in the room. This was not, as it happened, her betrothed. Ashford's eyes were fixed upon her, it was true, but his face was utterly devoid of expression. He looked as if he did not even recognize her.

That is good, she reminded herself, *it is progress*, but her words meant nothing to her quickening heart, to the sharp edge of panic building in her chest. Lydia looked desperately to the illustrious Lady Phoebe whose lips were parted in surprise, as if her jaw had been on the way to dropping before she had mastered it, before landing, at last, on the bearish gentleman standing next to her, who was wearing a broad smile of welcome.

'Welcome, welcome,' he boomed. 'Come in, come in . . .'

For a moment, Lydia's feet would not work. It was only the reassuring press of Pip's arm against hers, that had her moving forward.

'Good evening!' Lady Phoebe said, recovering her expression and giving them a wide, brilliant smile.

She was wearing an exquisitely simple gown of cerulean silk that fitted her to absolute perfection and contrasted brilliantly against the darkness of her hair. Unlike the plethora of ruby brooches upon Lydia's own gown, she was unadorned, save for the necklace around her neck, which bore the most magnificent array of diamonds that Lydia had ever seen in her life.

'May I introduce you to my husband, Sir Waldo? I do not believe you have yet met.'

'Pleasure to make your acquaintance,' Pip said.

'I hope we are not terribly late,' Lydia whispered. She had planned to call Sir Waldo by the wrong title, but in that moment, she could not force the words past her lips.

'I was beginning to worry you might be lost!' Lady Phoebe said.

'Easily done, I am sure,' Ashford said, coming forward with a smile upon his face.

'Just so,' Sir Waldo said. 'Remember how you used to do so when we first married, my love!'

He cast a beaming smile down to his wife, and she dimpled in return. Lydia watched them rather enviously. The courtship of Sir Waldo and Lady Phoebe was rather legendary. Not all of it could be true of course – he surely hadn't sent her three hundred freesias the night after their first meeting – but plainly, they were still deeply in love. It was possible, then, for the lucky ones.

'I must apologize,' Ashford murmured in her ear.

Lydia turned to regard him sharply. For one wild moment, she thought he had somehow divined what she was thinking and was apologizing for denying her just such a love match.

'We ought to have sent someone to escort you down,' Ashford clarified.

That was . . . kind. Had circumstances been different, Lydia might have been touched. Had she reciprocated whatever feelings had caused Ashford to propose, she would have been well pleased with such care.

Lydia regarded Ashford for a long moment, staring up into his grey eyes and searching deep within herself for any ounce of the affection with which Sir Waldo and Lady Phoebe looked at one another. Or, failing that, any portion of what she had felt, a fortnight earlier, upon meeting Captain von Prett – clammy palms, warming cheeks, quickening heart. She had to check, had to be absolutely sure . . .

But no. Nothing. It was almost miraculous. A handsome man smiling at her, and she felt quite as unmoved as if he had been a portrait. Lydia could not have asked for a timelier reminder of her purpose.

Sir Waldo gave a theatrical cough, and Lydia jerked her eyes away from Ashford's with a start, to find the rest of the room regarding them curiously. She took a minute step away from him and drew in a deep, fortifying breath.

The first stage was vulgarity. Use uncouth expressions, she reminded herself, speak on financial matters, reference their merchant roots.

'May I introduce my brother-in-law, Lord Dacre?' Lady Phoebe suggested brightly.

Lydia curtseyed again, and, as she rose, affected a start of surprise. She had known that Sir Waldo and Dacre were twins, of course, identical in all but their facial hair, for Dacre lacked Sir Waldo's side whiskers – but ignorance was far more useful.

'La,' she said. 'Am I seeing double?'

Use vulgar expressions – tick.

Sir Waldo gave a neigh of laughter, Dacre a small smile.

Pip raised his quizzing glass to inspect them.

'Twins,' Pip diagnosed. 'How . . . suspicious.'

Sir Waldo's smile faded a little. Lydia instinctively opened her mouth to intervene – a lifetime of easing over some of Pip's *faux pas* was not easily forgotten – but mastered herself just in time. *Eccentric relatives – tick.*

'How so?' Waldo asked.

'A jest?' Dacre suggested.

Sir Waldo's brow cleared.

'Oho!' he said, clapping Pip on the shoulder with such force, catching the delicate chain that held Pip's quizzing glass around his neck and breaking it so that Pip dropped the glass, which fell to the floor and skidded away on the dark wooden floorboards. Pip lunged after it with a muttered oath.

'Ashford is known to you, of course,' Lady Phoebe interceded. 'And Mr Brandon, too, I think? But not Lord Hesse – Hesse, may I present to you Mr and Miss Hanworth?'

Lady Phoebe beckoned to Lord Hesse, who edged past Pip, who was now groping about for his quizzing glass under a side table, to bow over Lydia's hand. Fresh to the title after the death of his father the previous year, the young Lord Hesse would have been handsome had it not been for the rather petulant cast to his expression.

'Charmed,' he said, without enthusiasm, his eyes straying to where Pip was stooping to peer under the side table, though he was prevented from turning his head by his shirt's collar points, which had been made to such height and stiffness that they pressed into his cheeks.

'Lady Hesse and Miss Hesse . . .' Lady Phoebe continued on, indicating Lord Hesse's mother and sister, and determinedly ignoring the commotion.

Very angular, very pale, with a faint silver dress and white-blonde hair edging towards grey, even Lady Hesse's smile was pallid yet sharp as she greeted Lydia and Pip. But it was her daughter in whom Lydia was more interested. Fair of hair, skin and eyes, and wearing a dress of shimmering ivory satin, Miss Hesse had more substance to her than her near-translucent mother and was such a vision that even Lydia was hard-pressed to keep her eyes away. Why on earth had Ashford never courted *her*?

'And who is this?' Lydia asked, gesturing to the creature in Miss Hesse's arms, deducing that it must be a dog, however much it resembled a coiffured rodent.

'Brutus,' Miss Hesse introduced, dimpling. 'He belongs to Lady Morton. Would you like to hold him?'

'I'm sure Miss Hanworth does not wish to risk damaging her gown,' Lady Hesse said. 'It is so . . . original, Miss Hanworth: one so rarely sees pink and green and red all together.'

Lady Hiss might be the more appropriate appellation. Even knowing she had dressed in such a way on purpose, Lydia's face warmed.

'La, I know,' she said, as proudly as she was able. Then, though she had to force the words out of her mouth, added: 'You should not *believe* how expensive it was.'

Openly reference money – tick.

Lady Hesse's cheeks puckered. Lydia could not help but cut her eyes to Ashford, but his attention was still caught by Pip, now on all fours and searching under the sofa.

'You look so very cheerful,' Miss Hesse said sweetly to Lydia. 'I wish I had a gown so bright.'

'Oh, your dress becomes you beautifully, Cynthia, there is no need to feel outdone,' Lady Hesse said. 'As I'm sure everyone can attest.'

'Yes of course, stupendous!' Mr Brandon said at once, but Lady Hesse did not appear to hear him, regarding Ashford expectantly instead.

'It's *there*,' Ashford muttered, pointing to where the quizzing glass lay against the sofa leg. Pip seized it and sprang back upwards as violently as a jack in the box. The whole party startled, save for Ashford, who had conjured a calm smile to his face he swivelled back to their conversation.

'Well, my lord?' Lady Hesse pressed him. 'Do you think Cynthia's gown becoming?'

'Why yes of course,' Ashford said, obediently.

'Mama thought you would,' Miss Hesse confided.

Lady Hesse gave a little choking sound, while a great peal of laughter came from the corner of the room. Lydia turned to see a lady rising from one of the low sofas. From the brilliant copper of her hair, this could only be Lady Morton, a dashing widow of five and forty years said to be a most prodigious flirt.

'Exposed, Letitia, exposed!' she crowed.

'I don't know of what you speak,' Lady Hesse sniffed.

'I could make my meaning clearer,' Lady Morton said, 'but I don't think you would enjoy that.'

Lydia looked from one to the other. Was Lady Morton suggesting that Lady Hesse wished for a match between Ashford and her daughter? Lydia would be happy to assist her in that endeavour, if it were true.

'Ladies,' Lady Phoebe chided.

'You must forgive us,' Lady Morton said to Lydia, reaching out to clasp her hands. 'We have all known each other *such* a long time, we can be dreadfully rude.'

In appearance, she could not be more different to Lady Hesse, all curls and curves she was, and yet her words worked to make Lydia feel just as excluded. There was no breaking into ranks such as these, they seemed to be telling her, they had shared nurseries and schoolrooms long before they had parties and ballrooms. It was a good thing, then, that Lydia wanted no part of it. She waited, watching and listening for her next opportunity, but it was proving difficult. Conversation was in full flow as Lady Hesse relayed a few choice morsels of gossip.

'. . . and then, it was revealed – the rubies had been false, all along!' Lady Hesse concluded, delight on her face to speak of such misfortune. 'Dupes!'

'Oh, you ought to have suspected,' Lady Phoebe said. 'If they were of such a size, her ears ought to have been on the floor from the weight.'

'That is why you are needed in London, my lady,' Lady Morton said, with a hand to Lady Phoebe's arm. 'Enough of this marital bliss – return to the trenches with us!'

Everyone laughed, as Lady Phoebe's cheeks pinked.

'La,' Lydia said quickly, before conversation could move on, 'you certainly have an eye for jewels, Lady Henley.'

She flicked her eyes pointedly to Lady Phoebe's diamonds.

As conversational gambits went, Lydia was rather pleased with this. To concertina a vulgarity, an impertinent question, and a mistitling all into one sentence – why, it was rather impressive. Lady Phoebe certainly seemed impacted, putting an uncertain hand up to her necklace, opening her mouth, shutting it, and then looking appealingly towards Ashford for help.

'Your necklace was a gift from Sir Waldo, I believe?' Ashford said, as if Lydia had not said anything in the least unusual.

'Diamonds for my diamond!' Sir Waldo concurred, laying a large paw upon Lady Phoebe's shoulder. 'It belonged to a Sultan, you know, and is quite the largest of its kind in Europe.'

As if to verify this, Pip raised his quizzing glass and leant forward. The sudden sight of his eye, grotesquely magnified to ten times its usual size, had Lady Phoebe flinching backwards.

'I have never seen diamonds so large,' Lydia persevered, keeping one eye upon Ashford.

'Yes, well it's a little impractical, really,' she said.

'I won it myself at Seringapatam,' Sir Waldo said, chest puffing out proudly.

'Won?' Pip said. 'Or stole?'

There were sharp intakes of breath across the room.

'I beg your pardon?' Sir Waldo said, the smile slipping from his face.

'You'll have to forgive my brother!' Lydia said, voice almost a yelp. There was impertinence, and then there was a criminal accusation. Pip could not very well aid her endeavours if he had been thrown from the house on the very first night. 'He acts as a consult to Bow Street and forgets that we do not all share the Runner sense of humour.'

Since most of Pip's 'work' occurred with Mr Simmons at various drinking locales – Pip returning in the early hours of the morning starry-eyed – consult was a rather grand interpretation, but she needed to say something to arrest Sir Waldo's budding outrage.

'A jest,' Ashford confirmed quietly, and Lydia shot him a grateful smile before she could stop herself. Recollecting herself halfway through, she abruptly broadened it to a smile *with* teeth – Aunt Agatha's second most crucial rule – and had the satisfaction of seeing Ashford's eyes widen under her toothy beam. That was something, at least.

'Thieves do walk among us,' Pip explained, with the voice of One Who Has Faced the Darkness of the World. 'As I know all too well.'

Sir Waldo began to chuckle. His brother followed his lead immediately, and Mr Brandon, too, was forcing a laugh even if confusion was still writ large upon his face.

'I had no notion you were such an original, sir!' Sir Waldo said, with a mighty slap to Pip's back.

'Nor did I,' Lady Phoebe said. 'Did *you*, Ashford?'

Perhaps it was wishful thinking, but Lydia felt there was a glare under Lady Phoebe's bright, bright smile, as she turned to her cousin.

'No,' Ashford said, his benign smile gone. 'No, I did not.'

'How interesting,' Dacre said, with avuncular kindliness. 'Have you been – ah – involved in anything we might have heard of?'

'Perhaps you read about Rundell and Bridge the jewellers'

affair?' Pip's air of theatricality heightened even further. 'It was my first case.'

The room regarded him, curiosity chasing away their outrage.

'You must be very brave,' Lady Morton said, moving to touch Pip upon the arm.

'Famous,' Mr Brandon declared.

Lydia breathed out a sigh, her heartbeat beginning to calm to its normal tempo.

'How . . . sordid,' Lady Hesse observed, mouth puckering as though tasting a sour plum, and Lady Phoebe shot Ashford a quick glare.

'I wonder that they could spare you for the week,' Lord Hesse said, in a tone caught somewhere between envy and sulkiness, 'given you are so important.'

'It was a difficult decision,' Pip said. 'But Mr Simmons – my . . . mentor – agreed I might use the house party as an opportunity to practise my investigating skills. If her ladyship does not mind?'

He looked enquiringly toward Lady Phoebe.

'You mean to investigate us?' Lady Phoebe said, looking as though she did not know whether to find this amusing or alarming.

'You will find us dull subjects, I am sure!' Sir Waldo said jovially.

'I do not think so,' Pip said. 'Everyone has secrets, after all.'

A strange shiver passed around the room. For a moment, not one person appeared to want to make eye contact with anyone else in the room.

'Ah, surely you are not suggesting . . .?' Ashford began.

'Everyone,' Pip repeated darkly. 'Especially those with moustaches.'

The moment broke.

'Oh, you rotter!' Sir Waldo said, slapping Pip upon the back again.

Laughter reigned again – all save Lady Phoebe, who was glaring at Ashford – and Ashford himself, who was gazing from Lydia to Pip and back again, blinking rather dazedly, as if trying to wake himself from a dream. At last, at *last*! Lydia was awash with sudden relief. Thank goodness for Pip. His methods might have brought them close to disaster, but they were undeniably effective, and Lydia opened her mouth to continue their momentum but—

'I think it must be almost time for dinner,' Lady Phoebe proclaimed, before she could speak.

As if in obeyance to her words, the grandfather clock behind her struck a single bell tone, and in the same moment the butler appeared in the doorway, giving her a significant nod. Lady Phoebe took in a deep breath, her shoulders relaxing down her spine, and held out her arms as if to conduct an orchestra.

'Please, won't you follow me?' she said, and, with a few deft movements, had them each paired for the walk to dinner, and the evening back under her control.

Everything in Lady Phoebe's life seemed to run perfectly to plan: the adoring husband, the wondrous home, the luxurious life. This house party would doubtless be the same: each moment designed according to her vision and executed to perfection.

It was almost a shame Lydia was going to have to ruin it.

5

Lydia's sense of victory in the drawing room had been precipitous. Pip might have rocked Ashford's indefatigable calm for a moment, but by the time they were seated in the West Dining Room, it had been entirely restored. What's more, Lydia's nerves had made a reappearance, too. For the grandeur of the dining room was such that she felt overwhelmed anew: panelled entirely in dark oak and hung in crimson damask, it boasted a glittering chandelier overhead and a gleaming mahogany table at its centre, laden with pies, pates, jellies, fondues and blancmanges past counting.

Lydia cast an evaluating eye to the fleet of footman lining the walls. Just how many hours of preparation had this opulent repast required?

'A sinful amount of housework,' her grandmother would have tutted, had she been there to witness such a display. Having begun life as a maid, Mrs Hanworth had a strong aversion to excess, and as Lydia took a seat between a beef tremblant and pigeon *à la Crapaudine*, she had never felt more in agreement. For even between ten of them, they should never finish all these delicacies.

Lydia had bigger concerns, however, as she, the lowest ranking woman, and Ashford, the highest-ranking gentleman, had been seated at opposite ends of the table, rendering most of her planned methods of revolting him impossible. She berated herself, furiously, for not considering this earlier. What on earth was there to do that he, so far away, would be certain of noticing? There was one wild moment, as the rest of the table began to sup on the mountain of dishes ladening the table and Lydia's hands hovered above the row of cutlery sitting either side of her plate. Did she have the gall to use the wrong fork?

Before she could act on the impulse, Lord Dacre had tilted towards her.

'I believe it's outside in,' he murmured in her ear, so quietly that not a single person other than she could hear him. It was such an unexpected piece of kindness that Lydia could not help but heed him, taking the correct cutlery in hand.

'Thank you,' she whispered. 'It is all just a little . . .'

'Daunting?' he said, in the same low voice. 'That is only natural. If you have any questions, you need only ask me – or Reeves, for that matter.'

He raised his voice minutely as Reeves drew between them, decanter in hand.

'You flatter me, my lord,' Reeves said, neutrally, though Lydia fancied the corner of his mouth rose just slightly, and Lydia's opinion of Dacre rose with it. He was certainly the least awful person here. Indeed, she had met both Sir Waldo and Dacre only this evening, and though the only physical difference between the two brothers was in their choice of facial hair, she felt that, even if blindfolded, she would have no difficulty telling the two apart. They held themselves so differently: Dacre's quiet assurance so much calmer than his rowdier brother.

Abandoning her schemes for the time being, there being very little else to do that Ashford would notice, Lydia spent the rest of the meal in observation. It was not often she broke bread with people she had hitherto only read about in gossip columns. Lord Dacre, on her left, seemed by far the steadiest, taking all of his brother's teasing with equanimity, while offering none of his own. Mr Brandon, with the exuberance and mane of a golden retriever, was certainly the liveliest, and angelic Miss Hesse the most agreeable. Lady Morton, bewitching and arch, had lived up to every inch of her reputation, flirting with an audacity only permissible when one was rich and titled and widowed. Though whenever her attentions fell upon Lord Hesse, Lady Hesse's lips pursed into a cat's bottom of displeasure that suggested she did not agree.

Next to all these characters, Ashford was . . . well, rather dull. He was not the loudest, nor the funniest – indeed, he barely laughed at all – and his only notable feature appeared to be an ability to maintain a civil expression even under the toothiest of smiles Lydia could send his way. It was rather irksome. Clearly, all momentum had been lost – if anything, Ashford appeared to be enjoyed himself, which was certainly not the point of Stage One at *all*.

It was a relief, then, when Lady Phoebe rose to lead the ladies away to drawing room, leaving the gentlemen to the port. There were only so many hours of the evening left, and Lydia was determined to make use of them.

She quickly found, however, that she was not the only person with an agenda. No sooner had Lady Hesse seated herself in an armchair than she had Lydia in her sights.

'It is so marvellous to make new acquaintances,' she said, fixing Lydia with a false smile and a gimlet eye. 'I rarely do so, these days. So tell me, Miss Hanworth, how *did* you and Ashford first meet?'

'At the Alcot ball,' Lydia said, after a beat of hesitation. She very much doubted Lady Hesse's interest was motivated by curiosity alone.

'Not long ago,' Lady Hesse noted, with a smile. 'And you are already invited to Hawkscroft!'

She was watching Lydia closely. Did she suspect the true reason behind Lydia's invitation?

'I have always believed in bringing new people together,' Lady Phoebe said, with a calm belied by the haste with which she was now pouring the tea. 'It makes everything so much livelier.'

'It certainly suits me,' Lady Morton said. 'I am at sixes and sevens to know which gentlemen ought to be appointed my flirt. You have delivered such an embarrassment of riches.'

Lady Phoebe and Lydia both laughed – one could not help it, such outrageousness was irresistible – but Lady Hesse's mouth puckered.

'Goodness,' she said acidly. 'You speak as if they are all yours for the taking.'

'Are they not?' Lady Morton said with a toss of her fine head. 'I count only one married man amongst them.'

'And my son,' Lady Hesse said frostily, 'who is only three and twenty.'

'Ah, a fine age,' Lady Morton said in a reminiscing sort of way. 'So much vim and vigour.'

Lady Hesse opened her mouth, as if to deliver a snapping retort no doubt, but was interrupted before it could pass her lips.

'Knock knock!' Sir Waldo boomed, peering his head around the door frame with a silly grin upon his face. 'Is it safe to enter? Ought we to bar our ears?'

He bounded into the room without waiting for a reply, with the rest of the gentlemen following behind. Mr Brandon made an immediate beeline for Miss Hesse, while Pip eschewed the sofas to begin a slow circuit of the room; Lady Phoebe took this in with a worried frown, before evidently deciding it was better to ignore him. Ashford, bringing up the rear with Hesse and Dacre, caught Lydia's eye as soon as he crossed the threshold, and sent her a smile. Lydia pretended not to see it. By the end of the evening, she vowed, he would not be smiling at her so.

'That was quick,' Lady Phoebe commented, as Sir Waldo seated himself heavily next to her. 'Was the port not to your liking?'

'Oh, I could not be without you for another moment, darling,' Sir Waldo said, taking her hand.

'Oh, you two,' Lady Morton said fondly. 'And I here, having not been paid a single compliment all evening.'

She cast Lady Hesse a wicked glance under her eyelashes. 'Surely *you* have noticed my new gown, Lord Hesse?'

'Oh, Hesse's notice is reserved for horses, cricket and cards,' Lady Hesse said before her son could answer.

'Mother,' Hesse said, 'I have long put away such frivolous pursuits, you know that.'

'I know, darling. In fact, I worry you work too hard! He has completely thrown himself into running the estate this past year,' Lady Hesse told them all proudly. 'Darling boy!'

'*Mother*,' Hesse said again, folding his arms across his chest. 'I am not a *boy*.'

'I have always admired a dutiful man,' Lady Morton said caressingly. Lord Hesse uncrossed his arms.

'I hope you will still have time to join us for a ride on the morrow, Hesse?' Ashford asked. 'The terrain around these parts is some of the best in the country.'

'I quite agree,' Miss Hesse whispered.

'Oh, what a pair you make,' Lady Hesse said. 'Both horse mad.'

Horse mad, was he? Lydia digested this piece of information consideringly. It made sense, now she thought of it, for Ashford could be seen riding in Hyde Park with a regularity that spoke more to passion than convention. Interesting. Yes, she could certainly work with this.

'I as well!' Mr Brandon said eagerly.

Lady Hesse appeared not to hear him. 'Do you ride, Miss Hanworth?'

It was a strange feeling, to feel so obliged to a person one disliked, and yet Lydia felt a rush of gratitude to Lady Hesse, serving such easy hits to her.

'Yes,' she said. 'Though I only learnt recently.'

This was not true, but there was already a budding plan forming in Lydia's mind.

'You did not ride as a child?' Sir Waldo asked.

'My grandfather did not trust horses,' Lydia said. 'Or horse-shaped people.'

This part *was* true.

'He sounds an original character,' Dacre said, smiling encouragingly at her, and what better prompt could there be? She opened her mouth to elaborate on just how original her grandfather was when . . .

'How wonderful it is to be here, altogether,' Ashford said, not loudly, but drawing all eyes to him, nonetheless. He raised his teacup to his cousin in toast. 'I feel very fortunate to be hosted so well.'

Lady Phoebe preened.

'I as well,' Mr Brandon agreed. 'I must say, I am intrigued as to what trickery you might have up your sleeve, Lady Phoebe.'

'I cannot think what you mean,' she demurred.

'Trickery?' Pip said, turning from his inspection of the mantelpiece. '*Deception?*'

Pip, at least, was having no trouble finding an opening.

'Mama said last year there was a surprise guest,' Miss Hesse said, turning enquiring eyes upon Lady Phoebe. 'Is there to be one this year, too?'

Lady Phoebe's smile widened. 'My lips are sealed.'

From beside Lydia, Lady Morton let out another delighted laugh. 'You are too cruel, my lady – I adore it!'

She turned to Lydia in dramatically confidential fashion. 'If last year is anything to go by, then I would prepare for this week to eclipse any house party you have ever attended, Miss Hanworth.'

'Oh goodness, you shall set me up for failure, Lady Morton,' Lady Phoebe chided her. 'I do not know with whose house parties I am to compete – for all you know, Mr and Miss Hanworth could have been hosted by the Prince Regent!'

'I have never attended any house party before,' Lydia announced.

There was a pause. The longest of the evening.

'I perceive that the Hanworths are more used to acting the host,' Ashford interpolated, reaching into his pocket for his snuffbox.

Could *nothing* she said shake him?

'You must have quite the country seat!' Sir Waldo said, accepting Ashford's explanation at once. 'Which county do you find it?'

'We don't,' Lydia said. Then, feeling it was time to up the ante, she continued: 'Grandpapa would never have countenanced spending so much time away from work.'

'*Work?*' Lady Hesse said, leaning a little backwards as if the concept was contagious.

Across from her, Ashford paused with his snuff halfway towards his nose, as if frozen in amber.

'Duties, perhaps?' Lady Phoebe suggested rather desperately.

'In a sense,' Lydia said. 'There is so much to do . . .'

She paused, for dramatic effect. For once, neither Ashford nor Lady Phoebe rushed to intervene. They were all staring at her, very much as one might find oneself helpless to look away from a carriage accident.

'. . . at the factory,' she finished.

The word 'factory' acted very much as a hot poker inserted suddenly somewhere uncomfortable. Everyone flinched backwards from her, eight faces arrested in shock and horror.

Lydia, her eyes upon Ashford, had the satisfaction of seeing him lower his snuff away from his nose, very slowly. For the first time that evening, he looked unnerved.

Yes, indeed. Ashford was well prepared for the next stage, upon the morrow.

6

Wednesday – Eight days remaining

Ashford waited in the stable yard, still and silent and seething. The church bell, from the nearby village of Melford, had just struck quarter past the hour and Miss Hanworth was nowhere to be seen.

Ashford had risen soon after dawn, of course, spending a few hours at his desk – running his and his father's estate at such a distance was no mean feat – before joining the breakfast table, where Miss Hanworth had been similarly absent. She was a late riser, it seemed, which was the latest in a very long list of unfortunate revelations about his bride-to-be.

Now, all around Ashford, the rest of the party was readying themselves for the morning ride, including Mr Hanworth. This was no great consolation, however.

The Mr Hanworth of Ashford's recollection had been a pleasant, regular sort of fellow. *This* Mr Hanworth, standing at the other side of the stable yard, had – sometime between dinner last night and breakfast this morning – sourced a notebook and pencil that he was currently brandishing at Lords Dacre and Hesse at the other end of the yard.

'He was not joking about this investigation business, then?' Mr Brandon said, from beside Ashford.

'No,' Ashford said, rather grimly. 'It appears not.'

Ought he to intervene? Dacre would not hold a grudge, but since coming into his title, Hesse's dignity was so easily wounded. Ashford understood, a little. Though his father was very much alive, after the loss of the duchess, Ashford had had to step into His Grace's shoes prematurely. At the tender age of sixteen he, too, had committed some oddities in the pursuit of being taken seriously, though he had thankfully never thought, as Hesse obviously had, that becoming a man of fashion should be one of them. This morning, Hesse wore his hair in painstakingly dishevelled curls, and breeches so closely fitted that they could hardly have been more revealing without being transparent.

'Pray, what has my childhood to do with anything, sir?' Hesse said, nose in the air. 'I'm sure I can hardly recollect it.'

'Shows inclination to evasion,' Mr Hanworth intoned, bending his head to make a note.

Mr Brandon snorted. Sir Waldo, standing beside Lord Hesse, bellowed a laugh and Lady Morton and Miss Hesse trilled out their own. It was fortunate that they seemed to consider him more a comedian than a madman, but Ashford had to question the world in which this was now a comfort to him. Had he only *known* . . .

'Fortunately, no skeletons in my cupboards,' Brandon said.

'Nor mine,' Ashford said, eyes still fixed – disbelievingly – on the gentleman who would soon be considered a member of his family.

'Truly?' Brandon said. 'None?'

'Do you wish to accuse me of something, Brandon?' Ashford said, turning to regard his friend with some bemusement.

'I am just curious,' Brandon said.

'About?'

'Well,' Brandon said, so casually that Ashford knew it to be forced, 'you did say you intended to marry this year. *Some* people have been wondering if perhaps you intend to court one of the ladies here. Miss Hanworth or . . .'

His eyes travelling to where Miss Hesse, a vision in palest pink, was stooping to pet at Brutus the Pekinese.

'Miss Hesse,' Brandon finished delicately. 'Yes, some people have been wondering.'

'These "people",' Ashford said. 'Anyone I know?'

'Friends of mine,' Brandon said. 'Not sure you are acquainted.'

Ashford suppressed a smile. Even if Brandon had yet to admit it aloud, the candle he held for Miss Hesse was obvious to anyone paying the least bit of attention.

'I am not courting Miss Hesse,' he said.

Brandon did not look convinced.

'She *does* meet all your requirements,' he said. 'I would understand if your heart had been caught.'

Ashford considered, for a moment, whether he might tell Brandon the whole truth. He was the closest thing Ashford had to a confidante, and already knew, after all, of Ashford's intention to wed and some of the difficulties he had encountered along the way, though Ashford had never fully explained his financial motives, nor His Grace's more sentimental demands. It was tempting, but no. To admit the duchy's financial difficulties was insupportable and he could not risk his father finding out the truth. For if the duke caught even a whiff of Ashford's true motives, he might well withdraw his approval and ruin the whole thing.

'I am not courting Miss Hesse,' he repeated, perceiving, from the worried cast to Brandon's expression, that he did need some further reassurance. 'I am, however, looking forward to getting to know Miss Hanworth better.'

Get to know her, discover what on earth was going through her mind, what the hell she was thinking – it was all much of muchness. To think, only yesterday, Ashford had thought Miss Hanworth sensible, pleasant, inoffensive.

'Oh!' Brandon said, much surprised. 'Oh! Yes, well, of course, she is, ah, *very* . . .'

He trailed off, plainly at a loss for how to conclude the sentence.

'Isn't she,' Ashford agreed pleasantly. She had been 'very', after all. Very strange, very impolite, very vulgar – the list went on.

'La,' came a voice from behind Ashford, 'what a fine morning.'

Brandon's eyes had widened as they looked over Ashford's shoulder, but even with this warning, Ashford was unprepared for Miss Hanworth's riding dress. It was a habit of bright green ornamented with a band of lilac stripes running down the front, and no less than five precariously drooping ostrich feathers emerging from a monstrously large hat. All in all, she bore a striking resemblance to the circus troupers who peddled tickets outside Astley's Amphitheatre.

For a moment, Ashford's mind was utterly blank. What did one say, to a woman so befeathered? It defied belief.

'A very fine morning,' he agreed at last, groping in his pocket for the reassuring shape of his snuffbox, as he always did when he wished to steady himself – in recent days, it seemed hardly out of his hand.

'And you are a confirmed bachelor, Lord Dacre?' He heard Mr Hanworth say from over his shoulder.

'He has you on the ropes now, brother!' Sir Waldo crowed.

'Oh dear,' Miss Hanworth breathed, gazing over Ashford's shoulder. 'He has a notebook.'

'He does,' Ashford confirmed.

Her eyes had widened in concern, and Ashford found the sight oddly reassuring. She had not lost all her commonsense, then.

'Everyone is taking it in good humour,' he reassured her, and her eyes moved back to him. As their gazes met, she seemed to startle.

'I am so nervous,' she confessed abruptly.

Ashford felt his vexation ease a little. The young lady he had known in London still existed, she was there, under the ostrich feathers – just besieged by nerves he had not thought she possessed.

'I did wonder if that might be the case,' he said, as gently as he could manage, 'but I assure you—'

'For the ride,' Miss Hanworth added, in a rather rude interruption. 'Do you think we will go far?'

'Oh, I should think only an hour or so,' Ashford said, 'and then, once we return, perhaps we might speak—'

'An *hour*?' Miss Hanworth interrupted again, and a snappish retort was on the tip of Ashford's tongue – would she not let him *finish*? – when the clattering of hooves had him turning. Soon, the yard was taken over with the business of mounting, made only noisier by Brutus, yapping furiously.

'Ought the little monster be shut inside?' Mr Brandon said, watching with concern as Miss Hesse's horse gave a nervous skip away from the noise, just as she was being helped into the saddle. 'He is upsetting the horses.'

'He's no bother,' Miss Hesse said, serenely, mastering her horse as beautifully as she did everything. Ashford fought the urge to scowl. He had meant what he had said to Brandon. He would never torture his friend by putting his hat in the ring, but after the events of the past day, Miss Hesse had never seemed more tempting.

'Let us be off,' Lady Phoebe declared, clapping her hands as she approached the gleaming thoroughbred that was Sir Waldo's latest purse-breaking gift. Her groom made to give her a leg up, but Sir Waldo shooed him away in order to throw her into the saddle himself.

'Sir Waldo cannot keep his hands off you,' Lady Phoebe,' Lady Hesse observed with indulgence.

'How sweet,' Lady Morton said. Then, with a pout, added: 'Does no one throw *me* into the saddle?'

She picked an imaginary piece of fluff from her overspilling bodice. Lord Hesse stepped forward so quickly his skintight breeches creaked under the strain.

'Your groom can assist you perfectly well,' Lady Hesse said waspishly, seizing her son's arm.

Ashford hid a smile behind his horse's neck, allowing the scent – leather, hay and horsehair all mingled together – to calm him for a moment. In his belief, there was no problem that could not be solved by an hour on horseback, and Miss Hanworth would be no different. He took the left stirrup in his hands and was just about to place his foot within, when he became aware of a flurry of commotion to his right.

'Miss? Miss?'

Ashford turned to see Miss Hanworth's groom standing, baffled, holding the reins of a cheerful-looking fellow of fourteen hands. Next to him, Miss Hanworth was wringing her hands.

'Is anything amiss?' Ashford asked, frowning.

Her horse turned curiously to regard her, as if he did not understand her behaviour any more than Ashford did and blew a soft snort of air in her direction. Miss Hanworth skittered back several steps.

'I cannot,' Miss Hanworth said. 'I simply cannot do it – I am too afraid.'

She seemed to be shaking, the ostrich feathers on her hat wobbling precariously.

'But I have seen you riding, haven't I?' Ashford said, perplexed. 'In Hyde Park?'

'Ashford?' Lady Phoebe called over from atop her horse. 'Is all well?'

Ashford and Miss Hanworth were the only ones not mounted now, and they were beginning to attract curious glances. Ashford felt a prickle of embarrassment run up his spine.

'You need not ride if you do not wish to,' he told Miss Hanworth, trying to keep the impatience from his voice. 'Perhaps you ought to—'

'See how he looks at me,' Miss Hanworth said, speaking over him – and truly, if she interrupted him once more he was going to lose his temper, he really was – 'Leering down his nose in such a way.'

'I think that is just the way all horses . . .' Ashford began, rather helplessly, for what could he say? Their noses simply *were* very long.

'What is going on?' Sir Waldo grumbled.

'I think she is a nervous rider,' Lady Phoebe murmured.

'Why *say* you can ride, if you cannot,' Lady Morton drawled in perfectly audible undertone.

'Darling, we must be sympathetic!' Lady Hesse said, loudly this time. 'Not every lady has been raised in the saddle, as we have!'

It was turning into a Scene and there was nothing in the world Ashford hated more.

'Remain here,' Ashford told Miss Hanworth. 'If you would prefer,' he added, hearing the peremptoriness of his own voice.

'Very well,' Miss Hanworth agreed. Then, turning limpid eyes upon him, she asked: 'Will you – will you remain here, with me?'

Ashford hesitated. It was such a fine day . . . Surely, if anyone should stay, it should be Mr Hanworth? But Mr Hanworth was seated upon his own horse, regarding his notebook with absolutely no ounce of concern for his sister's plight. Ashford repressed a rush of indignation. Recollect, he urged himself, spending time together was an integral part of courtship.

'Of course,' Ashford said, ungritting his teeth with some effort. 'Of course I shall. Phoebe, Miss Hanworth is not feeling well, so she and I will remain here.'

'Oh,' Lady Phoebe said, audibly disappointed. 'Oh, of course – perhaps you might ask Reeves to give you a tour of the house?'

Next to Lady Phoebe, Lady Hesse looked from Miss Hanworth to Ashford and back again with narrowed, suspicious eyes.

'You know,' she said, 'if you are to stay, Ashford, then will you take Cynthia with you, too? You did say you were feeling fatigued, didn't you, darling?'

'Yes,' Miss Hesse said agreeably. She slid off her horse, the very picture of good health as she sent a sunny smile Ashford's way.

'You know I think I am feeling peaky, too!' Mr Brandon said, throwing the reins of his own horse back to his groom.

'Truly, Brandon?' Lady Phoebe bemoaned, looking round at her riding party, halved in size in the work of two minutes.

'Afraid so – my throat, you know,' Brandon said. 'Miss Hesse, may I offer my arm? The ground is a little slippery.'

Ashford suppressed a sigh as the horses filed past them, skittish and fresh in the morning light. Then, taking in a deep breath, he turned back to Miss Hanworth. She looked, for someone who had just ruined his morning, remarkably cheerful, and he added 'obliviousness' to his mental list of her flaws. It was growing rather long now. Miss Callow's overuse of French phrases seemed practically charming, in hindsight.

'Shall we go inside?' he said, offering his arm to her and forcing his rising temper down into his boots.

There was no point in succumbing to anger or frustration. What was done could not be undone, and the only thing left was to make the best of it. He had eight days before he had to introduce Miss Hanworth to his father. Whether her strange new turn of behaviour was the result of agonies of nervousness or poor advice from her family, it did not matter. She could conduct herself well, for he had seen her do so with his own eyes. She would do so again.

He would not be felled by this. He refused.

7

'The central portion of the house is of Tudor origin, while the wings were added later as one can see from the rococo stylings...'

Reeves had pivoted to the role of tour guide rather impressively, escorting them through a rabbit warren of some thirty rooms for Hawkscroft boasted two dining rooms, three drawing rooms, a handful of saloons and parlours and a grand library to boot and had something interesting to say about each of them. Though he must have had a long list of other, more pressing duties to fulfil, not a shadow of exasperation passed across his face, no matter how irritating their band of deserters were, the ever-cheerful Mr Brandon whispering jokes into Miss Hesse's ear, the ever-yapping Brutus trotting at her heels, while the ever-irritating Lydia peppered the tour with a steady flow of inappropriate questions.

'Is Sir Waldo the wealthiest man in England?' she asked. 'I should think this house fit for several kings.'

It was an impertinence, but not an exaggeration. Even this room, a small parlour that could hardly see daily use, was decorated with finely crafted objects from the workshops of Chippendale and Haig. Lydia's grandmother would have clucked her tongue and dubbed it obscene, though Grandfather would certainly have been fascinated by the mahogany chests, rosewood tables, and Persian swords that constituted Sir Waldo's war loot.

'Of course, old houses have their idiosyncrasies, too,' Reeves said evenly. 'This parlour door cannot be closed in summer, for the wood would swell shut permanently.'

Again, Reeves had weathered Lydia's impertinence with no discernible sign of stress, which was commendable – as did Ashford, which was not. Lydia was not, however, as distressed by Ashford's implacability as she had been the day prior. She fancied there was a sour cast now to Ashford's benign expression – after all, one would surely have to be entirely made of stone not to feel some mortification at the scene she had made outside, even if he was able to suppress most signs of it. She just had to push him harder – and, fortunately, she had several weapons in her arsenal still to deploy.

'Here we have the library,' Reeves was saying, as they reached the end of the East Wing, and he threw open the doors to reveal a long hall of books that twinned with the West ballroom in size. It was fitted with the same elaborate taste as the rest of the house, with a gilded and painted and chandeliered ceiling, but it was the sheer number of leather-bound volumes standing upon its shelves that caught Lydia's breath.

'*Goodness*,' Lydia said, impressed into a genuine reaction. There was no shortage of public libraries in London, and some of them were rather beautiful, but this outdid them all. She drew in a great lungful of air, delicately sweetened by the indefinable scent of old books. Out of the corner of her eye, she saw Ashford do the same.

'There are just so many books!' Miss Hesse said with charming naivety.

'A splendid collection,' Ashford confirmed.

'Yes,' Lydia breathed, forgetting herself for a moment, before adding, hastily, but with all the flourish she could muster: '*C'est magnifique.*'

Despite the very best efforts of two separate language masters, Lydia could only recollect four French phrases, but fortunately, this was quite sufficient to suit the second stage of her attack: pompousness.

Beside her, every muscle in Ashford's body seemed to have stiffened.

'I did not know you spoke French, Miss Hanworth,' Mr Brandon said, a tiny shake of laughter in his voice.

'Yes,' Lydia said – for why not overegg her abilities, while she was at it? – 'I like to practise as much as I can.'

'How admirable,' Miss Hesse said.

'Yes,' Ashford said woodenly. 'Admirable is exactly the word I was reaching for, too.'

She watched him, sidelong, as they followed Reeves back up the grand staircase. He was on the precipice; she was sure of it.

'Here we have the portrait gallery,' Reeves said, leading them into a broad corridor, bearing a least two dozen portraits of stern gentlemen on its walls.

'My goodness,' Miss Hesse said, voice full of admiration.

'You will find three Reynolds upon these walls,' Mr Reeves said serenely, giving no indication of his own opinion on the subject, 'if you can spot them . . .'

Mr Reynolds, perhaps the most famous portraitist for several centuries, a household name in every house of quality.

'Who is that?' Lydia asked Ashford, with an innocent widening of her eyes – for why not throw a little of Stage Three (foolishness) into the ring now?

'Ah – an artist,' he explained. 'The first president of the Royal Academy.'

'I have never visited,' Lydia lied. 'Can't stand such stuff.'

'Oh, I love it,' Miss Hesse breathed.

'I as well,' Mr Brandon said at once. 'I wager I can find the Reynolds before you, Miss Hesse.'

They scampered off, as merry as schoolchildren, Brutus trotting behind, while Ashford set a more sedate pace. It was the most alone they had been since their engagement. Lydia stole an evaluating glance at Ashford. He did not seem the sort who would try to steal an arm around her waist, but one never knew, and they *were* engaged . . . On the pretence of adjusting her cuffs, she felt for the reassuring shape of the sharp pin hiding in the cloth there. Her grandmother had gifted it to her on her sixteenth birthday, with stern instructions that she must wield it liberally against lecherous gentlemen.

Ashford paused in front of a rather sensual depiction of a previous Lady Cavendish – Sir Waldo had purchased Hawkscroft's art collection along with the house – arranged suggestively on a chaise longue. She had plainly been as beautiful as she was full figured. 'What extraordinary brushwork,' Ashford observed.

Lydia released her pin. She was not going to need it.

'Are these all ancestors of the previous owner?' Lydia asked, with an expansive wave of her arm. 'Or are there any members of Sir Waldo and Lady Phoebe's family included, too?'

Ashford paused before the next painting. 'This is mine and Phoebe's great-great grandfather.'

Lydia took in the portrait. He was a stout man, and what could be seen of his expression – through the wiry hair that appeared to cover every inch of his neck, face and ears – was dour and dissatisfied. Long in the tooth both figuratively and quite literally, for his incisors protruded at an alarming angle from his mouth. He was, perhaps, the ugliest man Lydia had ever seen.

'I can perceive the family resemblance,' she said. 'Uncanny.'

There was a pause, during which Lydia worked to keep her face quite still.

'Resemblance to . . . me?' Ashford said.

Lydia nodded. 'I have a discerning eye for these things,' she said. 'I imagine it will not be above a few years before you could pass for twins.'

'How old do you think I—' Ashford began, then broke off with an irritable shake of his head, stepping onto the next portrait.

'And this is Charles Jenkinson, a relative to Waldo and grandfather, of course, to Robert,' he said.

Oh, how perfect.

'Grandfather to whom?' Lydia repeated, as innocently as she was able.

'Ah – our Prime Minister,' Ashford said.

'Another one?' Lydia said. 'Gosh, it does make it difficult to keep track, doesn't it – the way they constantly keep swapping new ones in.'

'Every four years, usually,' Ashford said, voice very, very neutral.

'Jenkinson . . .' Lydia said, tapping her finger upon her chin in thought. 'The name does sound familiar.'

'Perhaps you might have read about him in the papers?' Ashford suggested hopefully.

'No, that's not it,' Lydia said. 'Is he the one who was found in a state of undress with Lady Massey?'

'I shouldn't think so.'

'Then I give up,' Lydia said. 'Politics is so impossible to follow! I have enough issues remembering everyone's names and titles *here*.'

'Yes, I have noticed, that on occasion you can mix them up,' Ashford said. 'Very understandable, of course, but – ah – you may ask me, if you are ever in doubt.'

'In the middle of conversation?' Lydia asked doubtfully. 'I would have thought that a little rude, but if you think I ought, then I shall!'

'No, no,' Ashford said hurriedly. 'I meant more – a discreet aside – but perhaps not.'

'I can be discreet!' Lydia said very loudly.

'No!' Ashford snapped.

His tone, for the very first time since the visit had begun, was brusque and pointed. Perfect. Lydia affected a wobble of her lip.

'Y-yes of course – it w-was foolish of me,' she said, affecting a little choke.

Ashford looked towards Lydia, startled, eyes widening in horror at the sight of her rapidly moistening eyes. Even he, so poised, was not excluded from the general masculine fright at feminine tears. It was one of the few *faits accomplis* available to her gender, and Lydia could only be thankful she was able to utilize it at will. Her childhood ambition to become an actress – before Grandfather had informed her that this was an occupation for charlatans – was at last serving her well.

'Oh, I did not mean to . . .' Ashford said, putting out his hands as if to comfort her, and then snatching them back when he realized this would be entirely inappropriate. 'My apologies, Miss Hanworth, I did not intend to distress you – how insensitive of me to ever imply . . .'

As Ashford trailed off, helplessly, Lydia gave several great heaving sniffs.

'I should never wish to embarrass you,' she whispered tearily.

'No, of course not, of course,' he said.

Patting down his pockets, Ashford produced a beautiful silk handkerchief upon which she blew her noise, noisily and thoroughly. The force of it knocked one of her ostrich feathers askew once more.

'Better?' Ashford asked, maintaining eye contact determinedly, though the ostrich feather now hung perpendicular to Lydia's face. She held the handkerchief out to him.

'No, no, you may . . . you may keep it,' Ashford said, appearing to keep a grimace off his face with great difficulty.

They walked on in silence for a few moments. Several times Ashford took in a sharp intake of breath, as if he were about to speak, but did not. Lydia waited him out, with bated breath – was now the moment . . . ?

'I perhaps did not appreciate how nerve-wracking such an event as this might be,' Ashford said. 'It was thoughtless. I am sorry.'

'Oh,' Lydia said, in genuine surprise. She had not thought him the sort to apologize.

'I wish to help you feel more at ease,' Ashford said. 'How can I do so?'

'La, I am quite comfortable,' Lydia said.

Ashford did not look convinced.

'I hope you know,' he said. 'That you need only be yourself, even here.'

'Myself?' she said innocently. 'But I am.'

Ashford shot her A Look.

'I hope you don't mind my disagreeing with you,' Ashford said, 'but I do not think you have been.'

Lydia let out a sceptical snort.

'You think you know who I am?' she said, before she could stop herself.

'Miss Hanworth?' he said, brows raising in surprise. 'Is there something you wish to say?'

Lydia bit her lip, berating herself for allowing Ashford to see her mask slip.

'No, no,' she assured him. 'There is nothing.'

'Miss Hanworth, I do wish you would confide in me.'

He was not going to let it go – she had to give him something.

'Forgive me. It is just this is all so very new to me.' She gestured around them, at the portraits, the gallery, Hawkscroft itself. 'I confess I have been all of a quiver, ever since I arrived.'

'Yes, I noticed,' Ashford said.

'You did?' She widened her eyes again. 'But I have been trying so very hard to hide it!'

'Even so,' Ashford said. 'What is it that you find so daunting? Perhaps I can help?'

Oh, lord. What was she meant to say now? She had not planned for this.

'It is everything,' she said. 'There is so much I do not know.'

'It is not so complicated,' he said. 'We are not born with the knowledge – we all learn.'

'You do not wish to marry someone who already knows it all?'

Lydia was genuinely curious. He must know that she was not the most likely choice, however well she had behaved back in London. 'A lady who is already prepared for such a life . . . surely that would have been easier?'

She expected him to offer her a piece of flummery, some empty flattery entirely in keeping with what she knew of his two-faced character, but Ashford surprised her again.

'A troubling number of those ladies are my relatives,' he said confidingly.

Lydia was startled into laughter. She had not thought him to be amusing.

'If we ever once shared a nursery, I do not wish to marry them,' Ashford went on, smiling too. 'A little rule of mine, you see.'

'Incest is not quite as *a la mode* as it was,' she agreed, and this time he was the one to laugh. She had never seen him do so, before. It changed his face entirely and for a moment, she felt she understood better why he was so widely held to be charming and—

Lydia stopped her thoughts in their tracks. What was going on here? Were they *bonding*? No, no, no!

'I do find it difficult to understand why you chose me,' she said abruptly.

The smile slipped from Ashford's face.

'If you regret it,' she continued, 'I wish you would tell me.'

The words were not premeditated, but in the moment all she wished was to jolt them away from the easy warmth that had looked about to form.

'I don't . . .' Ashford broke off, looking away and down. Was he emotional? Surprised by her frankness?

'Miss Hanworth, I would not have asked you to marry me,'

he said, 'if I did not wish for it.' He looked back toward her. 'There may be much for us to learn about one another, but I am looking forward to it.'

He seemed so sincere, so heartfelt. Lydia held his gaze, struck despite herself. She did not know what to say.

There was the clearing of a throat. Reeves had approached without either of them hearing him.

'The riding party has returned,' he said. 'Lady Phoebe wishes to inform you that refreshments are being served on the terrace.'

'Thank you,' Lydia said.

'I can make your excuses,' Ashford told her, 'if you would prefer to rest or . . . change.'

'No, no.' Lydia shook her head, seeing out of the corner of her eye the ostrich feather droop still further. 'Let us join them.'

Ashford did not argue with her. They turned together to leave the gallery and then, so casually and subtly that Lydia would not have noticed had she not been paying him quite so much attention, Ashford reached up and tweaked her ostrich feather back into place.

And that was – well, it was kind. The apology: that too was kind. It was all rather kind, wasn't it?

And in the face of it, Lydia began suddenly to feel rather cruel.

8

Lady Phoebe allowed them only half an hour at the refreshment table before moving them briskly on to the next activity.

'Lawn billiards!' she declared, springing to her feet as if there was not a moment to waste. An hour before, Lydia would have shared such an attitude, but now she rose to obey Lady Phoebe's chivvying rather reluctantly. She did not wish to play billiards. She wished to think.

'Goodness,' Lady Morton said, fanning herself vigorously, sending wafts of red tendrils fluttering around her face, 'I am far too fatigued to participate.'

'Truly?' Lady Hesse said rather derisively. 'I have always thought you so . . . *robust* a woman.'

'I slept uneasily,' Lady Morton said.

'Uneasily? Or . . . guiltily?' Pip wondered, picking up his pencil and flicking his notebook to a fresh page.

'*Pip*,' Lydia entreated softly. Ought she bid him discontinue with this notebook business? It was certainly proving his eccentricity, but was he now going too far?

'Lady Morton does not deserve such insolence, sir!' Lord Hesse glared at Pip around another giant collar. 'I have a good mind to call you out!'

'Don't be silly, darling,' Lady Hesse said.

'*Mother!*' Hesse said through gritted teeth. 'I am not silly.'

'Was I being rude?' Pip asked Lady Morton, as if this had never occurred to him. It probably had not. Pip had many qualities, but self-awareness could not be counted as one of them. More than once it had fallen to Lydia to extricate him from a social misstep.

'Oh, I do not mind in the least,' Lady Morton said, appropriating herself of Pip's arm. 'Let us take a turn of the gardens together, and you may satisfy *all* your curiosity.'

The billiards pitch had been laid out on one of Hawkscroft's rolling lawns, with seats and parasols and several footmen to attend to them. Lady Phoebe divided them into pairs for the game, and Lydia was relieved to be given Hesse for a partner. Had she been placed with Ashford, she could not have wasted such an opportunity to perform more incomprehensible stupidity for Ashford's benefit, but after their tour, however, she was not sure she had the stomach for such tricks. It had been a great deal easier to plot Ashford's downfall before she had come to know him a little better.

'Are we ready?' Lady Phoebe said. 'Waldo, I think we shall begin!'

But Waldo was not attending. Reeves was speaking quietly in his ear and gesturing back towards the house.

'. . . he wishes for an audience.'

'Waldo!' Lady Phoebe called again, holding out a mallet towards him.

'I am afraid you will have to do without me for a moment,' Sir Waldo said. 'I have to attend to some business.'

'What business?' Lady Phoebe said, a tiny frown appearing between her eyes. 'We have guests, Waldo.'

'I warned you of this,' her husband replied.

'Did you?'

'Yesterday. You are so forgetful,' he said, reaching out to pinch her chin, and they gazed at one another so caressingly that Lydia had to look away.

Her eyes, almost against her will, sought out Ashford. As if sensing them, he looked up and smiled. Lydia shifted uncomfortably in her riding habit, and not merely because the thick wool material was too hot for such activities as this. She had forgotten, a little, how very pleasing he was to look at.

'Reeves, you will have to hold Waldo's place,' Lady Phoebe declared, holding out the mallet towards Reeves who took it after the tiniest beat of hesitation. Was this not just classic behaviour from Lady Phoebe – to change the rules on a whim, and then change them back? Was this a trick?

'I think not,' Ashford said firmly, and yes, *of course*, Ashford would not wish to play a game with a servant, because he was far too high and mighty to. Then, 'I hear Reeves was one of Wellington's best riflemen, which constitutes unreasonable advantage,' he said.

'The 95th regiment, wasn't it?' Dacre said, once again proving his exceptional manners. To have remembered such a thing about his *brother's* butler – not even his own – was quite remarkable.

'Are you a very good shot?' Brandon asked.

'I wouldn't go as far as that, my lord,' Reeves said modestly. However, by the end of his turn, he was receiving joking curses from all the gentlemen, even Ashford. What was happening, here? The man who had used the word 'Cit' was comfortable playing billiards with a butler?

Ashford and Miss Hesse took to the field next. Miss Hesse had not played before, and Ashford had to spend a little time talking her through the rules of the game. He did so patiently, of course, because apparently everything he did was patient. Patient and calm and unexpectedly *kind* and it was so irritating Lydia could *scream*. Where had *this* version of him been, during the Season? Or had he always been this person, and she had just been blinded by his poor first impression? Perhaps his words to Mr Brandon, in that corridor long ago – perhaps she had misunderstood them, remembered them for worse than they were? She had been frustrated, that day, hadn't she? Perhaps it had led her to judge him too harshly?

But where did that leave her? Even if he were not as bad as she had thought, she still did not love him, and that was what counted. But to continue to visit such humiliations upon him, knowing he did not deserve them . . . It did not make her feel a particularly good person.

'Miss Hanworth! It is your turn!'

Some might consider lawn billiards a relaxed sport. Not Lady Phoebe.

'Waldo is missing all the fun,' Lady Phoebe fretted. 'Ashford, will you fetch him? He'll listen to you.'

If Ashford thought it strange that he was being used as an errand boy, he did not show it. 'Brandon – I shall rescind my tutoring role to you.'

'Right you are!' Mr Brandon said, beaming at Miss Hesse.

'There are others who might wish for a turn,' Lady Hesse

intervened quickly, as Pip and Lady Morton approached, their circuit of the gardens now complete.

'Right you are,' Mr Brandon subsided gloomily.

Lady Morton took up the mallet gamely enough, giving Pip a wink of farewell.

'Can we speak?' Lydia said quietly to her brother. 'I am not at all sure what to do.'

'Fret not, I am,' Pip said, taking an evaluating glance around the group. 'This is our moment.'

'Our moment for what?'

'For investigation,' he said. 'While everyone is occupied out here, I shall begin my search.'

'Of the house?' Lydia said, a little alarmed.

'Stands to reason I'll find some clues inside.'

Lydia bit her lip. This was her fault. She had encouraged this, but she ought to have predicted that Pip would get carried away.

'Recollect no crime has actually been committed,' Lydia felt beholden to remind him.

'Yet,' Pip said darkly. 'But there's bound to be something – I've never met such smoky fellows in all my life, and Simmons *did* say I have prodigious instinct for such things.'

Lydia did not doubt that Simmons had said such a thing, but just as a lady ought to feel some cynicism for compliments given by a gentleman trying to win her favour, so too did she think Simmons' opinion on Pip's investigative skills ought perhaps to be taken with a pinch of salt.

'If you are discovered somewhere you ought not be,' she reasoned, 'they are quite likely to think *you* the smoky one. I do not think it wise.'

'I shan't be discovered,' Pip said, 'for you will be keeping watch.'

'But I— Oh, very well.'

He was not likely to change his mind, and far better that she be there beside him, to defuse whatever scrape he might fall into, than he go alone.

Lydia tugged an ostrich feather from her head and held it up to the group. 'Alas! My brother is going to escort me to change my hat!'

No one paid them any mind, for Miss Hesse had just managed to score a point and Mr Brandon raised both his hands in a whooping cheer.

'Will you be able to hold the fort for our pair, Lord Hesse?' Lydia asked. 'I'm sorry to abandon you.'

'Oh it doesn't matter,' Hesse said, raising his chin. 'A child's game, really – oh by Jove, good shot!'

He forgot his world-weary aloofness long enough to enthusiastically applaud Dacre's sportsmanship, while Lydia and Pip made their way back toward the house, through the open French doors, across the drawing room, and down the long corridor that led to the grand staircase.

'We shall pass directly by Sir Waldo's study,' Lydia warned Pip. If it would not have looked odd, they would have been better rounding the house and re-entering via the front door, so that they might climb the grand staircase directly, but no matter.

'Fact is, just need to appear nonchalant,' Pip said.

He began a strange sort of walk, sort of swashbuckling and duck-footed, as if his hips had become abruptly loosened from his waist.

'No, no,' Lydia said. 'Don't do that!'

They were about to pass Sir Waldo's study, the door to which was standing just slightly ajar when Sir Waldo's voice boomed out:

'—a complete disgrace!'

'Your advice is kindly meant, sir, but I do not require it,' Ashford said.

'You evidently do,' Sir Waldo said, 'if you can countenance marriage to such a terrible creature!'

Lydia and Pip paused, mid-stride. They exchanged a glance, and then, by silent agreement, pressed themselves against the wall to listen.

'I would thank you to speak more carefully of my betrothed,' Ashford said, and Lydia had never heard him speak so coldly.

'I cannot be silent,' Sir Waldo said. 'I consider you something of a younger brother, my lord.'

'You are older, I suppose,' Ashford said. 'But aside from that I am afraid I do not—'

'After all your family has endured, to make such a horrible choice as this!' Sir Waldo went on. 'I did not think you the type to lose your head over a pretty face.'

'I am in total control of my faculties,' Ashford snapped, 'and – rest assured – I always act in my family's best interests.'

'Is it the dowry?' Sir Waldo paid no heed to the anger in Ashford's voice. 'I understand the duchy is in a tough spot but—'

Lydia frowned. This was the first she had heard of such a thing.

'Who told you that?'

'Dear boy, one hears things,' Sir Waldo said, his voice full of condescending sympathy. 'How bad is it? You need capital, I take it?'

'The duchy will be fine.' It was the closest Lydia had ever come to hearing Ashford lose his temper. 'I have it all in hand.'

'Do you? This girl will debase your name! It is the very height of foolishness.'

'*Waldo*—'

'I know you have a devilishly difficult time with the duke, but you need not do this all alone. I wish you had consulted me.'

'I owe you no explanations, Waldo,' Ashford said in freezing accents, 'but you may be reassured that I consider my business dealings very carefully. Miss Hanworth's dowry is considerable, her family unobjectionable, and – ordinarily – her character is entirely docile.'

There was a pause. Lydia's heart was pounding so loudly that she could hear it.

Dowry. Docile. Business dealings. It was far softer than any of the insults Sir Waldo had levelled at her, but Ashford was her future husband. And he was describing her as if she were a – a *horse*.

'But her behaviour?' Sir Waldo moaned.

'Is motivated by nerves,' Ashford interrupted, 'which I assuaged this afternoon. I think you will find her far improved going forward.'

He had manipulated her, then. That little show of earnestness in the portrait gallery had been just that – a show.

'This shall be the last time we discuss the matter, Waldo. My mind will not be altered.'

The sound of footsteps had her jolting back.

'We must go,' she hissed to Pip.

'But—' Pip looked at her face and bit back his protest. 'Yes, of course.'

They hurried down the hall and back out onto the lawn.

'Docile?' Lydia whispered.

'Not good,' Pip said fervently. 'Not good at all.'

'He is worse than I – more than I . . .'

She did not have the words.

'A villain with a moustache,' Pip summarized. 'The most dangerous sort.'

'And to think I felt sorry for him,' Lydia marvelled. 'I thought he might actually . . . *care* for me.'

Her face burnt with mortification. She could not believe she had been so foolish.

Polite laughter tinkled lightly over them as they approached the billiards lawn and she remembered that she was meant to have changed her hat. Lydia reached up and plucked more feathers off her hat, discarding them in a convenient bush. One, two, three, four. She did it so violently that some of the velvet came loose with it, and Lydia could feel a new breeze on her head that was suggestive of a hole.

'Perfectly done,' Pip said.

'There you are!' Lady Phoebe said. 'All of you.'

They turned to see Ashford and Sir Waldo striding out onto the lawn behind them. Neither one was looking at the other.

Lydia had to fight to keep a glare from her face. How dare he! How *dare* he throw her life into such disorder and not even tell her why. He needed capital, did he? Why, he was no better than a common fortune hunter, and she had wasted time feeling sorry for him, had worried she was humiliating him unfairly – had questioned her intentions, her motives, her memory!

'It is your turn, Miss Hanworth!' Lady Phoebe called out merrily.

Lydia accepted her mallet, approaching the ball which had been left at a little distance. She examined it carefully, then hit it with a resounding smack and impeccable aim. It flew directly towards Ashford, forcing him to jump backwards with an undignified yelp, only partially avoiding the ball which hit him on the thigh rather than her original, far more painful, planned spot.

'Goodness!'

'By Jove, that's a hit!' Sir Waldo said enthusiastically.

'I'm not certain it's the right game, though,' Dacre murmured.

Standing upright with a wince, Ashford forced a laugh. 'Have I offended you, Miss Hanworth?'

'I am sorry, my lord,' Lydia said, smiling her toothiest smile.

'All is forgiven,' he said, 'as long as you promise to aim for the hoops in future.'

'I promise,' she said sweetly, and added, in the privacy of her own mind: *to make your life a living hell.*

9

'The yellow, tonight, Jane,' Lydia declared as she entered her chambers.

'I'm not sure the yellow is . . . suitable,' Jane said. Although now fully aware of Lydia's intentions to disgust Ashford, this dress was a step too far for the lady's maid.

'The yellow,' Lydia affirmed, grimly.

'Perhaps I could do something with it – take away the trimming, perhaps, there is so much of it . . .'

Jane, the daughter of a seamstress, could perform miracles with a needle and Lydia had no doubt she might be able to improve the dress if she set her mind to it. Alas, improvement was not on Lydia's agenda.

'It is absolutely perfect as it is.'

It was a gown of sickly yellow, cut in a style not seen in the *ton* for at least ten years past, and it might well have been designed to emphasize Lydia's very worst qualities: the colour brought out her sallowness of skin, the puff-capped sleeves broadened her shoulders, and the white feathered edging paid distinct homage to the goose. It was sufficient to render any gentleman distinctly nauseous, and so shockingly unflattering as to give Ashford cause, surely, to regret the day he was born.

Jane looked her over and grimaced. 'You do know the rest of the household thinks you quite mad? Elspeth – Lady Phoebe's maid – tells me that Lady Phoebe has been ranting and storming about your outlandish behaviour in her bedchamber.'

Lydia gave a nod of grim satisfaction. 'You might warn Elspeth that matters are about to become a great deal worse.'

Then, rigged out in the most unattractive ensemble known to man, Lydia sashayed down to the drawing room, head held high and proud. Everyone turned to look at her and she had the satisfaction of watching their faces light with surprise. Ashford, across the room from her, looked nothing less than aghast.

Stunning.

'Good evening, Miss Hanworth!' Lady Phoebe sang out, eyes upon the feathered trimming as if she could not help but look elsewhere. 'What a – magnificent dress.'

'It is so rare to see gowns of *such* a hue,' Lady Hesse said, hiding her smirk behind a peach lace fan.

'It reminds of one of that fruit . . . I forget the name,' Sir Waldo said musingly.

'Perhaps you mean a flower?' Dacre interceded.

'I meant what I said, brother,' Sir Waldo said, rather more crossly than the situation warranted. 'It was certainly a fruit, one I encountered upon my travels – you won't be familiar.'

'The mango?' Hesse suggested.

'Wrong colour entirely, sir.' Sir Waldo wagged his finger. 'It has an exterior skin of sorts.'

'The pineapple?'

'No, no, no.'

'Perhaps we could move on to another subject,' Lady Phoebe tried to cut in but to no avail.

'It shall bother me all evening if I can't think of it – what *is* it?'

'The banana,' Ashford supplied quietly.

Sir Waldo snapped his fingers. 'You have it, my lord!'

Lydia looked to Ashford. 'Is the banana an attractive fruit?'

Ashford, for the first time in her acquaintance, appeared lost for words.

'I was told it is all the rage in France,' she added. '*Très chic*.'

'Then doubtless we shall all be wearing yellows by the autumn,' Lady Phoebe said, trying to hasten the conversation onward.

'Wouldn't suit you, darling,' Sir Waldo said, shaking his head.

'Not with all the jewels you like to wear,' Lydia agreed. She gestured towards the diamond necklace once again sitting around Lady Phoebe's neck – for why not repeat a prior gambit, when it had been so successful the first time? 'I wonder you do not bruise from the weight of them.'

Across from her, Ashford closed his eyes briefly, as if asking for strength.

'Yes, well . . .'

'On occasion they do!' Sir Waldo said, proudly. 'Largest diamonds in Europe!'

Lady Phoebe gave up.

'Dinner is served!' she sang out, throwing an urgent glance towards Reeves who – face tightening in alarm – beat a hasty retreat toward the kitchen, as Lady Phoebe led the way a full fifteen minutes early.

'Tonight, I shall seat you a little differently,' Lady Phoebe suggested. 'It will all get dreadfully boring if we are seated next to the same person each night, shouldn't it? Miss Hanworth, you may move upwards; Ashford, do take your seat beside her.'

Lydia prepared herself for battle. When she and Pip had planned such moments as this, they had agreed she would restrict her *faux pas* to the verbal and fashionable, only. Anything more than that and she would risk horrifying the company sufficiently that stories of her gross inelegance would follow her back to London. But such soft techniques were no longer enough. Feeling Ashford's eyes upon her, she recklessly took a deep draught from her wine glass. Let the gossip reach Aunt Agatha, she did not care – in this precise moment, she wanted nothing more than to make Ashford feel just as bad about himself as he had made her feel.

For what sort of gentleman described their betrothed in such a way? Despite his words in Uncle Edmund's study, he plainly cared not a jot for her. When she had thought him led by sentiment, she could find some sympathy within herself for his bullheadedness, but now she perceived there was no such excuse. Her poor first impression of him had been correct – nay, entirely too fair. He was, in fact, nothing less than the most reprehensibly arrogant man she had ever encountered, and she must rid herself of all attachment to him with the utmost expediency.

Rounding her shoulders to a slovenly posture, and laying an elbow upon the table, Lydia reached for the jug rather than wait for a refill to be offered to her – tipsiness would be, she felt, helpful on all counts – except—

'Ah, may I offer you some lemonade?' Ashford said, sliding the jug away from her before she could reach it.

She looked up at him, narrowly. Had he done that on purpose? It was difficult to tell. His expression was almost entirely unreadable.

'Yes, please.'

She waited for him to fill up her glass, and then reached for the soup tureen. There would be no waiting for the gentlemen to serve her *this* evening.

'Ah, would you perhaps like some artichoke soup, as well?' Ashford said, hastily seizing the ladle in hand before she could even touch it.

'Ugh, no, thank you,' Lydia said a little irritably. This was not going to work if he kept getting there first. 'I hate artichokes.'

'You do?'

'They make me feel uncomfortable. Physically.'

Ashford cast her a sideways glance.

'I see,' was all he said. 'Would you like—'

'Uncomfortable,' she said, with a vague explanatory gesture to her stomach. 'In my . . . self.'

Ashford made a noncommittal noise that did not invite her to continue.

'Sometimes, even it causes me to—'

'You have my sympathies,' Ashford interrupted.

Lydia shrugged. '*C'est la vie,*' she said, with all the vim and flourish she could muster, and watched as Ashford's hand clenched around his spoon.

Perfect.

As the serving concluded, the table turned as one, in a movement so ingrained it resembled a dance, the gentlemen to their right, the ladies to their left. Everyone except Lydia.

'Miss Hesse,' she called across the table. Miss Hesse paused, midway through turning to Lord Dacre. 'Miss Hesse, did I see you at Captain von Prett's lecture last month?'

A shiver of discomfort went round the table, as when a cat is rubbed the wrong way. Miss Hesse opened her mouth, shut it, glanced to her mother, and then uncertainly back to Lydia. When one dined informally, it was allowable to converse with persons on the opposite side of the table. This was not informal dining, however, despite Lady Phoebe's assurances otherwise.

'I – yes,' she said, at last. 'Mama and I attended together.'

Miss Hesse tried to turn again to Dacre.

'What did you think?' Lydia persisted. and she could almost see the mental calculations passing across Miss Hesse's mind: to ignore a direct question, rude, to speak across the table in such a way, ruder.

'It – he – I . . .' Miss Hesse stammered, so uneasy that Lydia had to steel herself against a pang of guilt.

'Oh, isn't he wonderful?' Lady Phoebe sprang to assist. 'Sir Waldo and I met him at Burlington House, and his descriptions of the Americas were just fascinating, weren't they, Waldo?'

She sent the volley to the opposite end of the table.

'Eh?' Sir Waldo, slower upon the uptake, fumbled the return.

'It was his lecture you found enlightening, was it?' Ashford sprang to assist. 'Not his face?'

'I'm sure I don't know what you mean,' Lady Phoebe said coyly.

There were murmurs of laughter around the table, and the tension Lydia had caused subsided. With Lady Phoebe and Ashford leading the charge, the informality of a group conversation was deemed more permissible.

'Do I know this fellow?' Dacre asked.

Lady Morton batted him playfully on the arm. 'How have you not heard of him, Dacre?'

'Oh, Dacre has always been behind the times,' Sir Waldo said dismissively. 'He's a military chap, isn't he?'

'Originally,' Lady Hesse said, 'but now he's a prodigious explorer.'

'His writings have been in all the papers,' Lady Phoebe said, 'and he speaks wonderfully.'

'All the ladies adore him,' Mr Brandon explained in stage whisper.

'I have not met him,' Lady Morton said. 'But I saw his portrait at the academy this spring – *divine.*'

'He's rather a foppish young cub, isn't he?' Hesse said with a dismissive flick of his head. His curls, so weighed down with grease, moved not an inch.

'Displays little self-awareness,' Pip intoned softly, opening his notebook.

'Oh, the notebook has made it to dinner.' Lady Phoebe's smile grew more fixed. 'How amusing.'

'*Très drôle!*' Lydia agreed, rolling each 'r' for as long as physically possible.

Beside her, Ashford took in a sharp inhale and turned his head abruptly toward her, and for one moment, Lydia thought she might have broken him, thought he might be about to snap at her, in full view of the entire table . . .

'May I offer you a morsel of turbot?' Ashford asked.

Was that it? Was he so lily-livered as to let her get away with such behaviour – a coward *and* a cad?

'No,' Lydia said, disappointed. 'I do not eat any creature with scales.'

'Are you feeling quite well?' Ashford lowered his voice to encourage her to do the same. 'You are acting a little strangely.'

Lydia pretended she had not heard him.

'But Miss Hesse, what did you think of the talk?' Lydia called across the table again – as little as she wanted to distress the poor girl, she could not allow her *faux pas* to be brushed past so easily.

'Oh! I – I found it touching?' Miss Hesse said, and Lydia was about to question her further when Mr Brandon jumped into the fray, beginning a bantering conversation about horseflesh with Lord Dacre. Just as soon as that was concluding, Lydia readied herself again, but Lady Hesse picked up the reins, relaying the contents of a letter she had received just that morning from Lady Jersey. No one was looking at Lydia, anymore. It was as if they had all decided, by silent though unanimous agreement, to block her out of conversation. Lydia subsided back into her chair and – grumpily – picked up the wrong fork to cut up her chicken.

'Lady Phoebe, I must ask,' Lady Morton said, 'are we to expect our surprise guest tonight? Last year' – she turned to Pip in explanation – 'Melville made a surprise entrance on the second evening – we were all beside ourselves!'

'I thought Ashford would faint from excitement,' Brandon said.

'Something of an overstatement,' Ashford muttered.

'Embarrassed by emotion,' Pip recited doggedly, making a note.

'What does Ashford's adoration of Melville say about him, then, Mr Hanworth?' Mr Brandon said merrily. 'Is he a murderer?'

'I imagine it says I have excellent taste,' Ashford said.

'Oh, I quite agree,' Miss Hesse said, eyes shining as she turned towards Ashford. 'Melville is my absolute favourite poet.'

'Mine too,' Mr Brandon said hastily. 'Ashford and I were *equally* excited.'

'Yes, I seem to remember you weeping, did you not?' Ashford said.

'Do you?'

'Girlish sobs,' Ashford confirmed.

'Girlish sobs.' Pip's pencil scratched at his notebook.

'Wonderful,' Mr Brandon muttered.

'I do not feel shame for it,' Ashford said. 'Anyone who *isn't* moved by such literature must surely lack a soul.'

'I hate all poetry,' Lydia announced belligerently, casting aside her lifelong adoration of the form without a thought.

'All of it?' Miss Hesse said, aghast.

'A jest?' Dacre suggested.

'*Au contraire*,' Lydia said and beside her Ashford flinched. 'I think we are all beyond the age of nursery rhymes are we not?' she continued.

'Nonsense!' Pip said supportively. 'No need for it.'

'The theatre is worse,' Lydia added recklessly. 'Why should one *pay* to be bored?'

Lady Morton let out a great peal of laughter. 'Degenerates, the pair of you!' she accused playfully.

And, well, now felt as good a moment as any to debut her new laugh. It was a sound she had practised with Pip in the quiet of the grounds that afternoon. After half an hour it had become a thing of such violently grating proportions that Lydia felt it must surely be the very first of its kind in the history of the whole world.

In its aftermath, no one seemed to know quite what to do. Ashford was staring at her, eyes wide, grip upon his fork so tight his knuckles were white.

'Well,' Sir Waldo said, into the silence, 'this seems as good a time as any to make our announcement, my dear.'

'Does it?' Lady Phoebe said. 'I am not sure . . .'

'What announcement?' Lady Hesse said.

'I have received the most flattering offer,' Sir Waldo said. 'I have been asked, by His Majesty's government, to fill the role of Governor of Mauritius.'

There was a ripple of excitement around the table.

'By Jove!' Mr Brandon exclaimed.

'Oh, my goodness!' Lady Morton said.

Lady Phoebe had frozen in her seat.

'You kept that very quiet, Lady Phoebe, you humble thing!' Lady Hesse said.

'You did not mention . . .' Ashford's brow furrowed.

'Waldo only told me yesterday,' Lady Phoebe said. 'A marvellous surprise.'

'When do you leave?' Lady Morton asked.

'Waldo ships out at month's end,' Lady Phoebe said. 'We have not decided when I will join him—'

'We will *both* leave at month's end,' Waldo corrected. 'I cannot be without you for a day, my love!'

Lady Hesse cooed her approval.

'I believe this calls for a toast?' Dacre said, raising his glass. 'To the Governor!'

They held their glasses aloft.

'Lawks!' Lydia declared.

10

Lydia stood by her bedchamber door, her ear pressed to the crack, listening for footsteps. The ladies had all retired long ago, but it was only now that the gentlemen, who had elected for cards and cigars with Sir Waldo, were drifting towards their beds. Lydia's mind was far too rattled for sleep, and so she waited, until . . .

'Pip,' she whispered, recognizing his profile passing her doorway, and opening her door a crack. '*Pip!*'

He wheeled around, losing a little of his balance in the process. She beckoned him toward her, and as he slid into the room, the telltale scent of port wafted over her.

'Well?' she demanded. 'How did he seem?'

'How did who seem?' Pip said, wandering over to her dressing table and seating himself before the looking glass – seeming a trifle surprised to see his own reflection within it.

'*Ashford!*' Lydia said impatiently, then – when Pip seemed

bent upon adjusting his necktie – snapped her fingers at him impatiently. 'How did he seem?'

She was not foolish enough to think that Ashford would have broken down into public sobs over his Terrible Mistake, but there were other, subtler, signs of inner despair. Had she done enough? Had it worked? Was she free?

'Difficult to say,' Pip said vaguely. He appeared to be having a little trouble focusing his gaze on her. 'Not the chattiest fellow, is he?'

'Did he look at the end of his tether?'

Pip considered this. 'Not at the beginning of it, certainly. Stands to reason.'

'Pip,' Lydia said, trying to master the frustration rising within her, 'you are meant to be my eyes and ears. Is there nothing you can tell me?'

'Nothing is at it seems,' Pip said. '*That's* for certain.'

Turning to face her fully, he extracted his notebook from his pocket and fumbled to open it. 'Dacre, for example – the man's *too* pleasant, it makes no sense – suspicious, I tell you, the way he does not heed any of Sir Waldo's insults.'

Lydia held up her hands. 'Please may you just concentrate, for a moment?'

Pip closed his notebook, a trifle crestfallen. Lydia felt as if she had just kicked a puppy.

'I'm sorry, I did not mean to . . . it is just, this is my future. It is important.'

Pip nodded. 'I know that.'

'Do you?' she said. 'You have performed your role admirably, and I am grateful, but at times I feel as though you have forgotten our purpose entirely.'

Thrice today, she had tried to bend his ear on Ashford, but each time he could hardly bring himself to concentrate for a moment. Too busy daydreaming of mysteries to attend to her.

'I have had a great deal to do,' Pip defended himself. 'The investigation . . .'

Lydia restrained her temper with an effort. 'I need you to be serious now,' she said with tolerable composure.

While she had certainly made an impact upon Ashford this evening, it had not eased her agitation. She felt as if she was a bird flapping desperately at a closed window and the proximity of her escape was only making her more frantic. She had to be free of him, she had to!

But Pip would not yield. 'I am being serious. It is my work.'

Lydia's frustration burst its banks. 'There is no work, Pip! No crime, no mystery. Practising your investigation is one thing, but you are taking it all too far now.'

'Something fishy is going on!' Pip insisted. 'I can feel it in my bones.'

Lydia pressed the heels of her palms to her chin. 'Oh, dear lord!'

'Do you not believe me?'

Lydia lowered her hands very slowly. Pip's eyes were wide as he regarded her, expression stricken.

'I – I . . .' She did not know what to say.

Slowly, Pip reached his hand into his pocket for his pencil.

'How,' he said, opening his notebook to a fresh page, 'does one spell betrayal?'

'Oh, don't do that!' Lydia snapped. 'I did not mean. . . the situation is so precarious right now, Pip, for both of us. If I cannot rid myself of Ashford, then our plan – our life together – it will be ruined. I cannot leave you *alone*.'

'I do not need you to protect me, Lydia,' Pip said.

Yes, you do, Lydia wanted to shout at him. *How can you not see that?* But of course he did not, because that was Pip. Too open, too unselfconscious, too *himself* in a world which would only punish him for it.

'I am the elder,' Pip reminded her. 'Stands to reason, *I* do the protecting.'

She stared at him helplessly. 'I—'

A soft knock interrupted them. Lydia turned, just as Jane poked her head round the door.

'Miss Lydia, are you—'

She halted when she saw them. 'Oh good. You are both here.'

Lydia frowned. 'Is everything all right, Jane?'

Jane did not usually appear in Lydia's bedchambers until morning.

'No, it is not.' Jane pushed the door open. 'No, I – well *we* – need your help.'

She walked inside, leading by the hand another young woman, dressed in maid's uniform.

'This is Elspeth,' Jane said. 'Lady Phoebe's lady's maid.'

As the light of Lydia's candle illuminated their faces more fully, Lydia say that Elspeth's face was tear-stained, her eyes puffy.

'Are you hurt?' Pip rose from his seat.

Elspeth turned to Jane. 'Please, I did not think I *can* . . .'

'They can help,' Jane encouraged, squeezing her palm.

Lydia looked from one girl to the other and frowned. 'Help with what?'

Elspeth shook her head, fresh tears springing to her eyes.

'Feel better in a moment,' Pip encouraged.

'No, I won't,' she choked out. 'Not when I'm like to be killed.'

'Killed?' Lydia repeated, alarmed.

'Killed?' Pip repeated, excited. 'Whatever for?'

'I cannot say, miss,' She turned again to Jane. 'I ought not be speaking to them at all.'

'You can trust them,' Jane promised.

Lydia thought she might know what was going on here. 'Has Lady Phoebe been cruel?'

She could not imagine that her ladyship was the world's easiest mistress and house parties did put such pressure on household staff. All of their grandmother's worst stories were from events such as this.

'No, no Miss,' Elspeth refuted, visibly bridling. 'No, no, it is not her . . . It is my fault.'

Jane shook her head. 'No, it is not.'

'What is "it"?' Pip prompted.

Elspeth stared at them, tears still glinting on her face, the absolute picture of tragedy.

'It's the diamonds, sir,' she whispered. 'Lady Phoebe's diamond necklace. It's gone.'

Pip drew in a deep, ecstatic breath. 'You don't mean it's been *stolen?*'

He turned on Lydia triumphantly. 'I told you there was something smoky afoot – thievery! It is just as I suspected.'

'I didn't do it – I promise I did not,' Elspeth said. 'But I went to clean it tonight, after Lady Phoebe retired – and it's not there.'

'Perhaps it's lost,' Lydia said. 'Misplaced – fallen down the back of something.'

'It's always locked safely in the box,' Elspeth said. 'Sir Waldo is most specific for it's so valuable and he worries about thieves – and I have the only key because he says Lady Phoebe can't be trusted not to lose it.' She let out another sob. 'I have the only key,' she repeated. 'Everyone is going to think I took it.'

'Did you?' Pip asked.

'Pip!' Lydia smacked his arm.

'One has to ask the difficult questions,' Pip said. 'In my line of work.'

'Steal diamonds worth half the country?' Jane said. 'She'd be far better off stealing silverware.'

Indeed. For what servant would set such a rare and easily identifiable item in their sights, when the house was riddled with far easier treasures?

'I would never do such a thing!' Elspeth insisted.

'Then you have nothing to fear,' Lydia assured her. 'We shall go to Lady Phoebe and alert her there is a thief—'

'No! They will think it's me,' Elspeth said, 'and I'll be hung.'

Jane reached out and squeezed her hand. Lydia bit her lip. Servants often received severe punishments for egregious thefts, imprisonment or even transportation to foreign lands, for a mere moment of light-fingered temptation. The largest diamonds in Europe, Sir Waldo had called them. What would be the punishment for such a theft?

'You will not be hung,' Pip said, 'not if we can find the true thief.'

His dramatic, portentous tone filled Lydia with foreboding. 'Pip, we cannot promise such a thing.'

'May I remind you,' Pip said, a bite in his voice that she was not used to hearing, 'that I am a Senior Officer on Bow Street.'

He had promoted himself, since arriving at Hawkscroft. Lydia huffed out an exasperated sigh.

'Pip, I really do not think . . .'

Pip turned to Elspeth and Jane. 'Together, we will find the diamonds and catch the killer.'

'The thief,' Lydia corrected.

'The thief, yes,' Pip said. 'Exactly.'

'Do you truly think it possible?' Elspeth blinked up at him.

'Pip...' Lydia cautioned. To give the girl false hope – it would be unreasonably cruel. More to the point, would it not make her look more guilty, the longer the absence were concealed? 'Lady Phoebe will discover it missing herself if we tarry. What if she wishes to wear it on the morrow?'

'She doesn't,' Elspeth said. 'She says it is too uncomfortable, to put it away until the masquerade.'

'Then all we have to do is find the clues,' Pip said. 'Stands to reason we can solve it in time.'

Lydia grasped Pip's arm and drew him around to face her. 'We ought not to promise anything we cannot fulfil.'

'We have to *try*, Lydia,' Pip said, voice suddenly serious. 'Surely you can see that?'

Still, Lydia hesitated. 'I do not know...'

There was a headache beginning to throb between her eyebrows, and she pressed her thumb there, trying to think. There was an awful part of her that wished Jane had never brought this to their door, for Lydia did not think she could cope with more complications. And yet how could they say no? Pip would certainly not be able to let it alone and she would not be able to let him *do* it alone – but it was not as if she had nothing to do, herself! With the trap of her engagement tightening around her with every moment that passed, to be distracted at such a juncture could be fatal.

'It is too much,' she muttered, more to herself than the others.

'Miss Hanworth,' Jane said. The formality of her address had Lydia blinking in surprise. Jane usually only referred to her as such in front of Aunt Agatha. 'There is no one else who can help. Please.'

Her voice was entreating, almost pleading. Lydia had never heard Jane speak so and it broke her thoughts away from their selfish bent.

We are just the same as they, her grandmother used to tell Lydia at every opportunity, reminding her that, but for a few changes in circumstances, Lydia too would have grown up in domestic service. Such a thing as this could easily have happened to her, or Jane – an injustice, committed by another leaving one left to bear the consequences, alone and powerless.

'You need not be involved,' Pip said, 'if you do not wish to be.'

'If you're in it, I am too,' she assured all three of them. Pip beamed at her. 'Where should we begin? There are hundreds of people it might have been.'

Pip drew himself up to his fullest height. 'I believe no servant would be foolish enough to steal such a thing, and that leaves only our fellow guests.'

Guests who had been informed of the necklace's preciousness and value at great length.

'If Lady Phoebe is to wear the diamonds on our last night,' Pip said, 'we have eight days to find the thief and bring them to justice.'

'Truly?' Elspeth was looking at him as if he had hung the moon. 'You believe we can?'

'Fact is, I *know* it,' Pip said. 'I have already begun by questioning the suspects – Simmons says that is the very first thing one should do, you see. Then, we must search the rest of the house – every room, every bedchamber – for evidence.'

'What sort of things should I look for?' Elspeth asked breathlessly.

'We shall know them when we see them,' Pip said, with a dismissive wave of his hand.

'The house is crawling with staff,' Jane warned.

Lydia's brow wrinkled, feeling that this might be more difficult than Pip imagined. 'What if any of you are apprehended?'

A dozen disquieting scenarios sprang easily to her mind, but Pip only gave a dismissive wave. 'We'll think of an excuse.'

'What if you are apprehended by the *thief*?' Lydia demanded. 'They could be a dangerous person – do you have your pin, Jane?'

'Of course.' Jane withdrew from her lapel a pin the twin of Lydia's own. Grandmother had supplied all her maids with these weapons, knowing as she did how some gentlemen felt they might take liberties with the household staff.

'If we time the thing well enough,' Pip said, 'and use each other as lookouts, we will not be discovered.' Warming to his inspirational role, he added: 'We shall prevail! On this, and on—'

Lydia cut her eyes meaningfully to Elspeth. Just because they were united in this venture, did not mean they ought to reveal all their confidences, surely?

'The *other* matter,' Pip finished, with such significance that Elspeth looked between them, curiosity obviously piqued.

'You are making good progress,' Jane encouraged, with equal indiscretion. Lydia frowned at her. 'His valet reports he is going through snuff by the pound.'

However uneasy Lydia might feel about their loose lips, this was the piece of reassurance she needed. Lydia felt the hard knot in her stomach ease, a little.

'Good,' she said. 'That's good.'

Pip gave her an encouraging smile. 'We can do both, Lydia, I promise. There is time.'

She reached out to touch his arm. 'Thank you.'

He was correct. There *was* still time. And, if Ashford had not jilted her by the end of tomorrow, there was still one – very terrible – thing she had not yet tried.

11

Thursday – Seven days remaining

'I'm not sure I can do it.'

It was after dinner the following evening. The party had retired to the drawing room as they always did, and Lydia and Pip were drinking their tea in a pair of armchairs positioned at a little distance from the rest of the group.

'I'm not sure you need to,' Pip said. '*Look* at him.'

Across the room, Ashford was seated next to Lady Phoebe on a low sofa, looking distinctly careworn. As well he should. This past day, Lydia had launched an attack of unparalleled magnitude upon Ashford's defences. From breakfast to dinner, over toast and *blancmange*, she had interrupted him, misunderstood his witticisms, claimed an ignorance on any topic he raised and referred to him as 'your grace'. Twice. From the clumsy to the frankly ludicrous, no stone had been left unturned in a siege so thorough that even Reeves had a wary look in his eye when he regarded her.

'And yet he will not jilt me,' Lydia said. 'I need to do something to push him over the edge, Pip.'

Still, she was not certain she had the wherewithal to carry out what she was considering next. It was Aunt Agatha's most serious rule, and the only one Lydia had never had any difficult following.

'I would have to be very brave,' she said.

'It is everyone *else* who will have to be brave.'

'Do you have any other ideas?'

They were running out of time.

Pip did not answer. Lydia followed the direction of his gaze to where Lady Morton and Lord Hesse were deep in conversation.

'Conspiracy,' Pip identified darkly, raising his quizzing glass to regard them.

'Mere flirting,' Lydia said, shaking her head. 'I think she just does it to irritate Lady Hesse.'

'A ruse, perhaps.'

'There was nothing in Hesse's chambers,' Lydia reminded him.

Pip had managed to scour both Lord Hesse and Miss Hesse's chambers while everyone was enjoying a nuncheon that morning.

'I shall try Lady Morton next,' Pip said. 'She's practically dripping in jewels.'

Indeed, as Lady Morton turned back to face the room, Lydia could see a glint of rubies at her ears, throat and wrists.

'Doesn't that prove she can buy her own?' Lydia wondered.

'There are *other* motives for theft,' Pip said waspishly.

Lydia opened her mouth to argue but was forestalled.

'Shall we have some music?' Lady Morton suggested. 'We could do with waking up a bit.'

Lydia straightened up, a rush of nerves prickling down her spine. Here it was. Her chance, if she was brave enough to seize it.

'You cannot,' Pip hissed in her ear. 'Fact is, cannot let you.'

'It would be the perfect distraction for you,' Lydia whispered. 'You might slip upstairs while everyone is watching.'

Pip hesitated, clearly torn.

'Everyone is here,' she said, 'and the servants will all be at dinner, now.'

'Do you intend to entertain us, Lady Morton?' Sir Waldo said, with a wag of his eyebrows.

'Oh, you scallywag,' Lady Morton said. 'I am far too old for such exertions, as you well know.'

She smoothed her hands coquettishly down the closely fitting bodice of her cerise gown.

'I cannot allow you to utter such falsehoods, my lady,' Hesse said dramatically.

'She *did* attend your christening,' Lady Hesse told her son, twisting a smile in Lady Morton's direction. Lady Morton narrowed her eyes.

'I think music a famous idea,' Lady Phoebe interceded hastily. 'Don't you think, Ashford?'

'Perhaps something soothing?' Ashford said. He was leaning his head against the back of the sofa, uncharacteristically slovenly. At dinner, Lydia had concluded the meal with a lecture on her grandfather's factory, and he had yet to recover.

'Cynthia!' Lady Hesse said. 'Go and fetch your music.'

Miss Hesse gave a tiny, tired sigh.

'Miss Hesse has entertained us three nights in a row,' Mr Brandon pointed out lightly. 'Is she not fatigued?'

Was anyone going to ask Lydia? This was one scenario in which she could not barge blindly in. When word of this got back to Aunt Agatha, and word would, indeed, travel far, she wished to be able to say, '*They insisted, I could not refuse again without seeming ungracious!*'

'Oh, she's used to it, poor thing,' Lady Hesse said. 'When one has a voice that sweet, one can't hide it away.'

'Are you certain, Miss Hesse?' Lady Phoebe said. 'I should offer but—'

'No, no,' Sir Waldo protested. 'You cannot subject us to such caterwauling, it is too cruel.'

Lady Phoebe flushed.

'Twenty years of lessons, and she cannot hold a note,' Sir Waldo declared to the room with a fatuous chuckle. 'Not at all the thing for a Governor's wife!'

'I recollect your voice being rather fine, my lady,' Dacre said, in quiet support.

'You only say so because yours is even worse!' Sir Waldo said. 'Perhaps the two of you should duet! That would wake us all up a bit.'

He slapped his thigh, laughing.

'Not kind, Waldo,' Lady Phoebe said, though Dacre – giving an infinitesimal shrug – did not appear to have minded.

'I am jesting, my dear.' Sir Waldo patted Phoebe's knee. 'You need not take everything so seriously.'

'Perhaps Miss Hanworth would like a turn?' Mr Brandon said, smiling at her.

It was perfect. It was horrifying. If this did not cause Ashford to jilt her, nothing else would. She looked to Pip. He took in a deep breath and nodded.

'I should be honoured,' Lydia lied, her mouth very dry. She did not, even now, know if she could do it.

'I do so love to sing,' she said, and felt herself stand as if she were not quite in control of her own body. 'I'd sing every day if I could – but you will have to forgive me – my skill is not the equal of Miss Hesse's.'

Never had a statement been truer.

'You mustn't worry,' Lady Hesse insisted. 'Cynthia has the privilege of a unique gift and several excellent masters – we should none of us be so unjust as to compare you.'

'How kind you are.' Lydia inclined her chin modestly.

'Splendid!' Sir Waldo clapped his hands together.

'Have you any music?' Lady Phoebe asked. 'Ought someone fetch it for you?'

'I'm afraid I brought none,' Lydia said, entirely truthfully – for not in a thousand years would she ever have thought it would come to this. 'I shall have to play from memory.'

She stood and approached the pianoforte as if she were ascending the gallows, sat down before it and ran her hands over the keys in apology for what she was about to do. Pip, at the back of the room, slid out of the door. Ashford, placed in a chair quite near the pianoforte, had his eyes fixed politely on her face, entirely unaware of what was about to happen.

Lydia took in a deep, deep breath and opened her mouth . . .

To say the past few days had been trying for Ashford would be an egregious understatement. In truth, his cousin's house party – previously an event he associated with good conversation, excellent food, and the promise of relaxation – had begun to assume the proportions of a nightmare.

Every ounce of forbearance, patience and politeness he possessed had been brought to bear – strained and taxed and challenged as Miss Hanworth, his affianced bride, had tested him in ways he had not known were possible. Indeed, Ashford's nerves, a concept he had not previously believed in, might never recover, and yet he had remained outwardly calm throughout. He had retained a sense of positivity, weathering Sir Waldo's disapproval and Lady Phoebe's consternation, certain that the assessment of her character he had made those six weeks ago, could not have been so wrong, still sure that the Miss Hanworth he had previously known would soon re-emerge. She had not.

But the moment she began to sing, Ashford felt whatever vestiges of hope that remained leave his body in one fell swoop. It was not just the timing – a nervous young lady, performing in front of veritable strangers for the first time, could be forgiven for coming in a few beats ahead of where she ought – nor the inadequate mastery of the pianoforte, which had surely never known its keys to be jangled so aggressively in its lifetime. Those he might have explained away.

It was her voice. At turns a coarse rasp a full octave lower than the song required, punctuated by shrill screech whenever the song required a high C. And the song required many, many high Cs. In the second verse, some of Miss Hanworth's nerves appeared to have dissipated, and she became louder, more assured. But volume held no virtue for her, and the audience pressed themselves back into their seats, as if this extra distance would provide respite. Even those with the hardiest constitutions among them looked faint.

By the time the song appeared to be entering its final verse – Ashford had never noticed it had quite so many before – he felt as if he had lived a thousand lives. It was quite possible, in fact, that he had already died, and this was hell – pure, unending hell.

But worse was still to come.

For the final chorus, Miss Hanworth – who had thus far kept her gaze fixed upon the keys of the piano, as if she was trying very hard to get each one correct (and wasn't that a horrifying thought?) – lifted her head and looked straight at him.

Before today, Ashford wouldn't have said he particularly believed in the power of music to convey meaning. He was much more struck, on the whole, by literature and he certainly wouldn't have thought the simple country ballad Miss Hanworth was currently butchering – the tale of a country maid looking for her lost sheep – had any deeper meaning other than the literal. And yet, as he stared, almost mesmerized, into Miss Hanworth's eyes – as still as if she had turned him to stone – he felt a vision come upon him.

I do so love to sing – I'd sing every day if I could, she had said, just minutes before. And she would. He could see his future, his entire life, lying ahead of him, with the certainty and clarity of a vision from God.

Every night they spent together, rain or shine, guests or no guests, she would sing. And he would no more be able to stop her than he had been able to stop any of her outlandish behaviour this whole week. He would have to sit there, suffering not only from the humiliation of his friends and family witnessing such a spectacle, but also from the very real pain of his soul to hear a deplorable noise. She would sing, and he would listen, song after song, night after night and year after year – until the final, sweet release of death.

At long, long last, the final searing note resounded, wrenched from Miss Hanworth's mouth with all the subtlety of a plough oxen. In the silence it left behind, no one knew quite what to say, and, blinking their eyes in confusion, exchanged shocked glances with one another.

'Music has . . . such a power does it not?' Miss Hanworth said serenely, looking around at them with a gentle smile.

'Certainly,' Sir Waldo said. 'Certainly, it . . . does.'

'Shall I play another?'

'No!' Eight voices spoke over one another.

'I think we are all feeling a little tired,' Lady Phoebe said. 'Can I offer anyone a cup of tea?'

Ashford's recollection of the next hour was a little loose. He felt clammy, ill, as if he had caught a chill, and he fulfilled the duties of a guest to the very bare minimum. Fortunately, it was not long before everyone began to drift upstairs to bed.

'Sleep well, my lord,' Miss Hanworth said cheerfully to him, as she passed by him to fetch a taper from Reeves.

Ashford dipped his head in response – he could not trust himself to speak – and caught Mr Brandon firmly by the arm as that gentleman tried to pass him, frogmarching him towards the smoking room.

'Everything all right, my dear chap?' Mr Brandon asked, as Ashford shut the door behind them with a click. 'You need me for something?'

Ashford did not answer, walking briskly over to the liquor cabinet, and pouring out two very large glasses of brandy.

'Really, Ashford, I'm not sure I can manage a nightcap. It's been a long day.'

'No matter,' Ashford said, tipping first one, then the other down his throat. The warmth blazed a path down his throat, chasing away some of the clamminess from his veins.

'She's a madwoman,' he said at last. 'She is. There is no other explanation.'

'Who?' Mr Brandon asked, with forced innocence.

Ashford turned to look at him, not in the least convinced. Mr Brandon dropped the act.

'She's . . . eccentric! I think it charming.'

'That,' Ashford said, jabbing a finger towards the drawing room. 'Was not mere eccentricity – it was . . .'

Words failed him.

'I cannot believe I thought she would be a suitable bride,' he said.

'Perhaps it would be exciting,' Mr Brandon said quickly. 'One never knows quite what she will or will not say, after all – keeps one on one's toes! And lots of gentlemen enjoy having a wife not quite in the usual way.'

'Which gentlemen?' Ashford demanded.

Mr Brandon pondered this for a moment.

'Marlborough!' he said after a moment. 'That wife of his has a collection of ferrets unlike anything I've ever known – *very* eccentric – and Marlborough always looks happy enough, doesn't he?'

'He's always covered in bites,' Ashford pointed out. 'It's not a state to which I aspire!'

'I am trying to be positive.' Mr Brandon sighed. 'I do wish you might join me.'

'Oh, please!' Ashford snapped. 'You don't believe any of this – you're just worried I'll turn my attentions to Miss Hesse!'

'I must say that stings,' Mr Brandon protested, though he flushed a guilty red. 'If I am worried, it is just on the ladies' behalf! Who's to say you might not change your mind about Miss Hesse, too, the moment she sings a song a little flat?'

'A little flat? I have heard death knells with more musicality,' Ashford said. He shuddered. 'To think I am engaged to such a creature.'

The words slipped out before he realized what had happened.

'You are engaged?' Brandon said sharply.

Oh lord! Ashford pressed a shaking hand to his forehead.

'When did this occur?'

'Before we arrived,' he said. There was no point lying about it now. 'We had to keep it a secret, the duke wishes to announce it himself at the ball.'

Brandon went to pour brandy for each of them.

'I begin to appreciate the gravity of the situation. *Christ.*'

'She has not the smallest idea of how to behave,' Ashford said. 'She cannot sit through a single meal without committing the most horrendous *faux pas*, she calls everyone by the wrong title, no matter how often she is corrected, she hates all literature, she knows so little about so much, her *laugh*—'

He broke off, pressing a shaking hand to his mouth.

'The laugh is bad,' Mr Brandon acknowledged. 'But . . . just think how large your houses are! You would not hear it.'

As if that shrill cackle could not make its way through *miles* of stone and mortar.

'Oh, I'll hear it.' He jabbed a finger quite violently to his forehead. 'I can still hear it now.'

'Are you sure it's not you that's gone mad?' Mr Brandon asked.

'If I have, it is her that has driven me so,' Ashford said. 'Each day she gives new and different reasons for me to despise her company. I cannot bear it a moment longer.'

'But you must,' Mr Brandon said, voice suddenly serious. 'You made a promise, Ashford. You gave your word.'

Ashford heaved a great sigh, all the agitation seeping out of him in a great rush.

'I know,' he said. 'I know. I just . . . I do not know what to do.'

'Nothing you can do,' Brandon said. 'But when you are married, you'll solve it: you'll see.'

'How? By sending her to the madhouse?' Ashford said. 'What kind of asylum could fix her?'

Mr Brandon considered. 'One that provided singing lessons?'

12

Friday – Six days remaining

The next morning Ashford could not bear to look at Lydia. He had attempted it, once, but a single glance at her walking dress (a figured muslin gown of hideous orange to which Jane had added a dozen flounces) had him swallowing convulsively and fixing his attention determinedly elsewhere.

As the party readied themselves for the day's outing, he involved himself in a deep conversation with Lady Hesse, ignoring all Lydia's attempts to catch his eye. He even made sure they were not seated next to one another in the barouche that was to take them to a nearby village, where a picturesque walk would take them to the top of a ruined keep.

It boded well for the day – Lydia could taste victory on the air – but she would not get her hopes up prematurely and had a most diverting plan of attack for this outing.

'I believe you will find the ruins most interesting,' Lady Phoebe declared as Sir Waldo handed her down from the barouche. 'One can still make out much of the church and gatehouse, and there is some rather fascinating carved stonework that—'

'My darling girl, you will bore our guests to tears if you continue on in such a way,' Sir Waldo interrupted with a chuckle.

'Oh – of course!' Lady Phoebe said, pinking in embarrassment.

The whole party was in attendance, save for Pip, who had claimed to have caught a chill.

'Fact is,' he had said over breakfast, 'cough, cough.'

The household was by now too used to his idiosyncrasies to think this odd, allowing Pip to take advantage of their absence to continue his search. Lydia now sent a silent prayer that he not be discovered somewhere he shouldn't.

She pushed her concern away as the rest of the party paired up in predictable fashion for the walk, Mr Brandon offering his arm with prompt eagerness to Miss Hesse, before Lady Hesse could prevent it, and Lady Morton seizing Lord Hesse's arm before she could prevent *that*.

'May I walk with you, my lord?' Lydia said sweetly to Ashford. Ashford turned to regard her, valiantly managing a moment of eye contact before looking quickly away again.

'Of course,' he said, tugging unhappily at his cravat. 'In fact' – he lowered his voice as he offered his arm – 'I should be glad of a chance to . . . discuss some matters with you.'

And there it was.

Lydia had to work to keep the victorious grin from her face. Finally – finally. Today was the day he was going to jilt her! She sent another prayer, this time of thanks, to the heavens. At last. Deliverance was upon her – and ahead of schedule, too.

Ashford and Lydia brought up the rear; he walking at a slower pace than usual, brow furrowed as if deep in thought. Planning, no doubt, how he was going to break the news. Lydia remained quiet. Her work was done and all she had to do was wait for him to speak.

She concentrated her thoughts instead to what she and Pip would do afterwards. They would need to remain until the business of the diamond necklace was concluded, of course – having promised Elspeth their aid, Lydia was now as determined as Pip to see it through. At least once she was freed from Ashford, she could dedicate herself entirely to this cause. Pip had managed to see to Mr Brandon's rooms the night prior, but Lady Morton's had proved elusive – her lady's maid was the conscientious sort who rarely left her post, no matter what Elspeth did to tempt her away. Perhaps, with Lydia helping more actively, they might have better luck. Then, once they had found the thief, they could return to London and life would be open before them once more.

Her mood lifting higher than it had been in days, Lydia took in the scenery around her with genuine pleasure. However ill at ease she might feel in Hawkscroft itself, with its forbidding luxury and overly manicured lawns, it was situated in the most beautiful countryside. The path ahead wound through a forest of lush green, the branches above dappling the sunshine down through the leaves onto them, the only sounds to be heard birdsong – and the strident tones of Sir Waldo.

'The tarn is man-made,' he was explaining, as the gentle curve of the path took them in view of a wide pool of water, its surface thickly coated in bright algae. 'By old Capability whatsit, you know.'

'Capability Brown, in the year—' Lady Phoebe began.

'Goodness, another fact!' Sir Waldo said. 'You risk becoming quite the bluestocking, my love!'

Underneath her high-poke bonnet, Lady Phoebe's cheer dimmed, though Sir Waldo did not appear to notice that his teasing had hurt rather than amused on this occasion. Ashford, however, had his eyes upon his cousin's crestfallen face, a tiny frown between his eyebrows – and, really, Lydia could not have his attention so divided.

She slowed her pace to a dawdle, pretending to admire the tarn. Ashford huffed a sigh and slowed his pace, too. The rest of the party disappeared around a bend.

Lydia looked away from the tarn to take a sidelong view at Ashford under the brim of her bonnet.

'We ought not tarry,' Ashford said. 'We might lose our way.'

'Very well,' Lydia said, though she made no effort to quicken her steps. They had been walking in such close formation, and would Ashford really jilt her in the presence of eavesdroppers?

She took another evaluating glance at him. His eyes were fixed on the path in front of them, unmoving and unflinching, but what she could see of his profile was tired and wan. Every now and then, as it had done all morning, a shadow passed over his face, as if he were remembering some awful torment. Perfect. Everything was as it should be, so why did he not speak? Plainly he detested the very sight of her now; plainly he wished to end their ludicrous engagement, and yet even with a clear opportunity and complete privacy, he would not speak. What more did he need?

Lydia followed him around the edge of the tarn, frowning. A breeze fluttered the flounces on her skirts and then the festoon of organza ribbons securing her beehive bonnet. Lydia reached up to still the ribbons, then paused. Yes! She unravelled the strings and, watching Ashford to make sure his eyes were firmly on the path ahead, she threw her hat across the tarn with all her might.

'Oh no!' she announced. 'My hat has fallen from my head.'

Ashford turned. He looked toward the hat – incomprehensibly floating in the centre of the tarn – and then back toward Lydia.

'Oh dear,' he said without any emotional inflection whatsoever.

'I do not wish to catch the sun,' Lydia said, with a worried glance up to the sky.

'Lady Phoebe brought a parasol with her,' Ashford said. 'I'm sure she will allow you to use it.'

He made an encouraging hand gesture. Lydia did not move.

'It belonged to my mother,' she lied.

Ashford's gaze went once more to the tarn. Lydia understood his reluctance. It looked very murky. She would not wish to go in there, were she him. Unfortunately, however, she was going to make him.

'She gave it to me just before she died,' she added, the final cherry.

Ashford sighed. 'Fine. I shall fetch it for you.'

He looked down to his Hessian boots rather mournfully, as if evaluating the merits of soaking them beyond repair against how fussy he would appear if he took them off. Appearing to conclude 'boots on', he did, however, remove his coat of blue superfine and cast it gently on a nearby rock. Then, he took in a deep breath and stepped in to the tarn. It was a scenario in which there was no winning. A tentative, ballerina insertion of the foot would have made him appear ridiculous, but the determined stride he opted for – while altogether more masculine at first – ran him immediately foul of the slippery rocks on the lakebed. His arms windmilled furiously as he tried to step upright.

'Don't fall over now,' Lydia called.

'Very helpful,' she heard him mutter under his breath, as he regained his balance.

He began to tread carefully forward.

'How on earth did it go so far in?' he demanded. 'It is not even a very windy day.'

'It was one of those unexpected summer gusts,' Lydia said sagely. Then, when he stumbled again, added: 'It might be slippery!'

'Thank you so much,' he said sarcastically.

He was thigh deep in water before he got in arm's reach of the hat, which he grabbed quickly and turned back with a great sloshing sound.

Lydia clapped her hands joyfully.

'Oh bravo,' she said. 'Bravo.'

'Perhaps you might tie it a little more tightly this time?' Ashford began, with a poor excuse of a smile. 'Then we can catch up to the—'

Lydia never heard the end of the sentence. Ashford's foot had landed poorly, on something very, very slippery; with a shout of shock, his leg skidded out from under him, and he fell back into the water with an almighty splash. The tarn was just deep enough that his entire head went under for a moment, too, before he emerged, coughing and spluttering, water and algae pouring off him.

'Oh dear,' Lydia said, pressing a hand to her mouth to contain her laughter. 'Oh dear, it was rather slippery, wasn't it?'

'Yes!' Ashford said savagely, climbing to his feet with the grace of a newborn foal. 'Yes, it was, Miss Hanworth – rather slippery indeed.'

He dragged himself from the water, resembling a very cross sea monster.

'And now look at me!' he said, looking down at his tarn-soaked self and letting out a wild peal of quite deranged laughter. 'Just when I thought my lot could not get any worse!'

'You *do* look rather uncomfortable,' Lydia observed.

It was a comment that appeared to light the smouldering flames of Ashford's rage.

'Oh, do I?' he bit out. 'How fitting – how incredibly fitting – because I do, in fact, *feel* rather uncomfortable, Miss Hanworth.'

He brandished the bonnet at her somewhat violently.

'I had thought that you must, surely, have run the gamut of new ways to debase me,' he said. 'And yet here I am – soaked in fetid water – and my mortification is complete. Are you satisfied?'

He was almost shouting now.

'No, of course I am not,' Lydia lied, desperately trying to blink some tears into her eyes, for the situation could surely be exacerbated by tears. 'Indeed, I *am* sorry. I never meant for you to fall in so embarrassing a manner. You must feel so humiliated.'

Ashford did not appear to be listening. He leant down to tear off his left boot, tipping it upside down to clear it of water.

'It is not just the hat,' he said, watching an incomprehensible amount of water run out. 'It is *everything*.'

Hopping about on one foot – and truly, Lydia almost felt mortified for him, for the display was quite intensely unmasculine – Ashford replaced his left boot and then pulled off his right. Neither one appeared to have been in the least waterproof.

'Everything you have done since arriving here,' he went on bitterly, 'has been so impossibly deplorable that it defies comprehension. Indeed, I could almost accuse you of – of . . .'

Lydia had ceased trying to cry in favour of observing Ashford's meltdown as gleefully as one might watch one's horse win a race.

In fact, she had lost control of her own expression entirely, and it would prove to be her mistake.

For when Ashford raised his head to fix her with another accusatory glance, he did so to see her regarding him with a wide grin of triumph on her face.

'Of – doing – it – on – purpose,' he finished.

Lydia rearranged her face as quickly as she could, but the mask, once removed, did not go back on as smoothly. Ashford stared at her, rage tempered with incredulity upon his face, as realization slowly began to dawn. There was a long pause.

'You *have* been doing it on purpose,' he said.

'What on earth can you mean, my lord?' Lydia asked, all distressed confusion. Even to her own ears, it was no longer convincing.

'I thought you seemed different, right away,' he said, almost to himself. He raised a trembling hand to his forehead. 'Your gowns, your behaviour, your laugh . . . It makes sense, now. But why on earth would you *do* such a thing?'

Lydia bit her lip. She had not prepared for this eventuality.

'Was it some sort of test?' Ashford demanded. 'Did you mean me to prove my worth by – by driving me mad?'

What on earth should she say? What was the correct manner to manage this?

'Tell. The. Truth,' Ashford said, very deliberately.

And, well . . . Perhaps that was the only thing left to do.

'Not test you,' Lydia said. 'More . . . get rid of you.'

'Get rid of me?' he said, voice rising again. 'Get rid of *me*?'

'I do not wish to marry you,' Lydia explained. 'Thus I had to get rid of you.'

'But . . . *why?*' he said. 'I do not understand . . .'

'I imagine you do not,' Lydia said, 'given you think yourself such a prize that you reject women for French and capriciousness.'

Ashford mouthed at her wordlessly for a moment, as a goldish stranded on land.

'You heard our conversation, that night,' Ashford said at last. 'When I was—'

'Enumerating all the ways ladies were failing to meet your standards,' Lydia finished for him, 'as if we are chattels, there to be judged and found wanting?' She smiled sweetly. 'Yes, I heard you.'

He stared at her for a moment longer.

'Then why did you accept my proposal?' he said, at last. 'A simple "no" would have seen me off, I assure you.'

Lydia snorted.

'Decline you, the future duke?' she said. 'With my aunt and uncle present and barely two minutes to prepare for the moment? I could not.'

'You most certainly could.'

'They would have made my life miserable,' Lydia went on, 'and there was no telling what you would have done had I refused you.'

'I would have done nothing!' he protested. 'I would have respected your decision; why would you possibly think I would do anything else?'

'Perhaps because we never spoke of it,' she snapped. 'Why did you never think to speak privately to me first?'

'When exactly do you suggest I should have done so?' he said. 'At one of the hundred-person events at which we met? In the middle of the dance floor, as we changed partners every other moment?'

'Other gentlemen seem to manage it,' Lydia said.

Ashford fished furiously in his pockets for his snuffbox. He opened it with a savage flick of his hand, as he always did – and a puddle of water came out. He let out a strangled noise of rage, and snapped it shut again.

'You gave me every sign you wished to marry me,' he said. 'You danced with me, and spoke with me and walked with me . . .'

'Consider the power you hold,' she said. 'I do not think there is a single young lady in London who could refuse a dance, or a conversation, or a walk with you – a future duke – without causing risk to her reputation. Accepting a dance does not, however, constitute consent to marriage.'

'But you *did* consent!' he said. 'I asked if you wished to marry me, and you had every chance . . .'

'I barely had a chance to think,' she corrected. 'Did you not notice I was not exactly dancing with happiness?'

'I thought you were shy,' he protested. 'Your uncle informed me you welcomed my suit.'

'They would have me marry a goat if it had a title!'

'If you felt pressure from your family, then I am sorry,' Ashford said. 'But that is not my fault. You must admit that.'

'You never thought to speak to me first,' she said, 'because you never imagined in a thousand years I would not fall over myself to marry you. *You* must admit *that*.'

Ashford flushed a slow, incriminating red. 'And so, you came up with this scheme to humiliate me?'

'No!' she defended. 'Merely to show you that you had been wrong in choosing me.'

He gave a savage shout of laughter.

'Consider that very much achieved!' he said. 'I have never encountered such unfeeling malignance in all of my life – I can only thank God that I saw your true colours in time to avert such a colossal error.'

'Thank me, not God.' She folded her hands together demurely and gave him a sweet smile. 'It is I who has brought this about, not He.'

'You are monstrous,' he said.

'Oh, pish.'

'Pish?!'

'Your actions are preventing me from marrying my true love,' she said. 'I do not think my reaction so monstrous.'

Ashford stared. After a moment, he heaved out a sigh and ran a distracted hand through his hair.

'You ought to have explained you had a prior attachment,' he muttered.

Lydia faltered. Ought she to correct his assumption? She did not had have a specific gentleman in mind, after all. Though . . . 'And you would have understood?'

It did not matter that she had not yet met him, her true love. She knew he was out there.

'I am not heartless,' he said. 'Your family do not approve of the match, I take it?'

'Well,' she said, looking away and brushing some imaginary dust from her sleeve, 'I suppose the thing is . . . I do not know him, yet.'

Ashford frowned. 'What do you mean?'

'I did not mean you to take me so literally,' she said. 'It is the *opportunity* of which you rob me.'

'You do *not* have a prior attachment? This gentleman does not exist? He is fictional?'

'He certainly *exists*,' she snapped. 'I have met several possibilities already.'

'Have you? Such as?'

The scepticism in his tone and face made her wish to push him back into the tarn.

'Well . . . Captain von Prett for one,' she said boldly.

'Captain von Prett,' Ashford sputtered. 'The explorer?'

'Yes,' she said.

'The one who goes on and on about his tragic affairs?'

'The one,' Lydia corrected, 'who is honest and brave and is not afraid to feel.'

'Christ,' Ashford raised his eyes to heaven. 'Have you even met him?'

'Once,' Lydia admitted. 'But there was a moment of true connection and—'

'I wager he does not even know your name.' He looked as if he did not know whether to laugh or begin shouting again.

'He does,' Lydia insisted, though she was not sure of this herself. 'Besides, it is not about Captain von Prett. It is about what he symbolizes.'

'You have spent a week humiliating me in favour of the *symbolism* of another man?' Ashford demanded.

'I have spent a week humiliating you in order to secure my freedom,' she corrected.

He took in a deep inhale through his nose. 'You will write today and inform your guardians that you have ended the engagement,' he said with forced calm. 'And you will leave Hawkscroft in the morning.'

'No,' she said.

'*No?*' he said, jaw dropping. 'What on earth do you mean?'

'If I could have cried off, do you think I should not have done it at the very beginning of the visit?' Lydia said, irritated. 'I cannot, because of Mildred.'

'Who – who is Mildred?' Ashford asked, looking about wildly as if he expected her to appear. 'What has she to do with anything?'

'My other aunt,' Lydia explained. 'She's awful and I will be sent to live with her if I cry off. No, you must jilt me.'

He shook his head wordlessly.

'That is the whole point of this,' she stressed, stepping closer. 'I thought you understood.'

'I cannot jilt you.'

'You just said you wanted to!' she said indignantly, reigning in a desire to stamp her foot.

'I am a gentleman,' he said. 'It would be the height of dishonour.'

Oh, lord.

'Recollect no one knows we are engaged,' she pointed out, taking another step towards him. 'It cannot be *that* dishonourable.'

'Lady Phoebe knows,' he said. 'Sir Waldo, Mr Brandon.'

'It is supposed to be a *secret*,' Lydia said acidly.

'This is all your fault.' Ashford combed a distracted hand through his wet hair. 'If you had come to me, right at the beginning, and explained your position . . .'

'You had already left town!' she said. 'I could not.'

'Then I might have been able to prevent all of this,' he continued as if she had not spoken. 'But you did not, and now it is too late for anything but you to cry off.'

'And live with Aunt Mildred?' she said. 'She is awful.'

'At present,' he said. 'I could not care less if Aunt Mildred is a real-life ogre. You will cry off, today.'

'If enough people know to risk your honour,' she said, 'then it is sufficient to risk my reputation, too.'

No gentlemen, not even Captain von Prett, was likely to fall in love with an ostracized woman. No hostess was likely to invite an ostracized woman to dinner.

'You are young,' he said. 'Society will forgive you.'

'Oh yes, Society is just *so* forgiving of young, untitled women,' she said. 'I think not. You let the news out so you must lump the dishonour.'

He leant forward. 'No.'

'You simply must.'

'I simply will not.'

'You must.'

'No, *you* must.'

'No, *you*—'

Ashford broke off. They were practically nose-to-nose, each glaring fiercely at the other. His grey eyes – ordinarily so calm, so benign, so blank – were now alight with rage.

The moment stretched, then Ashford turned away to take a deep breath – Lydia did not know quite why he was bothering; they did not seem to be calming him down.

'The others will be wondering as to our whereabouts,' he said, his voice tight. 'Let us go. Later, we will discuss, calmly, our next steps over a cup of tea.'

'You may drink all the tea you like,' Lydia said, amazed her voice was so steady. 'I already know what my next steps are. If you will not cry off today, then I will have no choice but to continue.'

'Continue?'

'Continue showing you how very awful your life would be, married to me,' she said. 'I have a great many other things planned, you know.'

'Do you stoop now to blackmail?' Ashford said quietly.

'I will stoop to anything I need to,' Lydia said, raising her chin. 'For my freedom. I will sing every night—'

'Stop!'

'I will call Sir Waldo a duke and Lady Hesse a Miss, I will humiliate you in every single way I—'

'Oh, I *loathe* you,' he burst out, clenching both his hands round the sadly bedraggled hat as if he would quite like to throttle her instead.

'Then jilt me,' she said.

'No.'

'Then you will simply have to accept the consequences,' she said, and with that she turned her back and walked away, heart pounding but affecting complete nonchalance.

'This,' he called after her, 'is not over.'

13

'Again, Miss Hanworth, again!' Sir Waldo begged.

'I really don't think—' Ashford started, but Lydia was already windmilling her arms, screwing up her eyes and dropping her mouth ajar in a most unladylike imitation of Ashford's fall into the tarn.

'Careful!' Lady Phoebe said, as Lydia knocked a glass, though Reeves caught it neatly before it could fall.

Since the day was so fine, Lady Phoebe had requested the afternoon's refreshment be served on the front lawn, though the outdoor location did not in any way diminish the extravagance of the table. There were crystal jugs filled with lemonade and plates of delicate slices of fruits and cake arranged before them, with a series of parasols protecting the table from the sun. A selection of lawn games had been brought out, for further entertainment, and Lords Dacre and Hesse were batting a feathered shuttlecock back and forth with some energy.

'I had no idea you were so gifted an imitator!' Sir Waldo declared to Lydia, clapping his hands together.

The others seemed less willing to laugh at Ashford's expense, even with their host's encouragement, exchanging only tense smiles.

'Perhaps we ought to speak of something else,' Lady Phoebe began.

'Oh, it's just jesting, Phoebe,' Sir Waldo said. 'You need not be so tense – Lady Morton found it amusing, didn't you, my lady?'

But Lady Morton was not attending, her eyes having strayed over to Dacre and Hesse. In deference to the afternoon heat, they had shed their coats to play in their shirts and breeches, though were playing an energetic enough game to have a light sheen of perspiration.

'A fine jest,' Lady Morton agreed absently, ogling the gentlemen quite as much as if this were a performance organized for her benefit alone. It might well have been. Every time he struck the shuttlecock, Hesse shot her a glance over his shoulder.

'Yes, bravo,' Ashford said.

Having changed his dress upon returning to Hawkscroft, Ashford had valiantly regained some of his usual calm along with his superfine coat, but certainly not all of it. Sitting rigidly in his seat, hand clenched around his goblet of lemonade, he looked and sounded distinctly peevish.

'*I* do not think it so amusing,' Lady Hesse said. 'Do you, Cynthia?'

'No,' Miss Hesse said obediently. 'You must be very brave.'

'Thank you, Miss Hesse,' Ashford said, and was it Lydia's imagination or was he regarding Miss Hesse rather wistfully? She could understand why. Sitting there in her simple white gown of French cambric, doing and saying everything that was right and proper, Miss Hesse could not contrast more to Lydia if she tried. On Lydia's left side, Lady Hesse observed them smugly; to Lydia's right, Mr Brandon's face had tightened.

'Mr Hanworth!' Lady Morton called in greeting, looking over Lydia's shoulders. 'Are you feeling better?'

'Entirely better,' Pip said, taking a seat at the table and accepting a glass of lemonade. Lydia caught his eye, and he sent her a grimace – he could not have found anything useful then.

'Though I fear I may have a relapse,' Pip added hastily. 'Tomorrow morning, perhaps, while the rest of you are riding.'

'How specific,' Ashford said, and he was regarding Pip through narrowed eyes. 'What kind of illness did you say it was?'

'The erratic kind,' Pip said. 'Have I missed anything of note?'

'Your sister,' Sir Waldo said to Pip, 'was just entertaining us with a most amusing story. Miss Hanworth, you must do it again—'

'The jest has run its course,' Ashford interrupted. There was a decided snap in his voice that bordered on outright rudeness. Sir Waldo flushed a little and turned to look at Lady Phoebe rather accusingly, as if she were accountable for Ashford's behaviour.

'Oh, do learn to take a joke, Ashford,' Lady Phoebe said, springing immediately to her husband's defence. 'Recollect you once pushed *me* into a pond.'

'We were children,' Ashford said irritably.

'You used to be a terror,' Brandon said, in a reminiscing sort of way. 'Do you remember how we would sneak into each other's bedchambers to make apple pie beds?'

Ashford flushed. Miss Hesse let out a scandalized giggle. Lydia's insides pickled with second-hand mortification. Dear lord, was this truly her opponent?

'Such rascals,' Lady Hesse said indulgently.

'What else did you do?' Miss Hesse asked.

'Enough, Brandon,' Ashford said.

'Once,' Brandon said, 'I dyed all of his shirts pink.'

Miss Hesse giggled again, and Brandon's face lit up.

'He repaid me though,' Brandon said, 'by stuffing eggs under the floorboards of my bedchambers. You would not believe the scent they made!'

'Enough, Brandon,' Ashford repeated.

'What happened to that boy?' Brandon asked, still grinning.

'I grew up,' Ashford said, quellingly. 'Perhaps you might try it.'

'Sounds ghastly,' Brandon said.

Miss Hesse giggled again.

'May I offer you some lemonade, my lords?' Reeves said quietly, as Dacre and Hesse – game finished – approached the table. Hesse accepted a glass without comment, while ever-polite Dacre looked Reeves directly in the eye to smile his gratitude. By now, Lydia understood this politeness to be entirely characteristic of him. She had not witnessed Dacre make a single discourtesy to any of Hawkscroft's household staff, and she would wager he received an elevated level of service, as a result, for from dawn to dusk his cup never ran empty.

'Thank you, Reeves,' Dacre said, accepting a glass which looked marginally fuller than Hesse's. 'Though I am not sure I deserve it after my defeat.'

'You did not let me win?' Hesse checked.

'Would I do that?' Dacre protested mildly. Reeves suppressed a smile as he turned away.

'Do not fear, Hesse!' Sir Waldo said. 'I attest that Dacre's backhand truly is that weak.'

'True enough,' Dacre said, accepting this teasing as gracefully as he always did.

'Would anyone else care for a game?' Hesse asked.

Lady Morton rose to her feet, brushing down the skirts of her Pomona-green gown so that the delicate fabric clung even more closely to her shape.

'I do. Though I do not know the rules,' Lady Morton said, 'so you shall have to teach me the correct form.'

Lydia suppressed a smile. Such tutelage would surely involve a great deal of close contact.

'I think Hesse ought to rest,' Lady Hesse said, apparently thinking along the same lines as Lydia, 'the day is so warm.'

'Mother,' Hesse muttered, raking his hand through his pale locks. 'I am not a child.'

'Did you play pranks as a boy, Lord Dacre?' Miss Hesse said, turning enquiringly in his direction.

'Oh, I used to *torture* him,' Waldo declared proudly, before Dacre could answer. 'Once I took his cufflinks and—'

'Took?' Pip asked, leaning forward suddenly. 'Stole?'

'Only briefly,' Sir Waldo said irritated. 'No – don't write that in your little book, sir, it was only a prank!'

'Perhaps we might speak of something else.' Ashford pinched his nose with two fingers, as if to ward off a headache.

The table fell silent, all regarding Ashford a little warily. Over on the grass, Hesse was adjusting Lady Morton's hands on her racquet and her tinkling laugh made Lady Hesse's eye twitch.

'Lady Phoebe,' Dacre said after a brief pause, 'what will happen to Hawkscroft while you are in Mauritius? Will you shut it up?'

'There is still so much to discuss,' Lady Phoebe said, throwing

Sir Waldo a quick glance. 'It might be that I remain here, to look after the estate.'

Sir Waldo hooted.

'Look after the estate?' he repeated. 'You would run us into bankruptcy within the month, my dear, you have no head for business.'

'I settle all my own bills,' Lady Phoebe protested.

'Oh yes, hats and dresses,' Sir Waldo said, with an exaggerated nod. '*Exactly* the same.'

Lady Phoebe gave him a swat on the arm. 'I could learn. There are books on such things.'

'Are there?' Miss Hesse asked, wide-eyed.

'Yes,' Lydia said, before she could stop herself, for she could recollect her grandmother trying to locate such dry tomes at the library.

'See!' Lady Phoebe said triumphantly. She turned to Lydia. 'Are they good?'

Perhaps Lydia could turn this to her account. 'I do not know,' she said airily. 'But then, I cannot read.'

'Well, that's not true,' Ashford said.

'Yes, it is,' Lydia said.

'You *can* read.'

His cheeks were colouring in frustration.

'I think I would know.'

'I have seen you write.'

'I can write; I cannot read.'

'They are the same thing.'

'No, they are not.'

'Stop lying!' Ashford snapped, leaning forward to jab a finger at her.

There was a shocked silence, and Lydia willed her lip to tremble.

'Ashford,' Sir Waldo reproached, 'there is no need to shout.'

Blinking, Ashford looked around. Everyone was staring – at him, not at Lydia. Their shock at Ashford – perfect, controlled Ashford – behaving in such a way was writ clear upon their faces.

'Not everyone enjoys the same access to education,' Lady Hesse said softly, faint disapproval colouring her voice. She might toad-eat Ashford for her daughter's sake, but even he was not immune to the rules of polite behaviour.

Lydia cast her head down in apparent mortification, and Miss Hesse laid a comforting hand on her arm.

'I – apologize,' Ashford said. 'I – I don't know what came over me . . .'

'Perhaps you are coming down with something?' Lady Phoebe suggested.

'You *are* looking a little flushed,' Mr Brandon said.

'Did you catch a chill from the water?' Dacre suggested.

'I did not.' Ashford had balled his hands up into fists so tightly his knuckles had turned white. Just a little prod further and he would lose all control . . .

'An infection?' Lady Phoebe suggested.

'Could it be,' Lydia said, 'from that fish which bit you.'

Miss Hesse let out a shocked gasp.

'What are you *talking* about?' Ashford's jaw dropped. 'This is utter nonsense.'

'When you fell in the lake,' Lydia said. 'You remember?'

She windmilled her arms again. Ashford glared at her with real hatred.

'You did not say anything about a bite,' Mr Brandon said. 'One really has to be careful with bites, you know, Ashford.'

'Nothing bit me!'

'What did it look like, Miss Hanworth?'

'Purple, with yellow spots,' Lydia said.

She had not realized before today what a gifted improviser she was – truly, she ought to have had a career on the stage.

'Foreign,' Lady Hesse breathed in horror, fluttering her fan wildly. 'We ought to call for a doctor.'

'No!' Ashford insisted.

'A friend of mine was bitten by a snake, once,' Mr Brandon said. 'In France. Just came out of the grass – slam!'

He mimed a biting serpent.

'Then what happened?' Miss Hesse whispered.

'He had to miss the races,' Brandon said, heaving a grieved sigh. 'Poor chap was devastated – a cautionary tale if ever I've heard one, Ashford.'

'Is it?' Ashford said. 'Given it's the wrong animal and the wrong country and nothing ever bit me in the first place?'

'Would a doctor even be able to prescribe an antidote?' Lady Hesse wondered.

'If we can draw a picture of the fish, perhaps?' Brandon said.

'I can draw a picture,' Lydia offered. 'Pip, may I borrow your notebook?'

'There was no fish!' Ashford said explosively, rising to his feet and stepping away from the table. 'I have not been bitten. I feel perfectly well.'

They all leant minutely back.

'Right you are,' Sir Waldo said soothingly. 'Right you are.'

'Aggressive temper,' Pip intoned, writing in his notebook.

'I shall take a turn of the gardens,' Ashford said. He dug in his pocket for his snuffbox and took a pinch to each nostril.

'Very calming,' Lady Hesse approved.

'Miss Hanworth,' Ashford bit out, 'would you care to accompany me?'

'No thank you,' Lydia said.

He narrowed his eyes. 'I should like your company.'

There was nothing to be gained from allowing Ashford to voice whatever threats he was so clearly desperate to utter. Far better to let him marinate in this temper.

'I intend to rest before dinner,' Lydia said, affecting a little yawn. 'I imagine it is going to be quite the eventful evening.'

As everyone else returned to their conversations, she held eye contact with Ashford for a moment longer, giving him just the tiniest little glint of a smile.

She hoped he understood this for the threat it was.

Lydia was able to successfully avoid Ashford until near dinner time – imagining, with not insubstantial enjoyment, that his temper must now be pickling his insides. When the hour neared half past six, she dressed once again her yellow gown, for the only thing worse than wearing it once was, surely, to wear it upon two consecutive evenings.

As she left her room, Ashford appeared almost immediately, as if he had been lying in wait for her on the landing; his expression already stormy as he took her in.

'I suppose this garb is one of your stratagems?'

'You suppose correctly,' she said, walking directly past him.

'And your brother?' he asked. 'He is involved in this, I presume?'

'You presume correctly.'

'I knew it,' he said, hurrying after her. 'His bizarre behaviour – this investigating business . . .'

'Oh, that's all Pip,' Lydia said, quickening her steps. 'His eccentricity is entirely genuine.'

'I don't believe you,' he said, keeping pace with her. 'It can't be.'

She threw him a sunny smile over her shoulder. 'Would I lie?'

'Your deception knows no bounds,' he said darkly.

'Not everything has been a lie,' she said. 'I do hate fish. That was true, you know.'

'Oh well, thank goodness for that.'

'Once,' she said, tilting her head toward him confidentially, 'my Aunt Agatha forced me to eat a whole plateful of fish pie and I was quite incomprehensibly sick.'

Ashford elected to ignore this.

'Vomiting,' she clarified.

'Yes, thank you – and as reassured as I am—'

'And I truly cannot sing, not in the least,' she added. 'That was not acting.'

'My relief knows no bounds.'

They had reached the stairs. Lydia grasped her skirts – a few feathers puffed up into the air – and began to walk quickly down.

'Truly, you ought to be thanking me,' she said, 'not berating me.'

'I'm sorry,' he said, pausing in outrage at the top. 'Do you believe yourself to have done me some kind of favour?'

'It was certainly for your benefit as well as mine,' she said. 'It is not easy, you know, standing up in front of everyone, singing in such a way, but I did it – for us both. You would be miserable married to me. Come now,' she added, 'you can't dawdle there.'

'As I am beginning to perceive,' he said, stamping down the stairs towards her while she resumed her descent. 'You must be the most accomplished liar that I have ever encountered.'

'Oh, cease acting so injured,' Lydia said impatiently, reaching the hallway at the bottom and turning towards the next set of doors. 'You are far more deceitful than I.'

'*What?*'

'You pretend to be the perfect gentleman,' she said, 'whilst thinking everyone is below you.'

'I do not think—'

'You pretend to be polite and considerate and agreeable, whilst truly acting only according to your own interests.'

'I am not—'

'You maintain this perfect, pristine mask at all times,' she stressed, 'hiding who you really are—'

'I am hiding nothing!'

Lydia's temper was climbing, now.

'You pretended to feel something for me,' she said. 'You proposed in such language as to suggest your sentiments had been caught. Saying you felt *certain* of me – letting my aunt call it "love at first sight".'

'I could not exactly correct her!' Ashford said. 'It would have been so rude!'

Lydia let out a disbelieving laugh. 'Deception is more polite, is it?'

'When have I deceived you?'

'Oh, then I must be mistaken,' she said. 'You must have mentioned, in your proposal, that you only wished to marry me for my dowry. I must have simply forgotten.'

'What are you—'

Lydia stopped in her tracks, wheeling round to face him.

'I *heard* you,' she said. 'I heard you tell Sir Waldo that you had thought me unobjectionable and biddable, and my dowry considerable. I heard that the duchy needs capital, which I assume is the only reason you offered for me, whatever you said in your proposal.' She jabbed an accusing finger at him. 'I heard it all.'

Ashford stared. 'You were eavesdropping *then*, too? Is no private conversation safe?'

'I am glad I did,' Lydia said. 'It seems to be the only time you speak honestly. Were you ever going to tell me the duchy was in "dire straits"? Or was that a surprise you were saving for our wedding night?'

'I – I did not—' he broke off, pressing a hand onto the balustrade as if to steady himself.

'Do you deny deception now?' she demanded, with another jab for good measure.

He recoiled away. 'It does not make me a villain to consider marriage a matter of business,' he said defensively.

'If it is business, then I must have missed the negotiation,' she said. 'You never *said*—'

'One does not discuss such things with one's bride,' he said defensively. 'It is not done!'

'How terribly convenient.'

'This is the way of the world!' he protested hotly. 'It is the entire purpose of the Season! It is why we were all *there*.'

'It is not why *I* was there!' Lydia said, so angry she felt she might cry from the frustration of it, and she turned to walk away from him, but Ashford seized her hand before she could.

'Whatever our disagreement,' he said urgently, pressing her fingers between his own, 'we have to be sensible. Let us call a truce and speak properly.'

'No.'

'I cannot think properly with you behaving so wildly!'

'That is rather the point.'

'But if I could,' Ashford continued, 'I am sure there is a way we could both get what we want.'

'I am already getting what I want,' Lydia said doggedly, trying to pull her hand from his grasp.

'You have not thought this through,' Ashford said. 'You have embarrassed me, I admit it. You may continue to do so, I am sure, but you will certainly harm your reputation in the process. Where will that leave you?'

Lydia did not answer. In the past few days she had, she could admit, pushed her behaviour far past the boundary of what caution ought to allow, but she could not de-escalate, could she? Not now when the great advantage of Ashford's cluelessness had elapsed. She had to show strength.

'What will it cost me,' he said, 'to cause you to cease this madness?'

Lydia lent towards him.

'I thought you were poor?' she said, voice so mean and soft she herself was shocked to hear it.

Ashford flinched.

'I have been very clear about what I want,' she said. 'Jilt me, and I shall leave you alone. Do not and . . .' Her voice trailed off meaningfully.

He looked at her, a muscle ticking in his jaw. 'You ought not make an enemy of me,' he said eventually.

He meant it, she could see that. Lydia raised her chin, heart beating fast.

'Yes, well, as much as I do fear the apple pie bed and floorboard eggs,' she said acidly, 'make all the threats you will, my lord, but in truth, you have no leverage, no bargaining power. Any humiliations you might visit upon me only further *my* agenda. You may as well give in, now.'

'Never,' he said.

'Then brace yourself,' she said. 'For I have much in store for you.'

She wrenched her arm away and turned towards the drawing room – Ashford hot on her heels.

'I will see you regret this,' he hissed, as they crossed the threshold.

'What was that, my lord?' Lydia asked loudly. 'I could not quite hear?'

Under the enquiring eyes of Lady Phoebe, Ashford wilted.

'I said I was looking forward to dinner,' he said sulkily.

Lydia smirked. She had never felt more powerful.

Most of the party were gathered before the windows, admiring the golden sunset, and Lydia hastened over to their side, Ashford trailing petulantly behind.

'I too am looking forward to dinner,' Lady Phoebe agreed, with more than mere politeness. Her face was flushed with excitement, her smile wide. 'But before then, I have a surprise for you all!'

She raised her voice to carry over the room, and everyone turned to regard her.

'I am so delighted to announce,' she said, 'that we have an addition to our party, this evening, who will be joining us for the rest of the week.'

There were murmurs of interest from around the room. Lady Phoebe paused coquettishly, relishing the moment.

'May I welcome my very great friend, Captain von Prett!'

14

For a moment, Lydia wondered if she had taken leave of her senses. Had the pressures of the past days sent her over the edge? How long was she to be beset by such incredibly vivid hallucinations? For there was Captain von Prett, stepping into the room and looking just as striking as he had at the lecture where she had first encountered him, with the famous cowlick that fell just so, heavily marked brows and a distinguished aquiline nose. His evening attire was perfect in its simplicity: his dark blue coat lay across his shoulders just so, and his satin knee breeches had not a single crease.

For the third time in as many days, Lydia felt her mind grind to a complete, shocked halt.

'A coup indeed,' Lady Hesse murmured, watching as Lady Phoebe ushered the captain over the threshold.

'Oh, my goodness,' Miss Hesse whispered.

'Such a pleasure to have you with us!' Sir Waldo boomed with his usual volume, seizing von Prett's hand in a vigorous handshake. 'Such a pleasure.'

'I did not know he looked like *that*,' Lady Morton said *sotto voce*, stepping away from the window and reaching up to adjust her bodice a touch lower.

'Lord Dacre, my brother-in-law,' Lady Phoebe continued, moving Dacre forward.

'Is he so special looking?' Lord Hesse said in peevish undertone.

'I've never truly seen the appeal, myself,' Mr Brandon muttered.

'You have eyes, don't you?' Lady Morton said.

Lydia tore her eyes away from Captain von Prett to look around her. Everyone else was staring, too, whether in admiration or churlishness. Even Lady Hesse was trying to subtly fluff up her curls. That clinched it. Von Prett was real. He was here, in the flesh, and for one long moment, Lydia felt awash with excitement. She had so wished to renew their acquaintance! Fortune was smiling on her at last and—

'How *interesting*.'

Ashford's voice was extremely close, intimate in tone. Lydia turned to him slowly, knowing that she would not like what she was about to see.

'I believe *that*,' Ashford said, a seraphic smile sweeping across his face, 'might constitute some leverage, don't you think?'

And Lydia remembered where she was.

Remembered why she was here.

Remembered what she was wearing.

'It's moments like this,' Ashford said, as Lady Phoebe began to walk Captain von Prett around the room, so quietly only she could hear him, 'that one does indeed believe in the power of divine intervention. Would you introduce me to your paramour,

Miss Hanworth? As your betrothed, I should so love to meet him.'

This was bad. This was very bad. Too many thoughts were flying around her mind to focus on any single one, and all she was aware of was the sound of her heartbeat in her ears. She could not have predicted this, this was utterly new territory now, the kind that required several hours to properly absorb, and then several days to re-strategize, but Lady Phoebe was approaching, and Ashford was bowing and Lydia had no more than five seconds before she was going to have to speak to Captain von Prett, and it was becoming very difficult to breathe . . .

'May I present Miss Hanworth?' Lady Phoebe was there.

It took Lydia a moment to remember how to curtsey, and even longer to remember how to speak. She rose, staring – gaping, really, for her mouth was open and she could not seem to close it.

'A pleasure to make your acquaintance, Miss Hanworth,' Captain von Prett said, bowing in turn.

'I – we – we've met, before,' Lydia stammered.

'Oh!' Captain von Prett said, a flicker of a frown quickly wiped away. 'But of course! It was at the, er . . .'

'Perhaps you do not recollect the exact encounter?' Ashford suggested happily.

'You meet so many people,' Lydia said, wishing it were appropriate to elbow Ashford in the side. 'Of course I did not expect—'

'At Darracott house,' Captain von Prett said, snapping his fingers in realization. 'We spoke after my talk.'

'You remember?' Lydia beamed. *Take that, Ashford.*

'Of course,' Captain von Prett said. 'You wished to know more about my dear Emmeline, did you not?'

The captain had lectured on some of the far and foreign shores he had visited, so vividly that one felt one had accompanied him. For Lydia, however, it had been his earnest description of Emmeline, his first love who had tragically died before their marriage, which had made the most impression.

'Yes,' she said, rather faintly. His smile was very warm, and in such close proximity, the effect was rather overwhelming. He had remembered her. It was more than she would have dared to hope.

'I can only wonder that I did not recognize you at once,' the captain said. 'Have you have changed your . . .'

His eyes swung down to the yellow dress and widened.

'If you are wondering of what the gown reminds you,' Ashford put in, 'we decided it was a banana.'

Lydia had never hated anyone as much as she did Ashford in that moment.

'May I introduce Lady Hesse and Miss Hesse?' Lady Phoebe said, moving swiftly on.

'Good evening, sir,' Lady Hesse said crisply, keeping a protective hand on her daughter's arm. Miss Hesse was already blushing, as she came forward – prettily, of course. Blast. Charmingly attired in a muslin gown of the softest shade of pink, she looked as fresh as a newly bloomed rose.

'We have met before, too, have we not?' the captain asked Miss Hesse, bowing low over her hand.

And if he had spoken to Lydia with the same warmth, he was certainly looking differently at Miss Hesse. Blast, blast, *blast*. There had never been a worse moment to resemble a fruit.

'Yes, once,' Miss Hesse breathed, bobbing a demure curtsey. 'I am honoured you remember.'

This was *not* ideal. What on earth was Lydia to do now? A moment before, her plans for the evening had run the gamut from slurping her soup to referring to Ashford as Your Highness, but she could not very well do that *now*, in front of the only gentleman for whom she had ever felt a *tendre*. She could not embarrass herself in such a way, with Miss Hesse dimpling such sweet smiles and Lady Morton thrusting forward such impressive bosoms.

'This makes matters far more complicated,' she said to Pip, as he escorted her to dinner a short while later.

'Not really.' Pip twirled his quizzing glass around his finger. 'Von Prett can't be the thief – wasn't here. Stands to reason.'

'For *me*,' she said. 'I need to rethink everything.'

The atmosphere, as they filed into the dining room, was thick with excitement. Once again, Lydia was seated towards the lower end of the table, with Ashford on her right, while Captain von Prett was at the other end, in the seat of honour next to Lady Pheobe. On the whole, Lydia felt this was to her benefit. As much as she might wish for further conversation with von Prett, she and Ashford had unfinished business.

'About that truce,' she began, very quietly, as they seated themselves.

'No.'

'*You* suggested it!'

'You ought to have agreed when you had the chance,' Ashford said, and he was smiling. 'I imagine all your little plans are a trifle more complicated with Captain von Prett here to observe.'

Lydia could have throttled him.

'Before we begin . . .' Lady Phoebe beamed around at them all, plainly delighted by the stir the new guest had caused. How long had she been planning this very moment? Days? Weeks? 'I would just like to say—'

'A toast to our newcomer!' Sir Waldo cut across her, raising his glass. 'Welcome, sir!'

'Welcome,' they all intoned, raising their glasses with him.

'Welcome,' Lady Phoebe said, a beat later, her smile deflated.

'Thank you so much,' Captain von Prett said, pressing a hand to his chest, as if to emphasize how very much he meant it. 'There is nothing more joyful in the world than breaking bread with one's friends. I am so glad to be here.'

Spoken by anyone else, the words would have been saccharine, but somehow they did not seem so spoken by von Prett. Having spent so long surrounded by cutting tongues, hidden motives and double meanings, it felt gloriously refreshing – but Lydia was not the only one struck down by admiration.

'And yet you have deprived us of *days* of your company,' Lady Morton said with a pout. Her burgundy gown was trimmed with a festoon of lace at the bodice, drawing the eye inexorably to her teetering bosoms – both of which she now directed towards Captain von Prett. From further down the table, Hess glowered.

'My apologies,' Captain von Prett said with a smile. 'I had a speaking engagement in Herefordshire.'

'Oh, how marvellous!' Lady Morton said rapturously.

'I have been to Herefordshire,' Hesse muttered, 'for several important meetings.'

'A less perilous journey than your usual adventures, I should imagine?' Dacre said, managing to direct an encouraging smile towards the captain and a grateful one to Reeves (refilling his glass) in the space of a single moment.

'Oh, I do not know,' the captain said. 'After all, mileage is no guarantee of adventure.'

All the ladies deemed this Very Profound – Miss Hesse even let out a rapturous sigh – the gentlemen significantly less so.

'Come, sir, mileage does help a little,' Sir Waldo protested. 'I ought to know!'

The captain shook his head gently. 'In my experience it is the journey within that matters most. "Knowledge dwells in heads replete with thoughts of other men; wisdom in minds attentive to their own."'

'William Cowper?' Lydia leant forward to catch his eye.

'Yes,' the captain said, turning to beam at her. 'He is my very favourite poet.'

'Mine too,' Lydia said eagerly. Goodness, if that was not a sign then she did not know what was.

'Forgive me,' Ashford said. 'But I thought you hated all poetry?'

Lydia had almost forgotten about Ashford.

'You must be thinking about someone else,' she said without looking at him.

'You disavowed the whole form just yesterday,' Lady Morton confirmed.

'Such wonderful memories you all have,' Lydia said through gritted teeth. 'I was jesting – my apologies, I thought that was clear.'

Fortunately, the serving finished before Ashford could argue the point. Around the table, everyone turned, and this time, Lydia did not disrupt the natural flow – but she must do something. Captain von Prett's head was turned away, deep in conversation with Lady Phoebe at the far end of the table. Perhaps . . . Perhaps, with a great deal of care, she might be able to progress two objectives at one time: show Captain von Prett what a marvellous lady she was, while continuing to make Ashford's life difficult.

With one eye on the captain, Lydia reached her hand towards the wrong utensil and—

'No,' Ashford said, pressing her hand back against the table under his own.

'Unhand me!' she hissed at him.

'If you try to eat your soup with a fork,' he said out of the corner of her mouth. 'I shall scream.'

Mere minutes ago, this prospect – mutual public humiliation – would have thrilled her, but now . . . She tried to peel his fingers off her hand. It was surprisingly difficult. He placed his other one on top of that.

'What on earth are you both doing?' Sir Waldo asked.

The table turned to regard them.

'A little game,' Lydia said. 'Though I don't think I understand the rules, my lord – where should I put my hand next?'

'That is not what I . . .' Ashford flushed and extracted himself. 'The soup is delicious, Phoebe.' He sent Lydia a vitriolic look.

'I could not agree more,' the captain said. 'I appreciate it all the more after so many months on the road.'

'How long do you remain in England?' Lydia ventured – cross-table talk having been opened by others, it felt permissible to continue.

'I have only a few more engagements to fulfil,' the captain said, 'and then . . .' His spread his hands out. 'Who knows?' he said. 'There is still so much to discover.'

This week was it, then. Lydia's only chance to get to know him.

'I think you very brave,' Lady Phoebe told him warmly. 'To travel so far from home – I cannot imagine it.'

'Soon that shall be us!' Sir Waldo said. 'Lady Phoebe and I are bound for Mauritius in a few weeks.'

'Oh, how wonderful,' the captain said. 'You must be beside yourself with excitement.'

'A little nervous, too,' Lady Phoebe said, with a weak smile. 'I have no head for languages, you see.'

'You'll pick it up,' Sir Waldo said robustly. '"May I buy this hat" cannot be so difficult to learn.' He gave a hoot of laughter at his joke.

'I speak only French – apart from English, of course,' the captain reassured Lady Phoebe. 'Kindness is the same in every language.'

'How admirable,' Lady Morton breathed, leaning so far toward him that her bosoms looked in danger of falling into the chicken fricassee.

'Fascinating,' Miss Hesse said, fluttering her long eyelashes.

'Very,' Lydia agreed, not to be outdone.

'Don't you speak French, Miss Hanworth?' Ashford said.

Lydia clenched her hand so hard around her spoon that her knuckles turned white.

'You do?' the captain said, turning in her direction.

'No,' she said.

'But we have heard you!' Sir Waldo encouraged.

'Not really,' she corrected – for she did not think looking a liar was exactly attractive, either – 'The tiniest amount.'

Three phrases, to be exact.

'Oh, you are being too modest,' Ashford said, and there was an evil glint in his eye. 'We must all begin somewhere – I am sure the captain would not mind practising with you?'

'*Bien sur!*' von Prett said. '*Passez-vous une bonne soirée?*'

Lydia's face flamed red.

'Go on,' Ashford said. 'How do you answer him?'

'The second course already!' Lydia said loudly. 'Goodness, Lady Phoebe, this is an elegant spread.' She gestured to the table, which seemed even fuller than usual. There were beefsteaks in oyster sauce, a baked trout in a caper dressing, a fricassee of chicken, accompanied by broiled mushrooms, French beans and dishes of asparagus so succulent they must have been cut by the kitchen-gardener moments before cooking.

'Thank you,' Lady Phoebe said, a little startled – thus far, Lydia had purposefully not offered such praise. 'Please do not feel you need to eat everything.'

'But of course we will!' the captain said. 'To refuse such fare, when you have gone to such trouble, would be such a discourtesy.'

'A slice of the carp for you, Miss Hanworth,' Ashford asked, depositing an enormous portion onto her plate before she could answer.

'Thank you,' she said through gritted teeth.

Ashford spooned another great portion. The smell threatened to turn her stomach.

'Enough,' she hissed. 'Or I shall be sick.'

'That is your issue,' Ashford hissed back. 'Not mine.'

'I shall be sick on *you*,' she said.

By the end of dinner, every muscle in her body ached with tension and her mind was fraught with the effort of trying to out-think Ashford at every juncture of conversation. It was untenable.

Everyone rose from the dinner table as one. Tonight they were discarding tea and port to proceed directly to the ballroom. Though there were too few of them for any but the simplest arrangements, everyone was full of cheer at the prospect of some dancing, however informal – everyone except Pip who, with an unconvincing cough, claimed his intention of getting an 'early night' while sending Lydia a very speaking look. Tonight, the objective was Mr Brandon's rooms.

'May I speak with you?' Lydia said to Ashford, as they stood.

'Oh, now you wish to speak?' he muttered, but he lingered with her, as the rest of the party left, and then looked around to the footmen. 'May we have the room?'

Once they were finally alone, Ashford leant back against the table, removing his snuffbox from his pocket and tapping it against his other hand. 'Well? I have only a moment.'

Plainly, he was going to make this as difficult as possible for her, and the urge to hit him across his stupid, smug face became almost overwhelming.

'Why must you continue to ruin my life?' she demanded instead. 'If you were not here, Captain von Prett and I would probably be halfway to love by now.'

'If I was not here, neither would you be.' He sounded infuriatingly calm. 'And you must certainly think a lot of yourself to imagine your mere presence enough to make him fall in love. I, for one, don't quite see it.'

'At least I am not so arrogant as to assume everyone in Christendom wishes to marry me!.'

'It is only *you* that seems to find the idea so repulsive,' Ashford said, smug smile falling from his face.

'Perhaps the others have not had the occasion to speak to you at length,' she said, anger driving her a step forward. 'I'm sure that would cure them of the notion speedily enough.'

'I will have you know I am widely considered,' he snarled, stepping forward too, 'to be *delightful* company.'

'Oh, well now you've explained it to me,' she said, 'I find myself absolutely overcome with attraction.'

There were only a few inches between them now, and they held each other's glares, neither one looking away. If anyone were to walk in on them right now, they would surely assume themselves to be interrupting a lover's tryst. They might think it romantic, the way the flickering candlelight was casting Ashford's face into half-shadow, drawing the line of his cheekbone and jaw into stronger relief. Not knowing any better, they might even believe Lydia and Ashford – standing as close as they were, scandalously unchaperoned – on the point of a kiss. How misled they would be. For if Ashford's eyes were darkening as they stared into hers, if Lydia's heart was beginning to beat rather wildly, it was out of anger, not desire. And he was the last gentleman on earth she could be prevailed upon to kiss.

'I am not going to back down,' she said hoarsely. 'And I will prevail, even if circumstances are more difficult.'

'Will you?' Ashford cocked his head slightly. 'Even while everything you do to me also affects your chances with Captain von Prett?'

Lydia fought the urge to scream. He was right. She had no answer.

'You must face it: you have now run out of road.'

Lydia had had a very trying day, and the white rage that burnt through her in the face of Ashford's smug face left no space for rational thought. She merely acted, reaching over to the table, picking up her still-full glass of lemonade and throwing it over him.

Ashford sprang back in shock.

'What are you *doing*.'

He grabbed a napkin and tried to dab himself, but it appeared tan breeches were very absorbent.

'Oh, dear,' she murmured. 'How clumsy of me.'

'You child,' he said. 'You absolute harpy!'

She stepped neatly around him and made for the door before he could think to retaliate, hastening for the ballroom where she would have some time to speak to Captain von Prett without Ashford listening, for it would take him ten minutes at the very least to refresh his outfit.

Matters were not that simple, however. Though Lydia hastened down the corridor to the Great Ballroom where a hundred candles were burning brightly, and a quartet of musicians stood, bows aloft, by the time she arrived, she was already too late. Von Prett was thick in conversation with Miss Hesse and Lady Morton – Mr Brandon and Lord Hesse looking worriedly on – and it was all laughter and tossing hair and touching each other upon the arm.

Blast, blast, *blast*.

'We appear to be rather heavy on the gentlemen.' Sir Waldo looked round the room rather disapprovingly. 'You ought to have considered that, Phoebe.'

'I'm sure we can manage,' Lady Phoebe said lightly. Her ability to throw off such comments from Sir Waldo (whose lack of organizational contribution to the house party did not prevent him from criticizing hers) was truly admirable. She clapped her hands, and the musicians sprang to attention. 'We have five couples here. I do not know where Ashford has got to, but we shan't wait.'

Lydia took a hopeful step towards von Prett as Lady Phoebe began to pair them up – but with no luck. As the dancing began – Waldo leading out Lady Phoebe, Mr Brandon pairing with Lady Hesse, Miss Hesse escorted by her brother, Dacre bowing over Lydia's own hand and Lady Morton triumphantly partnered with

Captain von Prett – Lydia divided her time between watching the captain and stealing anxious glances back to the doorway, with poor Lord Dacre's toes suffering as a result.

'How are you getting on?' Dacre said, as they began to twirl.

'Yes,' Lydia said vaguely, for she was not attending.

How long did it take a person to change their breeches? And how could she prevent the other ladies ensnaring the captain, when she herself was so deplorably distracted? It was impossible. Ashford had been correct – as matters stood, he had the advantage.

'Where is Lord Ashford, Phoebe?' Lady Hesse called, as the five couples finished up a country dance that had them all flushed and panting. 'Cynthia would like to save him a dance.'

And there it was. Of course. Lydia ought to have pursued this seriously from the beginning. Miss Hesse was certainly well-dowered enough to suit his mercenary needs. If she could just make Ashford *see* how perfect she was, then perhaps jilting Lydia would seem more appealing.

Yes. It was time for Miss Hesse to make herself useful. As Mr Brandon led her into the next dance (Captain von Prett having been ably snared by Lady Hesse for Miss Hesse's hand), Lydia's mind whirred with this new direction. By the time Ashford did appear, it had been more than half an hour – time enough to change breeches ten times over – and Lydia had still not managed to speak or dance with von Prett.

'Ashford!' Lady Phoebe called in welcome. 'At last. Perhaps you might lead Miss Hanworth out for the cotillion – Waldo, you don't mind sitting this one out, do you?'

Sir Waldo – flushing red, clenching his jaw and stomping over to the side of the room as an overgrown child – plainly *did* mind, though Lady Phoebe was too busy curtseying to Dacre to notice.

Lydia, meanwhile, narrowed her eyes at Ashford as he approached. There was a self-satisfied curl to Ashford's lips that she could not like.

'What has you looking so pleased?' she muttered at him as she lightly placed her hand in his to be led to the starting position.

'Oh, you know.' Ashford squeezed her fingers just a shade too tightly. 'Oncoming justice, the promise of retribution – the usual fare.'

Lydia frowned. 'What have you—'

But the music began before she could finish the question. They bowed and curtseyed to one another.

'I fear you shall find me a most clumsy partner,' Lydia warned, teeth bared in her most fearsome smile.

'Funny,' he said, with a matching grimace. 'I was just about to warn you of the same.'

15

Saturday – Five days remaining

Lydia awoke the next morning to aching toes and the overwhelming scent of fetid trout. She sat bolt upright and looked wildly about the room, half expecting to see a pail of fish at the foot of her bed, for what else could have caused such a stench? There was no pail, only Jane, standing before the fireplace, hands pressed against her face.

'What on earth is that smell?' Lydia gasped.

'I don't know,' Jane wailed through her fingers.

Lydia's stomach gave a threatening heave. She scrambled out of bed and dashed across the room to throw open the nearest window, thrusting her head out to take in a great gulp of fresh air.

'Did something crawl in here to die?' she said, trying to calm her rolling stomach.

'I shall go for help,' Jane called, running for the door.

Lydia turned back to the room to take a tentative inhale. The hour was nearing ten, and she needed to dress for breakfast.

Perhaps the smell would not be so bad, now . . . She gagged and turned swiftly back to the window, cursing her own bad luck. She had spent hours last night awake in bed, replanning her campaign, and not one of her plans had included missing breakfast. She could not cede the field to Ashford so early in the day!

By the time Jane reappeared, Reeves in tow, the situation was bad enough that Reeves – who had hitherto expressed no emotion stronger than a mild smile – physically flinched, before ordering a fleet of maids and footmen to move Lydia to another set of chambers at once. By the time *this* was achieved, however, and Jane could finally help Lydia into her dress – a gown of simple, unadorned blue crepe of Aunt Agatha's selection that would, she hoped, drive all thoughts of bananas out of Captain von Prett's mind – it was nearing eleven. Breakfast would almost be at a close.

'I can still smell it,' Lydia said, wafting her hands back and forth in front of her face.

'It lingers on your gowns,' Jane said, sniffing and wincing. 'Perhaps a spritz of lavender water . . . ?'

There was a knock at the door and Lady Phoebe swept in full of apologies, and closely followed by a maid bearing a tray of bread rolls and chocolate.

'I shall send over a gown for this evening while your others air,' Lady Phoebe offered through the handkerchief pressed to her face, while Jane began dousing Lydia in lavender water. 'With some swift altering they will suit.'

'Thank you,' Lydia said, blinking with surprise. It was a piece of kindness that – given Lydia's behaviour this week – she could not have expected.

'You might find them a trifle . . . simple for your preference,' Lady Phoebe warned. 'My wardrobe is sorely lacking in flounces.'

A piece of kindness with a slight sting in the tail.

'And you will wish to remain at Hawkscroft to recover your energy after this horrible start, of course,' Lady Phoebe went briskly on. 'Most of the party is bound for a shopping expedition, but Sir Waldo intends to remain here, so you shall not be entirely alone.'

'No, no,' Lydia said hastily. 'I shall join you.'

'Are you certain? You have not had breakfast . . .'

Lydia took a hasty sip of chocolate and a bite of a roll.

'I am ready,' she insisted.

She could not abandon the field of battle for the entire day, not for a little fishiness. With a reluctant nod, Lady Phoebe acquiesced, and together they walked briskly along the corridor and down the grand staircase – though Lydia did notice that after a few steps, Lady Phoebe made certain there was slightly more than an arm's length between them.

'I have no idea what could have caused this,' Lady Phoebe muttered, her face pinched with stress. 'Short of a fish rotting somewhere, I cannot *think* what caused that most awful smell.'

'Nor I . . .' Lydia broke off as they swept out onto the front steps. The rest of the party were milling in the morning sunshine, awaiting the arrival of the carriages. There was Captain von Prett, ever-correct in buckskins, top boots, and a close-fitting coat of navy blue standing on the lawn and laughing gaily with Miss Hesse, the picture of lovely innocence in a gown of ivory cambric, while Mr Brandon hovered close by. There was Lady Morton, ravishing as always in a novel walking dress of Pomona-green poplin, flicking a small piece of fluff from Hesse's many-caped driving coat while a peevish Lady Hesse looked on. There was Reeves, standing to attention at the base of the steps, looking on, eyes slightly narrowed at where Pip was examining an unperturbed Lord Dacre through his quizzing glass.

And there, waiting on the bottom step, was Ashford, an expectant air about him, looking up with eyes aglow as Lydia appeared. His expression was smooth and pleasant. Too pleasant.

Lydia narrowed her eyes. The night before, when the party had broken up for bed, Ashford had been the one to hand her a taper candle to take upstairs.

'Sleep well,' he had said, with a smile that, upon recollection, she realized had been deeply suspicious.

'*You* sleep well,' she had said in – admittedly immature – riposte.

'Oh, I shall,' he assured her.

'Well, I'm *glad*.'

At the time, Lydia had felt gratified at stealing the last word. Now, as a breeze ruffled her gown and disturbed another waft of fish from the material, another recollection rose to the forefront of her mind. What had Mr Brandon said the afternoon prior? *Once he stuffed rotten eggs under the floorboards of my bedchambers... you would not believe the scent they made!*

'Where have you *been*, Phoebe?' Sir Waldo said petulantly, bounding up the stairs toward them. 'I have been waiting to speak to you.'

Lady Phoebe paused to lend him her ear, and Lydia began to descend without her, her glare intensifying with each step she took.

'Good morning, Miss Hanworth,' Ashford said. 'I hope you enjoyed a restful night?'

Another breeze had 'eau de fish guts' drifting from her and Ashford's neutral expression broke as he tried, unsuccessfully, to bite back a smile as he recoiled.

'I suppose you think yourself clever,' Lydia hissed.

'I have no notion what you mean,' Ashford said loftily. 'Though – an entirely unrelated topic – I am not sure that I care for your perfume. New, is it?'

'I shall make you sorry for this,' she warned.

'Perhaps you could do so while standing downwind?' Ashford asked. 'I'd be most grateful.'

'Is everyone ready?' Lady Phoebe called, skipping down the steps, and clapping her hands to attract everyone's attention. 'I think you will like Eagleton; it is—'

'We can all hear you, my dear,' Sir Waldo interrupted. 'No need to shout.'

'Oh, goodness, was I?' Lady Phoebe faltered – though Lydia had thought her speaking at quite a normal volume. 'Well . . . Eagleton is not the largest of towns, but it has several interesting shops, a splendid jeweller, and a milliner that has the most prodigious array of ribbons.'

'I do love ribbons,' Lady Morton said, 'but I am afraid I have decided to remain here, my lady. I received some correspondence this morning that begs my attention.'

'Oh,' Lady Phoebe said, crestfallen. 'Will you not be terribly bored, all alone? Sir Waldo is seeing to business all day, I'm afraid.'

'That is true,' Lady Morton said, with a concerned pout. 'Unless I can persuade another strapping gentleman to entertain me?'

Her eyes were on the captain, but he had raised his face to enjoy the feeling of the sun upon it and was not attending.

'I shall,' Hesse offered eagerly. 'I have several letters, too – important ones! On important business matters.'

'Perfect,' Lady Morton said before Lady Hesse could object.

'Lady Hesse, you have raised such a kind son, you do have my compliments.'

'Thank you,' Lady Hesse said frostily. 'You know, I am persuaded Cynthia and I shall remain as well. She could do with some quiet. All the excitement is too much for her.'

Miss Hesse smiled vaguely, idly spinning her parasol in her hand.

'That is half the party gone,' Lady Phoebe bemoaned.

'Would you not rather rest, too, my dear?' Sir Waldo asked. 'You are looking run ragged.'

Lady Phoebe wavered.

'I should like to see Eagleton,' Ashford put in.

'As would I,' Captain von Prett said valiantly. 'One cannot allow adversity to alter one's path. Are you certain you will not join us, Miss Hesse? I think you would look very fine in a new ribbon hat.'

And as much as Lydia could not like the attention he was bestowing upon her, she would prefer Miss Hesse within touching distance, too – how else could she throw her and Ashford together?

'Yes, you would,' Lydia agreed. 'Were you not saying the same just this morning, Ashford?'

Lady Hesse turned to regard Ashford sharply. 'Were you?'

'Was I?' Ashford asked Lydia.

'Did you?' Mr Brandon asked Ashford rather grimly.

'Yes,' Lydia told the entire group of them.

'Oh, well,' Lady Hesse said, smile spreading across her face. 'Far be it for us to disappoint you, my lord – Phoebe, can I leave Cynthia to your charge for the day?'

'Yes, indeed,' Lady Phoebe beckoned to Miss Hesse as the first barouche drew up. 'Come along.'

They were handed into the barouche by a footman, who leapt up alongside the driver, followed quickly by Mr Brandon, and Lord Dacre was about to join them when Sir Waldo grasped his arm.

'Do not let her ladyship out of your sight,' he instructed.

'Waldo lives in fear of my being stolen away,' Lady Phoebe explained with a tinkling laugh, as she adjusted her skirts around her.

'Do you fear bandits in Eagleton?' Dacre quizzed him, though his smile dimmed a little under Sir Waldo's severe frown.

'We are ready to leave, Waldo,' Lady Phoebe said impatiently. 'The rest of you may take the carriage.'

'I think you might sit beside with Miss Hesse, Lord Ashford!' Lydia suggested. 'There is a little space . . .'

'Yes, Cynthia can shift over!' Lady Hesse encouraged – really, Lydia's dislike of the lady was vanishing by the second, for she was being so very helpful.

'I am afraid I would not dare to crowd her and sadly cannot sit backwards as Mr Brandon does,' Ashford said evenly. 'A cursed affliction – after you, Miss Hanworth?'

He gestured towards the second carriage pulling up. Lydia scowled at him but accepted his hand into the carriage. Pip followed closely behind, taking the seat opposite her and pulling out his notebook to flick through it. Lydia frowned at him.

'Is today not a good opportunity for the search?' she asked, voice low and quick. 'With so many of us away from the house?'

'I'm lying low,' Pip said. 'Yesterday, I was caught trying to get a nosey in Dacre's rooms.'

'By whom?' Lydia said, alarmed.

'Reeves,' Pip said. 'Managed to smooth it over – said I was

lost, you know – but he's been watching me closely ever since. As if *I* am the suspicious one!'

'What are you going to do?'

'Going to have to be more careful,' Pip said. 'But Simmons suggested in his letter would be a good thing to have a snoop around the town, anyhow – never know what one might come across.'

'You are writing to one another?' Lydia whispered. 'Is that wise?'

Private correspondence was night impossible, here. With Lord Dacre, Hesse and Ashford franking all the billets – removing the price of postage – and Reeves organizing their passage to the mail coach by way of a post-boy, there several pairs of eyes upon each letter that left the house.

'Everyone knows he is my mentor.' Pip's eyes returned to his notebook, unconcerned. 'They will not think it abnormal. Gentlemen do write to one another, you know.'

Lydia bit her lip. '*Gentlemen* do – but will such frequent correspondence raise brows on Bow Street?'

Indeed, was it so unlikely that one of the billets be opened, even by accident? And how difficult would it be for prying eyes – of Simmons' fellow detectives no less – to divine more than mere friendship between the lines?

'But the billets are not signed by me,' Pip said, turning the page with a frown, 'but by Miss Philippa Higglepiff – a widow of unimpeachable honour with an interest in detective fiction, with whom Simmons struck up a friendship in Lyme Regis last year.'

Pip raised his head from his notebook to give her a theatrical wink.

Only partially reassured – could Pip not have landed on a

more inconspicuous name for his alias? – Lydia leant back as Ashford entered the carriage, depositing himself next to her and wrinkling his nose in distaste at the close quarters experience of her fishiness.

'It serves you right,' she muttered. 'You could be having a lovely conversation with Miss Hesse at this moment, but instead you had to be difficult.'

'I see,' Ashford said. 'Today's plan of campaign, I take it?'

'No,' she muttered disconsolately.

'I'd expected a grander manipulation.' Ashford settled back next to her, his arm brushing her own in a rather distracting fashion. Distracting in how – how *vile* it felt. Yes, that was it. Vile.

'Are you running out of ideas, Miss Hanworth?'

'Certainly not,' she said, leaning away from him. 'I have hundreds – thousands.'

'Very convincing.'

They quietened as the captain leapt in after them, taking the seat next to Pip.

'Sir Waldo is still advising Dacre on best care for his lady. Truly, is there anything so joyful in the world as love?'

He turned a beaming smile upon Ashford, who did not return it. Could there be two men more different? The captain sitting there, with a heart as open as his smile, while Ashford, across from him, had all the warmth of a thorn.

'Yesterday it was friendship,' Ashford noted.

'I agree entirely, Captain,' Lydia said, frowning at Ashford. Did he have to be such a prig?

'Oh, do call me Prett,' he said. 'All my friends do.'

Lydia beamed at him.

'Such blue skies,' Prett said, gazing out of the window. 'It puts one in mind of a quote from Blake – goodness, what on earth is that smell?'

'Miss Hanworth's perfume,' Ashford said. 'Lavender with notes of – ah – trout? It's all the rage in France.'

'Oh – oh I see, how modern,' Captain von Prett unwrinkled his nose with great effort.

'Lord Ashford jests,' Lydia put in hastily. 'There was this incident with a fish, and then cotton does so absorb and . . .'

The noise of wheels on gravel prevented further explanation as the carriage drew off. After a beat, the captain opened the carriage window and turned his face further into the breeze. Ashford looked away to hide his smile, and Lydia had to restrain herself from throwing an elbow into his side.

It did not take them above half an hour to reach Eagleton, a pretty town whose prosperous market, priory and nearby motte and bailey Castle kept it well populated by residents and visitors alike. It being a Saturday, the streets were busy, and more than a few curious glances were directed their way as the shining equipages made their way from the outskirts to the centre.

'I fear I may be recognized,' Captain von Prett said, leaning his head out of the carriage. 'Ever since my miniature portrait was copied, the places I can travel without some stranger approaching me are few and far between.'

Next to her, Ashford tried and failed to hide a grimace of distaste, but in Lydia's view Mr von Prett appeared more fatigued than boastful.

'That sounds difficult,' she said. 'Do you find it so?'

Captain von Prett turned to regard her. He did not appear to mind the fish smell anymore – perhaps he had grown used to it.

'You are so kind to ask,' he said. 'I own, it does take its toll, but . . . I must honour my audience. I have been fortunate to experience the world in such a way. It feels my duty to share it.'

'How beautifully put,' Lydia said.

'Well, I hardly think you at risk of recognition here,' Ashford dismissed – but he was proven wrong not five minutes later.

They had checked at a junction when three young ladies approached the carriage window in transports of excitement.

'Excuse me, sir, but are you Captain von Prett?' they asked.

'Why yes, yes I am,' Prett said, smiling in welcome and leaning almost his whole torso out of the carriage to greet them. 'Driver – may we pause? How wonderful it is to meet you – my signature? Yes of course.'

'Good God,' Ashford muttered.

Lydia glared at him.

'I think it a very charitable thing,' she said. 'To be so kind to strangers.'

'Yes, *that's* what motivates him,' Ashford said, watching Prett accept kisses to his hands. 'Charity.'

After a minute more of observing the scene, getting visibly crosser, Ashford grew so impatient that he abruptly slammed a hand up into the carriage roof causing the driver to set the horses to so quickly that Pip dropped his notebook and Prett almost fell out of the window.

'I say, you might have given some warning!' Lydia said indignantly.

'It is all for the best,' Prett said, tugging his coat back into position. 'I do try to wrap up such encounters quickly, but it is difficult . . .'

Ashford let out a sceptical snort, and this time, Lydia did not stop herself. She threw a reprimanding elbow into his side.

'Ow,! Ashford complained.

Prett's eyes swivelled to him, enquiring.

'Miss Hanworth has just elbowed me,' Ashford explained, making a great show of rubbing his side. 'Miss Hanworth, how have I displeased you?'

The captain's brows shot up and Lydia flushed.

'I did not mean to,' she said at once. 'The – ah – bumps in the road, you know.'

'But it has been an entirely smooth journey,' Ashford said. 'Is this another one of your eccentric turns? Sporadic acts of violence?'

'Goodness,' Prett said.

'I am not violent or eccentric,' Lydia insisted.

'We all have our faults,' Prett said sympathetically.

'I am not—'

'There is no need to be ashamed,' the Captain von Prett said. 'To love oneself is a great act of bravery.'

'That on your family crest, is it?' Ashford said, his smugness fading into irritation.

Prett only smiled gently.

'It would be jolly good if it was, I think,' Lydia snapped. 'Usually mottos are so frightfully boring.'

'Yes, "persevere" and "persist" and all that rot,' Pip agreed, looking up from his notebook.

'What are *yours*, my lord?' Captain von Prett asked.

'"Honour always",' Ashford said.

'Bad luck,' Pip said sympathetically.

'"Fortune brings in some boats that are not steered".' Prett quoted with a sage nod.

'I'm not sure I understand the relevance, here, sir,' Ashford began.

'It is *Shakespeare*,' Lydia hissed. '*Cymbeline*.'

'You have a good memory,' Prett praised. 'Impressive.'

Lydia preened.

'Even more so,' Ashford said. 'Given she cannot read.'

16

The party dispersed as quickly as dandelion seeds, just as soon as they arrived into Eagleton. In one moment, Lady Phoebe had appropriated Dacre's arm and borne him off on some unnamed errand, merrily instructing them to meet back at the carriages in two hours. In the next, Pip had slid off, muttering darkly about jewellers, and almost immediately after *that*, Prett had been approached by a clutch of nervous young women bearing autograph books.

'Yes, tis I!' he declared, spreading his arms in welcome.

'I refuse to watch this,' Ashford said.

'To the ribbons?' Mr Brandon suggested.

'Yes,' Lydia agreed. Furthering her acquaintance with the captain could wait until her scent had improved, and in the meantime, this was a serviceable opportunity to push Miss Hesse in Ashford's direction. 'Perhaps, Mr Brandon, you and I could . . .'

But Mr Brandon had already offered his arm to Miss Hesse

with an extraneous flourish, leaving Ashford no choice but to offer the same to Lydia. He held out his arm with far less enthusiasm than Mr Brandon, and Lydia took it without any at all. Matchmaking was proving far more difficult than she had expected – she had new respect for Lady Hesse's plight, and found herself wishing, though she scarce would have predicted it only a day before, that this lady be present to help.

Though Eagleton was not a large town, it boasted an impressive high street, counting a jeweller's, stationer's, library, printshop and several establishments devoted to raiment amongst its offerings. Of these, Burton's was the grandest and busiest: serving as a linen-draper, milliner and haberdashery united, one glance into its window showing it to be already thronging with people.

'There is not room for us all to enter at once,' Lydia said. 'Mr Brandon perhaps if you and—'

The end of the sentence had been 'I', but Mr Brandon interceded before she could finish.

'A famous idea,' he said promptly. 'Miss Hesse and I shall lead the way!'

Foiled again. Lydia resisted the urge to stamp her foot.

'How is it all going?' Ashford said, voice thick with faux sympathy, as the bell over the door dinged behind them. 'Not well?'

'Oh, hush,' Lydia snapped, turning to glare at him. 'You are such a – such a *sneaksby*.'

The insult slipped out before she could stop it – borrowed, as all her best insults were, from her grandfather's lexicon, and long forbidden by her aunt – and Ashford raised his eyebrows.

'I am not familiar with the term,' he said coolly, 'though I gather it to be a vulgarity.'

'Well, *someone* had to tell you,' Lydia said, turning her back to him and pretending to admire the flower display around the shop window.

'We may be at odds, but that is no excuse for discourtesy,' Ashford said, with infuriating primness. 'May I remind you that cordiality is the bedrock of a civilized society?'

'You may,' Lydia said, flashing him a fierce look over her shoulder. 'If I might then *cordially* invite you to cease making such an incredible ass of yourself?'

A passing promenading couple – overhearing Lydia's less than ladylike words – cast them an affronted glance, and Ashford flushed in second-hand embarrassment.

'Perhaps it is best we do not speak,' he said, turning to look out onto the street.

'Certainly,' Lydia said – some of her cheer restored, for she felt she had won that battle, even if the war was looking rather risky.

She peered in through the shop window. From what she could tell, Mr Brandon and Miss Hesse appeared to be making a full tour of the shop, dawdling away the minutes in admiration and indecision. She huffed a sigh. They might be here for some time. She glanced up at Ashford, who was apparently ignoring her in order to watch a gaggle of children rush past in a close game of steeplechase.

'I used to love such games,' she confided after a beat. 'I think it unfair that they are abruptly deemed inelegant once one attains twelve years, don't you?'

'May I encourage you to share such confessions with a diary?' Ashford said.

'I suppose you would never have done something so undignified, even as a child,' Lydia continued, ignoring this set down, and reaching out to pluck out a wilting peony spoiling the display. 'Did you exit the womb reciting Latin conjugations?'

Ashford made no reply.

'Or perhaps you were a sadly wild child.' She began to pull the browning petals from the flower, one by one. 'Until you decided to mend your ways and become the ponderous prig whom we all know and – well, whom we all know.'

Ashford still did not speak.

'Though if Mr Brandon is to be believed,' she said, attempting to flick the petals onto Ashford's sleeve, 'you were full of vim and vigour as a boy. What happened, to pop all that fun out of you?'

Ashford brushed the leaves away with the smallest of huffs and reached into his pocket for his snuffbox.

'Come along,' she encouraged, batting his arm playfully with the stem of the now-massacred flower. 'Do be a good sport.'

'Do you imagine I am going to have a chitchat with you about my childhood?' he said, finally provoked into speech. *'You?'*

'Will you not indulge my curiosity?'

'No,' he said, glancing at her grimly. 'You are only hoping that I might confess some childhood fear with which you would then torment me.'

'You think *I* would resort to such childishness?' she said, with pointed emphasis.

Ashford turned away to regard the square again.

'Did you have any childhood fears?' she asked, after a beat.

'*No.*'

'Not even of beetles, perhaps?'

'No.'

'Not even a little?'

'I'm ignoring you.'

'What about a *bedful* of beetles?'

Ashford opened his snuffbox rather than answer. As ever, something about the way he did it – slow, unhurried, dismissive – prompted a rush of irritation in Lydia and her hand clenched around the stem.

'My grandfather used to say,' she said, as Ashford took a pinch to his nostril, 'that taking snuff was a habit reserved for loose fish and lechers.'

Ashford inhaled rather sharply and spluttered.

'A charming adage,' he said, in a passable imitation of his usual calm – though his eyes were watering. 'He would not have approved of me, I take it?'

Lydia snorted.

'On the contrary.' She examined the ruined flower in her palm. 'He will be dancing in his grave at the thought of our marriage.'

'The apple fell quite far from that tree, then.'

'I resemble my grandmother more,' Lydia said defensively. 'She had a great deal of integrity' – *Why* was she still speaking? – 'and she felt very strongly, too.'

'If you say so,' Ashford said.

'I suppose your relatives are all cut from your cloth,' she said scathingly, dropping the floral remnants on the pathway and pushing them towards the gutter with one slippered foot. 'Duty and honour and hearts of stone.'

'You are wrong,' he said. 'My father is very sentimental, in truth, and so is – *was* – my mother.'

It was difficult to say who was made more wrongfooted by this statement: Lydia – for she could not exactly argue with him now that he had brought up his deceased mother, could she? Or Ashford himself, who had flushed uncomfortably. Lydia had never heard him speak of his mother before, though in London rarely a day went by when she did not see her referred to in the papers or hear her named to in conversation – usually accompanied by a rapturous sigh. The late duchess had been famed in her lifetime, beautiful, kind, and one half of a marriage that – before Lady Phoebe and Sir Waldo – had been quite the most lauded love match for a century. It was rare for a person to live up to such a reputation, and yet, according to Lydia's grandmother – who had had the felicitation of meeting the great lady as a child – she had been quite the sweetest creature imaginable. As this encounter had occurred in her previous life as a maid, the Hanworths could hardly boast about it – much to Aunt Agatha's chagrin.

'I heard she was—' Lydia began softly.

'Everyone in the family is very proper, too, of course.' Ashford's priggishness, briefly vanished, made a swift return. 'Tradition and duty are paramount to us all.'

'It can't be that paramount,' she said, 'if you offered for *me*.'

'Then, if you recall, you were a great deal more elegantly behaved,' Ashford reminded her, 'and spoke a great deal less cant.'

'I am still a Cit's granddaughter.' She surveyed him for a moment before asking, impulsively, 'Does His Grace truly approve of me?'

Ashford hesitated. 'While your family history is, ah, a little different to what he is used,' he said carefully, 'he was happy enough to approve, given the extenuating circumstances.'

'Ah,' she said. 'Your poverty?'

Ashford frowned down at her. 'That is hardly accurate.'

'Well, how am I meant to know,' she said, 'unless you will tell me?'

'It is private family business,' he said.

'I am your betrothed,' she reminded him.

'Not for long.'

'On *that* we agree.'

He turned again to regard the street. Lydia turned away from the window and followed his gaze. The game of steeplechase had ended, and the children were now embroiled in a healthy scrap. As they watched, one of the little girls began thwacking her opponents with her tiny parasol.

'I don't understand how you can need my money,' she said, after a pause. 'Your family has acres and acres of land.'

'Land is expensive,' Ashford hummed. 'And even the oldest families can fall.'

'Did your father order you to marry a wealthy girl?' she hazarded a guess. 'Threatening to disown you, if you did not comply?'

She had read of such things happening.

'This is not the dark ages,' Ashford said irritably. 'Of course not.'

Lydia nodded dubiously, not at all sure that she believed him. 'Very well, but when you cry off from our engagement—'

'When *you* cry off,' Ashford corrected.

'He will be disappointed?'

'Very,' Ashford said grimly.

'There is always the little Season, in the autumn,' she encouraged. 'Or house parties are, I see now, a very fine way to meet eligible persons.'

'They are almost finished,' Ashford interrupted brusquely, nodding over her shoulder to the shop window, where Miss Hesse and Mr Brandon had reached the counter. They both turned to look, and then faced each other directly.

'Why,' Lydia went on, as if she had just been struck by a New and Interesting Thought, 'had matters been even a little different,

I imagine you would have been most pleased to be spending the week with so eligible a young lady as Miss Hesse.'

'I suppose you think yourself very clever,' Ashford said, deeply unimpressed. His eyes, as they looked down at her, were almost as dark as they had been last night, in the dining room.

'You – you do not disagree with me though,' she said, feeling oddly unsettled by his continued gaze. 'We are ill-suited, are we not? Will you not consider some kind of—'

'Swap?' he said, stepping back again and rolling his eyes. 'And I am the one who treats women as chattels? Do Miss Hesse's wishes figure in this, at all?'

'Of course they do!' Lydia snapped. 'I am merely asking you—'

'The answer is no.' He shook his head. 'So you may cease trying.'

'She is superior to me in every way,' Lydia persisted.

'Believe me,' Ashford said, 'I am quite aware of that.'

And even though Lydia had been the one to say it first, it still felt a blow, and her cheeks stung red.

'My apologies, we did run on didn't we?' Mr Brandon said, appearing at their side and puncturing the tension. 'It was just that Miss Hesse seems to suit so many colours! It is quite miraculous, really.'

'You are too kind,' Miss Hesse said, smiling.

'Miss Hesse, would you accompany me inside now?' Lydia said abruptly. 'I would so value your opinion.' She needed to be away from Ashford, now.

'Very well,' Miss Hesse said agreeably.

She showed no hint of boredom as they moved around the room, looking at the trinkets and sheets of material as if she were looking for the first time. Perhaps she truly was quite as incomprehensibly good-natured as she seemed, which was a blessing, in many ways – but it did make Lydia's task rather difficult.

As much as she did not wish to admit it, Ashford did have a point. What were Miss Hesse's wishes?

'Is there anything in particular you are looking for?' Miss Hesse asked. 'You like feathers, do you not?'

'Yes,' Lydia agreed, without truly paying attention. 'Your mother wishes you to marry Lord Ashford, doesn't she?'

If Miss Hesse was alarmed by such a bold conversational turn, she gave no sign of it. 'Yes,' she said, placidly.

Lydia waited, but no more information appeared forthcoming.

'What do you think of him?'

'He is very nice,' Miss Hesse said.

'Do you *care* for him? More than other gentlemen?'

Miss Hesse's nose wrinkled in confusion. 'What do you mean?'

'How do you feel for Mr Brandon?'

'He is very nice.'

'And Captain von Prett?'

'He is *very* nice.'

Lydia's heart sank. 'Do you like any of them enough to marry them?'

'I must marry well,' Miss Hesse said. 'It is my purpose.'

Lydia, a little queasy at the phrasing, persevered.

'What does marrying well mean . . . for you?' she asked. 'Not your mama.'

Miss Hesse considered. 'A pug,' she said at last.

Lydia thought for a moment she must have misheard. 'A . . . pug?'

'Yes, a little pug all of my own,' Miss Hesse said dreamily. 'Mama sneezes around dogs, you see, so we have never had one – but once I am married, she says my husband might buy me one.'

Lydia stared at her. For days she had wondered what was going on in Miss Hesse's beautiful, sweet head – she would never have guessed that what was going on was . . . pugs.

'For clarity,' she said. 'The sum total of all your worldly desires, your greatest dream – is a pug?'

'My greatest dream,' Miss Hesse gave a charming little giggle, 'would be to have *hundreds* of dogs – but no gentleman is likely to share in that. So, a pug.'

'I see,' Lydia said, digesting this. 'And so, if Ashford promised to buy you a dog . . .'

'A pug,' Miss Hesse corrected.

'A pug,' Lydia agreed. 'You would be happy to marry him?'

Perhaps this was a better-case scenario than Lydia could have hoped for – a marriage of convenience, with both parties happy with their end of the bargain. Ashford, the prettiest and richest girl of the Season; Miss Hesse, a pug.

'Do you think he would?' she said. 'He barely looks at Brutus, you know.'

'Brutus?'

'Lady Morton's Pekinese.'

'I see,' Lydia said. 'Yes, a worry for us all, I am sure, but—'

'And Mr Brandon called him a monster,' Miss Hesse said. 'In the stable yard.'

'Unkind,' Lydia agreed. 'But—'

'I simply could not countenance a dogless future.' Miss Hesse paused. 'Captain von Prett used to have a dog of his own, you know. While he was travelling through the Americas.'

'Oh, yes – Cassie, or something,' Lydia said, recollecting this from the talk.

'Yes, who he tragically lost in darkest Peru,' Miss Hesse's eyes were shining now.

'So when you said that you thought his talk moving,' Lydia said slowly, 'it was the dog that you meant?' *Not the loss of his wife?*

'Yes, of course,' Miss Hesse said with a delicate sniff. 'A man who speaks like that would certainly like a pug, wouldn't he?'

'I think I'm finished in here,' Lydia said brightly, rather than answer.

They made their way back slowly, by way of several more shops, so that by the time they arrived at the carriages, Pip and Dacre were already waiting for them. Lydia caught Pip's eye and sent him a questioning look. He shook his head. Nothing of use, then. Lydia was not much surprised. Surely, any thief accomplished enough to steal such a prize as the diamond necklace, would not entrust its sale to a provincial jeweller?

'Have you seen Lady Phoebe?' Dacre asked. 'I lost her in the print shop.'

'And we lost von Prett to his adoring public,' Mr Brandon commiserated. 'A careless bunch, aren't we?'

'There they are!' Miss Hesse said brightly, pointing to where Prett was sauntering up to the carriage, Lady Phoebe on his arm. Even now, heads still turned in his direction – his visage quite as recognizable, it seemed, as he had warned them it would be.

'Oh good,' Brandon said. 'I was worried we might never see him again.'

'Let us be off, shall we?' Lady Phoebe said brightly, and they dutifully climbed back into the carriages.

'Would you believe,' Prett said, as their wheels moved off, 'that I found a shop actually selling my miniatures?'

For the first time, Lydia noticed the brown paper bag he was holding in his hand. 'Oh?'

He opened the bag and pulled out a whole stack of wooden

engravings bearing his visage. Both Lydia and Pip bent forward to take a closer look, while next to her, Ashford sat back with the faintest of harrumphs and extracted his snuffbox once more. As ever, the act prompted a rush of antipathy from her. There was something so incredibly arrogant in the way he took snuff, as if to suggest he was so infinitely above everyone and everything around him, and as she watched him take a delicate pinch to each nostril she wished, vehemently, that she could exchange the tobacco inside for pepper, to teach him a lesson and . . .

Well, it might not be her most *elegant* idea, but for now . . . The idea of causing Ashford any discomfort was certainly appealing.

'Look!' Lydia said, thrusting one of the tiny Pretts toward Ashford who, reluctantly, was forced to lay his snuffbox to the side in order to accept it.

Casually, Lydia placed her reticule gently on top and shortly after, when they exited the barouche at Hawkscroft, she swept both neatly into her hands.

Perfect. The day held hope, yet.

17

Having called for a bath to be brought to her new bedchambers, Lydia spent a full hour that afternoon scrubbing herself from head to toe – then toe to head for good measure – with vigour sufficient to remove an entire layer of skin, as well as the last of the trout odour.

It was unfortunate that the same could not be done for her clothes, but true to Lady Phoebe's word she had sent over a selection of evening gowns that Jane had spent the afternoon altering with Elspeth's help.

Despite Lydia's initial misgivings, they had swiftly taken Elspeth into their full confidence, and thus far she had had no cause to regret it. Indeed, Elspeth – so grateful for their assistance – had immediately offered to help in any way she could.

'The thing to do,' Pip mused, from where he was lounging upon the window seat, twirling his quizzing glass, 'is to think thief.'

'And how does one do that?' Jane asked, without raising her head from her needle.

Pip considered the matter. 'If you were a criminal . . .'

'Which I am *not*!' Elspeth piped up.

'Which *we* are not,' he agreed, 'how would you sell a diamond necklace?'

'You'd break it into pieces, would you not?' Lydia said, from her own position, at the dressing table. Jane had fetched salt and pepper from the kitchen for her, and now Lydia was engrossed in mixing small amounts of each into Ashford's snuff mixture. Sufficient quantities that, upon inhale, were likely to cause one a shock, but not so much that one might immediately tell upon looking that it had been tampered with. 'Far easier to dispose of it that way, without detection.'

'You seem to know an awful lot about it . . .' Pip said, turning his head slowly to regard her.

Lydia looked up, laughing. 'Am I to be a suspect now?'

'No stone unturned,' Pip said. 'Though it would pain me to send you to prison, Lydia.'

'Oh, that's all right then.'

'Which rooms remain unsearched?'

'Just Lord Dacre's and Lord Ashford's,' Elspeth said. 'There was nothing of note in all the rest.'

'These will be our objectives tonight,' Pip vowed, 'while everyone is in the drawing room before dinner. Do you think you can keep everyone there, Lydia? We shall need a clear half hour.'

Lydia nodded her assent. 'There,' she said, regarding the snuffbox with satisfaction. 'Done.'

'As are we,' Jane said, shaking out Lydia's dress. 'Will you try it on, Miss Lydia?'

An hour later, with dusk setting in outside, and the last alterations made, Lydia turned to view her reflection, smoothing her hands down her dress rather nervously. It was a gown Lady Phoebe must have kept from her own maiden years, for the sarsnet was a paler blue than a married woman would ordinarily wear, draped over a petticoat slip of finest white satin and fastened with clasps of sapphire and pearl. It was the finest, and certainly the most expensive, dress Lydia had ever worn, and she fancied she had never looked better either – and yet why was it, given all this finery, that she felt so much more vulnerable than she had in her yellow monstrosity?

But there was too much to do to be distracted by such insecurity now, and Lydia banished such thoughts from her mind. She had a task to complete. She must replace the snuffbox in Ashford's pocket and as soon as possible, too, for who knew whether they would be seated together at dinner. Thus, for the first time since she had arrived at Hawkscroft, Lydia left her bedchambers early, dawdling slowly in the corridor, until he appeared.

'Ashford,' she said, as soon as he exited his room.

He gave a little start, turning, and then openly grimaced to see her.

'Have you been lying in wait for me?' he said. Then, in quite a different voice, and with a deepening frown, added: 'A new gown? Is this for Captain von Prett's benefit?'

'It is certainly not for yours,' she said.

'Well . . .' he paused. 'The colour . . . becomes you.'

Lydia blinked. Was this to wrong-foot her? 'Oh, well – thank you, I suppose I . . .'

What inarticulate demon had seized her tongue? She recalled her plan with an effort.

'Ashford, I need to speak with you. Privately.'

Standing a good four feet apart, she had no chance of slipping the box back into his pocket. Some kind of tête à tête would be much easier – but Ashford had already turned to walk towards the stairs.

'It will have to wait,' he said. 'Unlike you, I *do* mind being late.'

'It shall not take above a minute,' she said, hurrying to catch up. 'It is *important*.'

She seized his arm, tugging at it entreatingly. He resisted for a moment, before sighing and allowing her to pull him into the second-floor parlour.

'For someone who doesn't wish to marry me,' he said. 'You certainly spend an awful amount of time trying to get me alone.'

He extracted his arm from her grip and moved a little further into the room, putting an entirely unhelpful amount of space between them. *Rats*. That wouldn't do at all.

'Well?' he said. 'What is it, that simply could not wait?'

'Regarding Miss Hesse,' she began (two birds, one stone), taking a step forward and trying not to look him over too obviously. Where exactly were his pockets?

'No,' he said.

It was obviously not in the plan for Lydia to become distracted, but it was impossible not to be, when he was being so *maddeningly* hypocritical.

'Will you not consider paying your addresses to her? That way, you would still be engaged before your father comes home!'

'I see, I see,' he said. 'Forgive me, there are just a few small matters you are forgetting.'

'Which are?'

'Miss Hesse?' he said. 'Her desires? Is any of this ringing a bell?'

'As long as you purchase for her a pug she will not mind,' she assured him.

'Oh, well, now you have explained it to me in such a way,'

Ashford said, throwing his hands up in the air, 'I shall immediately comply!'

'Truly?'

'*No*,' he said. 'What of Mr Brandon?'

Lydia bit her lip. 'It's obvious he carries a candle for her. But Lady Hesse appears to hold him in such low account – do you truly think she will approve the match?'

'Perhaps not,' Ashford said. 'But poor friend I would be if I stood in his way. If that is all . . .?'

He moved towards the door. She sidestepped into his way.

'I have not finished!'

'I have!'

He made a bid for the door again. Quick as a flash, she kicked out the doorstop.

'Don't!' Ashford jumped forward, but a second too late. The door closed with a resounding slam.

'You ninny!' he said. 'This door jams in the heat. Were you not listening, during Reeves' tour?'

'Of course not,' she said. 'Was *anyone*?'

Ashford reached around her to tug at the handle. It did not budge. He heaved at it. No movement.

'Have you tried turning the handle and pulling at the same time?' Lydia asked.

Ashford stepped back and gave sarcastic little wave. 'By all means, try this magical technique.'

'There is no need for that tone,' she said, muscling him out of the way, and giving it a go herself.

It didn't budge.

'It's stuck,' she said.

Ashford reached round her and began pounding his fist on the door.

'Stop making a hullabaloo,' Lydia said crossly. 'We don't want people to find us.'

'Don't we?'

'Not alone, behind a locked door – they'll think you were after my virtue.'

'Believe me, I want nothing less in the world than your virtue,' Ashford muttered.

'And then we'll *have* to marry, which neither of us want in the slightest.'

Ashford let his hands drop. 'It would appear dreadfully improper,' he admitted. 'Unless it is someone we could trust to remain discreet . . .'

'If Pip were to pass by – or my lady's maid,' Lydia agreed. 'Then we might attract their attention without concern.'

She laid her ear against the door, listening hard. But then, of course, Pip was not going to be walking down to dinner yet – by now, he would be trying to sneak into Dacre's rooms, and she was meant to be keeping all the lords and ladies safely downstairs. She had to escape this room, and quickly.

'This is utter nonsense.' Ashford took an irritable turn about the room. 'A pointless exercise.'

'And do you have any bright ideas?'

Ashford paused, thinking, and then made his way over to the windows. They were very large, beginning just above his knee and running right up into the ceiling. Ashford unhinged the latch and pushed both panes open, and Lydia leant round him to stick her entire torso out – or at least she tried, but she had no more stuck out her head, when Ashford had looped a hasty arm about her waist and tugged her back.

'Do you mind?' she demanded. Distinctly flustered, she began slapping at his arms.

'Do you have a death wish?' he said tightening his hold. 'We are three floors up!'

'We are two,' she said, hands pressing his chest away. Her heart had begun to beat rather quickly and she had the absurd fear he might be able to feel it. 'I'm just *looking*.'

He relaxed his hold, though reluctantly, and Lydia briskly stepped out of his arms and leant out again, to review the distance between the window and the ground – glad to be away from him and his . . . silly arms. She was correct – they were on the second floor, ten feet above the ground if her eye was correct – far enough that one could certainly not jump.

'Perhaps we could tie some sheets together,' she said, recollecting a plot from one of her favourite books. 'In a rope of sorts, and one of us climb down.'

'There are no linens in this room from which to make rope.'

She looked out once more, peering down to the long tresses of lilac flowers cascading down the walls below – wisteria, Sir Waldo had called it, boasting that the twining vines had been imported all the way from Canton.

'I think this would hold a person,' she said, giving the wooden trellis beneath the blooms an experimental tug.

'You are not climbing out of the window,' Ashford said, and he had his hands half held out again to prevent her.

'Of course, I'm not,' she said. '*I'm* wearing satin.'

She turned and gave him a winning smile.

He heaved a sigh, raising his eyes to the heavens.

'It does have a certain sort of inevitability about it, doesn't it?'

'I truly believe there is no other choice,' she said. 'We will be late to dinner – and if they find us in here, alone . . .'

Ashford heaved another sigh and began to take off his coat.

'I am spending too much time with you. You are beginning to sound sensible and that does not bode well for my mental state.' He held out his coat towards her.

'Why, pray, am I to act as your coat rack?' she asked.

'Because I am the one risking my life,' he said. 'And because this cost ten guineas.'

'And people say women are vain,' she muttered, accepting the coat with a show of reluctance.

Ashford hoisted one leg out of the window, eyeing the trellis with a great deal of misgiving.

'If I die, doing this,' he said, 'I shall never forgive you.'

'If you die, doing this,' she said, 'all my problems will be entirely resolved, and I shan't think of you again for a moment.'

'Not if I come back to haunt you,' he said, swinging the other leg out. 'I have not done anything such as this since I was a boy – this is entirely undignified.'

'You are doing wonderfully,' she assured him, going across to the other window, so that she might lean out of it and observe. 'It looks easy, if anything. All you have to do is put your foot there and there – make your way a little across and down to the window below, and then even if you fall, it is only a little hop, skip and a jump to the ground.'

He placed a foot on the trellis, testing it for a moment and then, with an inhale, lifted himself entirely off the windowsill onto the trellis. Lydia tensed, watching. For a moment, her courage fled entirely, and she was about to shout that he should come back in, now, and hang the consequences but there was not even a tremble on the vines and Ashford began to climb, hand over foot, down towards the ground. He was surprisingly strong, for one so lean.

'Not too quickly,' she advised. 'Don't get over-confident.'

Ashford muttered something under his breath that Lydia assumed was not flattering.

He was eight feet from the ground when there was the unmistakeable sound of the French doors below creaking open.

'Stop!' she hissed. 'Someone is coming.'

Ashford froze, pressing himself into the canopy of leaves, just as Sir Waldo and Lord Dacre sauntered out onto the gardens.

Lydia crouched hastily down, so that only her eyes were peeping over the windowsill.

'Can you truly not tell me the whole?' Dacre was asked. 'I might be able to help.'

Lydia's heart was in her throat. If they looked up, even for a moment, they would see Ashford there – and what could they do then? This was, of all the options, the most damaging way possible to be caught. It would appear as if Ashford were fleeing the scene.

'You *can* help,' Sir Waldo said impatiently. 'I am telling you how.'

'It is a lot to ask, without explanation,' Dacre noted.

Lydia frowned. What were they speaking about?

'I expect you to help me. Stand by me, as I have stood by *you*, all these years.'

Dacre made no reply.

'Come,' Waldo said impatiently. 'I do you the favour of keeping your secrets. Surely you can do me this favour in return?'

What on earth – what secrets?

But suddenly Lydia could see the wisteria trembling and her

attention was entirely distracted as a few tiny tremors begin to rock the trellis. Ashford was not going to be able to hold on for much longer. He pressed himself closer to the house, face lost amidst the leaves.

'We'll be late for dinner,' croaked Dacre. Lydia had missed the last exchange, but finally, finally, they moved back inside.

'They're gone,' she whispered.

The ivy began to shake in earnest.

'Ashford?' she said, alarmed. 'Ashford, it's shaking dreadfully.'

But when Ashford extracted himself from where he had pressed himself within the blooms, she could see he was laughing as he began to descend again.

'This is ridiculous,' he said. '*We* are ridiculous.'

'Speak for yourself,' she said, laughing herself now – she had not heard Ashford laugh before, she realized, and it was surprisingly infectious. 'You're the one with wisteria in your hair.'

He was almost to the ground when a branch finally snapped under his foot, and he went crashing down. Fortunately, he was only two feet aloft by this stage – and even more fortunately, he landed on the grass, flat upon his back.

'Are you all right?' she called down, half whispering even now.

He began patting himself down.

'Arms, yes,' he said. 'Legs, yes. Dignity – no.'

She snorted and turned back to seize his coat, remembering, only at the very last moment, to tuck the snuffbox back within it – she had almost forgotten about her initial purpose entirely. Folding the coat into a more throwable size, she leant back out the window.

'Catch!'

He did not catch. The coat landed in a tangle upon his head.

'Ten guineas!' came the muffled protest, before he rose with a groan. Shaking the coat out, he raised his head to look up at her consideringly.

'This seems the right moment to ask you to let down your hair, or some such,' he said.

'Did you knock your head?' she asked. 'You must go before anyone sees you, you dolt.'

'Gosh,' he said. 'I should think you might be a little more polite, given you are still trapped.'

'I'll climb down, too!' she threatened. 'Probably ten times faster as well.'

He grinned. 'We'll come to fetch you,' he promised, before disappearing back inside.

True to his word, it was not above five minutes before there was a great deal of commotion outside the door. She could hear many voices – Ashford and Lady Phoebe, but also Reeves, Dacre and Prett.

'Miss Hanworth?' Lady Phoebe called. 'Can you hear us, Miss Hanworth?'

'She is locked in, not turned deaf,' Ashford said, his voice irritated. 'Miss Hanworth, a great many people – not all of them necessary – have come to your aid, never fear.'

There was the rattling of the doorknob.

'Would you believe, Captain, I did try the door,' Ashford muttered.

'I believe, gentlemen,' came the calm voice of Reeves, 'that we might benefit from some assistance – I shall return presently.'

'By that time,' Prett said. 'She might well have fainted.'

'There is no need for dramatics,' came Ashford's voice. 'She is quite well.'

'You cannot be certain of that,' Prett said. 'Fortunately, a similar event occurred to a lady when I was on a boat, sailing for Sardinia, and—'

'An essential detail, is it?' Ashford said.

'Dacre, will you assist me?'

'What would you have me—' Dacre began. 'Oh, is that not a little dramatic, sir?'

'Very dramatic,' Ashford said. 'And highly foolish – I do not think—'

But Lydia did think – nothing this exciting had ever happened to her before and she rather thought she wished to see the end of it.

'The air feels very thin,' Lydia called through the door. If one was to be cast in the role of damsel in distress, then one might as well do it properly.

'Say no more!' Prett said. 'Come Dacre, with me – stand away, Miss Hanworth!'

'This is ridiculous,' Ashford began, but then there was the sound of running footsteps, and cracking wood, as the combined force of Prett and Dacre hit the door and it burst open with a resounding crash.

18

'Do you need another cushion, Miss Hanworth?' Prett asked solicitously.

'If it is no trouble?' Lydia asked, in a voice she hoped was attractively feeble – though across the room, Ashford's raised eyebrows told her she was overshooting it.

She did not care. She was seated next to Prett – Prett! – upon a low sofa, being supplied with calming tea and biscuits to soothe her frazzled nerves. To think, only a few hours earlier she had feared the day a failure! Further, though she had arrived to the drawing room later than she had promised Pip – who was, at this very moment, performing a search of the bedchambers – the whole company was thankfully present. Disaster had been averted on all counts.

'Truly, I cannot thank you enough.' Lydia blinked guilelessly up at the captain.

'Oh, it was nothing,' Prett said, with a careless wave of his hand.

'You were magnificent,' Lady Morton told him throatily.

The only issue of the whole affair was the effect Prett's heroism had had upon all the other ladies, too, for Lady Morton and Miss Hesse were almost beside themselves with admiration, and even Lady Hesse had deigned to express praise for his actions.

'You are too kind,' he said, brushing hands down his waistcoat, though there was no dust to remove.

'You ought to have fetched me, Phoebe,' Sir Waldo said, rather peevishly, as he accepted a refill of Madeira from Reeves. 'As host, I would have taken on such a task myself.'

'You were in your study,' Lady Phoebe said, 'and not to be disturbed, you said! Besides, the captain and Dacre handled it marvellously.'

'I don't know what I would have done without you,' Lydia said, not to be outdone on the compliments.

'Solved the matter in a calm, less destructive fashion, perhaps?' Ashford suggested sourly.

He would get his comeuppance soon enough, though it was nearing the hour for dinner and still he had not taken any snuff. Ordinarily, he would have done so once, if not twice, by such an hour, but this evening, he appeared too distracted, and Lydia was beginning to worry she would miss the moment.

'Perhaps we were a little excessive,' Dacre said, as Reeves refilled his glass. 'I hope we did not cause too much mess, Reeves?'

'Not in the least, my lord,' Reeves said. 'I myself thought it admirable.'

Dacre pinked.

'I would never have suspected you of such mettle,' Sir Waldo said. 'Father used to say the day you were born was your first and final act of boldness.'

Dacre's smile became rather fixed. 'Yes, ah, his favourite little jest.'

'Tonight was very bold,' Prett encouraged. 'I would have you in the 95th regiment in a moment, my lord.'

'The 95th?' Dacre repeated.

'That was your regiment, Reeves, wasn't it?' Lady Phoebe exclaimed in delight, looking towards Reeves.

'Yes, my lady,' Reeves said without inflection.

Sir Waldo hooted. 'By God! Do you know each other?'

Von Prett looked a little unnerved. 'It was a large regiment...'

'I do not think we served at the same time,' Reeves said.

Von Prett relaxed minutely. 'Yes, indeed.' Another smile spread across his face. 'Did you find, dear Reeves, that war changed you? For me, it was a *transformative* experience – nothing was the same afterwards.'

'Oh it would take more than war to ruffle Reeves!' Sir Waldo said, before Reeves could make an answer. 'He faces worse each day from our Cook!'

He hooted at his own joke.

'Indeed, sir,' Reeves said. 'Speaking of which... I am afraid, my lady, that dinner is to be a little delayed this evening. However, Alphonse assures me that the flambe will be well worth the wait.'

'Will you keep until then, Miss Hanworth?' Prett asked, all solicitation. 'You are not feeling faint?'

'I think I shall survive,' Lydia said, with the air of someone triumphing over adversity against the odds.

'Might we have some music?' Lady Morton suggested.

'Before dinner?' Lady Hesse said. 'How unusual.'

'Only in England, my lady,' Prett said. 'The rest of the world does not curtail themselves so, I assure you.'

'I could listen to Miss Hesse at any time of the day,' Mr Brandon said gallantly.

'You sing, Miss Hesse?' Prett said, turning his eyes away from Lydia to Miss Hesse. 'I ought to have known. You have such an aura of musicality.'

'Miss Hanworth sings, as well,' Ashford put in, an evil glint in his eye. 'Does she have an aura, too?'

Oh no.

'She has an unforgettable voice,' he said.

'Well, I should like to hear it!'

Lydia cast Ashford a look that could, if not kill him, at least cause some kind of long-term punitive disease.

'No, I don't think I could sing tonight,' Lydia said, firmly. 'I quite wore my throat out from calling for aid.'

Prett subsided at once, patting her comfortingly upon the arm. Miss Hesse, after a few pointed nudges from her mother, walked over to begin playing softly at the piano.

'Perhaps the gentlemen ought to join the burden of such entertainment, this evening?' Lydia suggested.

'A famous idea!' Lady Morton clapped her hands together.

Sir Waldo chortled. 'What say you, Ashford? Shall you and I attempt to harmonize?'

'I don't think so,' Ashford said.

'You have not inherited your mother's ability?' Lady Morton asked. 'She sang so sweetly.'

The smile vanished abruptly from Ashford's face.

'No, I'm afraid not,' he said.

'Reeves, do tell Alphonse we have waited long enough, now,' Lady Phoebe said, eyes tense upon Ashford.

'A beautiful voice, indeed,' Lady Hesse said. 'Does not the

story go that it was with her voice that the duke first fell in love?'

Mr Brandon and Miss Hesse both let out rapturous sighs.

'Something to that effect,' Ashford said and now, at last, he was reaching into his pocket in a familiar motion, though Lydia did wish – with a pang of something uncomfortably akin to guilt in her chest – that the conversation could have been on something different.

'We miss her very much,' Lady Hesse said, bringing a handkerchief to her very dry eyes.

She ought to have saved herself the effort, for Ashford's entire attention appeared now to be on his snuffbox, which he was turning over in his hands. Did he recognize that it was rather heavier than it had been earlier? Surely not, though now Lydia found herself wishing he might. For as much effort as she had put into the scheme, it felt rather cruel to cause him physical discomfort at such a moment.

'By Jove, is that a Sèvres snuffbox?' Prett asked, eyeing the box with interest.

Ashford paused. 'I'm afraid I do not know. It was a gift from my father.'

Oh lord and now she might be besmirching the memory of his one living parent – was it possible to be a worse person?

'May I see?'

Ashford handed it over, agreeably, and Prett turned it over a few times in his hands before returning it.

'I have taken a recent interest in the practice you see,' Prett said. 'Now they are to release a whole range with my portrait upon them. I could gift you one, if you should like.'

Ashford paused, appearing to search for an answer that meant 'absolutely not' but in more polite terms. Then, horrifyingly, he flicked the box open with one finger. 'Would you care to try some?'

Prett reached out a hand.

No. No.

'Gosh,' Lydia cut in, interrupting Lord Dacre mid-flow. 'I should not think Prett likely to indulge in so unpleasant a habit!'

Several frowns were dashed her way. Prett looked entirely taken aback.

'In many cultures,' Prett said reprovingly, 'the sharing of tobacco is a hallowed act.'

'It is a compliment, indeed!' Sir Waldo boomed. 'Ashford has never honoured me so!'

'You may have some, too, if you like,' Ashford said. 'All are welcome.'

Oh God. No. No! But now it was not only Prett taking a pinch, but Sir Waldo and Mr Brandon were accepting the offer, and Hesse was stepping eagerly forward too.

'Do you know how to do it, dear?' Lady Hesse asked her son solicitously. 'Don't take too much.'

'I have taken snuff before, mother,' Hesse insisted. 'We're always doing it, at my gentleman's club.' He took a sidelong glance at Lady Morton. 'White's, you know.'

Only Dacre refused. 'A kind offer, Ashford, but it doesn't usually agree with me.'

'Oh, don't be such a milksop, Dacre,' Waldo said derisively. 'Here, you must have some.'

After a beat of hesitation, Dacre obeyed.

'It looks a little odd, don't you think?' Lydia squeaked. 'Perhaps it has gone off?'

'Miss Hanworth,' Lady Hesse said, 'I am certain Lord Ashford does not keep bad snuff – it is bought from Fribourg & Treyer's I assume, my lord?'

Across the room, the gentlemen were raising the snuff to their noses. All except Ashford, turning to answer Lady Hesse's question.

'Indeed. This is their new European blend.'

'I really think . . .' Lydia raised her voice in one last desperate attempt.

It was too late. As one man, the gentlemen inhaled.

In polite society, when one felt shock or any unpleasant physical experience, one was taught to express this in as polite a way as possible. Aunt Agatha had, for example, recommended that Lydia and Pip limit any public expressions of shock to 'Oh my' or, under very, extreme circumstances, 'Pon rep'.

Needless to say, under the experience of a particularly strong pepper being inhaled sharply into one's airways, such lessons of conduct were quickly and abruptly abandoned.

'Jesus Christ!' Sir Waldo expostulated at the top of his voice.

'My God!'

'What in *hell*?'

The ladies of the party near jumped out of their skin, Miss Hesse in her shock playing a series of jarring, discordant notes.

'I beg your pardon!' Lady Hesse said, outraged. 'There are ladies present!'

'Dear lord . . .' Ashford regarded them, horror-stricken.

None of the gentlemen saw fit to apologize as they all began, with every means available to them, to expel the ticklish powder from their noses.

'Waldo!' Lady Phoebe said, as they coughed, sneezed and hacked, all bent double, eyes streaming. 'Whatever is the matter?'

'Ashford's new blend does not appear to be sitting well,' Lady Morton said, a gleeful smile upon her face.

'Is it a disease?' Lady Hesse demanded, moving towards the door, as though poised for flight. 'Does it feel contagious? Get back, get back I say.'

'Some water, please?' Lydia called to Reeves. 'I am so sorry . . .'

The apology slipped out without conscious thought, but no one heard it – no, indeed, as the spluttering and coughing subsided, three glares that were no less accusatory for their wateriness, were directed instead toward Ashford.

'What the devil do you mean by giving us such vile stuff?' Sir Waldo demanded.

'I don't – I didn't—' Ashford said, looking down at his box as if it might step in to help him explain.

'So damned *peppery*!' Brandon agreed. 'Near burnt my nose off.'

'Mine too,' Prett said through watering eyes. 'And I have a high tolerance for spice, after my time in India.'

'Is this some kind of prank?' Sir Waldo said hotly.

'Waldo, Ashford did not mean—' Lady Phoebe said, but Sir Waldo ignored her.

'Well, sir? How do you answer?'

'Dear lord, Waldo, it is not my intention to embarrass you,' Ashford said.

Reeves had arrived back with two other footmen, bearing goblets of water upon trays.

'Are you well, my lord?' he said, handing the first to Dacre, who accepted it gratefully.

'I am not embarrassed!' Sir Waldo said, his face now maroon with rage and, well, pepper. 'But insulted! In my own home!'

Lady Phoebe attempted to lay a calming hand upon Sir Waldo's shoulder, but he shook her off angrily.

'Did you know of this?' he demanded of her. 'A little plot, to humiliate me?'

'Of course not,' Lady Phoebe exclaimed.

Lydia stared. Sir Waldo presented as somewhat of a buffoon but was otherwise jocular and friendly; who knew he had such a temper as this?

'I'm sure Ashford is very sorry, aren't you?' Lady Phoebe said, a tight smile upon her face.

'Of course,' Ashford said, but he wore an incredulous look as if he, too, could not believe the extremity of Waldo's reaction. 'Perhaps you are not used to continental blends?'

'That is not,' Mr Brandon looked up, eyes watering, 'a continental blend.'

'I heard such blends are all the rage in France this year,' Lydia put in rather weakly. Her trick might not have worked quite in its intended manner, but no one could argue with its *efficacy*.

Ashford turned his head, very slowly, to stare at her. Comprehension dawned upon his face.

'Dinner is served,' Reeves announced quietly. Ashford was quick to take Lydia's arm to escort her to her chair.

'I hope you're happy,' he hissed at her as they journeyed the hallways. Prett and Mr Brandon had retired to splash recovering water on their faces, while Sir Waldo soldiered on, red-faced and blinking. 'What on earth possessed you to *do* such a thing?'

'Well, I didn't know you were going to offer it around!'

'Now everyone thinks I am trying to poison them – a low blow even for you!'

'You put a fish in my room!'

Too enraged for words, Ashford threw himself into his chair and pulled himself in with a screech. Barely waiting for the rest of the party to seat themselves, he seized Lydia's bowl and began aggressively spooning fish stew into it.

'Oh no, too much soup.' She narrowed her eyes. 'Whatever shall I do.'

Lydia would be the first to admit that matters got rather out of hand, after that. Ashford's next spoonful did not make it into the bowl, splattering instead onto her lap, so that Lydia was forced to jerk out of the way, thanking the lord she had already placed her napkin over her knees.

'This is your cousin's dress!' she hissed.

Ashford ignored her, continuing to serve only her most abhorred dishes – until she spilled her wine glass over his shirt sleeves, staining their pristine white, at which point he could ignore her no longer.

He retaliated by serving her horseradish instead of stewed spinach, causing her to sneeze violently in the midst of Prett telling the table his account of the Battle of Waterloo. Lydia answered this by referring to each person at the table by every appellation under the sun save for the correct one, which irritated Ashford to such an end that he burst out a correction in the midst of carving the chicken, at which point Lydia affected a few suppressed tears which won the entire table (already regarding Ashford a little sniffily) over to her side.

The evening was concluded by the *pièce de résistance* of Lydia causing a small fire with a well-placed napkin near the candle which Ashford had to put out with the wine-soaked remains of his ten-guinea coat.

By the time she retired to her bedchamber, Lydia was

tired, dishevelled and not at all certain who had come out the winner.

'Was he impressed?' Jane asked, helping her with her buttons.

'Hard to tell,' Lydia said gloomily. 'He was angry, certainly, but the whole endeavour didn't quite turn out as elegantly as I had hoped.'

'I meant the dress,' Jane said. 'And Prett.'

'Oh – oh,' Lydia said. 'Yes, I think so – certainly an improvement, but I do not know what I shall wear tomorrow, now.'

'Sunday requires something simple,' Jane said. 'I altered a few cambrics this evening – if you can bear to try them, now?'

Lydia stood wearily, and helped Jane try dress after dress – though she would rather have reached her bed, she knew she must help Jane put together a fish-free wardrobe for the next few days.

'Did you have much luck with the search?' Lydia asked, as Jane stooped to adjust her hem.

'Some. We made a complete exploration of Lord Dacre's chambers – nothing to report – though we could not access Lord Ashford's. His valet was practically guarding the threshold.'

Lydia's brow wrinkled.

'How is Elspeth holding up?'

'The fun of the hunt is providing a distraction.' Jane gestured for Lydia to turn. Lydia obeyed, staring toward her bed.

'I will vouch for her,' Lydia promised, 'if it comes to that.'

'Miss Lydia, I am not certain your good word means much to these people, right at this moment,' Jane said, needle flying through the material at Lydia's feet. 'Dare I ask what you have planned for tomorrow?'

'Nothing,' Lydia said. 'Yet. It has to be something brilliant.

Something so exceptional that he cannot help but be entirely impressed – distressed, I mean.'

'I should certainly like to distress that valet of his,' Jane muttered. 'You'd think he was the King himself, the way he swaggers about. He made *such* a performance today of instructing the laundry maids on how to wash his lordship's shirts tomorrow – you'd think they'd never seen cotton, the way he was going on about what his lordship would do if they were not perfect.'

'Perhaps Ashford has the most terrible tantrums if his shirts are not exactly pristine,' Lydia theorized, 'and his coats not perfectly . . . tailored . . .'

She trailed off. She watched Jane's hands fly over the garment in her lap, quicker than any seamstress she had ever known.

'How long would it take to alter a gentleman's riding dress?' she wondered aloud.

At this, Jane paused in her sewing.

'What an evil idea,' she said.

'*Isn't* it?' Lydia enthused.

19

That night, long after Jane had extinguished the candles and left for her own quarters, Lydia lay awake, her mind turning, turning, turning, too busy to allow for sleep. In London, if such insomnia struck her, she would light a candle and read until her eyelids were straining with the effort of staying awake. But there had been no space for books in her trunk – a good thing too, given her recent proclaimed illiteracy – and she was left defenceless, now. She wished it were appropriate for her to spend a few uninterrupted hours in Hawkscroft's grand library. But to wander the halls, at nighttime, in her nightgown – it would be improper and foolish. She would simply have to wait for sleep to come, patient and restful . . .

Her bedroom door creaked as it closed behind her, loud in the hush of the house, and Lydia flinched to hear it. Hawkscroft, forbidding enough in the daylight hours, became almost frightening in total darkness. The fragile light of the taper candle sent long, flickering shadows ahead of her, turning the suits of armour from grand to ghoulish, the portraits upon the wall from smiling to sinister. She crept down the hallway, the flagstones very cold against her feet – she ought really to have worn slippers – and down the grand staircase.

She had to brace her shoulder against the oak to open the doors to the library. A single step inside however was reward enough for the effort, and as Lydia inhaled a lungful of old books and old wood, she felt a wave of calm wash over her. Her bare feet made no noise on the flagstones and though it was even darker here – the rows of bookcases did not allow her candlelight to travel far – it was no longer frightening. Lydia picked a book from each row she passed through, some old favourites, some titles she did not recognize and then wandered in search of the hearth, where she recollected there were several armchairs with vague pretensions to squishiness. Yes, there they were – a few wing-backed chairs, clustered around a fireplace that was still glowing. Perfect. Lydia rounded the chair, ready to collapse into it – until she realized, with a jolt of horror, that it was already occupied.

She let out a shriek of surprise, dropping several books with a loud thud as she leapt backwards, clutching at her taper. The figure in the chair gave their own shout of surprise, startling violently and knocking over their own candle.

'Damnation!'

'Ashford?'

'Dear. God.' Ashford said, releasing a hand from his chest to pat himself down as if he were expecting to find a bullet wound upon his person.

'What on earth are you doing *lurking* in such a way?' she demanded.

'I do not lurk,' he said, with more hauteur than she would have thought possible from a gentleman wearing sheepskin slippers and a woollen house robe.

'You ought to make more noise when you walk,' he muttered, mopping up the spilled wax from his sleeve. 'I might have hurt you.'

'What would you have done? Thrown your slippers at me?'

Ashford abandoned his mopping to glare at her.

'Leave,' he instructed. 'I'm here to find some peace.'

Whatever calm Lydia had gathered in the past few minutes dissipated into irritation.

'You have no right to order me around in such a way. Perhaps I am here to find peace, too.'

'It is not proper for us to be here alone. We are in our nightclothes.'

'As attractive as your dressing gown is,' she said, 'your virtue is perfectly safe, I assure you. If you are concerned, *you* may leave.'

She sat down mulishly in the seat opposite him.

'Shrew,' he said.

'Clodpoll.'

'Harpy.'

'Bufflehead.'

Ashford paused. 'Bufflehead?' he asked, reluctantly curious.

'Stupid,' she said. 'But worse.'

'Wonderful. Now – begone.'

'*You* begone.'

She leant forward to pick up the book at the top of his stack, holding it up to her candle so that she might read the title.

'This is one of my favourites,' she said, surprised.

He looked at it. 'Mine as well.'

'Though it was written by a woman?'

Ashford leant forward to snatch the book back. 'I do not actually hold women in low account.'

'Really?' she said, rather derisively. 'You can understand why I would disagree, given what I overheard on our very first meeting.'

'I should never have said such things if I knew anyone was listening!'

'Do you see how that makes it worse?'

'Everyone has a right to hold an opinion,' Ashford said. 'Is it such a crime to evaluate the characters of the women I might marry?'

Lydia laughed. 'Very well,' she said. 'Tell me something you learnt of these ladies' characters – beyond whether they know who the Prime Minister is.'

'What do you mean?' Ashford's brow furrowed.

'Does Miss Callow have a favourite novel?' Lydia suggested, in the sort of tone one might use to speak to a particularly slow child.

'I don't—' he broke off.

'Miss Mablethorpe's sister was wed last year,' Lydia said. 'I wonder, does she miss her, now she has left home?'

Ashford stared. Lydia leant forward.

'Could you tell me the name of Lady Evelina's new niece?' she asked.

There was a long pause.

'No,' Ashford admitted.

'I suppose their characters were not important to you,' Lydia said. 'So long as their dowries were considerable and their families unobjectionable.'

Ashford scrubbed a hand across his face. He seemed shaken. 'It was more than . . . I did not have long to make my choice and I . . .' Ashford stammered out. Lydia had never seen him so tongue-tied.

'It is rather damning,' he admitted after a pause. 'When one lays it out in such a way.'

'Thank you,' Lydia said. 'It was meant to be.'

She tried not to preen at this win, but Ashford sent her a narrow-eyed glance.

'Are you always such a smug winner?' he asked.

'No,' she said, 'but well done on asking a question.'

He gave a reluctant snort of laughter.

'I do not mean to excuse myself,' he said. 'But it has been rather a trying year.'

Lydia raised her eyebrows in challenge, waiting. If he wished to absolve himself, she was not going to help him.

Ashford held her gaze for a moment, pressing his lips together and tapping his fingers consideringly upon the arm of his chair.

'The marriage mart is treacherous ground,' he said at last. 'When one is . . .'

'So very eligible?' Lydia suggested.

'That is not what I was going to say,' he muttered, then – raising his voice over the sound of her snort – continued: 'but there *are* many who covet my title for their daughters or nieces, and they are forever throwing lures into my path.'

He was speaking more quickly now.

'Then, there is the fact that I cannot *speak* to a young lady for more than five minutes before the gossips begin predicting matrimony,' he said, the tapping of his fingers becoming more of an agitated drum. 'I thought making swift judgement would avoid unnecessary scrutiny to myself or any young lady, but now . . .' His hands stilled. 'I suppose it was rather cruel,' he admitted.

Lydia sat back a little in her seat, regarding Ashford with less rancour than she had in days. Here, in the candlelight and with no one else around to observe, he seemed far softer, somehow – a person, not a monster. It was difficult to find someone intimidating, when they were wearing slippers – not impossible, but difficult.

'How then, did you come to choose me?' she asked, with genuine curiosity. 'There are ladies better born, by the score, and some of them just as wealthy. Surely you might have found *one* who was not pompous, nor foolish or eccentric, who would have been a less controversial choice?'

Ashford sent her a peevish glance. 'Recollect your behaviour was rather different, in those halcyon days.'

Lydia shook her head. 'It cannot just be that.'

Ashford spent a moment plucking at his cuffs, as if to adjust a crisp cotton shirt and not a dressing gown.

'What harm can the truth do now?' she entreated. 'I just wish to understand. You were not, I think, overcome by my beauty?'

She waved a hand self-deprecatingly over herself. Ashford's eyes followed the movement down to her dressing robe and then – as if recollecting their mutual state of undress anew – tore his eyes away to stare up at the ceiling.

'Yes, well, I did not – I was not *displeased*, by how you look – *looked*,' he said stiffly. 'Your gowns, in those weeks, were more – were less . . .'

'Banana-ish?' she said helpfully – for the effort of finishing such a sentence looked as if it were hurting him.

'*Much* less,' he agreed, eyes flicking back to hers and it was rather remarkable, how they changed according to his feelings.

Darker, when angry; lighter, when amused – as he was now. Both so much more superior to the wooden vacancy of the expressions he had worn earlier in their acquaintance.'

'I offered for you,' Ashford went on, and Lydia jolted back to conversation to realize she had been staring, 'because I thought my father more likely to accept a controversial choice than a traditional one.'

Lydia furrowed her brow. She did not know the duke, of course, but generally weren't such figures meant to be rather austere? Committed to respectability and such?

'I don't understand,' she admitted.

Ashford gave his cuffs a last tweak, and then laid down his hands. 'My father is insistent my marriage be a love match, as his was. Every other suitable young lady I have suggested to him, he has rejected, feeling that my feelings were not sufficiently attached. And so, I decided to . . . pretend.'

Lydia swallowed the retorts that sprang to her tongue. Whatever spell had him speaking so honestly – whether it was the midnight hour, or the softness of the firelight – she did not wish to break it.

Ashford paused, struggling to collect his thoughts. 'You accused me, yesterday, of deceiving you – I truly had not considered it in such light, though I perceive now that is cold comfort. I was so fixed on solving our predicaments, you see, and . . . I assumed you would be getting what you desired, from the match, too.'

'A leg up in the world?'

He held her gaze with admirable fortitude. 'I have been beset by those who wish themselves or their daughters to be a duchess, from the moment I came of age,' he said quietly. 'Earlier, even. If it never occurred to me that you would not have an interest in my title, then it is because you may indeed be the first.'

Lydia found this oddly flattering. 'I am one of a kind,' she said, preening a little.

'As I have borne witness,' Ashford agreed, a trifle grimly.

'And His Grace . . . believed you?' she said. 'He thinks you in love with me?'

He nodded. 'He deemed the gap between our stations proof enough of my feelings.'

Lydia sat back further into her armchair, allowing its squashy warmth to claim her. She did not know what to think. A thousand questions fought for precedence in her mind.

'Such deception,' she said. 'Such effort.' She did not know whether to be more appalled or impressed. No one could accuse him of laziness, at least. 'Is marriage truly the only way you can solve your situation? It seems so very convoluted.'

Ashford extended a palm in invitation. 'By all means, if you have another idea.'

'Don't you have a grand house, such as Hawkscroft?' she said. 'Why don't you sell it?'

Ashford retracted his palm. 'I think not.'

'You would be sure to get a good price,' she encouraged. 'And then you might buy a cottage or some such and be done with all the expense of it.'

'A cottage?'

'Well, it could be a big one!' she said. 'Lots of rooms. Thatched. Charming. I can see it in my mind's eye.'

'No.'

'It does not have to be the estate you sell,' she said – he was far too small-minded to consider it, clearly – 'they say you have countless houses. A townhouse in London, a hunting lodge in Scotland, apartments in Brighton when you wish to visit the sea. Surely you do not need them all?'

'No . . .' Ashford said, drawing out the word slowly. He leant his head back in the chair, looking up at the ceiling. 'My father has too much fondness for each of them to countenance selling. The London townhouse is where he and my mother met, after all. The Scottish lodge is where they honeymooned, and the house in Brighton is where, he believes, they were happiest.' He huffed out a laugh. 'It is impossible to argue with him on the subject.'

'Oh,' Lydia's heart twisted. 'Oh, how sweet.'

'How impractical,' Ashford corrected. 'How maddening. It has put me in such a bind – never mind the *hypocrisy* of such a—'

He broke off, jerking his head as if to silence his own anger.

Against her will, Lydia found herself feeling a rush of sympathy for him. However understandable it was for the duke to treasure his wife's memory, he could not have considered how it was affecting his son. She watched Ashford, whose eyes were now on the dying fire, his expression shot through with a melancholy she was not used to seeing on his face. Was it possible that he felt just as trapped as she did, by their predicament? Just as robbed of the possibility of great love?

'You are giving up a great deal,' she said. 'I am sorry.'

Ashford quirked his eyebrow at her, not seeming to understand.

'A marriage of convenience is quite the sacrifice,' she explained.

'Oh!' Ashford said in realization. 'Oh no, no it isn't. Not for me.'

Lydia's brief empathy vanished.

'My father notwithstanding, it is not often that people of our station marry for love,' he continued. 'One chooses for duty, not for sentiment.'

'What is wrong with doing both,' Lydia said, 'if one can?'

He twitched his head as if to rid himself of an irksome fly. 'It is an unrealistic aim.'

'Is it?' she said. 'Lady Phoebe and Sir Waldo do not seem to find it so.'

'Oh yes, the very *picture* of happiness.'

Lydia's attention was immediately diverted. 'What do you mean by that?'

'Nothing. Pray, disregard it.'

Lydia frowned. 'They adore each other.'

'Yes, I have seen the fawning.' Ashford's voice did not sound as if he shared her admiration. 'But they are exception. Besides, one day I shall inherit the duchy. The expectations for me are higher.'

But that was not right either.

'But your parents . . .' Lydia argued, for their love match was still spoken of with sighs of admiration.

'Another exception.'

'Which are beginning to stack up, aren't they?' she said, half smiling. Why was he being so difficult? 'Why do you believe it so impossible for yourself?'

'I simply do not wish for it.' He sounded bored, as if this was a topic he had debated a hundred times before.

Lydia could not comprehend it. 'How can you not?' she asked, sitting up in her chair. 'The happiness your parents shared – people still speak of it.'

'It did not exactly end in happiness, did it?' Ashford muttered.

'Ah,' Lydia said.

'What do you mean "ah"?' Ashford asked.

'I do not mean anything by it,' Lydia said. 'It was just an "ah".'

'It obviously was *not*.'

'I am not trying to antagonize you,' Lydia said. 'I just wish to understand. It is so different to how I feel, you see.'

'Yes, yes,' Ashford said, 'you wish to fall desperately in love with Prett, I recall. Though how you can still possibly desire him, when he is such an almighty fool?'

'He is not a fool!' Lydia said indignantly. 'He is everything I hoped he would be – heartfelt and earnest and *himself*, while you—'

'The way he *speaks*,' Ashford went on, 'forcing his travels into conversation with the most spurious links!'

'He is an *explorer*,' Lydia said. 'It is noble and brave and—'

'We all enjoy travel,' Ashford said. 'I do not see that it makes him so special.'

'Do you honestly feel yourself above him?' she said. 'You, who have had everything handed to you on a gilded plate, above he, who has had to work every day to reach such a station?'

Ashford flushed red.

'I think myself above him,' he snapped, 'because he is the most singularly self-obsessed man I have ever had the misfortune to encounter – and *I* spend my Christmases with Sir Waldo.'

'You are wrong about him,' she said. 'And about love, and – and *everything*.'

'Oh, is that all?'

'You will see,' she threatened. 'I will show you.'

She could not believe that a moment before she had felt sorry for him, when clearly he was too disagreeable to deserve sympathy.

'By all means,' he said. 'Once you cry off from our engagement, I will watch your courtship avidly.'

Lydia raised her chin. 'I am not going to cry off.'

'You mean to continue your foolishness?'

'Unless you would like to wave the white flag?'

'Not in the least.'

'So we are in agreement?'

'We are.'

The grandfather clock struck one.

'It is late,' Ashford said. 'Let us retire.'

The library felt colder as they wound their way back through the bookcases and along the corridor. They climbed the staircase in silence, save for the swoosh, swoosh, swoosh of Ashford's slippers. He paused when they reached the second-floor landing.

'I trust you can find your bedchamber from here?' He spoke with all the politeness, as if they were concluding a formal promenade in Hyde Park. 'Or do you require further escort?'

Lydia sniffed. 'I do not. Besides, if we were seen, people might think us in the middle of some sort of – of assignation.'

In the flickering light of their candles, he gazed down at her, expression unreadable. Without quite knowing why, Lydia flushed.

'Which would be – be *disgusting*!' she added, rallying.

Ashford raised his brows, but otherwise made no reply, and the silence lingered for a long moment. Why did this feel so much more intimate than sitting in the library together?

'Well, goodnight,' she whispered.

Without waiting for an answer, she hastened down the corridor towards her bedchamber. She was about to push open her door when she heard a faint rustling sound up ahead then the door to the servant's staircase opened and out popped Pip, closely followed by Elspeth.

'Hallo!' he whispered in greeting.

'What are you doing?' she said, glancing back to check Ashford was out of sight. 'You have not been searching bedchambers at this time of night, have you?'

Lydia had visions of Pip breaking in on their fellow guests in various Intimate Moments and shuddered.

'*No,*' he said. 'But it's a good time to search the rest of the place, isn't it? No one about. Stands to reason.'

For the first time, she noticed both Pip and Elspeth's hands were covered in flecks of ash.

'Have you been rooting around in the fires?'

'Looking for clues,' he explained. 'Sort of thing people do – burning things, I mean – when they're hiding something.'

'Look what we found,' whispered Elspeth, 'in the dining room hearth!'

Pip's worldly logic was eternally optimistic – and incomprehensibly, often true, for he opened his palm to reveal several fragments of parchment, yellowed and burnt.

Checking the corridor was still clear, Lydia opened the door to her room and ushered them both inside. She used her taper to light more candles while Pip deposited the fragments on her dressing table. Together, the three leant in closely, poring over the tatters. The letter was almost unreadable. The sender's address – 16 Ravens Road, London – was visible, as was their signature, a Mr Villars, but for the contents of the letter, only a few phrases here and there were fully legible.

'"Last chance to answer terms",' Lydia read, frowning and bringing the scrap even closer to her face. '"Leave us no choice" "Lord something" – Pip, what is this?'

'I don't know,' he said. 'But fact is, sounds awfully close to blackmail. And . . .'

He put his finger to the page, over a word Lydia had hardly been able to make out.

'Diamonds,' she breathed. 'To whom do you think it was addressed?'

Elspeth and Pip exchanged glances.

'He says "Lord",' Pip said. 'Stands to reason that can only be three persons.'

'And Mr Hanworth has already searched Hesse and Dacre's rooms,' added Elspeth. 'Which only leaves . . .'

Lydia balked. 'Ashford? I hardly think he is the thief.'

For all of Ashford's faults, thievery was surely not one of them.

'Why not?' Pip said. 'He needs a fortune, doesn't he?'

'That is a secret!' Lydia told Elspeth hurriedly. 'You mustn't tell anyone.'

She was not sure why that felt important. If anything, it would be within her interests to spread such embarrassing gossip about him – only, in the light of the honesties they had just shared, it felt dishonourable somehow.

Elspeth gave a derisive sniff. 'As if I needed telling, Miss Lydia. I would never betray Lady Phoebe – or her family – in that way.'

'I have not yet searched his rooms, so he cannot be ruled out,' Pip said bracingly.

'Yes, the damned valet,' Lydia said, remembering Jane's words from earlier.

Elspeth sniffed again. 'Dreadfully high in the instep, that one – won't let anyone else touch his lordship's things.'

'We shall have to change that,' Lydia said, thinking of the half-cooked plan she and Jane had discussed hours before. 'For Jane and I need access to Ashford's rooms on the morrow, too.'

20

Sunday – Four days remaining

Some people might feel some moral discomfort about carrying out such schemes upon the Lord's Day. Fortunately, Lydia did not count herself amongst them.

Less fortunately, neither did Ashford, and he too appeared to have spent some part of the night planning, and if his techniques belonged more to the schoolboy than the sophisticate, one could not argue against their efficacy.

Directly after returning from church – and an hour-long sermon on the Virtue of Charity – Ashford had swapped her sugar for salt at the refreshment table, causing Lydia to douse the table, and Captain von Prett's arm, in regurgitated tea. She retaliated swiftly, sticking out a leg to trip Ashford as he rose from the table and as he very almost took a nose-dive into Lady Morton's decolletage, she felt him justly served.

In this manner, they had tripped, spilled, mimicked, insulted and inconvenienced one another all day until somehow it was nightfall and Lydia had still not managed to enjoy a single conversation with Prett alone while Miss Hesse had had several. Even now, they were seated next to one another on the low sofa, quietly conversing, and though they were too far away for Lydia to hear them, she did not like the smiles on both their faces. Even more damningly, Prett had Brutus upon his lap. *Rats.*

She stabbed a needle moodily through her embroidery hoop. As usual, they were all arranged in the drawing room after dinner, though in respect to it being Sunday, they were engaged in calming activities: Lady Morton and Dacre playing a quiet game of cards together, Lady Hesse reading a letter, Sir Waldo a newspaper, and Lady Phoebe had a novel in her hand but looked on the point of falling asleep.

Lydia's eyes fell on Ashford, sitting next to his cousin, to find him looking at her. The last move having been his – calling over Prett to admire Lydia's appalling embroidery – he had been rather twitchy for the last half hour, impatiently awaiting her retaliation. But Lydia could be patient in her revenge. She might be sitting quietly in the drawing room, primly seeing to her embroidery, but elsewhere Pip, Jane and Elspeth were carrying out God's work.

'I found out from his lordship's groom that his valet has a terrible weakness for sugar plums,' Elspeth had told them all, early this morning. 'Alphonse keeps a supply in the pantry.'

She was to waylay him with the plums after the servant's dinner, allowing Pip and Jane access to Ashford's rooms where Pip could complete his search and Jane could kidnap Ashford's trousers.

Lydia smiled just to think of it, still looking at Ashford. He gave her a sarcastic smile in return. Lydia broadened her smile to a beam. He stretched his to an unpleasant grin.

'Are you well, my lord?' Lady Hesse said, eyeing him in some concern.

Ashford hastily restored his face to normalcy. 'Yes, certainly. I was merely . . . exercising my face.'

Lydia snorted. Ashford threw her a glare. Her role was keeping an eye on Ashford and Reeves, both of whom were present in the drawing room and both of whom she had to keep there, by any means necessary.

Ashford rose from his seat.

'Where do you go, my lord?' Lydia asked at once.

'To fetch my book,' he said. 'If that meets with your approval, Miss Hanworth?'

It did not at all meet with Miss Hanworth's approval.

'Can someone not fetch it for you?' she asked.

'I am happy to—' Reeves began, but Ashford waved him off.

'I have been seated still too long,' he said.

'As have I,' Sir Waldo said, laying down his paper with a sigh, though Lydia had not seen him turn a single page all evening. 'Phoebe, surely you have more planned for us this evening than all this sitting about?'

Lady Phoebe blinked away her tiredness.

'Ought we not to rest ahead of our expedition?' she said. 'Recollect we are riding out to Chaffington Castle in the morning.'

'This is the first I've heard of such a scheme.' Sir Waldo's brows furrowed.

'We spoke of it just yesterday, Waldo,' Lady Phoebe said.

'It's the first I've heard of it,' Sir Waldo repeated. 'Chaffington is a little far, don't you think?'

'We can rest ourselves and the horses at Melford, surely,' Ashford put in, frowning a little in Sir Waldo's direction.

Lydia remembered the sharpness in Ashford's voice when he had spoken of his cousin's marriage. Was this what he had been referring to? Did he think Sir Waldo not supportive enough of Lady Phoebe's endeavours?

'Yes indeed!' Lady Phoebe threw Ashford a relieved smile. 'I thought it could be an adventure.'

'Ah, adventure,' Prett said. 'Is there anything more essential to the human soul?'

'I cannot wait,' Lydia agreed.

A sea of incredulous eyes turned toward her. In hindsight, the fuss she had made at the beginning of the week now seemed a little shortsighted.

'Are you certain you wish to join us?' Lady Phoebe said. 'After your distress the other morning.'

Lydia waved a hand. 'Oh, I think my mount was merely too headstrong for me.'

'He did seem rather headstrong,' Ashford agreed, nodding sagely. 'Pudding was his name, wasn't it?'

'Perhaps I might borrow from your stable,' she said to Lady Phoebe, ignoring him. 'A very calm horse.'

'Do you have one that does not leer, cousin?' Ashford asked.

Lydia took in a slow, calming inhale. Would it be *so* obvious if she threw her embroidery hoop at him?

'We need an activity, now,' Sir Waldo said, boring of the conversation. 'Resting is dull.'

'Would anyone volunteer to read to us?' Lady Phoebe suggested.

'Dull!'

'Perhaps a game of charades?'

'You are terrible at charades,' Sir Waldo said, shaking his head.

What was *wrong* with him this evening? Were he and Phoebe having a quarrel?

'I remember her being quite adept, actually,' Ashford said. 'I say we play a round.'

Well, Lydia had no particular skill at the parlour game in which each person recited a riddle, and their audience had to guess the word – but if it would keep Ashford in the room . . .

'Marvellous,' she said.

'We did play a rather interesting version at Burlington House last year,' Lady Phoebe admitted.

'Wellington's residence, you know,' Sir Waldo put in, cheering up at the chance to name-drop.

'We are familiar,' Lady Hesse sniffed.

'Instead of describing the word by riddle,' Lady Phoebe continued, 'one *acts* the word.'

'How amusing,' Lady Morton said at once.

'How fatiguing,' Lady Hesse said.

An impasse.

'Perhaps I might read to you?' Prett said. 'I have just finished my newest piece for *La Belle Assemblée*.'

'Charades it is,' Mr Brandon said promptly. 'Shall we do teams?'

Out of the corner of her eye, Lydia spotted Reeves making quietly for the door.

'Perhaps Reeves should act as master of ceremonies,' she suggested hastily, 'so that we might all play?'

'Wonderful,' Lady Phoebe said, her usual briskness returning as she sprang into organizational action. Within two minutes, she had split the party into two and bade Reeves write out some simple words and concepts on folded pieces of parchment. Lydia's group, headed by Sir Waldo, and rounded out with Prett,

Miss Hesse and Mr Brandon, were to go first, and they huddled outside the drawing room and watched as Sir Waldo unfolded the parchment.

'Misfortune,' Sir Waldo said. 'Hmm . . . How would one act that out?'

'I would suggest a tale from mine own life,' Prett said, 'but I do not think I could perform without weeping.'

'I wish you wouldn't,' Mr Brandon muttered.

'You may cry if you wish,' Miss Hesse said, laying a gentle hand upon his arm.

'Perhaps something simpler?' Lydia interceded.

'What about the Battle of Seedaseer?' Sir Waldo suggested. 'That *would* have been misfortunate, had I not been there to save the day – though I was almost a boy at the time, you know.'

'Perhaps a little ambitious?' Lydia wondered.

'We would need a full theatrical cast,' Mr Brandon agreed incredulously. 'Let us keep the matter simple: the first syllable is "mis".'

'We are misses,' Miss Hesse said to Lydia. 'Perhaps we might . . . promenade or some such, in a missish manner?'

'Perhaps,' Lydia said dubiously, 'though the spelling . . .'

'Your time is up,' Reeves bade them from the other side of the door.

'It shall have to suit,' Mr Brandon said hurriedly. 'We shall have to improvise "fortune".'

They re-entered the room. The others had gathered together around the fire and watched as Lydia and Miss Hesse linked arms and began walking towards them. Lydia flushed to have so many eyes upon her – she could only hope that Pip and Jane were getting on well upstairs, to justify such humiliation.

'Have we any clues, Reeves?' Dacre asked.

'My lips are sealed,' Reeves told him.

'Noun? Adjective? Adverb?' Dacre persisted.

Reeves merely smiled.

Lydia held up a single digit.

'First syllable!' Hesse said at once, leaning on the edge of his seat, world-weariness vanished in favour of boyish enthusiasm.

'Walking.'

'Promenading.'

'A stroll!'

Lydia gestured to herself, pointedly.

'Oh, I see,' Ashford said, with dawning comprehension. 'Shrew.'

Lydia glared.

'Ashford!' Lady Phoebe said. 'Why on earth . . .'

'The way she was pointing,' Ashford said, all faux-innocence. 'Shrew?' Malignant shrew?'

'I am *not*!'

'The actors oughtn't speak,' Sir Waldo reprimanded from behind her. 'Carry on trying!'

Lydia gestured again to herself, even more pointedly than before.

'Witch?' Ashford wondered instead.

Lydia encompassed Miss Hesse in her gesturing.

'Witch*es*?'

'Excuse me?' Lady Hesse said sharply.

'It is just a game, my lady,' Lady Phoebe said soothingly.

'Nonetheless, Lord Ashford is risking incivility,' Lady Hesse said.

Ashford did not seem to be attending.

'Bufflehead!' he said, with a decisive snap of his fingers, and suddenly Lydia was biting back laughter.

'I think your time is up!' Lady Phoebe said shrilly.

The second group had better luck. Re-entering the room full of decisiveness, they collected several cushions and placed them in a line.

'Props are surely not permitted?' Sir Waldo muttered.

'It is just a game, Waldo,' Lady Phoebe reminded him.

Lord Hesse handed his mother over the row of cushions, followed by Dacre, who handed across Lady Phoebe.

'A bridge?'

Lydia bit her tongue as Ashford joined them. However tempting it might be to return his insults, she would not demean herself by stooping to his level . . .

'Bracket-face!' The word burst out of her before she could stop them. Several people turned to stare at her, utterly scandalized, while behind them Ashford was fighting back a grin.

'His expression,' Lydia explained.

'You are cold,' Ashford advised.

'Maggoty?'

'Am I?' Ashford asked, rather injured, and it was so ridiculous that Lydia could not help but laugh, this time, though she was still being regarded with alarm from all sides.

'Simple words and concepts,' Lady Phoebe trilled. 'Think "rice", "flour" and such.'

'Don't give it away, Phoebe,' Sir Waldo said crossly.

The game swiftly descended into chaos after that, though Lydia and Ashford were not the only culprits. Admittedly, their insults became increasingly creative whenever the other appeared on 'stage', though by the time Lydia was accusing Ashford of being a 'muckworm' he appeared to be more amused than offended by it. Meanwhile, however, Sir Waldo's competitive spirit was sliding into boorishness, as he turned his criticisms onto the performers, guessers and even Reeves.

'These words are too difficult,' Waldo berated the butler.

'I think they are rather good,' Dacre said.

'Thank you, my lord,' Reeves said.

'They are not!'

'It is just a *game*, Waldo,' Lady Phoebe reminded him, while everyone else began retreating from the conflict.

'Do I want to know what a muckworm is?' Ashford's low voice startled Lydia, for she had not noticed his approach. 'My instincts suggest it's not flattering.'

'Your instincts are correct,' Lydia said, keeping her gaze elsewhere, while he took a seat next to her. She had returned to the small sofa and for a moment Ashford seemed to hesitate, perhaps realizing how small the space was and how closely they might be positioned together. 'Finally.'

'Captain von Prett, perhaps you wouldn't mind reading your piece, after all?' Lady Phoebe asked, returning to her chair, defeated.

'Of course!' Prett said, hastening over to the table, where he began rifling through his papers. 'It is a tale of my perilous journey from the mountains of . . .'

'Oh lord,' muttered Ashford, his arm brushing Lydia's as he passed a hand over his eyes. 'I cannot listen to this.'

'Coward.'

'Yesterday that insult might have hurt me,' he said, 'but after "muckworm" I find it somewhat lacking.'

They sat quietly together for a few moments; Lydia trying

most diligently to concentrate on her lacklustre embroidery rather than the warm press of his thigh against hers. The clock on the mantelpiece chimed eight and at almost the same moment the larger, louder clock from the village church could still be heard faintly through the windows. It was too early. Pip and Jane would surely need more time.

'Here we are!' Prett said triumphantly. Ashford made to rise from his seat.

'You must stay,' she said, lifting her gaze from her embroidery and – finding their faces even closer than she had thought – flushing. This close, she could see a tiny ring of blue around the edge of his irises. There was a long pause while they assessed each other.

'For someone who wishes *not* to marry me,' he murmured at last, 'you seem to spend an awful amount of time requesting my company.'

'You flatter yourself.' She broke eye contact, and resolutely turned back to her stitching.

'Do I?' he said. 'There is nowhere I am free: you follow me into the library, you lock me in parlours. If you wish to spend time with me, Miss Hanworth, you need only say.'

'Well, I don't,' Lydia said. 'In fact, I should rather wish you at Jericho – off you pop there now.'

'Shan't,' Ashford said cheerfully. 'I have a good mind to listen to this talk after all – perhaps I might learn something.'

'Perhaps you might,' she said, with a savage jab of her needle. Ashford leant to peer over her shoulder, close enough now that a slight woodsy scent wafted towards her. It was rather pleasant. Did gentlemen wear perfume, she wondered, breathing it in, or was the scent all his own?

'And what animal, pray, is this meant to be?' Ashford said, regarding her embroidery hoop with some amusement.

'A squirrel, of course,' Lydia said loftily.

Ashford eyed it doubtfully. 'I don't think so. A deranged fox, perhaps?'

She jerked the hoop away, just as Prett approached the fireplace, notebook in hand. The glow of the fading fire cast a warm glow across Prett's face as he looked about the room, making eye contact with each one of them in turn – and as their gazes met, Lydia was reminded, forcibly, quite why she had been so taken with him in the first place.

'This is only a first draft,' he said, looking down to his pages. 'So I must ask forgiveness for any clumsy wording.'

Lydia thought she could listen to him speak each night, quite happily, for the rest of their life. She could picture them, in fact, as husband and wife, sharing a fireside much like this, taking it in turns to read aloud to one another. She from whatever novel she was reading, he from whatever article he was writing. How wonderful that would be.

'"The solitary midnight traveller, long wandering the labyrinth of hopelessness",' Prett began, in low portentous tones, '"approached the lonely dwelling—"'

'Oh Christ,' Ashford muttered, sinking down in his seat.

'"The natives are not blessed with the comforts of our more temperate climes",' Prett said. '"Unacquainted with both spring and autumn, and yet a welcoming people . . ."'

'They would not be if they knew the terms in which he is describing them,' Ashford muttered.

'Hush,' Lydia whispered, her stitching set aside so she could better focus on the words.

They were far enough away from the rest of the party, and sitting at close enough quarters, that Ashford's whispering would not be attended – but that was beside the point, for she wished to listen.

'Imagine having someone to stay at your home, and afterwards they publish an article patronizing you in such a way,' he said, body now entirely slouched down so that his head was resting against the back of the settle. 'I'd be *livid*.'

Lydia shushed him again. Could she not have found any other way to secure his presence in the drawing room?

'"Until the vivifying orb of the day . . ."'

'What is a vivifying orb?' Ashford whispered.

'The sun,' she whispered back. 'Obviously.'

'Then why not just say that?'

'Because this is *not* a bedtime story.'

'I wish it were,' Ashford complained. 'I should prefer that.'

Lydia ignored this, trying to concentrate.

'Little Red Riding Hood, perhaps,' Ashford whispered to her. 'My mother used to do a marvellous job with the voices.'

'Your mother read to you?' Lydia asked, looking away from Prett with surprise.

'Yes?' He blinked up at her. 'Why so shocked?'

'I don't know,' she said. 'I would have supposed you to be handed off to a nurse after only a few hours.'

'Well, you would be wrong,' he said. 'She read to me, just as yours did.'

'Ours did not,' Lydia corrected. 'She and my father were hardly in the country, really.'

Not that they did so when they *were* at home, either. There was a certain irony in it, truly, that Ashford's parents had indulged in such tenderness, when hers had not – for it was Mr and Mrs

Hanworth's dogged pursuit of upper-class behaviour that had caused them to hand their children's care almost entirely over to the various governesses and tutors who had tutored them in the deportment of the gentry.

'You were fortunate,' she said reflectively. 'I did not think such affection common, in your set.'

'I suppose not.' Ashford's voice was strange. 'I am . . . sorry.'

'There's no need to be sorry,' Lydia said, rather revolted. She did not wish for his *pity*. 'Pip was an excellent storyteller.'

'That does not surprise me,' Ashford said.

'Though,' Lydia confided, 'I am not certain he always kept to the script.'

Prett's eyes flicked in their direction, and Lydia lowered her voice further, gaze back upon Prett but inclining a little toward Ashford so that he might still hear her.

'When you were read Little Red Riding Hood,' she asked, 'did the grandma turn out to be colluding with the wolf all along?'

'No,' Ashford said, and she could hear the smile in his voice. 'Though that sounds a great deal more exciting. Truly, Mr Hanworth is . . .'

Lydia whipped her head sharply round to regard him. 'Yes?'

'One of a kind,' Ashford finished.

She narrowed her eyes at him, and he put up his hands in appeasement.

'Is that acceptable?' he said.

'Yes,' she said reluctantly. 'I suppose it is.'

He gave a pleased little nod. 'I do not at all recollect him behaving in such a way in London.'

'He is more . . . curtailed in London,' Lydia said. 'My aunt and uncle keep him on a tight leash.'

'Ah,' Ashford said. 'She is not pleased by his involvement with Bow Street, I take it?'

'Not in the least.' Lydia sighed. 'It smells far too much of trade for them. He tried to bring Mr Simmons to dinner – his mentor, you know – and they almost had an apoplexy.'

Their objection, of course, had as much to do with Aunt Agatha's suspicion that there was more to Pip and Mr Simmons' relationship than mere mentor and mentee. It had been a horrible afternoon. Lydia had made it so much worse, of course, leaping to a defence Pip had not asked her to deliver, and after – when all the worst words had been exchanged, and Pip had left the house rather than spend another moment amongst the arguments – she had felt so guilty and so lonely, too, that there was not a single other person with whom she could share her worry.

'Nothing can make one feel more helpless,' Ashford said quietly from beside her, his eyes searching out Lady Phoebe across the room, 'than worrying over one's family.'

It was so close to where her own mind had travelled that Lydia turned to him in surprise.

'Yes,' she said. 'That's it, exactly.'

The firelight was glancing across his face, too, and at such close quarters, the effect was . . . not unappealing. The moment stretched between them. It was almost a waste that their engagement was such a sham. For now, again, they found themselves in a scenario so intimate that, were the situation different, one might easily call romantic. Sliding closer and closer on a low sofa, speaking in soft voices on softer subjects. It struck her as strange, all of a sudden, that only days ago she had not comprehended why anyone would find him attractive. She understood it now.

It was not until Ashford raised his eyebrows enquiringly that Lydia realized she had been staring.

'Not that I suppose you to worry overmuch about others,' she said, turning her face quickly back around to Prett, feeling suddenly crotchety.

'. . . "the shrouded clouds vanished, the larks ascending as the great beast reveals itself."'

'You have caused me to miss something crucial,' she hissed.

Why did he have to ruin everything?

'We are in the mountains,' Ashford said. 'Everything is going fabulously.'

'"Until it opened its great maw",' Prett said, voice building in drama and volume, '"and I saw in its eyes nothing but hatred . . ."'

'Everything is not going fabulously,' Ashford corrected himself.

'. . . "so fierce and so venomous",' Prett went on, '"that even the serpents fear her".'

'I did not know he had met Lady Hesse upon his travels,' Ashford said very quietly.

Lydia snorted despite herself. Lady Phoebe turned to glare at them, and they straightened their faces hurriedly.

'Oh dear.' Lydia worked to keep her lips from turning up again. 'You are in her bad books.'

'I am behaving abominably,' Ashford said. 'Even if it is all your fault.'

'I agree with half of that sentiment,' Lydia said.

'Good of you.'

They fell silent, at last, but this did not make it any easier for Lydia to concentrate upon Prett's words. Having lost track of the plot, there was only flowery language and Prett's visage to sustain her. And, though she would not admit it to Ashford in a thousand years, the description was a little overblown, wasn't it? Perhaps they would not, if they married, do this every night – it might be rather wearing; and now she was watching Prett more closely, his expression looked more pompous than humble.

Her attention drifted back to Ashford once more. For even when he was not speaking, he managed to be distracting. Somehow, in the course of their whispered conversation, they had moved close enough together that their shoulders were now brushing together, and all of Lydia's attention had narrowed to that single point of contact – the rough wool of his jacket catching against the bare skin of her arm on his every exhale.

A round of applause brought her attention back to the room with a jolt. Prett was taking a deep bow.

'You are too kind,' he said. 'Too kind. The solitary traveller is solitary no more.'

'Tell me,' Ashford said, still speaking as quietly as before, 'when you were imagining this great romantic fellow, thoughtful and heartfelt and brave, did you also foresee he would refer to himself in the third person?'

Lydia jerked her shoulder away from his. The clock was nearing ten. She had given Pip and Jane two hours and that was surely sufficient.

'I am going to bed,' she said, standing.

'The Earl believes he has won that round,' Ashford intoned quietly, and Lydia stalked away rather than retort – chiefly because she could not think of one.

'Mr Hanworth found nothing,' Jane said, when Lydia reached her room again.

Lydia was not surprised – but where did that leave them? That was the last guest chamber he had to search. Was it time to admit defeat and call in reinforcements? Pip was exchanging almost daily letters with Mr Simmons – surely he would come, if asked?

'But our mission went very well,' Jane went on with a proud smile. 'I have never sewed more quickly in my life. Lord Ashford is going to look quite ridiculous.'

'Perfect,' Lydia breathed. That ought to make him less smug.

'Was it difficult?' Jane asked. 'Keeping him in conversation?'

'No,' Lydia said, truthfully, not quite able to meet her own eyes in the mirror as she set about unpinning her hair. 'No, it wasn't.'

21

Monday – Three days remaining

When Ashford stepped into his riding breeches, he suspected something to be amiss. When his valet helped him on with his jacket, he knew something was very wrong.

'Dear God,' he said, looking down upon himself, 'have I grown? Can that happen?'

Walter stared at him, dumbfounded. 'I – I do not know . . .'

Ashford cast a glance into the looking glass. He looked as though he had just climbed into the clothes of a schoolboy.

'Is this a new fashion?' he said. 'I wish you might have consulted me, Walter – it is not very flattering.'

'It is not my work,' Walter said indignantly. 'I should never do such a thing.' He pulled back the sleeves to examine the cuffs. 'This is not my stitching!'

'What do you mean?'

'Someone has altered it,' Walter said, perplexed. 'But I cannot think who—'

'I can,' Ashford said, rather grimly.

How on earth had she done it? He had barely let her out of his sights the past day but this was most certainly the work of Miss Hanworth.

'It has been done to all of them,' Walter said, rifling through Ashford's wardrobe. 'All your riding wear.'

Of course it had. Miss Hanworth did not do things by halves, did she? It would be admirable if it were not so very vexing.

'Can you unalter them?' Ashford asked, though he suspected he already knew the answer.

'The stitching is so tight,' Walter said, shaking his head. 'It has been done by a clever hand – it will take me hours to unpick.'

Ashford took a swift look at the clock. They had all breakfasted in their rooms, that morning, so that they might begin their expedition to Chaffington promptly at nine. Since Ashford did not believe a gentleman should spend more than ten minutes dressing, it was now five minutes to the hour.

'You might wear your morning breeches, though they are entirely the wrong colour,' Walter said, shuddering a little at the thought. 'But . . .'

The clock struck nine. Ashford groaned. He would pay her back for this – with interest!

'It will have to do,' he said grimly.

Fortunately, his top boots would cover most – if not all – of his calf. There was no helping the jacket.

'Can you not say you are ill?' Walter asked. 'Your reputation – *my* reputation!'

Ashford shook his head. To do so would be to admit defeat, and he could not do that – besides, he had other reasons for not wishing to miss today's ride.

He strode out of the house as best as he could with a sliver of shin exposed to the world. Of course, it was noticed immediately. First by Miss Hanworth, who would have known to look for it — her eyes sprang to his, down to his clothes, and then back up to his face, utter delight writ large. She herself was looking finer than he had seen her, dressed in an elegant habit of fine blue merino cloth and a tall-crowned hat set at a raffish angle, the peak almost obscuring the vision of one, very merry, eye.

Ashford returned her gaze with complete neutrality. This was only humiliating if he allowed it to be.

'Coat coming up a little short, isn't it, Ashford?' Sir Waldo said loudly.

Ten further sets of eyes turned in his direction. A week earlier and such a moment as this would have constituted something of a nightmare. Ever since he had been in smallclothes, turning oneself out in neat and acceptable dress had been a stalwart of gentlemanly behaviour, and yet here he was, facing down the *ton*'s finest with barely more than a prickle of embarrassment running down his spine. Miss Hanworth was a victim of her own success. After the humiliations she had already visited upon him, what was a short pair of trousers to signify?

'It's the all the rage in France,' he said blandly.

'A fashion for ill-fitting jackets and mismatched breeches?' Hesse sniffed. '*I* have not heard of it.'

'Given the state of your shirt points,' Ashford said. 'That does not particularly surprise me.'

'Let us ready ourselves,' Lady Phoebe said, clapping her hands. She appeared to have recovered some of her usual energy overnight and was dressed in a habit of pale green cloth resembling the uniform of a hussar, with golden epaulettes on the shoulder and braiding up each arm in matching thread.

Ashford was glad for it – the murmurings of guilt within him rose every time he saw her blink tiredness away from her eyes, for he and Miss Hanworth must be adding so much stress to her week. The guilt was not enough to cause him to cease, however.

It could not equal the rush of exhilaration he felt, besting Miss Hanworth.

The sound of hooves had him turning his head eagerly toward the lady in question. He wished to see her expression, when she realized what *he* had done.

'Now, Miss Hanworth,' Lady Phoebe said, in a voice pitched low so as not to embarrass her, 'I was concerned we did not have a placid enough mount for you, but Ashford came up with the most marvellous solution!'

Miss Hanworth turned very slowly to regard Ashford. He had been looking forward to this precise moment since yesterday and made no effort to hide his glee. She narrowed her eyes.

'Ah, here we are,' Lady Phoebe said. 'This is Bumper. As you can see, he is not in the least frightening.'

Miss Hanworth took Bumper in from top to bottom. It did not take long. Amongst the hunters, gathered gleaming and tall and impressive in the yard, the shortest amongst them fifteen hands, Bumper was so remarkably short and stout that he could well be mistaken for a donkey. She turned to regard Ashford again, pressing her lips together as if she did not know whether to scowl or smile, as if she did not know if she were more angry or impressed.

It was, he realized, an expression he had become rather addicted to, these past days.

'I know he has a stubborn look about him,' Ashford said, 'but indeed, that is just his face. Shall I hand you up?'

Bumper was short enough that assistance seemed barely necessary, but Miss Hanworth could not easily refuse in front of so many witnesses, though her eyes – when he approached – promised retribution.

'I cannot believe you,' she muttered, as she placed her left foot in the palm of his hand.

'I cannot believe *you*,' he said, boosting her upwards with such force she near toppled over poor Bumper's low back, then standing back to observe the image they made. 'So sorry, I did not realize how little height you required to mount.'

Girl and horse both stared him down – stared him out, indeed, for she was hardly much higher than he standing in his boots – as if daring him to laugh. Ashford pressed his lips together.

'A fine steed!' Prett called over to her, 'a perfect pairing!'

As much as Ashford did not like the fellow, it was rather perfect timing and he turned quickly to his own horse to hide his laughter. He might be dressed as the village idiot, but she was riding a glorified donkey, so at least they were both dunces.

It became almost immediately clear that Bumper had neither the ability nor desire to keep up with the gleaming destriers that their companions were riding. Try as Miss Hanworth might to chivvy him up, he would not be chivvied, and the riding party was forever having to wait for her to jostle up, red-faced.

'Do you wish to turn back, Miss Hanworth?' Sir Waldo called, a little irately. Though it was only morning, the day was warm with promise, and there was already a shine to his cheeks.

'Waldo!' Lady Phoebe muttered in reprimand.

'What?' he said crossly. 'It is not my fault that—'

'Perhaps you ought to be led,' Ashford suggested, all faux sympathy. 'Would that make you feel more comfortable?'

This proved to be an overstep.

'Thank you so much, my lord,' Miss Hanworth sang out sweetly, 'that would be marvellous.'

'I did not mean—' Ashford began, for plodding along at Bumper's speed was not exactly his idea of a good ride.

'It is *so* kind,' Miss Hanworth said. 'That way, I need not trouble the rest of the group to wait for us.'

'A famous idea,' Sir Waldo said cheerfully.

'Very kind of you, Ashford!' Mr Brandon said, reaching over to clap him on the back as he passed.

Ashford ceded to his fate, accepting the reins when they were taken over Bumper's head and held out to him without further complaint.

'Congratulations,' he said, once the rest of the party was out of earshot. 'You have managed to ruin even riding.'

'This is your design, not mine,' Miss Hanworth said. 'You should have thought ahead.'

'I could lead you into a bog, you know,' he threatened, brandishing Bumper's reins at her.

Bumper, taking exception to his tone, drew to a stubborn halt and began yanking his head this way and that.

'Give me back the reins,' Miss Hanworth instructed him.

'He's a stubborn mule,' he warned her, tossing them over.

'He just dislikes *you*,' Lydia said. 'That, in my view, makes him a very good judge of character.'

'The enemy of mine enemy,' Ashford said, smiling a little despite himself.

Released from Ashford's hold, Bumper deigned to move on, and they jostled along in silence, at radically different heights but with identical grumpy scowls.

Ashford could not help it: he began to laugh.

Miss Hanworth turned to look at him.

'What?' she demanded.

'We must look as though we have escaped the circus,' he said, gesturing between them. 'A stranger pair of riders I am certain I have never seen.'

She began to grin, too – and it suited her even better than the scowl.

'Where did you find him?' she asked. 'I can't imagine Sir Waldo buying a horse named Bumper.'

'He didn't,' Ashford said. 'We had to borrow him from one of the farmers.'

'I hope you went to a great deal of pain and effort,' she said.

'As much as you did,' he said, 'organizing my current wardrobe.'

Her smile widened to a grin. 'I cannot believe you are wearing them.'

'You did not leave me much choice,' he said. 'Though I warn you, if your hat ends up in a pond, again, you shall be retrieving it yourself – there is no world in which I will be removing my boots.'

'You do not wish everyone to see your ankles?' she said, with mock gravity.

'I should hate to cause a stir.'

'A stir? Are they very fine ankles?'

'I suppose that depends upon your definition.'

'Delicacy, in a female,' Miss Hanworth asserted, 'is why Aunt Agatha's so aggrieved by mine own. Boxy, you see.'

Ashford cleared his throat for want of a better response. In all his etiquette lessons, he had not been sufficiently prepared to handle conversations with Miss Hanworth.

'Have I offended your sensibilities?' she asked, seeming more pleased than worried.

'If I had pearls, I should be clutching them,' Ashford said. 'I do not make a habit of discussing ankles in public.'

Miss Hanworth looked pointedly left and then right. There were only deserted fields all around.

'Are you afraid of what the sheep will think of you?'

'The gossip rags do have spies everywhere,' he said. 'Better to be safe than sorry.'

'It must be so very dull, always behaving correctly,' she observed. A week earlier and he might have considered this rude, but after the past few days, Ashford was somewhat inured to her incivility.

'You would be cautious, too,' he said, 'if you were as observed as I.'

'Do you truly care so much about what people say about you?'

'Is that an honest question? Or are you simply trying to annoy me?'

'Can it not be both?' She gave an impudent grin. Bumper, perceiving her inattention, made a lunge for a nearby verge of grass. 'Have you considered deciding *not* to care?' she said, wrestling him back under control.

'Oh, what an excellent suggestion,' he said, voice thick with sarcasm. 'I cannot believe I did not think of it before, now all my problems are solved.'

'Mature,' she said.

'I do try.'

'I just think,' Miss Hanworth continued doggedly on, 'you are young, you are titled, you are not terrible to look upon . . .'

'Thank you so much.'

'What harm can they do to you? Truly?' She wafted her hands around as she said 'they' as if to indicate the world.

'Harm does not have to be physical,' Ashford said. 'Imagine yourself in my position, for a moment. I cannot make a single step, without it being gossiped over.'

'Everyone loves you—'

'That is no accident,' he interrupted. 'I cannot be seen at a disreputable locale, without my character being called into question – so I do not frequent such places. I cannot dance with a lady twice without my marriage being speculated over – so I spread my attentions evenly. I cannot misspeak without it being noted and discussed and exaggerated – so I do not misspeak. I am careful, every moment, and you may think it dull or deceitful, but one's reputation can take on a life of its own if one does not control it, and *that* can make one go mad – why, it almost killed my—' He broke off. Even now, he did not like to say the words.

'I'm sorry,' he said roughly. 'I did not mean to say all of that.'

'Do not apologize,' she said at once. 'I had not thought – not considered—'

'Why would you,' he said, without heat. 'I am not some tragic figure – my life has been a very comfortable one, but . . . It is tiring, living with so many eyes and expectations upon one.'

'Yes, I suppose it is,' she said thoughtfully.

'I cannot imagine what they will say about me,' he said, 'if we start selling up the duchy.'

It ought to be strange to discuss such subjects with her, given her role in them, but somehow it was not.

'A great many horrible things, perhaps,' she said. 'Though I still do not think that should rule you.'

'It is not only that,' he said. 'We Ancasters have held that land for twenty generations, you know.'

It was a boast his father was fond of quoting, whenever he was in his cups – though pride in the longitude of his family line had yet, in Ashford's experience, to translate into any active participation in trying to rescue it. Whenever Ashford tried to raise the topic, the duke would chastise Ashford for his dullness as if Ashford were not trying his best . . .

'And what of those before that?' Miss Hanworth interrupted his reverie.

'What do you mean?'

'The twenty-first generation,' she said. 'Where did those fellows live?'

'They came over with the Norman conquest,' he said, raising his chin loftily.

Miss Hanworth gave a sceptical snort.

'It is true! You may look at my family tree, if you do not believe me.'

'No, thank you,' she said, promptly. 'It sounds a rather dull use of time.'

'Were you about to make a point,' he said, 'or do you wish to be distracted by insults?'

'My point was,' she said, 'matters change.'

'So wise,' he said. 'Shakespeare, is it?'

'Oh, ha ha,' she said witheringly. 'I am being serious.'

'Inspiring, too.'

'Even your family has not been here forever,' she said. 'And not everything has to be the same, forever, to have value.'

'But . . . legacy,' he said. 'Tradition.'

'I'm sorry,' she said. 'Your sentence is missing its verbs.'

'Do you feel no attachment to it?' he said. 'Surely even your family—'

'Even my family?' she repeated, with a crow of outrage. 'And what pray, do you mean by that? The scaff and raff don't understand tradition, is that right?'

'It was not meant to be a—' He stopped, tried to regroup. 'It is just that you do not have land, exactly . . .'

'Wrong!' she trilled out. 'What pray, do you think the factories were built upon?'

He capitulated. 'My point stands: you feel a connection to that . . . heritage, don't you?'

Conversation paused for a moment as they negotiated their way through a gate – the others were so far ahead that they had obviously elected to shut it, in case of wandering livestock.

'I don't know,' Miss Hanworth said, thoughtfully. 'Grandfather's achievements *were* considerable, but we were never encouraged to speak of them, or take pride in them, outside the home.'

Ashford recollected, vividly, the look on Lady Hesse's face when she had heard the word 'factory' from Miss Hanworth's lips.

'Why did he take such an attitude?'

'Oh, he wished us to be genteel, refined, to go where he could not.' She smiled to herself rather wryly. 'But . . . though we all owe him a great deal, I do not feel the same obligation, as you do.'

'You do not feel you should honour what was built for you — seek out social ascension, if that was his desire?'

He watched as she considered it, thoughts passing across her face as ripples on a pond.

'My mother did,' she said, after a long pause, 'and my aunt, but for me . . . No. If anything, it is my grandmother I wish to honour. She was a maid, you know.' She shot him a quick, evaluating glance. 'And that is a secret.'

'I shan't tell anyone,' he promised easily. Then, obeying his curiosity, prompted: 'She was a household maid?'

'She began in the scullery, then the house, before becoming a lady's maid.' Miss Hanworth pronounced this last title with the same pride others announced knighthoods. 'Which is very difficult, you know.'

Ashford could not pretend he had spent much time considering this, but he tried, now. 'I imagine it would be. How did she – ah – adapt, to her new position?'

Was position even the correct word? After all the missteps and assumptions she had observed in him, thus far, he did not wish to offend any further. As strange as it was, he found he wanted her to think well of him.

'I do not think she changed at all,' Miss Hanworth reflected. 'None of it mattered to her, really. She loved Grandfather so greatly that it would not have signified to her if he had been a pauper.' She titled her head backwards to look directly at him under her hat. 'That is the better legacy, I think.'

Ashford did not think he had ever heard anyone speak in such a way. In his circles, one did not openly discuss one's family, voicing their complexities and oddities. It was too vulnerable, too soft – and yet hearing her do so now was having rather the opposite effect. It made him feel brave.

'My mother felt very similarly,' he began. 'I—'

'Ho!' a bellow from up ahead interrupted him, and they looked up the path ahead to see the rest of the party clustered together at the next gate, waiting for them.

'What were you going to say?' Miss Hanworth prompted, for they were still a hundred yards away.

But the moment was lost and he felt momentarily dizzy at how close he'd been to divulging far more than was wise. 'It's getting warm, isn't it?' he said and spurred his horse onwards.

What had he been thinking, sharing such things with her? He was at risk of turning into von Prett – or even his father, speaking endlessly of his own feelings as if the whole world shared in his own fascination . . .

The party reached Melford soon after and drew to a halt outside the inn where they were to partake of refreshment, relieved, for the heat was building progressively as the hour neared midday.

'We ought to have left hours earlier,' Ashford overheard Sir Waldo muttering to Lady Phoebe. 'It is far too hot for such a long excursion – this was a very foolish idea of yours.'

Ashford clenched his jaw as Phoebe blushed, but Sir Waldo was not alone in his antipathy. After some discussion inside the inn, they decided to cut the expedition short.

'No castle is worth such discomfort,' Sir Waldo declared with finality, as they remounted their horses and turned for home. 'Come along!'

'Where is Brandon?' Lady Phoebe said.

'I'm coming!' Brandon called. He was hurrying outside the inn, carrying a bowl of water.

'What are you doing,' Sir Waldo demanded irritably. 'Come on, sir, we are waiting for you.'

Mr Brandon placed the bowl in front of a stray dog taking shade under a nearby tree.

'Charitable,' Mr Hanworth muttered, from a little way behind Ashford. 'Unlikely sort to conspire against a maid.' There was a pause. 'Unless that's what he *wants* us to think . . .'

Ashford threw him a quizzical look. What on earth was he talking about?

'My apologies for the delay,' Brandon said, hastening over to them.

'Oh, do not apologize,' Miss Hesse breathed. 'It is so kind of you.'

She stared at Brandon with new, admiring eyes – and well, well. Brandon's star was on the rise at last.

'A noble hound,' Prett said, heaving a great sight. 'She does so remind me of my Cassie. She would have accompanied me over every distant sea, every wilderness, mountain and valley.'

'Oh, that is so wonderful,' Miss Hesse said, turning shining eyes back towards Prett. Mr Brandon's face fell.

By the time they turned back into the gates of Hawkscroft, all were looking distinctly worse for wear, bearing the distinct and inelegant evidence of perspiration.

'I should think we will all be very glad for some more lemonade!' Sir Waldo announced, looking – by now – as if he had had a rather long and fully clothed swim in the lake. He pulled to a stop and began to swing his leg over the saddle. 'I really do feel—'

But whatever Sir Waldo really did feel, they would never know, for just at that moment, Brutus the Pekinese came running across the yard, barking his high-pitched salute, and Sir Waldo's horse pranced away in surprise. Sir Waldo – mid thigh sweep – was in too precarious a position to bring his mount under control. He slipped and crashed to the ground, landing in a dishevelled heap at his horse's feet – a fall only cushioned by his own derriere.

'Waldo, are you all right?' Lady Phoebe scrambled to dismount from her own steed.

Sir Waldo scrambled to his feet, struggling to adjust his jacket, his hair clustered wetly around his perspiring face. He had never looked less dignified, and it might have been funny had his face not also been so entirely alight with rage that he was almost unrecognizable.

'You stupid, stupid animal!' he snarled, and he snatched his whip up from the floor, pulled his arm back and delivered a heavy thrash to the horse's neck.

'No!' Miss Hesse breathed.

'Waldo, stop!'

'Learned its lesson now, I think, sir!'

Sir Waldo ignored their protests, wrapping his hand around the bridle to pin the horse in place and delivering another blow that had the horse skittering backwards with a pained bray.

'We must stop him,' Miss Hanworth said, as she tried to untangle herself from her stirrups.

Some of the shock cleared from Ashford's head, and suddenly his legs moved as he swung off his own horse – throwing out his reins to Miss Hanworth without warning and she caught them from him instinctively. Ashford lunged towards Sir Waldo as he was trying to pull the poor animal back towards him to deliver another terrible blow, seizing his arm just in time.

'Cease!' he said, bearing Waldo's arm downwards with all the strength he could muster. '*Cease.*'

'Remove your hands,' Sir Waldo snapped. 'It needs to learn!'

'This teaches nothing,' Ashford said. 'Cease, sir.'

'A rotten animal,' Sir Waldo said. 'I shall shoot her myself – the worst forty guineas I have ever spent.'

'I shall give you sixty for her,' Ashford said, leaning round to tug the reins out of Sir Waldo's grasp. 'Martyn!'

Ashford's groom sprang forward.

'We have an addition to our stable,' Ashford said, tugging the horse further from Sir Waldo's reach. 'See what you can do to make her easy.'

With a sharp nod, the groom took the reins from Ashford, and led the horse away with a soothing series of clucks.

'Do you mean to humiliate me, sir?' Sir Waldo said, a vein throbbing in his beetroot-red forehead. 'In my own home?'

'You humiliate yourself,' Ashford said quietly.

'Waldo, I think you had best go inside and cool off!' Lady Phoebe said shrilly, her face white and afraid.

Something was very amiss here. As if in agreement, Brutus let out another stream of high-pitched barks.

'That animal!' Sir Waldo snarled, taking a sharp step forward to Brutus this time, violence still writ on his face.

Ashford stepped into his path – and for one moment he truly thought Waldo might hit him and braced himself. Brandon and Hanworth certainly thought so, too, for they were dismounting from their own mounts, Hesse becoming tangled in the capes of his coat in his haste to join them. But it was Dacre who came quickest, reaching Sir Waldo's side in two quick strides.

'Brother,' he said, clasping a hand upon his shoulder. 'Why don't we go inside and partake of a little lemonade, hmm?'

'Unhand me!' Sir Waldo tried to shake him off, but Dacre held fast. It was one of the rare moments where one appreciated that Dacre – so much more level-headed than his twin – still had every inch of the same breadth and brawn.

'You treacherous cur!' Waldo turned on Dacre, face full of recrimination and opened his mouth as if to shout – before suddenly appearing to perceive the shock and horror on the faces of his audience. He paused, took in a deep inhale, made a deeper exhale and appeared to wrestle his temper back under control.

'My . . . apologies,' he said, with great difficulty. 'The heat of the day – I must change my dress.'

He stalked off toward the house, leaving a horrible silence behind him. Lady Phoebe looked around helplessly. Ashford took a step toward her, but she warded him off with a raised hand.

'We all know . . . the horror of losing one's temper . . . don't we?' Lady Phoebe said, into the tense silence of the morning.

'Yes, of course,' Lady Morton said at once. 'Do you remember that time my cane broke at Vauxhall?'

She launched straight into the involved and amusing tale, as she was helped off her horse, managing – by sheer force of personality – to ease some of the tension in the air. Though Ashford noticed, as she picked up Brutus, that her hands were trembling.

One by one the party handed their horses to the grooms and began to trail towards the house, leaving only Ashford and the Hanworth siblings in the yard.

'Goodness,' Miss Hanworth said, face stricken and eyes very wide. '*Goodness.*'

She sounded just as Ashford felt, entirely winded. He had had his fair share of arguments with Waldo – but he would never have expected such violence from him.

'That was awful,' Miss Hanworth said.

'Fact is,' Mr Hanworth said, staring after Sir Waldo, a frown gathering upon his face, 'suspicious.'

For once, Ashford found himself in complete alignment with them both.

22

The atmosphere was strange that evening. Not subdued, for that would have been natural after such an afternoon. Instead, the party maintained a continuous patter of almost incomprehensible merriment that Lydia found profoundly unsettling.

Lady Phoebe and Sir Waldo led the way, as ever: Sir Waldo's brash cheer entirely restored as if nothing had occurred to upset it in the first place, and Lady Phoebe's frequent trills of loud laughter communicated quite clearly to all that she would rather not dwell. The rest were perfectly willing to comply, laughing and chattering, eating and drinking, generally brushing the afternoon's events firmly under the rug.

But for the first evening since Lydia's arrival, she remained quiet. She had never seen such a grand display of falsity in her life, and the overall impression was entirely depressing. She caught Ashford's eye across the table and, without quite knowing why, gave a little grimace – not, as it had been in days past, to communicate rampant dislike, but rather solidarity. For he alone – aside from Pip, who was taking furious minutes in his notebook – was not participating in the false cheer. Even Prett, for all his chatter about authenticity, was happy enough to pretend nothing had gone on.

To her surprise, Ashford had neither returned Sir Waldo's grins nor laughed at his jests. He did not aid Lady Phoebe in maintaining an easy flow of polite conversation, as he had worked hard to do when it was Lydia upsetting the status quo – merely observed proceedings with sharp eyes and a set jaw.

It was all very discombobulating.

After dinner, they retired to the drawing room, and Lady Phoebe, with new heights of effervescence, began corralling as many people as possible into a kind of choir, while Prett demonstrated his mastery of Himalayan throat singing.

'It sits deeper in the chest,' he explained to anyone who would listen. 'One projects from the diaphragm as *so* . . .'

'Lovely!' Lady Phoebe said. 'Do you think you could do it to the tune of "The Jolly Young Waterman"?'

Lydia's eyes travelled over to where Ashford stood by one of the great windows. Though the hour was late, the sun was just only setting, and the fading light had turned the rolling lawns of Hawkscroft pink. After a moment – feeling unaccountably nervous and hating herself for it – she crossed the room to stand next to him, following his gaze out into the gardens.

'You do not wish to join them?' she asked quietly.

He shook his head. Behind them, Sir Waldo launched raucously into the first verse.

'Has he . . . apologized?'

There was no need to clarify to whom she was referring.

'No, of course not,' Ashford said. 'To do so would be to admit something untoward occurred – if anything, he probably expects me to apologize to him.'

'How can he?' Lydia said. 'After he behaved so?'

Ashford lifted his shoulders in a tiny shrug. 'I perhaps could have handled the whole with a little more elegance. I was not thinking.'

'Well, I think it suits you,' Lydia said. 'Not thinking.'

She kept her gaze resolutely fixed upon the lawns as she said it, yet still felt it when he turned his head to look down at her.

'Does it?'

'I think was . . . admirable, what you did,' she said, maintaining a light tone by sheer force of will; somehow, she felt quite as exposed as if she had been cut open.

'Was that a compliment?' Ashford put his hand to his chest in a mockery so much gentler than all others they had hitherto shared that she found herself blushing.

'Well, you need not be so smug about it,' she said tartly, reaching for irritation as an armour.

'As I live and breathe,' Ashford marvelled. 'Well, that is kind – but I do not deserve such abject admiration—'

'Would we call it abject?'

'—for in truth I acted more in defence of Waldo than the animal.'

'You did?' Lydia said, looking quickly up at him.

'I saw you about to dismount from Bumper,' he said, with the hint of a smile at the corners of his mouth. 'And thought I had best intervene first, for who knows what *you* would have done to him.'

'Did you know he had a temper?'

Ashford shrugged. 'Not beyond mere crotchetiness. Though we do not know each other that well.'

'He is married to your cousin,' Lydia objected.

'They married so quickly,' Ashford said. 'You have never seen such a courtship: gifts, letters. You know, he sent her two hundred freesias, the night after they met?'

'That story is true?'

'Yes,' Ashford said. 'My uncle was furious – he sneezed for days – but approved the match, of course, and then . . . They disappeared here.'

'Really?' Lydia said, surprised. From the little she had seen of Lady Phoebe, this week, she would have supposed her to be very sociable.

'There are house parties, of course, and Christmas celebrations, but mostly they are alone in marital bliss.'

Lydia raised her brows at the faint edge of rancour in his voice.

'I do not mean to sound bitter,' Ashford said quickly. 'I just – I have missed her, this past year.'

'And now she will be leaving the country,' Lydia said.

She turned back to face the room, eyes travelling to where Sir Waldo, von Prett and Lady Phoebe were singing together by the piano. Ashford followed suit. Despite Sir Waldo's teasing the day prior, Lady Phoebe had a lovely voice, which harmonized rather beautifully with his. One might struggle to find a couple more visibly in love.

The sight should have prompted a jealous sigh from Lydia, but she found herself frowning instead.

'So long as she is happy,' Ashford said. 'That is what matters . . .'

He did not sound certain.

'*Is* she happy?' she asked. 'She seems so cheerful, but how can she be, after what has occurred today? And if she can hide disquiet after something like that . . .'

What else might she be hiding, under her unflappable cheer and beautiful smile?

'You underestimate our powers of repression,' Ashford said lightly. 'Our family is famous for it.'

'Ashford,' Lydia said reprovingly, 'pray, be serious.'

'I am being serious. One can never tell, with Phoebe,' he said. 'She is like my mother in that way.'

'Oh?' she said, as casually as she was able, feeling that any wrong word would break the moment entirely.

'She can be absolutely beside herself,' he said, 'and still look as though she is having the time of her life rather than put anyone out by showing it.'

He fell silent. Lydia waited a beat before speaking.

'You know,' Lydia said. 'My grandmother met her – your mother, I mean. When she was a small child.'

Ashford turned to look at Lydia, his expression unreadable.

'When Grandmother became a lady's maid for Lady Selby,' Lydia said, 'all the Daubneys came to visit. They were quite the handful, apparently, but very sweet – your mother laughed a great deal.'

'Yes,' Ashford said. 'She did that.' He looked back to the window. 'We all did, once.'

Once . . . 'Did His Grace have to . . . harden his heart, afterwards?' she guessed. Perhaps that was the source of Ashford's dogged adherence to duty, inherited from a father striving for order in the face of grief.

Ashford gave a soft snort. 'No, certainly not. He follows his heart resolutely, to this day. He is something of a family outlier, in that sense.'

Lydia's forehead wrinkled. 'You do not say that as if it is a good thing.'

Ashford hunched one shoulder. 'I just think it striking how often his heart leads him away from tasks he would rather not fulfil.'

He seemed rather surprised by the bitterness in his own voice. Unbidden, Lydia's arm reached out to him, as if to reassure, until the song, finishing with a resounding crescendo of voices, stayed her hand. Prett's throat singing the last note heard.

'Famous playing, Miss Hesse!' Brandon said, clapping his hands together, as Prett's final note at last concluded in a long throaty warble. 'Come, Ashford, let us sing a duet!'

Lydia – who had previously felt only liking for Brandon – would have readily wished him to the devil in that moment.

'No thank you,' Ashford said promptly.

'Oh, do be a good sport,' Brandon said, taking a few bounding steps toward him.

'Does he mean to capture me?' Ashford asked Lydia, eyeing Brandon's outstretched arms with some misgiving.

'It appears so,' Lydia said, edging out of the way.

'Recollect I am the faster runner, Brandon,' Ashford said.

'That is such a lie!'

'I wonder if I might take the opportunity,' Prett declared, 'since it is our last night together before the Grand Masquerade, to distribute a few little gifts?'

'Gifts!' Lady Morton clapped her hands with delight.

'Oh, you shouldn't have,' Lady Phoebe said.

'Nonsense!' Prett said, 'I must say thank you, from the bottom of my heart, for such a wonderful visit.'

'Brace yourself, Brandon,' Ashford murmured, recognizing the little brown bag at the same moment Lydia did.

'Would you believe there was a shop selling miniatures in town,' Prett was saying, 'which had two of my portraits in stock?'

'You shouldn't have!' Sir Waldo said, accepting one of the miniatures.

'This one, my lord, was dubbed "The Grecian Profile",' Captain von Prett said, handing it over to Ashford.

'You shouldn't have,' Ashford said, in quite a different tone.

'What,' Mr Brandon said, voice low enough that only Ashford and Lydia could hear him, 'am I meant to do with this?'

'I think,' Ashford said, 'that one . . . carries it around. Or I have seen persons display them on their mantelpiece.'

'Does he truly think I will display this?' Mr Brandon muttered.

'It takes a great deal of skill to paint such a thing,' Lydia said, primly. 'You must admire the Grecian Profile.'

'I do not,' Ashford said, 'and cannot, admire the Grecian Profile.'

Across the room, Lady Morton was in loud transports about her own miniature, declaring her intention of wearing it about her neck.

Ashford and Brandon began to snort with laughter.

'Neither of *you* have brought gifts for everyone,' Lydia hissed at them.

'Well, now, how can you be sure?' Brandon said. 'I might have done.'

'Just yesterday, in fact,' Ashford said, 'Brandon began embroidering his face onto some handkerchiefs.'

Mr Brandon nodded gravely. 'So that every time you blow your nose, you may think of me.'

Lydia lost the battle with her own self-control. She began snorting herself, just as Lady Morton, by accident, upset the box of miniatures, so that the remaining three fell onto the floor.

Quick as a flash, Brutus had picked one up and run off with it. There was laughter all round as Lady Morton and Captain von Prett gave chase, Brutus leading them on a merry dance around the pianoforte. In the end, it was Miss Hesse who scooped the thief up, and managed to wrest the miniature from his mouth.

'He has quite mangled your face,' she told Captain von Prett apologetically.

'Oh, there's an idea,' Mr Brandon whispered to Ashford. 'Here, smuggle him mine too.'

Prett could not quite maintain his usual air of relaxed abstraction as he regarded the remains of his miniature. 'Oh, you . . . naughty thing,' he said, bopping Brutus on the nose with a finger. Miss Hesse took a wary step backwards.

'You know dogs,' Lady Morton said airily, 'so mischievous.'

'My Flossie was the same,' Prett said, and Lydia waited for Miss Hesse to melt, as she always did when the animal was mentioned.

'I thought she was named Cassie?' Miss Hesse frowned.

'Oh yes, Cassie,' he said. 'My wretched memory.'

Miss Hesse's frown deepened. 'You do not remember her name?'

'It was a long time ago,' Prett said.

'She followed you for a hundred miles.'

'Yes, yes,' Prett said rather impatiently. 'But really – Flossie—'

'Cassie,' Miss Hesse corrected.

'Indeed, Cassie – was more a metaphor than anything else, for the trust I had lost in my fellow man. That is the point I wish audiences to take from it.'

The glowing eyes Miss Hesse usually pointed in Prett's direction were absent. Instead, she surveyed him as if she were seeing him clearly for the first time and did not like it a jot.

'A dog,' Miss Hesse said, with a disapproving sniff that was suddenly reminiscent of her mother, 'is not a metaphor.'

'I wish this portrait were a metaphor,' Mr Brandon said mournfully, looking down at his miniature, entirely unaware that his greatest competition had just been vanquished. As had Lydia's, of course. But as she waited to feel something, relief or triumph or gladness, that Miss Hesse was no longer to be vying for Prett's attentions, she felt . . . nothing.

Lydia looked to Prett, standing there – looking so very handsome with that infamous cowlick – and felt nothing. Ashford had been right. Prett was not who she wanted, at all.

23

That night, Lydia did not even try to fall asleep. She merely lay there, waiting, until the clock had struck midnight and she fancied that the whole house must be asleep. Then, she rose, threw on a nightgown and slippers, lit a taper, and padded downstairs towards the library. If she had been asked how she knew that he would be there, she could not have answered satisfactorily. Call it intuition, a hunch, or even just a hope – she felt certain he would be there.

And he was, seated in a winged-back chair observing the fire, a single taper candle on the table. This time he looked up at her without surprise and indicated the seat opposite with a wave of his hand, as if he had expected her just as much as she had expected him.

She sat, putting her candle down, then busied herself with angling her head to look at the title of his book rather than meet his eyes.

'Have you read it?' he asked, holding it up so she could better read its spine.

'Yes,' she said. 'A long time ago.'

'And . . . what did you think?' he asked.

Lydia raised her eyebrows. 'Another question. Are you trying to get to know me, my lord?'

'Well, I shan't, if you are going to be so damnably patronizing about it.'

'And now you have sworn in front of a lady,' she said sadly. 'Not very gentlemanly at all.'

He chuffed a laugh. 'What did you think?' he said, raising the book again. 'I should like to know.'

She flushed, without really knowing why.

'I enjoyed it,' she said. 'I should like to read it again – but there is a long waiting list at the public library.'

She looked around the walls and walls of books about them.

'If I had such a library as this,' she said. 'I would fill the shelves with all of my favourites.'

Ashford cleared his throat. 'I have one, grander than this.'

'Oh, yes?' she said. 'Do you wish for some time to boast about it?'

She did not quite know why she was trying to antagonize him so determinedly. She had sought him out by choice, after all. Had left the comfort of her bed specifically because the draw of speaking with him – privately too – was too powerful to ignore. But now the earnest cast to his words and expression was making her so nervous her heart might beat out of her chest. But Ashford did not rise to the bite in her voice, merely regarding her in a measuring sort of way, as if he were deciding something.

He took in a deep breath, sat up straight and placed his book to the side. Lydia's breath caught.

'I have had occasion to think, this past day,' he began, 'and—'

He froze. Lydia did as well, for she had heard it, just as he had. The gentle scrape of oak on flagstones.

'The door,' Lydia whispered.

Someone else had entered the library.

They stared at one another for the briefest of moments: alone, in their nightclothes, in the dead of night. Were they to be caught in such an encounter... In one move, both leant forward to blow out their candles, plunging them into darkness. Ashford seized Lydia's hand in his, pulling her to her feet and together they edged towards the walkway which ran down the middle of the room, bisecting the two lines of ten bookcases which separated them from the doorway. With the light of the corridor illuminating him from behind, they watched as the outline of a man turned to close the library door behind them.

'Come now,' Ashford whispered, and they dashed down the walkway as silently and quickly as they could, putting one, two, three, then four stacks between them, darting behind the fourth, pressing their backs against the bookshelves, trying to quieten their heavy breath. They listened, holding themselves very still, for footsteps. There were none. Had the person left, and they had simply missed the sound of the door this time? Or were they browsing the stacks closest to the door?

'If they come this way,' Ashford whispered, 'I shall distract them while you hide again.'

He spoke so quietly that Lydia would have had no hope of hearing him had they not been standing so close together, had he not turned his head to whisper directly into her ear. She could hardly see him, even so, for the glow of the fire could not reach them any longer, and the moon, visible in the far window, caused more shadows than it did light. She could feel, though, the brush of his shoulder against hers every time he took in a breath, the warmth of his palm against hers. They were still clasping hands, she realized. She had never held a gentleman's hand, without gloves to stand between them – and suddenly, she was thoroughly distracted from the unknown gentleman. Breathless for an entirely different reason.

'What were you about to say?' Lydia asked. 'Before?'

She should remain quiet and still, she knew this – and yet, it felt abruptly important, now more than ever, that they finished their conversation, that Ashford voice whatever declaration had, surely, been on the tip of his tongue.

'Sssh,' he said. 'Not now.'

'I just—'

'Quiet! We cannot risk discovery – it is nigh, we are entirely alone—'

'Fact is,' came a hoarse whisper from deeper within the stacks, 'not *entirely* alone.'

Ashford and Lydia near jumped out of their skins. Wheeling around in the direction of the voice, they stared into the darkness, making out – for the first time – where the outline of another figure was tucked against the wall.

'Pip?!' Lydia whispered. 'What on earth are you doing?'

'Nighttime wandering – suspicious,' Pip whispered, nodding towards Ashford. 'Slipped in through the servants' stairs.'

'You were following me?' Ashford whispered, with nonetheless audible outrage. 'The effrontery – it is beyond the pale!'

'Is it?' Pip hissed, in a rare flash of temper. 'Since you appear to have scheduled an assignation with my sister – quite *within* the pale, I would say.'

Ashford's outrage converted instantaneously to contrition, and he dropped Lydia's hand as if it were scalding. Lydia fought the urge to grab for it again.

'We can explain,' Ashford whispered, holding out his hands in supplication.

'Hush,' Lydia hissed.

At last, she could hear the sound of footsteps moving through the room, could see the flicker of a taper candle on the floor heading towards the fireplace. They fell silent, turning to peer through the shelves as children playing hide and seek. A moment later the person came into view: a man making his way cautiously toward the fireplace, casting looks left and right as if he was as afraid of detection as they. The taper held beneath his chin cast such strange shadows across his face that Lydia did not recognize him until the light of the smouldering fire provided further illumination. Reeves.

Beside her, she could feel the tension in Ashford's frame relax, and she understood why – Reeves was sensible and discreet. Even if he did discover them, whatever his private views, he might be trusted to remain silent. But no sooner had the thought crossed her mind than the sound of the library door could be heard again; they all tensed, nerves renewed. All save for Reeves, who looked up, expectant but unafraid. The sound of hurried steps, less careful, less stealthy than Reeves' had been, and then the new figure was revealed: tall, wide, unmistakeably bearish in frame.

Lydia's heart leapt into her throat. Sir Waldo would surely not take kindly to his butler making use of the library at nighttime, nor to catching the three of them out of bed at such an hour.

But then the firelight revealed the whiskerless face, and Lydia could relax again. For it was not Sir Waldo, but the infinitely preferable Lord Dacre.

'Oh *ho*,' Pip whispered.

Dacre paused, a few steps away from Reeves. He did not look surprised to see him. Lydia frowned, trying to see more of their expressions from between the stacks.

The gentlemen gazed at one another for a moment, then Reeves extended an invitatory hand. Dacre took two quick strides towards him and drew him into a close embrace.

Lydia felt her eyes widen. Beside her, Pip shifted on his feet. *Oh.*

'What a *week*,' Reeves said, when at last they parted.

'I should be very glad for it to be over,' Dacre agreed, 'if it did not also mean leaving you.'

'How long before you might visit again?' Reeves spoke into Dacre's neck, voice muffled but still audible.

'I do not know,' Dacre said. 'I might concoct some excuse about helping Waldo and Phoebe pack up the house, but . . .'

'It has been a year of sneaking around,' Reeves said. 'Barely satisfied by whatever visits, moments and scraps we can find.'

A year? Directly under Waldo and Phoebe's noses?

'I know.' Dacre sounded tired and pained. This, more even than the embrace, made Lydia feel abruptly uncomfortable with their eavesdropping – they should not be witnessing such emotion, only revealed under the assumption of privacy. She cast her eyes to the ground, determinedly, but she could not do the same with her ears.

'We must consider our approach.' When freed from the trappings of deference, it was far easier to hear the military in Reeves' voice. 'Before, I could not leave Lady Phoebe, but now . . . Are you in need of a new butler?'

She heard the whisper of Dacre shaking his head. 'Waldo would be suspicious.'

'Is it not worth taking the chance?' Reeves entreated.

'Not when it is your *life* endangered,' Dacre said, in tones fiercer than any Lydia had heard him use. 'My title and standing protect me, but you have no such shield. We have discussed this.'

'We have,' Reeves agreed, 'but . . . I do not think I can be satisfied with scraps any longer, Dacre – caution bedamned.'

'A few nights ago, you were the one instructing me to be more careful. What has caused this change?'

There was the sound of hands scrubbing across a face – whether Dacre's or Reeves', Lydia could not tell.

'I am not suggesting we be foolhardy,' Reeves said, 'but – it is just – well, in truth, I have not been able to cease thinking of what von Prett said to me.'

Dacre let out a surprised snort. 'Our dear captain? I thought you believed him a shammer.'

From behind the bookshelf, Lydia frowned. What did he mean?

'Oh, he is – that fraudulent popinjay has not spent a single minute on the battleground, I would swear my life upon it,' Reeves said contemptuously. 'If he speaks of Waterloo once more, I shall not be able to prevent myself from shooting him.'

'I know, I know,' Dacre said, with the fond indulgence of one who had heard this grievance many times.

'If only there was a way I might reveal his true colours . . .' Reeves broke off, taking in a calming breath. 'He was correct on one count, however,' he said, more slowly, 'war did alter me, Dacre. Having survived it, I vowed not to live according to fear any longer – a vow I am in danger of forgetting.'

There was a pause – a pause so long that Lydia could not prevent herself stealing a quick glance through the shelves, watching as Dacre reached out to clasp Reeves' hands.

'We are free men,' Reeves said. 'How should Waldo stop us? Would he truly expose his own brother?'

'In one of his rages, anything is possible,' Dacre said heavily. 'You saw him today.'

'I do not understand what has made him so. He does not usually lose control in front of company.'

Dacre shook his head rather than answer.

'Does it have anything to do with Mr Villars?' Reeves said.

'He has told you of that?' Dacre asked.

'No,' Reeves said. 'But he receives letters from them by the handful. What is going on?'

'I do not know the whole, myself; Waldo is too proud to unburden himself. I have helped him as much as I can afford to, but—'

'What?' The word burst from Reeves as if he could not hold it back. 'Why would you help him – when he treats you so abominably?'

'You know why,' Dacre said quietly.

'The way he *speaks* to you—'

'I weather his teasing, and he keeps my secrets,' Dacre interrupted. 'These are the rules by which he and I have always lived.'

'It is not teasing,' Reeves said staunchly, 'and it does not have to be that way. We can work toward a different future – we *can*.'

Lydia's breath caught as she waited Dacre's response.

'I want that, too,' he said quietly. 'I do.'

There was another pause, but this time for a kiss.

'I have swept the house, and no one wakes,' Reeves said, after, voice lower and gentler, now. 'Let us to bed.'

They left the library hand in hand.

Even after the door shut, Lydia, Ashford and Pip did not move, straining their ears for any signs they might be returning. Then, a full minute later, they let out three identical gusts of air.

Lydia turned to look at Ashford. She could not make his expression out, in the darkness, but she could feel the tension in his frame – and she had a sudden sense of horror at whatever he might be about to say, or do. For what would Ashford – dutiful, proper, traditional Ashford – think of what they had just witnessed?

'Suspicious,' Pip said, breaking the silence. 'Very.'

'We did not see that,' Ashford said abruptly. 'Do you understand?'

Pip was not attending.

'Waldo is in trouble,' he was saying to himself. 'Dacre knows – letters from Villars—'

'Mr Hanworth,' Ashford said, and his voice was hard and firm, 'I understand you believe yourself to be upholding the law, but we say nothing of this, do you understand?'

'Pip understands,' Lydia said. 'Don't you?'

'Yes, yes,' Pip said, flapping a dismissive hand at Ashford. 'Why would I say anything?'

'You are not listening,' Ashford said. 'This is serious.'

'*You* are not listening,' Pip said with uncharacteristic sharpness. 'Why would *I* say anything?'

He gave Ashford a speaking look. Lydia's heart near beat out of her chest as she watched Ashford's eyes widen with realization, felt her muscles clench and harden as if she were about to physically battle him. She would, if it came to that – whatever fragile conversation had been about to unfold between them, she would hang it all in a moment if he was going to be a danger to Pip. For Pip was not Dacre – he did not have the rank or the title or the connections to insure against any accusation that might be made.

'Oh,' Ashford said. 'Then you . . . appreciate the need for discretion?'

Lydia felt the fight leave her in a rush. She placed a hand on a bookshelf, to steady herself.

'I do,' Pip said. 'More importantly, I have come to a Big Conclusion.'

'What is it?' she asked rather weakly. She did not think she had the energy for any more revelations.

'It all makes sense, at last,' Pip said.

'What are you talking about?' Ashford said, looking from one to the other.

'We should tell him,' Lydia said. 'He might be able to help.'

'You trust him?' Pip asked.

'Yes,' she said.

Ashford turned sharply to regard Lydia, as though this were a far grander confession than it was.

'Very well,' Pip said. 'Fact is, it is *Waldo*. Waldo took the diamonds.'

24

'This is nonsense,' Ashford said. 'Another farce.'

'It is not a farce,' Lydia said. 'I promise.'

Ashford scrubbed a hand across his face. They were seated in front of the fire again and had just finished relaying the whole tale to him.

'If the diamonds are gone, why have you not informed Lady Phoebe?'

'Because suspicion would fall upon Elspeth in the first instance,' Pip said. 'She has the only key.'

'It was not her,' Lydia said. 'That you must believe.'

'Of course it wasn't,' Ashford said. 'She'd have been better making off with the silver teaspoons – and you know, Phoebe would have believed her.'

'But would she believe it's Sir Waldo who's taken the necklace?' Pip demanded.

'No, because that's ridiculous,' Ashford said. 'Waldo gave it to her in the first place – why would he then take it?'

'Would it even count as stealing?' Lydia wondered. 'If he bought it in the first place.'

'Well, yes,' Ashford said reluctantly. 'All Waldo's engagement gifts were named as Phoebe's in the marriage settlement – in the case of his death or their divorce, they belong to her, not the estate.'

'You see!' Pip slapped a hand upon the table.

'It proves nothing,' Ashford said. 'I am still not certain it constitutes a crime.'

'Even if it does not,' Pip said, 'it's still a *mystery*. You heard Reeves – Waldo is receiving letters from a Mr Villars, the same name as on the letter I found. I don't know who this Mr Villars is, but he's blackmailing him for something.'

'You and I also heard Waldo asking Dacre for money,' Lydia said to Ashford, 'threatening him.'

Pip looked up, sharply.

'When was this?' he demanded.

'When we were stuck in the parlour,' Lydia said. She turned to Ashford, appealing. 'Do you remember?'

'I do,' Ashford said, reluctantly.

'Something is afoot!' Pip said triumphantly. 'And it involves the diamonds, that's for certain.'

'Is it?' Ashford said. 'It's loose, sir, very loose.'

'If we do nothing,' Pip said, uncharacteristically serious, 'and something is afoot – Elspeth's life is at risk.'

'And he is about to leave the country with your cousin,' Lydia said. 'On a six-week voyage to a place where she knows no one. Don't you wish to know the truth before she leaves?'

'He adores her,' Ashford said. 'He has a temper, but . . .'

'But . . .' Lydia agreed.

She thought of the naked rage in his eyes as he had struck the horse, the redness of his face when he had lost his temper over snuff, the mean bite to his tone when he had threatened Dacre. Remembered all the little ways he had put Lady Phoebe down over the course of one weekend alone. Individually, the incidents might be small, but as a collective . . . They built an unpleasant image.

'Elspeth has definitely checked everywhere in the room?' Ashford asked weakly.

Pip stared at him, then to Lydia, and then back again.

'Not sure you're cut out for this work,' Pip said. 'Double checking is the *first* thing one does. Stands to reason.'

'Then the next thing we must do, is find this Mr Villars,' Ashford said. 'You may leave the matter with me. Once the house party is concluded I shall return to London and—'

'Fact is, no time,' Pip interrupted.

'Lady Phoebe intends to wear the necklace at the masquerade,' Lydia said. 'If it is discovered missing before we have answers . . .'

'I could make it to London and back in time, with a fast horse,' Ashford said. 'Assuming Villars – whoever he is – tells me anything.'

'Perhaps I ought to go,' Pip said. 'I can get Mr Simmons to join me, and they'll have a hard time denying Bow Street.'

'Meanwhile, we will continue searching here,' Lydia said. 'For the necklace or other proof – perhaps the letters Reeves mentioned.'

'If there are any remaining,' Ashford said, 'they will be in his study – which he keeps locked at all times.'

'Lock's unpickable,' Pip said. 'I already tried.'

'Then we shall get inside some other way,' Ashford said. 'Won't we?'

He looked to Lydia for confirmation, and something about the way he did it – with utter confidence in their ability to achieve such a thing together – had Lydia's heart clenching.

'Yes,' she said.

Pip rose from his chair.

'Very well,' he said. 'I shall leave at first light.'

'We will make your excuses,' Lydia promised.

Pip nodded and hastened towards the door, closing it softly behind him.

'I cannot believe I am indulging him,' Ashford muttered to himself. 'It's pure conjecture, riddled with holes – the ramblings of a madman.'

'Perhaps,' Lydia said. 'But Pip is correct. Whatever is going on, the consequences look set to land upon Elspeth – and perhaps Phoebe, too.'

'Why are *you* indulging this?' Ashford said. 'You have only just met these people.'

'I know,' she said. 'And there was a moment where I doubted it just as you did. But it would not be right to leave Elspeth and Phoebe to weather it alone. If we can help, we must try – Pip has shown me that.'

She walked over to the fire, holding her taper candle to the embers. She did not much relish trying to find her way back in the dark.

'You did not seem surprised,' Ashford said, 'about Mr Hanworth.'

'No,' she said. 'I knew.'

'Are he and this Simmons character . . . together?' Ashford asked.

She understood his curiosity but though she had discovered she trusted Ashford, more than she would ever have expected at the beginning of the week, there were some confidences that did not belong to her.

'You did not seem that surprised, either,' she said instead.

'It is not uncommon,' Ashford said. 'I have a cousin who prefers the company of men, as well – in our circles, it is easier, I think. People generally know to look the other way, though it is not spoken of openly, of course, the stakes being so high.'

The stakes were mortal.

'How hard it must be,' she said, thinking of Dacre and Reeves, 'to hide their love in such a way.'

She finally got the taper to light, and turned back around, cupping her hand around the flame.

'It makes what we've been doing seem rather trivial,' she said, not looking at him.

'I suppose it does,' he said after a pause, stooping to light his own candle against hers.

'Do you think we shall be able to do it, tomorrow?'

'I do,' he said. 'When we are not behaving deplorably, we work well together.'

'You think so?'

'I do,' he said. 'Given the circumstances surrounding our engagement, I think we get on rather well.'

It was the first time he had referred to their engagement without frustration. It was the first time she had heard it without feeling anger.

She took an unsteady inhale. 'That's true.'

'We can speak on many subjects,' he added.

'We can,' she agreed.

'And while I proposed without knowing much of the real you,' he said, 'I do, now.' Raising his eyes from the candle, he looked directly at her. 'My father arrives tomorrow, intending to announce our engagement at the masquerade.' He paused. The longest pause of Lydia's life. 'I wish to let him.'

'You – you do?' she breathed, hardly daring to believe her ears.

'Yes. In fact, I . . .' He took in a steadying breath. She waited, heart in her throat, not sure what she wanted him to say only that she would not interrupt, now. Could not, had her life depended upon it.

'I think – I think we might be friends,' he finished.

Lydia felt as if she had been doused with water.

'I think we might be friends, if we allowed ourselves,' he said. 'I think we might deal well together.'

Lydia looked down. It was not disappointment. It was not. It could not be, because she did not – she did not –

Except she *did*, didn't she? Lydia could not pinpoint the exact moment she had begun to look at Ashford differently, but she could no longer deny that her sentiments, somewhere along the line, had undergone a change. Perhaps there *was* no single moment, rather a collection of tiny instances – biting exchanges and shared laughter, lingering glances and unexpected confidences, brushing shoulders and quickening heartbeats – strung together as beads onto a necklace, and now . . .

Perhaps it ought to be reassuring that he no longer hated her, but somehow, Ashford's tepid words hurt far more than any of the insults he had ever thrown at her.

Lydia opened her mouth, closed it, then opened it again. 'Friendship is not quite what I am after.'

She was proud of the steadiness of her voice. It was a far cry from how she felt.

'It is a fair foundation to build a marriage,' he said, cheeks flushing. 'It is more than most people have.'

'That is true,' she allowed, for it *was*, and she knew, too, what was said – that deeper affection would grow, in time.

But friendship was no substitute for what Lydia had always wanted from life – what she now realized she wanted, from him.

And yet . . . She hesitated, trying to parse through her confused thoughts, her conflicting instincts. After all her effort to be rid of him, after all the horrid things she had done and said, in the pursuit of freedom, it should feel easy to decline his offer – yet now it came to it, she found she did not wish to lose him, after all.

'But I am not most people,' she said, at last. Lydia raised her gaze, again, to look him directly in the eye. 'It is not enough for me.'

However much had changed, these past days, this had not. However much it hurt to deny him, she could not betray herself in such a way.

'Is this about Prett again?' he asked. 'Surely you do not . . .?'

'No, I do not,' she admitted. 'He is not who I thought he was, but that does not mean that I cannot fall in love elsewhere.'

Her cheeks reddened to speak so openly, but she raised her chin and held his gaze nonetheless.

'How even you have swallowed such stuff!' Ashford muttered, running a hand, agitated, through his hair.

'Swallowed?' she repeated. 'You think I have been . . . duped in some way?'

'It is not your fault,' he said. 'Ladies have such unrealistic ideals shoved at them from the moment they are born, books and tales and talk of romance – it pains me that you are so enthralled by it, for it prevents you from rational decisions.'

'You think us so gullible?' she asked. 'Such fools?'

'I think you are allowing sentiment to distract you from considering marriage a business deal,' he said. 'One you should consider and negotiate for the changes to your life that it will bring.'

'How charitable you are,' she said. 'To have our best interests at heart – do give yourself a pat upon the back, my lord.'

Rising temper sent sharpness back to her tongue.

'I am on your side,' Ashford insisted.

'Perhaps,' she said. 'And yet here you are, a man, still telling me, a woman, how I ought feel, and behave. You'll forgive me if I struggle to tell the difference.'

'That is not what I—' He broke off, frustrated. 'We are two adults, who can speak honestly with one another, who might enter into such a union with open eyes. If we might agree upon a deal that works for us both – why, that would be a rare and beautiful thing, Miss Hanworth.' He stopped, and stared at her, expression entreating. 'Surely you understand that?'

'Here is what I understand,' Lydia said. 'You are asking me to marry you. To take your name. To legally cease to exist as a person myself. You are asking me to leave my family and absorb myself into yours, to leave my life and fold myself around your habits, your needs, your preferences. You are asking me to walk one step behind you, for the remainder of my days, to hand my freedom and my finances into your keeping.'

He opened his mouth, but she held up a hand to forestall him.

'You are asking me to risk my life bearing your children. Children, who at first breath would not belong to me, but to you, to be raised and educated and moulded according to your vision and desire. You are asking for all this and more. And I – I only ask for one thing: for love. For dancing, courting, flirting . . . Yet you think I am the one with unrealistic expectations? Tell me, Ashford, were the situation reversed – would you take that deal?'

She held his gaze and the silence. He did not try to speak.

'Once Pip and I both come of age, I will have income enough to live out my days unmarried,' she said. 'The only reason I should ever consider entering the matrimonial state would be for some grand love affair. When the risk to my life and happiness is so high, why ought I settle for anything less?'

Ashford looked as if he were having difficulty swallowing.

'I own, I – I had never thought of it in such a way,' he said, at last.

'That much is very clear,' she said. 'Those are my terms, my lord. How do you answer?'

Even after all his damning utterances thus far, there was still a part of Lydia which harboured some morsel of hope as she stared at him, waiting for his response.

'I could not,' he said, at last, though his eyes would not meet her own. 'I could never give you such a thing.'

'Never?'

'If I had thought there the veriest chance of such a thing,' he said. 'I should never have proposed in the first place.'

She tried to speak, but – finding she could not quite remember how – nodded, then nodded some more for good measure.

'I see,' she managed eventually. 'Well, I – I am feeling rather tired, now. I will bid you goodnight.'

'Miss Hanworth, I—'

'We shall have a truce, tomorrow,' she instructed. 'Until we solve this diamond business – but after that, we are adversaries once more. Everything will be exactly how it was.'

He reached out an arm to halt her – but she was already walking away.

25

Tuesday – Two days remaining

Very little of the plan went well, of course. Pip slipped out of the house easily enough, leaving vague excuses for his hosts that they did not receive until gone eleven o'clock. After the diversions of the day before, and ahead of the planned revelry of the night coming, Lady Phoebe had suggested they all rise late and breakfast outside.

As Lydia approached the table, she saw that the only empty seat remaining was next to Ashford. Of course it was. A few hours of snatched sleep had done little to soothe her and the memory of their conversation still stung fresh in her mind, and so she seated herself without looking at him, busied herself with buttering a warm roll of pillowy bread.

Lydia leant forward to take up the sugar bowl – and Ashford seized her hand before she could take it. Lydia jumped half out of her skin.

'I'm sorry,' he said under his breath. 'I forgot – it is salt again.'

Lydia shot him an acidic look.

'How embarrassing,' she said. 'To reuse an idea.'

'Is it?' Ashford said. 'Given how effective it was last time?'

Lydia flushed in remembered embarrassment and opened her mouth to retort.

'Let us not argue,' Ashford muttered, 'we have a truce, recollect.'

'Perhaps you might let go of my hand, now,' she said through clenched teeth.

He let it go with a start.

'The post has arrived,' Reeves announced quietly from the head of the table, and – as he had every morning since their arrival – took a silver tray bearing billets around to each person. Ashford, with only one look at the handwriting upon his, noticeably paled.

'Who is it from?' she said sharply.

He tucked the billet into his breast pocket without opening it.

'The duke?' Lydia guessed. Ashford did not answer, which was as good as confirmation. Their eyes caught, and Lydia was the first to look away.

'Are you excited for this evening, my lady?' Dacre asked Lady Phoebe, taking a billet from Reeves with a small smile of thanks. Reeves' expression meanwhile, was even and neutral and a hundred miles away from the open warmth with which he had looked at Dacre the night before.

Once again, Lydia marvelled at it. With all the adversity facing them, they had chosen to be together as best they could, no matter what. What she would not give for that kind of clarity. She had never felt so confused, in all her life.

'Yes, though there is still so much to do!' Lady Phoebe said. 'We have invited all the local gentry and every room in the house will be thrown open and made common.'

'So many nooks and crannies for us to explore,' Lady Morton said, with a sidelong look to Lord Hesse.

'I do hope Mr Hanworth feels better soon,' Lady Phoebe called down the table to Lydia. 'We do not wish him to miss the masquerade, do we Waldo?'

'Hmm?' Waldo said, without looking up from his billet, which he was frowning over.

'Is there ought amiss, Waldo?' Lady Phoebe asked, frowning in concern.

'Of course not' Sir Waldo said. 'Just an invitation I should rather not deal with – bound directly for the fire.'

Ashford and Lydia tensed.

'To what?' Lady Phoebe said. 'Am I invited, as well?'

She leant in, but Sir Waldo twitched the billet out of reach.

'We cannot attend,' he said. 'I will decline.'

'Without telling me what it is?' Lady Phoebe said, voice teasing. 'How mysterious.'

'What difference does it make? We are going overseas. We shall have to decline everything.'

'Oh, stop, I cannot bear to think of it,' Lady Hesse said.

'Neither can I, so I shan't,' Lady Phoebe said merrily. 'Today, I am not spending a thought on the future.'

'I commend you, my lady,' Prett said. 'If my life has taught me anything, it is that one should endeavour to live in the moment.'

He looked to Miss Hesse for a reaction, but she did not appear to be attending, sneaking Brutus slices of ham from her plate.

'I myself have too many relying on me,' Hesse said, 'to take so cavalier an approach.'

'"Heavy is the head that wears the crown,"' Lady Morton quoted, looking up from her letters to send him a caressing smile.

'We should discuss a plan of action,' Ashford muttered in Lydia's ear, so close that his breath tickled her neck.

Lydia twitched hastily away.

'Sir Waldo!' she said across the table. 'Reeves told us, upon the tour, that you have a Ming vase in your study.'

'I do,' Sir Waldo confirmed, puffing out his chest proudly – good humour restored at this opportunity to boast. 'A gift for Lady Phoebe. It cost the moon – Dacre has never forgiven me for outbidding him!'

'It was I who told you about it in the first place,' Dacre protested, good-humouredly. 'It did seem a bit rich for you to then outbid me.'

'You bottled it,' Sir Waldo said. 'You always do.'

Dacre's smile faded.

'I should dearly love to see it,' Lydia persevered. 'I am so interested in the study of – ah – that particular time period of . . .'

When was it?

'Fifteen-century China,' Ashford muttered in her ear.

'Fifteenth-century China,' she finished.

'Commendable!'

'Do you have a moment today to show it to me?'

Sir Waldo hesitated for a moment but then shook his head.

'Not today,' he said. 'I'm afraid I have too much to do.'

'Perhaps Lady Phoebe could show me?' Lydia persevered.

'Oh, Waldo doesn't permit me in his office,' Lady Phoebe said.

'You would only cause a mess,' Sir Waldo said, spearing another sausage onto his plate. 'Another time, Miss Hanworth.'

Frustrated, she rose from her seat to approach the nearby serving table, pretending to examine the plates of grilled ham and clusters of boiled eggs.

After a moment, Ashford joined her.

'That was your plan?' Ashford muttered. 'Asking him?'

'It's better than you asking him,' she whispered, keeping her voice very low as she accepted a fresh bread roll from a helpful footman. 'Recollect he hates you now, because of the horse palaver.'

'Oh, it's palaver now, is it?' Ashford said. 'Yesterday you were all for anointing me a hero.'

'I was *not*,' she said.

'We are meant to be a team,' he hissed at her. 'You are being careless and hot-headed and it is going to ruin everything.'

'I suppose we should do it your way, should we?' she hissed back. 'Act on such bizarre and cautious logic that no one ever gets anything they actually want?'

'Oh, for goodness' sake!' Ashford said.

The truce was not going so well.

They took their seats again in mulish silence until the party began to rise from the breakfast table – murmurs all around about enjoying a ride or a stroll or a rest ahead of the festivities.

'You take a turn,' she muttered, 'if my ideas are so stupid.'

'Well, I will,' he muttered back. 'Waldo!'

Waldo had already made it halfway back to the house, and Ashford strode purposefully after him, Lydia following as closely behind as she could, without looking as if she was doing so.

'Waldo!' Ashford called again.

'What can I do for you old boy,' Waldo said, so cheerfully that Lydia could hardly believe it. Did he not remember in what terms they had spoken yesterday?

'I was wondering if we might speak, about yesterday,' Ashford said.

'Oh, no need, no need,' Sir Waldo said, slapping him on the shoulder. 'The heat of the day, no need to apologize.'

Oh, the gall of it! Despite her own frustrations towards him, Lydia felt a rush of anger on Ashford's behalf.

'Nonetheless I must,' Ashford said, through gritted teeth. 'Perhaps we might go somewhere to speak.'

'Speak away,' Waldo said.

'Somewhere . . . private,' Ashford said. 'Your study.'

'Perhaps later then, old boy,' Sir Waldo said. 'I'm afraid I promised my lady I would perform a full check of the grounds before tonight.'

He pulled out his pocket watch, to see the time and there, on the same chain, was a ring of glinting keys.

'It is past midday,' he said regretfully, placing the watch and the keys back inside his coat pocket.

Lydia scurried forward as fast as her legs could take her.

'Sir Waldo! Beware – a bee!'

It was the first thing which sprang to mind.

'Eh?' Sir Waldo said.

'It has flown inside your coat!'

'Yes, I saw it too!' Ashford said, catching on. 'You must take off your coat at once lest it—' He broke off and made a violent, jabbing gesture with his right hand.

'I really don't think . . .' Sir Waldo began.

'Men can die of such things, you know,' Lydia said.

'Come, Waldo, this is no moment to play the martyr,' Ashford said briskly. 'Lady Phoebe will not forgive me if I allow you to be stung – come, off with your coat.'

Sir Waldo let out a frustrated sigh but began unbuttoning himself.

'Yes, there it is,' Ashford said.

'Allow me to take your coat,' Lydia said, pulling on Waldo's sleeves.

'Hang on, hang on . . .' Sir Waldo said.

Ashford began slapping his hands over Waldo's torso.

'I say, you will anger it!' Sir Waldo said indignantly.

Quick as a flash, Lydia had her hands in his pocket and pulled out the ring of keys and – for want of her own pockets – thrust it quickly down her bodice. Over Sir Waldo's shoulder, she gave Ashford a surreptitious nod.

'There, its flown away,' Ashford said.

'Well, thank goodness,' Sir Waldo said. 'You were beginning to get rather handsy, my lord!'

He let out a great guffaw at his own joke, adjusted his coat, and made off. As soon as he had turned round the corner, Ashford and Lydia turned to each other, giddy with victory.

'You have it?'

'I cannot believe that worked!'

'The bee – how did you think of it so quickly?'

'How did you understand what I intended?'

They were speaking over one another as excitable as puppies, hardly able to contain their glee, until . . .

'We make a good team,' Ashford said.

Their smiles suddenly faded, excitement elapsing into awkwardness as the memory of their conversation the night before resounded in both their minds.

Ashford cleared his throat.

'To the study, then?'

By now, Hawkscroft was abustle with activity: the front drive noisy with the wheels of tradesmen's carts, four footmen laying a red carpet down the front steps under Reeves' exacting eye, while four more were arranging a series of gigantic potted palms around the entrance hall, and innumerable maids and errand boys were flocking up and down the staircase and to and from the ballroom. One could not have asked for a more distracting atmosphere, though Lydia still waylaid Elspeth and Jane to find something to do at each end of the corridor and act as lookouts. If they were caught, in Sir Waldo's study, there would be no talking oneself out of it.

'How long do you think we have?' Lydia asked Ashford as they approached the door.

'Perhaps ten minutes?' he said.

Nodding, Lydia slid a hand into her bodice.

'What are you doing?' Ashford expostulated.

'*Hush!*' she reprimanded him sharply. 'The key, recollect! Goodness, it has fallen deep.'

'Quickly,' Ashford said, voice strained, eyes staring determinedly up at the ceiling.

'There!'

'Is it out?' he asked, still holding his eyes aloft, as if the sight of her rummaging would turn him into stone.

'Yes, yes,' she said impatiently, thrusting what she hoped was the correct key into the lock. For a moment, she did not think it fitted, but after a few moments of Ashford's careful jigging, the door at last creaked open. He shut it carefully behind them, leaving it just a sliver ajar. 'Just in case this door sticks too.'

It was tempting to throw open every cupboard and utterly ransack the place, but they forced themselves to remain calm and systematic and began with the grand mahogany desk that stood at the very centre of the room, which was covered in sheafs of disordered papers, pens, ink and wafers.

'Such disorganization,' Ashford said critically.

'Your desk is as neat as wax, I take it.'

'I certainly would not leave it in such a state as this – how is one meant to find anything?'

'It is almost as if he does not *wish* us to find anything,' Lydia said, picking up a stack of papers, and beginning to leaf through. Beside her, Ashford did the same.

It became quickly apparent that most of the papers were bills. Even knowing Sir Waldo and Lady Phoebe's extravagance as she did, the sheer quantity was still shocking. There were bills for servant's wages, for coal, for liveries, candles and wine. There were bills from the coachmaker, the butcher, the florist and the tailor, all jostled amongst one another in hopeless confusion. As Lydia progressed further through the pile, she began to see duplicates, reminders, politely worded final warnings that the credit was overdue.

'This is a mess,' she said, and she meant more than just the desk. 'How can one couple spend so much money?'

'Quiet,' Ashford hissed. She turned sharply. He had stilled, cocking his head to one side.

'Good afternoon!' Elspeth called loudly. She had been stationed far down the corridor, so as to give us as much warning as possible.

'Quick – hide!' Ashford instructed.

'Where?' she said, looking wildly about.

'Get behind the curtains,' Ashford said. 'I'll think of some excuse to explain my presence.'

The sound of footsteps from outside.

'I'll be discovered straight away,' she hissed. 'It will look more suspicious.'

'Will you stop arguing for once in your life?'

'I am right, and you know it!'

'Do you have anything *better*?'

There were audible footsteps along the hallway now. Lydia and Ashford stared at one another, naked panic in their eyes.

'We shall say we were having a liaison?' she said. 'Waldo will be so shocked, he won't—'

'A liais—?'

Lydia was not sure who was more surprised when she kissed Ashford. As the door began to creak open, she threw herself bodily toward him with such force that he had to put his arms about her just to keep her from falling to the ground. He made a muffled noise of shock against her mouth but after a single frozen moment where she was doing rather the lion's share of the work – which was not the most sensible division of labour, given she was certainly the lesser experienced of the two – he began to return it. Quite convincingly, actually – and yes, she rather thought she understood what the books had all been going on about now, for this was truly rather—

'What on *earth* are you doing?'

They leapt back from one another in shock. For a moment, Lydia had entirely forgotten the purpose of such a stunt, to shock Sir Waldo out of any suspicion. But it was not Sir Waldo standing in the doorway.

It was Lady Phoebe. And sitting around her neck was the stolen diamond necklace.

26

'How did you even get in here? You cannot use Sir Waldo's study for clandestine entanglements!' Lady Phoebe hissed. 'Ashford, I cannot believe—'

'The necklace,' Lydia said blankly. 'You have it.'

'On the day of our masquerade, of all days you could have chosen for such a stunt as this!'

'The necklace,' Ashford repeated. 'It is not stolen.'

'What are you talking about?' Lady Phoebe said.

'We were wrong,' Lydia said, turning to look at Ashford. His hair was disordered, one hand still a little outstretched toward Lydia, as if he had frozen on the point of drawing her back towards him. Unbidden, Lydia pressed a hand to her mouth and watched as Ashford's eyes followed it.

'Come, now, away,' Lady Phoebe said. 'If Waldo finds us in here!'

Her face was pale, and she kept glancing fretfully over her shoulder.

'Come, *now*!' she insisted.

They followed her beckoning hand out of the room and Lydia locked the door with shaking hands – Lady Phoebe's eyes half bulged out of her head to see Sir Waldo's keys in her possession – and just in the nick of time, too, for no sooner had they taken a few steps back from the door than Sir Waldo rounded the corner.

'What, ho!' he said, cheerfully surprised and stopping short at the sight of them. 'What's going on here? Some kind of corridor meeting?'

He chuckled at his own joke, and then, appearing to register the slightly strange mood in the air, his eyes flicked from each of them in turn, to the door to his study, and the smile slid off his face.

'Phoebe?' he said. 'Is all well?'

'Yes, yes of course!'

'Is there a reason,' he asked slowly, 'that you are waiting outside my study?'

'We were just discussing,' Lady Phoebe said, 'if we ought to throw open your study, as well for our guests.'

'Yes,' Lydia said. 'I suggested it – a fine idea, don't you think?'

'I'm afraid not,' Sir Waldo said. 'My study is the only room in the house that must always remain locked – as my lady wife knows very well.'

He looked so large standing there, shoulders filling up almost the entire hallway, and for the first moment since arriving at Hawkscroft, Lady Phoebe appeared terribly small – and without quite knowing why, exactly, Lydia stepped forward to stand alongside her.

'Yes, yes of course.' Lady Phoebe gave a trill of a laugh. 'Silly of me even to countenance it.'

'Very silly,' Sir Waldo agreed, and he walked forward, reaching out to take Lady Phoebe's chin between his thumb and forefinger and lifting her face.

'You are wearing my gift.'

'I was – I was just trying on my dress for tonight,' Lady Phoebe faltered, flinching a little away from his grasping hands. 'I thought – a special occasion.'

'Diamonds for my diamond. Do you not think it foolish to wear it with so many tradesmen coming and going?'

He still had not let go of her chin. Ten days previous, this might have seemed charmingly intimate to Lydia's eyes, but now . . .

Lady Phoebe pulled a smile to her face. 'Oh, no one would dare steal from you, Waldo!'

This appeared to please him.

'That's true,' he said with a nod. 'You will wear the blue gown, tonight?'

Lady Phoebe shook her head. 'The pink.'

'You know I prefer the blue.'

'I did not know you were such an expert on evening wear, Waldo,' Ashford said, and he was stepping forward, too. 'What colour do you think *I* ought to wear?'

At last, Sir Waldo dropped Lady Phoebe's chin.

'I'm sure you will always do exactly as you wish, Ashford,' he said. 'If you will excuse me, I have to attend to some business.'

He nodded toward his study and, to Lydia's horror, reached a hand into his pocket for his keys. Keys which Lydia still had grasped in her hand. Sir Waldo frowned, encountering only emptiness within.

'What?' he muttered.

Lydia did the only thing she could think of. Stooping, she pretended to pick something off the ground.

'Are these your keys, Sir Waldo?' she asked. 'They were on the floor.'

'Must have dropped them,' he said. 'Thank you, Miss Hanworth.'

Lady Phoebe clapped her hands together.

'Well, time is ticking on,' she asked brightly. 'Come, Miss Hanworth, and I shall show you your domino.'

They walked away.

'Would you prefer a lilac domino?' Lady Phoebe asked chattily. 'Or a green?'

'Phoebe—' Ashford began, but Lady Phoebe cut across him.

'I am the only one wearing red, of course – the hostess' prerogative.'

The smile on her face was rictus and false, and the bright sparkle of the diamonds, which eight nights previous, had only added to her lustre, now only emphasized the pallor of her face, the darkness under her eyes that not even powder could quite cover.

'Phoebe, what is going on?' Ashford said.

'What do you mean?' she said. 'Nothing is going on!'

'I don't – I – I don't even know what I am meant to ask,' Ashford said. 'But something is very wrong and you must tell me, so that I might *fix* it.'

'Stop talking!' Lady Phoebe said. 'Stop – we will be *heard*.'

Muttering an oath, she seized Ashford's arm, pushed open a door and pulled him into a side room. Lydia followed, uncertainly – this felt as if it was a family matter, but she was not about to miss it unless she was told otherwise.

Lady Phoebe took a hasty turn about the room, biting at her thumbnail.

'Phoebe . . .' Ashford said again. 'Speak.'

With a discernible effort, Lady Phoebe drew herself to a stop. 'I'm leaving.'

'Leaving what?'

'Everything,' she said. 'This house, my life, Waldo – all of it. I can't do it anymore.'

'I don't understand.'

But Lydia did. She looked from Lady Phoebe, down to the necklace, and back again.

'The necklace *was* missing,' Lydia said slowly. 'But you took it, didn't you?'

Lady Phoebe's eyes filled with tears.

'I need it,' she said. 'The money it will bring me will buy a whole new life.'

'But you wanted to marry him,' Ashford said. 'You *wanted* this.'

'I thought I did,' she said. 'It was such a whirlwind. You remember. The gifts, the letters, the *flowers*. No one had ever treated me in such a way before, with such devotion, but now . . .'

'Now?' Ashford prompted.

'I did not know it would be like this,' Lady Phoebe said. 'He wants to be with me, always. He did not wish me to attend the Season, but even when I am here, he needs to know where I am, always. If I leave the house, he tells the footmen not to let me out of their sight – he asks them, afterwards, where I have been, who I have visited.'

She paused, marshalling herself. Ashford opened his mouth to speak, but Lydia placed a hand upon his arm to forestall him.

'He thought me so perfect, at the beginning,' she said. 'And now, if I do not live up to his ideal, even for a moment, he lets me know I have disappointed him. When he is happy, life is good,' she said. 'When he is not . . .'

'Has he hurt you?' Ashford said sharply.

'Not physically,' Lady Phoebe. 'Not yet – I don't know, if he ever will, but I . . . cannot, anymore, cope with it. I am so tired of trying to be everything he wants.'

Lydia stood very still. It felt as if one wrong movement would frighten the truth away, somehow; would have Lady Phoebe pinning a smile back on her face and pretending all was well, again.

'Do you know,' Lady Phoebe said, giving a strange little laugh, 'I do not even like freesias?'

'Why didn't you tell me?' Ashford asked, his voice breaking. 'I would have helped you.'

'I know you would.' Lady Phoebe dashed across her face. 'You would have taken it on yourself, as you always have done, for the family – but what could you have done? I belong to him, Ashford.'

'I would have removed you from this house,' Ashford said. 'Spoken to him – ordered him that he could never—'

'I would still have had to go back,' she said. 'Eventually. It is not as if you would support my divorcing him, would you?'

Ashford paused, lips parted. Divorces were almost unheard of amongst the aristocracy, granted in the rarest and most salacious circumstances – with the shame following your family for evermore.

A bitter smile curled Lady Phoebe's lips 'That's a rather harder question to answer, isn't it?'

'I will speak to him,' Ashford said. 'You don't need to do anything drastic. There will be another way.'

'He will not let me go.' She shook her head, sadly. 'He will fight and make scenes and cause a thousand scandals rather than let me go.'

'You would spend your life running, instead?'

'With the diamonds, I shall have enough to flee, properly. I took the necklace to be valued in Chippenham last week, and it is worth more than you can imagine.'

'Of course,' Lydia murmured, as much to herself as to the others. 'It went missing the same night Waldo announced you were leaving.'

Lady Phoebe turned to her, frowning. 'How do you know all this?'

'Elspeth noticed,' Lydia explained. 'She feared she might be accused of its theft.'

'And she came to *you* for assistance?'

'To Pip, actually. He has been searching for it, but—'

Ashford interrupted her with an impatient slash of his hand through the air. 'And then what? You can hardly take such an item to a pawn shop, Phoebe – you would be discovered at once.'

'In England, yes,' Lady Phoebe said. 'But I shall not be here. I have saved enough pin money to get to France, and once there I shall organize it to be broken up and sold.' She looked back to Lydia. 'I was going to leave a note, explaining everything. Elspeth would never have been in danger.'

Ashford combed a hand through his hair, agitation not in the least appeased by this explanation. 'Where will you stay?'

'With your mother.'

For a moment, Lydia thought she had misheard or that Lady Phoebe was making a very poor, very crass joke. She turned sharply toward Ashford, who had gone quite as pale as if he had seen a ghost.

'You wouldn't,' he said, voice choked.

'I wrote to her.' Lady Phoebe gazed resolutely at Ashford. 'I thought she would understand, out of everyone, my desire to escape – and she did. She offered me shelter.'

'But isn't she—' Lydia began.

'She's not dead,' Lady Phoebe announced baldly.

'Phoebe, don't!'

'Oh, she ought to know if she is to be your wife,' Lady Phoebe said. 'My aunt did not die, Miss Hanworth, she ran away. Of course, we could not tell people that, could we?'

Lydia turned to look at Ashford, hardly able to believe her ears.

'You told everyone she *died*? When she is alive, still?'

'I did not,' Ashford snapped. 'I was only sixteen – but my uncles insisted, my father . . . She was everything to him. He could not face it. The shame of it would have been too much – it would have dogged us for generations.'

'That is purest insanity,' Lydia said, appalled beyond comprehension. 'Have you seen her, since?'

'Never,' Ashford said.

'She writes to him,' Lady Phoebe said. 'He does not even read them.'

'*Ashford*,' Lydia said. 'That is—'

'Do not speak of what you do not understand,' Ashford said. 'We could not have told the truth, it would have ruined us.' He turned to Lady Phoebe. 'As you risk doing so, too,' he accused. 'You have not considered the consequences. This is not just about you.'

'Isn't it?' she said. 'It is *my* life.'

'So, we should all just go about acting in our own interests,' he said. 'Never mind duty and family and—'

'What about *me*?' Tears had sprung to Lady Phoebe's eyes. 'Do I not signify?'

'I – I . . .' Ashford pressed a shaking hand to his forehead. 'I – I cannot. I do not . . .'

Lady Phoebe reached out an imploring hand. 'Please,' she said. 'You must understand . . .'

He backed away towards the door. 'I – I need to think,' he said. 'This is not – this cannot be the only way.'

'Ashford . . .'

But Ashford's hand was on the doorknob and in another moment he had gone.

There was silence, in his wake.

'Well,' Lady Phoebe said, with a sad little laugh, 'that went better than I expected.'

'Did it?' Lydia asked, rather incredulously.

'He believed me. There is that, at least.'

She walked over to a low sofa and sat down with a sigh. Lydia went to sit next to her.

'I just hope Ashford can recover his calm before this evening,' Lady Pheobe said. 'Waldo is watching me more closely than ever – and once you all leave there will be nothing to distract him and' – she was speaking faster and faster, thoughts spilling out of her in an anxious tumble – 'and I do not know how I shall ever get away under such scrutiny!'

She pressed her hands to her face. Lydia watched, frowning and thoughtful. Lady Phoebe was so brittle that one wrong word would shatter her. Lydia would have to speak carefully.

'I think you are a fool, to waste such an opportunity as this,' she said. Carefulness had never been her strong suit.

Lady Phoebe turned her head very slowly to regard her. 'Excuse me?'

'If you are concerned about distraction,' Lydia said, 'then what is tonight if not the grandest, most glittering distraction you could ever have asked for?'

Lady Phoebe stared at her.
'You mean . . . leave tonight?' she said.
Lydia nodded.
'How?' Lady Phoebe's voice was fragile with doubt and hope.
'Well, I – I think I have a plan.'

27

Hawkscroft shone that evening, each room radiating with chandelier light, each fireplace rolling with snapping flames, each glass glittering with the finest champagne. At nine o'clock, as the first carriages began swinging in through the gates, all the members of the house party descended the stairs, each dressed in masks and dominoes which would – all being well – utterly mask their identity.

'How thrilling,' Lady Morton said, looking round at them all. 'Masked in such a way, one feels *anything* could happen.'

'Indeed,' Hesse said, with a meaningful raise of his brows.

'The mask permits freedom in every culture,' Prett announced portentously. 'It is the same all around the world, you know, for in—'

'It is a domino,' Lady Hesse said waspishly, 'not a mantle of invisibility. All the usual rules do still apply.'

'*I* certainly plan on disappearing,' Lady Morton said. 'Without

Brutus at my heels, you will have no hope of identifying me, Lady Hesse.'

'Where is Brutus?' Miss Hesse asked anxiously.

'Safe and sound in my rooms,' Lady Morton assured her.

'A good thing, perhaps,' Lady Phoebe said. 'Lady Laleham will bring her pug no doubt – can't go anywhere without it – and we do not wish for a territory scuffle.'

'Oh, what fun,' Brandon said, with apparent genuine enthusiasm. 'Sweet things.'

Miss Hesse's head turned in his direction.

'Now, which dance shall we begin with, my lady?' Brandon went on.

'Do you like pugs, Mr Brandon?' Lydia interrupted, for she could not live with herself if she allowed him to pass by such an opportunity.

'Oh, well,' Brandon said, 'ordinarily I prefer larger hounds, you know, but pugs . . . My mother has one. Looks like a bruiser but is the dearest thing.' He smiled bashfully. 'But then, I'm certain I would have a hundred dogs were it not dreadfully eccentric.'

Miss Hesse's breath caught. Her eyes, behind her mask, were very round and Lydia had to fight the urge to clap her hands. At the eleventh hour! Mr Brandon did not even know what he had done. She looked around for the only person who would be as pleased as she by what had occurred – but he was not there.

'Would you save me your first waltz, sir?' Miss Hesse said, in a sudden breach of convention – ladies did not customarily request dances.

'Why – yes, of course,' Brandon stammered, cheeks pinked.

'My dear, you forget – Lord Ashford requested the first waltz,' Lady Hesse said quellingly.

'He is not here, however,' Miss Hesse said, more firmly than Lydia had ever heard her speak before.

Ashford had not been seen since that afternoon. Lydia had searched the grounds in case he was lurking sulkily in some alcove, but to no avail. She could only thank goodness that there were others she might turn to, for with Ashford and Pip absent she and Lady Phoebe would otherwise be quite alone. As soon as she had explained the day's revelations, Jane and Elspeth had swiftly offered their assistance for the evening's tasks. Their support was bolstering indeed, but Lydia was still hopeful that she might yet persuade Ashford to join their cause, for surely, he would reappear at dinner?

But he did not.

How disagreeable of him to make himself scarce when they had not discussed the events of the afternoon: Lady Phoebe, and his mother, the imminent arrival of the duke – and that kiss . . . Lydia brushed a hand across her mouth. Had it truly happened?

'I do hope Ashford recovers from his migraine,' Lady Phoebe said airily, now, 'in time to greet the duke.'

As did Lydia. She could certainly not meet Ashford's father before they had had a chance to decide, together, what they wished to do. He had spoken so firmly against love, last night – but after what they had shared this afternoon, perhaps . . .

'I am greatly looking forward to meeting His Grace,' Captain von Prett pronounced. 'I sense he may be a kindred soul.'

'I shall present you,' Lady Phoebe promised. 'And, indeed, you must remind me to bring you to Colonel Lynton – he oversaw the 95th, as you of course know, and has been *very* desirous of resuming your acquaintance.'

The captain's serene expression faltered, briefly. 'The colonel?' he said weakly. 'Oh how – how wonderful.'

'Reeves, do remind me to make the introduction,' Lady Phoebe instructed. 'I mustn't forget.'

'Certainly, my lady,' Reeves said, with a grim sort of satisfaction.

Across the room, Dacre turned his head towards the wall to hide a smile.

'What illness did you say Ashford had?' Lydia heard von Prett asking, as they made their way to the ballroom. 'For I too am feeling a little . . .'

As vast as the house had seemed to Lydia on her first day, by half past ten it felt veritably crowded from the crush of persons within, and so loud with laughter and chatter that even when one was in the ballroom, one could hardly hear the music. Lydia circled through the rooms with watchful eyes. Save for the servants, there was not a single person in attendance without a mask, and amongst the sea of gentlemen wearing mantles of blue, black and grey and the oceans of ladies in lilacs and pinks, it was almost impossible to recognize anyone. Almost. For Lady Phoebe was the only lady to have worn a bright and shocking scarlet, Sir Waldo would always be recognizable for his height and breadth and –

'Miss Hanworth?' Ashford said, behind her.

She turned, sharply. He was wearing a simple navy domino, with matching mask, but Lydia had no trouble recognizing him. She had spent a whole week making a complete study of every tiny variation of his expression, after all.

'You are here,' she said, stupidly.

'Where else would I be?' he said.

'I have not been able to find you, anywhere.'

'You were looking for me?'

'I was . . . concerned,' she admitted.

'About me?' he said. 'I am touched.'

He held two glasses in his hands and offered one to her. She was strangely startled by the gesture. 'Oh – thank you!'

She stared up at him. After spending all day beset by the questions and thoughts and concerns she wished to ask and relay and share with him, she did not know where to begin. Lady Phoebe, of course, was the most urgent, certainly, but now her thoughts were fixed on a very different direction . . . The light from the closest chandelier cast him in such shadow, but Lydia still felt his gaze upon her as a physical thing.

'It was quite the day,' she said, clearing her throat. 'Did you – do you wish to speak of it?'

'No.'

His unhelpfulness prompted Lydia back to herself, a little.

'Yes, perfect,' she agreed. 'Bottle it all up, every bit. That sounds sensible to me.'

'The good news is, I did not ask for your opinion,' he said, irritated himself. 'And thus . . .'

'Nevertheless, you must receive it.'

A lady passing in a green domino turned sharply at the sound of their voices.

'My lord, there you are!' Lady Hesse, for it was she, clutched at Ashford's arm. 'You owe my daughter a dance!'

Lydia felt a rush of impatience at the interruption.

'Do I?' Ashford said.

'She was most disappointed when you were not here for the waltz,' Lady Hesse said. 'Let me find her and you can make up the next set . . .'

Lydia had to get rid of her.

'It is so difficult to keep track of persons, tonight,' Lady Hesse said, peering this way and that. 'I have not seen Hesse for several minutes.'

'I have,' Lydia said. 'He and Lady Morton went to find a quiet spot to . . . rest.'

Lady Hesse swung her head round to regard Lydia.

'Which way did they go?' she said sharply.

Lydia pointed vaguely down the corridor, and Lady Hesse bustled off.

'Liar,' Ashford accused softly.

'It's probably true,' Lydia argued. 'You might thank me for getting rid of her, you know.'

She drew him backwards from the dance floor, so they might avoid further interruptions, next to the shielding leaves of a gigantic potted palm, though turning a little so that she might keep Sir Waldo and Lady Phoebe in her eyeline.

'We have sent your brother on a fool's errand,' Ashford said. 'He is wrong about Waldo.'

'Is he? Waldo might not be a thief, but I believe he is still a villain. Perhaps you might wish to have another conversation with your cousin?' Lydia suggested, as lightly as she was able.

'I do not think,' Ashford said, 'I have anything else to say at this time.'

'Truly? Even after a whole afternoon to yourself?'

'Do not joke.' Ashford irritably batted away a palm leaf that kept attaching itself to his shoulder. 'If she is not careful, she will ruin herself – and the family.'

'You are making a mountain out of a . . .' Well, it was not quite a molehill, was it? 'Medium hill,' she settled upon. 'I know this is very alarming for you, given your . . .'

Lydia tried to work out the most tactful way of phrasing this – but she had too much on her mind to make the attempt. Out of the corner of her eye, she saw Sir Waldo accept another glass of champagne. This would be his sixth, now.

'Given your mother ran off . . .'

'You should never have been told that,' Ashford said, coldly. 'And I would ask you to not speak of what you do not understand.'

Now Sir Waldo was leading Lady Phoebe towards the dance floor, again. They had completed several dances together, already – Sir Waldo taking advantage of the masks to avoid the usual hosting duties.

'You might know the facts,' Ashford said. 'But that still gives you no right to think you understand a single thing about my life.' He had her full attention, again. He had not used such a cold tone with her in many days, now. He made as if to leave. 'If you will excuse me . . .?'

Lydia grasped his arm before he could take a step.

'Of course I do not understand,' she said urgently. 'Until today, I thought your parents to be a great love match – I can barely believe that was a lie, let alone—'

'It wasn't a lie,' Ashford interrupted. 'They *did* love one another, in the beginning. My father still does – it is only her mind that changed.'

He set his jaw, as if the words had escaped without his permission. A decade of secrecy was not easily forgotten, it seemed. Lady Phoebe had told Lydia earlier that – even in privacy – the family did not speak of the scandal. Lydia imagined a younger Ashford having to suffer such tangled circumstances in silence – a loss, but not in the way everyone thought – and felt her chest tighten.

'It must be hard, to keep up such a pretence all these years,' she said, with a gentleness she did not know she possessed. 'For you, and His Grace.'

Ashford leant away, as if in bodily rejection of such sympathy. 'You need not feel sorry for him,' he muttered. 'He prefers the lie, I think. It suits him better. The way he speaks about her,' he continued, as if, now he had begun, it was difficult to cease. 'Even now, as if she is some angel who could do no wrong, recommending I seek out such torture?'

He shook his head in disbelief. 'Sentimentality blinds him. She ruined him – he loved her, and she left him, and she left *me* . . .'

She had never heard him speak in such a way, with such rawness in his voice.

'And now Phoebe is leaving too,' he said, looking away and down.

'I am sorry,' Lydia said. 'I am so sorry.'

She stepped closer to him, tilting her head to try and catch his eye.

'I do not know everything that happened with your mother,' she said quietly. 'I cannot pretend to, but with Phoebe . . . I do not think she has a choice.'

'There is *always* a choice.' Ashford's mouth was set and resolute. 'We all choose and I am here, choosing duty again and again while they consider themselves *exempt*, somehow, while they take the easier, pleasant route of choosing oneself!'

'I hardly think,' Lydia tried to be gentle in her reproof, 'that Lady Phoebe's route can be considered easy.'

Ashford deflated.

'No, I know.' His voice was suddenly tired. 'Waldo has pushed her to it – but it is complicated.'

'It isn't.' Lydia shook her head emphatically. 'Truly, it is simple. She is your family. You must help her.'

'This cannot be the only way to do so,' he said hoarsely, almost pleading. 'I do not know what the correct action is, but it cannot be this. Leaving us – leaving me – it's wrong!'

Lydia wished, suddenly, that they were not wearing masks, for she wanted more than anything in that moment to be able to see his face. For him to see hers.

'Sometimes the wrong thing,' Lydia said, hoping he could read the sincerity in her eyes, 'is the right thing.'

He stared at her through the slits of his mask.

'On occasion,' he said, 'you can be very profound.'

She smiled more in relief than in amusement. 'I astound even myself.'

He chuffed out a laugh.

'I cannot believe I am having such conversations with you, of all people,' he said, shaking his head a little. 'You must be very shocked at all this – you are not exactly seeing me at my best.'

'I have already seen the worst of you,' she said. 'And it does not scare me.'

He looked away and down.

'I will speak to Phoebe tomorrow,' he said to his shoes. 'I am not . . . proud of how I reacted.'

'Perhaps you might speak to her tonight,' Lydia said.

'I hardly think she would thank me for that,' Ashford said. 'Tomorrow would be more proper.'

'Or tonight,' Lydia suggested again.

Ashford paused.

'What are you . . .' he began. 'Why? She is not leaving this evening?'

Lydia bit her lip. She and Lady Phoebe had agreed not to say anything, to anyone – but she could not bear the idea of the cousins leaving each other on such terms as they had today.

'Please . . . do not try to stop her,' she said, placing a hand on his sleeve. This time, he did not try to shake her off. 'It is her only real chance.'

'In front of all these witnesses?' he said. 'It is the height of foolishness.'

'It is perfect,' she corrected. 'Sir Waldo is already half drunk, can be easily distracted. By the time anyone notices her absence, she will be halfway to Dover.'

'He has not let go of her all night,' Ashford said. 'You would be lucky if she gets halfway to the stable before he is calling for her.'

'You forget – this is a masquerade,' Lydia said. 'She and I are to swap dominoes so he will not notice her absence. To his mind, she will never have left.'

Ashford was silent for a moment, dumbfounded, she assumed, by her brilliance.

'This is your plan?' he asked.

'Yes.'

'It is . . . good,' he said, begrudgingly.

'Thank you,' she said. 'Now I have only to wait for the correct moment – as you say, he has not left her side.'

Ashford lifted a champagne flute from a passing tray.

'If I have learnt anything from our battles this week, Miss Hanworth,' he said, 'it is that one should never wait for the right moment.'

He offered her his arm and bore her off towards Lady Phoebe.

'Cousin!' he declared loudly, bowing before her.

Lady Phoebe turned in surprise.

'Ashford!' she exclaimed. 'Good evening – I hope you are enjoying yourself?'

'Of course,' he said. 'I was blue-devilled this afternoon, but I have realized I was wrong to feel so.'

Lady Phoebe paused. 'I am – so glad,' she said.

'Such a magnificent event,' Ashford said. 'But that is no surprise: you have such good instincts and always know . . . exactly the right thing to do. About parties,' he added, after a beat.

Lady Phoebe's eyes, through the slits of her mask, were wide and shining. 'Thank you – it means a great deal to me.'

He took her hand in his, laying a kiss upon it.

'I am at your service, tonight and always,' he said. 'If ever you should need me – I hope you know that.'

'Such gallantry!' Sir Waldo boomed. 'Ought I to be jealous, Ashford!'

He let out a great heehaw of laughter, and somehow, without it being quite clear how it had come about, the edge of Lady Phoebe's lace under-dress got caught under Ashford's foot. There was the sound of rending fabric.

'My dress!'

'Clumsy, Ashford!' Sir Waldo said, scowling.

'Oh no!' Ashford said. 'Miss Hanworth, you had best take Lady Phoebe to pin it up.'

'I will indeed!' Lydia said at once, putting her own arm about Lady Phoebe's waist and leading her away. As soon as they were out of the ballroom, they hurried off in search of the nearest empty parlour. As they passed down the corridor, they ran into Lady Hesse.

'Ah, Lady Phoebe,' Lady Hesse said. 'Have you seen my son? I have been looking for him.'

'No!' Lady Phoebe said, without the tiniest shred of politeness. 'Quick, here!'

She pulled open a door and she and Lydia took a step inside – only to see the room already occupied by a couple locked in a close embrace.

'I say!' Lady Phoebe said in surprise. Then, again: 'I *say*.'

'Lady Morton?' Lydia said, as the couple sprang apart – for who else could have such red hair?'

'Humphrey!' shrieked Lady Hesse, appearing over Phoebe's shoulder. 'What is going on here?'

'Now,' Lady Morton said, hastily rearranging her magnificent bosom in the confines of her bodice, 'let us all try to be calm and sensible.'

'Sensible!' Lady Hesse shrieked, taking a step into the room and jabbing an accusing finger at her. 'You are twice his age!'

'We are in love!' Lord Hesse declared passionately.

'Oh, dear lord,' Lady Morton muttered.

'The scandal this could cause!'

'Well, this really does seem a family matter,' Lady Phoebe said, edging backwards.

'Lady Phoebe!' Lady Hesse reached out a hand to forestall her. 'I must insist you remain!'

But Lady Phoebe and Lydia had already escaped, half running down the hallway now.

'For such a thing to happen at my house party,' Lady Phoebe gasped. 'Lady Hesse will never forgive me.'

'Fortunately,' Lydia panted, 'that is soon not going to matter anymore.'

They pulled open another door and, this time making certain no one was inside, began tearing at the clasps to their dominoes, pulling off their masks, and then handing them to the other.

'Elspeth has my things packed,' Lady Phoebe said. 'I shall go directly to the stable yard.'

'We will give you as much time as we can,' Lydia promised. 'All being well, you should be clear until morning.'

She pulled Lady Phoebe's vivid red domino around her, and Lady Pheobe helped her tie the loo mask.

'There!'

'Now go,' Lydia ordered. 'Now!'

Lady Pheobe hesitated.

'I wish to say thank you,' she said. 'I have been so cross with you this week – I thought you difficult and vulgar and rude and—'

'Is this your first time trying to thank someone?'

'But I am glad,' Lady Phoebe continued as if Lydia had not spoken, 'that Ashford chose you.'

Lydia swallowed, smiled as best as she could, and bade her farewell.

28

Lydia had spent enough time in Lady Phoebe's company to perform a passable enough imitation of her. As she re-entered the ballroom she pushed her shoulders back, pinned her widest smile to her face and tried to look about the room with the satisfaction of knowing one owned most of the things within it.

'Lady Phoebe!' Lady Hesse called, hastening towards her. Lydia turned and hurried in the opposite direction, but within two more steps she found herself hailed again.

'Phoebe, darling,' Lady Morton said, appearing at her right-hand side, closely followed by a flushed Hesse, 'if I could just bend your ear for a moment? As much as I hate to admit it, Lady Hesse does have a point regarding discretion . . .'

Dear lord, could she have no peace?

'Not now,' Lydia trilled in her best Lady Phoebe voice, and changed direction again.

'Phoebe!'

She looked up to see Sir Waldo ahead, beckoning her towards him. She affected not to notice, turning in yet another direction to wind through the ballroom in a complete circuit of the room.

This part was going to be difficult. Ideally, she needed to be within his sights for as much as the evening as possible, whilst avoiding actually speaking to him for as long as possible. Her imitation might be good, but she did not care to test it face to face with Lady Phoebe's husband until he had several more drinks under his belt. But that decision was not up to her, and as she nodded and smiled her way around the room, she became aware that she was being pursued by a flushed and sweating Sir Waldo. Dear lord. She sped up, watching as new couples began to flock to the floor for the waltz and tried to scan the crowd for someone she might force to be her partner.

Ashford appeared at her side just in the nick of time.

'He is coming,' he said. 'Dance with me.'

She accepted his hand, and they joined just as the musicians began to play the first notes.

'Where is he now?' Lydia asked, taking his hand in hers as Ashford placed his arm about her waist.

'Watching,' he said.

'Villainously?'

'Yes. I hope I am there, when he finds out she is gone – I should like to see the look upon his face.'

'Don't get ahead of yourself,' Lydia said. 'We have the whole night to get through, still.'

She could not help but sigh at the thought. 'What a day.'

'It does feel many moons since we were trying to hide in that study,' Ashford said.

They looked at each other and then away.

'We kissed, earlier,' she said, for if they were both thinking of it, they might as well speak of it, surely.

'Can we strictly call that a kiss?' Ashford wondered.

'Our mouths touched,' she said. 'I'm not sure what else you would call it.'

'Romantic.'

'I ought to apologize,' she said. 'I should have asked permission.'

'It would have been the gentlemanly thing to do.'

'I am not a gentleman.'

'That much,' he said, 'I had already noticed.'

They turned, and turned, and turned again.

'Well, I'm sorry,' she said belligerently.

'You need not be.' He looked down at her and then quickly away. 'I do not regret it.'

Lydia inhaled sharply.

'Ashford—' she began, but the next turn had her facing towards the doorway, and there was Pip, no mask on his face, his gaze significant and intense.

'Oh lord,' she breathed. 'There is Pip – I forgot all about him.'

'Poor chap,' Ashford said. 'He's been on a wild-goose chase this afternoon.'

Another turn, and she craned her neck to see him again.

'No.' She frowned. 'He looks . . . excited.'

His eyes were bright with it. The last notes of the song played and they drew apart.

'He is beckoning us,' Lydia said. 'Let us go at once.'

Ashford nodded, and made an immediate beeline for him, Lydia close behind until her arm was seized.

'Phoebe!'

She was turned forcibly around with a hammy arm, to look

into Sir Waldo's face. His eyes, through his mask, were glassy with alcohol, something stronger than champagne on his breath.

'Dance with me!' he instructed.

'Waldo!' Lydia said, in her best, breeziest impression of Lady Phoebe. 'Yes, of course – I should like nothing better, but I just need to—'

He shook her arm and she glanced desperately over her shoulder for Ashford, but he had disappeared into the crush of people.

'You have been trying to shake me off all evening,' he said. 'But I should like to dance with my wife.'

'Of course,' she said, trying to extricate herself again.

'Look at me when I am speaking to you!' he said, with another shake, harder than the first, that had her mask slipping. She put a hasty hand up to halt its progress.

'Stop.' She tugged at his arm again. 'You are making a scene.'

'Let your mask off,' he said. 'I wish to look at you.'

'You will ruin the magic of the evening! she hissed. 'No!'

His eyes were narrowed with anger.

'Do not tell me what to do,' he began, reaching up with one motion to pull the mask from her face, then blinked. 'Miss . . . Miss Hanworth?'

'Sir Waldo,' she said. 'You appear to have mistaken me.'

'I – I thought you were my wife,' he said, rather stupidly.

'Evidently,' she said. 'May I request you unhand me?'

He did not.

'You were speaking like my wife,' he said. 'And . . . that is not the domino you were wearing earlier.'

'You are drunk, sir,' she said. 'You know not of what you speak.'

Hurriedly, she placed her mask back on her face, in the vague hope that might confuse him further, but the fog was clearing from his eyes, now.

'You wished me to believe it was her,' he said. 'Why? Miss Hanworth, where is my wife?'

'How am I meant to know?' she said, and she meant it to be airy, but he was still holding her arm, squeezing tightly, and his face was red with anger, and so she could not help the edge of fear that entered her voice.

He pushed her arm away firmly enough to cause her to stumble back, then he turned on his heel and stalked toward the door. Lydia craned her head to search for Ashford, but she could not see him or Pip. It was down to her, and her alone, to decide what to do now.

She ran after him.

Sir Waldo stalked purposefully through the rooms, cutting through the crowds as a knife through butter, whereas Lydia – smaller and so much less intimidating – had to weave and apologize her way through, losing precious seconds of her chase with every delay. She hoped that he might run upstairs, to look for his wife in her quarters, but no. With the instincts of a predator he was making directly for the stables, with such strides as Lydia almost lost sight of him.

'Lady Phoebe!' Lady Hesse tried to grasp her arm as she passed. 'I must speak with you.'

Behind her, Lady Morton was hurrying through the crowd, too.

'Go away!' Lydia snapped, too harried for politeness.

'I beg your pardon?'

She sped up, almost tripping over Reeves, and startling him into knocking over his tray of glasses.

'I'm sorry!' she said, skittering backwards.

'My lady?' Reeves said. 'Are you well?'

'I . . .' Lydia began.

'Miss Hanworth?' He frowned in sudden recognition. 'What is . . .?'

'I cannot stop,' she said, picking up her skirts to avoid the glass. 'It is Lady Phoebe – she needs my help!'

She pictured Waldo's bulk bearing down upon Lady Phoebe with all the violence he had shown against that poor horse only a day before, as intractable and unstoppable as the tide. What help would she even be?

'Reeves, you must fetch Dacre,' she told him urgently. 'Please, fetch Dacre to the stable yard – he might be the only one who can stop him!'

And then she was running through the entrance hall and dashing down the front steps. Behind her, she could hear the echo of people calling her name – Phoebe's name – but she ignored them. In the distance, she could see the Henley carriage almost at the gates, but it had checked, the groom pausing the horses – for Sir Waldo was running after it, waving his arms and bellowing his wife's name.

'Stop!' Sir Waldo was shouting, and as he reached the carriage, he pulled open the door and thrust an arm inside.

'Waldo,' Lady Phoebe said, her voice high and nervous carrying back to Lydia, still yards away. 'I was just – I was—'

But he was not listening, jerking her forcibly from the carriage.

'Unhand her!' Lydia tried to call, but she was panting too hard to get the words out.

'What the blazes are you doing, Phoebe?' Sir Waldo was pulling his wife down the carriage steps. 'You foolish, foolish girl. How *dare* you.'

He began shaking her furiously, his face red with rage, Lady Phoebe's neck flying this way and that in his hold. Finally, Lydia reached them and seized one of Waldo's arms, but he shook her off easily.

'Stop! Stop!'

Behind her, more voices were clamouring, but she could not pay attention. With fumbling hands, she extracted her grandmother's pin from the cuff of her puffed sleeve and darted forward again, jabbing every part of Waldo she could reach. Against his bulk, however, she was as a fly bothering a great horse. She could not even tell if he noticed her. But then, from within the carriage, Elspeth tumbled out to assist. She seized the groom's whip from where he stood helplessly, unsure whether to protect his master or his mistress, and in one swift move laid a great thwacking blow across Waldo's back.

That he *did* appear to notice, giving a howl of pain and letting go of Lady Phoebe for a brief moment.

Lady Phoebe, dazed but still standing, took her reticule from where it hung on her arm and threw it with all her might towards his head. Her aim was true – lawn billiards had its uses – and from the way it clunked as it hit Waldo upon the head, there were heavy coins within. Sir Waldo barely flinched. It was only a moment before he was advancing again, pushing Lydia aside, seizing Elspeth's whip to toss it away and bear down upon Lady Phoebe, murder in his eyes. Lydia and Elspeth grasped at his arms once more – but this time they were not alone.

There was the sound of running footsteps and then suddenly more hands were joining theirs. Together they wrenched Sir Waldo away from Lady Phoebe with such force that he stumbled and landed in the dust, and Ashford, Dacre and Pip stood there, panting. Behind them, more footsteps as Reeves, Hesse and Ladies Morton and Hesse hastened their way.

'How dare you!' Sir Waldo was spluttering, raising himself onto one knee. 'What is the meaning of this?'

'Quiet!' Ashford snapped, pushing him down again. 'Phoebe – how are you?'

'What on earth is going on?' Dacre demanded. 'Waldo – what are you doing?'

He reached out a hand to grasp Waldo's arm, whether to raise him up or keep him down, Lydia didn't know, but Waldo threw it away.

'Don't touch me!' he spat. 'No one touch me.'

'How are you, Phoebe?' Ashford asked again.

She nodded rather breathlessly. 'I am well.'

'What is going on?' Lady Hesse demanded. 'Sir Waldo, I cannot believe your behaviour.'

'*My* behaviour!' Sir Waldo said incredulously, raising himself to his feet. 'This is a private matter, between me and my wife – I have been attacked, in my own home, by these madwomen!'

He pointed accusingly at Lydia – stooping to retrieve her pin from the ground – and Elspeth, who was still holding the riding crop threateningly aloft.

'They are not madwomen,' Ashford said.

'I was not attacking you,' Lydia said. 'I was defending her!'

'And I,' Phoebe said, 'do not wish to be your wife, any longer!'

A resounding silence followed in the wake of this declaration.

'I intend to divorce you.' Lady Phoebe spoke again, raising a wobbling but resolute chin.

Sir Waldo laughed. 'On what grounds?'

'Cruelty.'

'There is not a judge in the world who would grant such a thing,' he said. 'No one would believe it: I am a pillar of society!'

'Now that,' interjected Ashford, 'is not strictly true, is it, Waldo?'

He smiled at Waldo so benignly that Lydia half expected him to offer a pinch of snuff.

'What are you inferring?' Waldo spluttered.

'Mr Hanworth can enlighten you,' Ashford said evenly.

Pip raised himself up to his full height.

'Fact is,' he said, 'Sir Waldo has almost bankrupted himself. That Mr Villars who keeps writing to him is a moneylender. Wants his dues.'

'What on earth is he talking about?' Lady Morton frowned.

Sir Waldo had gone white as a sheet.

'Is that why you needed money, Waldo?' Dacre asked. 'Truly?'

Pip nodded. 'Your payment appeased them, but it will not for long – so Waldo promised them the necklace.'

'But you never had any intention of giving it to them, did you, Waldo?' Ashford said. 'That's why you decided to go to Mauritius.'

'And you had no intention of coming back,' Pip said.

'This is nonsense,' Waldo said. 'Madness.'

But his hands were shaking.

'Waldo?' Lady Phoebe said. 'Is this true?'

'A mere trifling spot of financial bother.' Waldo brushed at a speck of dust on his sleeve, not meeting anyone's eye. 'It is not serious.'

'Did you truly keep such a thing from me?'

'What good would there be in telling you?' he barked. 'You've no head for business.'

'As you have told me, again and again.' Lady Phoebe shook

her head. 'I almost believed you, but all this time – what about my money? My dowry?'

'Do not stand on your high horse with me!' He jabbed a finger at her. 'You were leaving – running off with some lover, no doubt. It runs in the family, I see!'

He sent a sneering look toward Ashford, whose jaw tightened.

'I want you to go,' Lady Phoebe cried, pointing a finger down the driveway.

'Go where?' Waldo's face twisted into an ugly smile. 'This is my home, Phoebe. It belongs to me. *You* belong to me.'

'I don't care about any of it,' she said. 'Go to Mauritius without me – go anywhere, but leave England. Forever.'

'Waldo,' Dacre said, his quiet voice carrying over his brother's spluttering. 'I think perhaps it is best if you do leave now. Spend tonight at the White Horse and then we will discuss it all in the morning.'

'And you turn on me as well?' Sir Waldo demanded. 'After all I have done for you? After all I could *say* about you?'

Dacre paled.

'I am not scared of you – any of you,' Waldo looked around at them all with an unpleasant look in his eyes. 'A collection of gossips and gabsters and degenerates, no more. You all have your own secrets to hide too, don't forget. The things I could let slip . . .'

He glared at the assembled company, each hesitating as if weighing their own secrets in the balance.

'Oh Waldo, tut tut tut.' Lady Morton broke the silence, stepping forward from where she and Lady Hesse had been standing. She ranged herself alongside Phoebe, taking her arm in her own, and shook back her red mane. 'You might *try* to play the conjecture game, but truthfully, some of us have been doing this for years.

The things I could say about *you* – why, it would not be more than a day's work to ruin you.'

'If that,' Lady Hesse said, and she too stepped forward. 'A few letters in the right hands . . .'

'A few whispers in the right ears,' Lady Morton agreed. 'You are quite right, Waldo, we *are* gabsters and gossips – and what's more, we're good at it.'

Lady Hesse inclined her head. 'We can send whispers of your doings all the way to London, and still have time to change our dress for dinner.'

'With nothing but some powerful adjectives, a few sheets of paper, and coins for postage.'

'Shan't need postage!' Hesse piped up, puffing out his chest. 'I'll frank 'em for you!'

'Very helpful,' Lady Hesse praised. Her smile slipped from her face as she looked back at Waldo. 'Women may not hold the houses, or the purse-strings, Waldo, but we *do* own the secrets. So unless you wish the *ton* to begin whispering your name, removing your name from invitations, rescinding the memberships of your clubs, not to mention Bow Street bearing down . . .'

Pip gave an emphatic nod of support.

'Do you think you shall be received in Mauritius if they knew of your hideous behaviour?' She went on, her smile was chillingly pleasant. 'If I were you, I would do as Lady Phoebe asks.'

'Phoebe,' Waldo said, focusing all his attention upon his wife, 'you are confused . . . not thinking clearly. Let us all go inside and discuss it – I am happy to reassure you . . .'

'No.' Lady Phoebe's voice shook. 'I do not wish you to re-enter the house.' She looked to Lydia, entreating. 'I do not wish him to re-enter the house,' she said again, louder, more panicked.

'Then he will not,' Lydia said promptly. 'Why, there are two inns in Eagleton alone.'

'Your valet will meet you there,' Ashford said, nodding.

'Let us be serious,' Waldo said. 'You cannot mean to banish me as if we are in some medieval play! Phoebe . . .' He held out a hand toward her, his face soft and entreating. 'Phoebe, you do not wish to do this.'

She was very pale and trembling like a leaf, something about his softness appearing far more threatening than his anger.

'I – I do,' she said. 'I will.'

'Phoebe . . .' he said again, taking a step forward.

But then Ashford was in front of her, and so too were Pip and Reeves, and Elspeth raised her riding crop once more, and Lydia brandished her pin as a very small sword.

'Go, Waldo,' Phoebe instructed, firm now. '*Go*.'

Finally, Dacre took a purposeful step forward. 'I should prefer not to stoop to such incivility as to strike you,' he told him. 'But I will, if I need to, Waldo.'

'Brother!' Waldo said, half in entreaty, half in accusation.

'You have always been a bully.' And if there was sadness in Dacre's voice, there was no uncertainty. 'No more.'

'If we ever hear a whisper of your presence on these shores again, you shall speedily regret it,' Lady Hesse said crisply.

Sir Waldo looked as if he were going to be sick.

'I . . .'

'I do not wish to look upon you for a second longer,' Lady Phoebe interrupted. 'I will sell the diamonds and pay your debts, so you may live easily in your new life. You will give me power of attorney to do so.'

The driver opened the door to the chaise with a suggestive creak.

'Go,' she said. 'And do not return.'

Sir Waldo looked about them all, from face to face, examining them for any weakness.

'This is not over,' he snarled at last, stalking past them. He leapt into the chaise and slammed the door hard enough to make the glass of the window shake threateningly.

The driver set the horses, too, and they watched as it swept down the front drive – silent, implacable and united.

29

'Well, you have outdone yourself, my lady,' Lady Morton said, patting Lady Phoebe's hand as the carriage left the front gates. 'I am certain I have never attended a more eventful house party.'

'It is a miracle we were not observed,' Lady Hesse agreed, turning to regard the empty lawns behind them. 'If any of this gets out, the whole of Kent will be gossiping for years.'

Lady Phoebe let out one, very constricted sob.

Ashford laid a hand on her arm.

'My lady,' Elspeth whispered.

'I think we can all understand the need for discretion, can't we?' Lydia said carefully. She made eye contact first with Lady Hesse, then Lady Morton.

'Fact is,' Pip said. 'There's rather a lot we would *all* like to keep quiet, is there not?'

'Yes, I think so,' Lady Morton said.

'There is no need, in fact,' Lady Hesse said, turning a gimlet eye upon her son, 'to speak any further on *anything* that has occurred this week – if we are all in agreement?'

'Yes,' Dacre said.

'No,' Hesse said, looking from his mother to Lady Morton. 'That won't do for me at all – I wish you to marry me, Lady Morton.

'Oh, do not be preposterous!' Lady Hesse said.

Lady Morton pouted. 'But it has been so long since I have been able to call anyone Mama.'

'If you *dare* . . .' Lady Hesse seethed.

'Oh, you are too easy!' Lady Morton said. 'Hesse, darling, it's been a great deal of fun, but I'm not in the least interested in marriage.'

'But – but I love you,' he declared.

'Understandable,' she said. 'I'm sure I'm very fond of you, too – but it ends here. You would not wish your mother to suffer a heart attack – ladies of her age must be vigilant.'

'You—'

'Yes, I'm terrible,' Lady Morton said mischievously. 'Come along, Dacre, you owe me a dance.'

She twined a hand through Dacre's arm and bore him off towards the house, Lady Hesse and her son trailing behind.

Lady Phoebe made a half-hearted move to follow them.

'Perhaps you ought to have a rest, my lady,' Reeves suggested quietly. 'I can fetch some—'

But in the next moment Lady Phoebe was shaking her hair back and standing tall.

'No, no,' she said. 'We have guests, Reeves! And the fireworks are soon to start. Miss Hanworth, I will need my domino and loo mask back. Elspeth will fetch you others.'

'Yes – of course,' Lydia said, unfastening the buttons of the cloak, and handing it over.

Lady Phoebe clapped her hands, briskly, and began leading the way back to the shining windows of Hawkscroft House.

Ashford and Lydia followed, at a slower pace.

'Thank goodness you arrived when you did,' Lydia marvelled.

'You were incredible,' he said.

'So were you,' she said.

'The bravery . . .'

And they were talking over one another, as they seemed always to do, but gabbling and giddy rather than cross and crotchety.

He put a hand to her arm, stalling her.

'Thank you,' he said. 'I mean it – thank you. What we would have done, if you had not been here . . .'

He shook his head as if to rid himself of the possibility.

'You were incredible,' he repeated and Lydia, not usually one for blushing, felt her face turn blisteringly warm.

'Come along!' Lady Phoebe's voice beckoned them imperiously from the entrance hall. They both startled.

Ashford exhaled around a laugh. 'We had best go inside.'

They paused only for Lydia to accept from Elspeth a new domino and mask which she hastily put on in the deserted entrance hall, before following Lady Phoebe's procession towards the ballroom. There, the festivities were still in full swing. The band still playing. The candles still burning. No one seemed to have noticed anything was in the least amiss.

'Well then,' Ashford said. He turned to Lydia and gave a superfluous wave of his hand. 'May I have this dance?'

Lydia made a great show of looking left and right for another partner – pretending to consider a florid gentlemen wearing a domino of bright emerald green standing nearby – before placing her hand in his.

'Good of you,' he said.

'Young ladies of quality ought to partake in charity every now and then,' she said primly, and he snorted a laugh as they swept together onto the dance floor, arm in arm.

Lydia felt suddenly awash with the relief of it all, the tension that had knotted her spine ever since she and Ashford and Lady Phoebe had met in that drawing room releasing with every exhale.

'I can hardly believe it,' she said, as they took their places opposite each other.

There was so much contained with the sentiment. *I cannot believe it is over* and *I cannot believe it happened* but also, *I cannot not believe* anything *that had happened*, these past nine days.

'I know,' Ashford said, and she believed he did know. For who else could understand exactly how she was feeling, in that moment, than he?

The musicians struck up a lively tune, one of Lydia's favourite country dances, so full of spins and jumps and hops that on the most ordinary evening one could not help but smile. Tonight, so very much no ordinary evening, they had hardly begun the first shape before she began to laugh, her giddiness rising and rising as they began turning, swapping partners and returning to one another – and she saw that Ashford was laughing with her. Not the modulated laugh he commonly gave when appreciating a witty comment, or the forced chuckle when amusement was socially wise, but something rather more helpless, spilling out of him as if he could no more contain it than keep the world from turning. The sound of his delight made Lydia's exhilaration ratchet even higher, and as they stepped towards one another again, clasping hands and spinning once more, faster and faster, Lydia felt she might burst from the joy of it all.

The dance ended too soon.

'Another!' she demanded, even before she had risen from her curtsey. 'Let us remain for another.'

'Two dances, consecutively?'

Ashford had never, to her knowledge, ever danced with a lady twice in one evening. He tried to raise his eyebrows in his usual sardonic manner – but the breathless grin on his face rather undercut the effect.

'It is a masquerade,' she reminded him. 'Your usual rules need not apply, surely?'

'I suppose not,' he said, and they stood still as the couples changed all around them, catching their breath after the exertions of the dance, though when the music began again, Lydia's heart began immediately to quicken anew. For it was the waltz . . .

Ashford moved slowly towards her, encircling her waist with one arm, taking her hand with his other. The last time they had danced so, Lydia had made a game out of how many times she could stamp upon his toes. She could not believe that had only been a few days earlier. Everything was so different, now.

'Are my feet to be safe tonight?' Ashford murmured in her ear, thoughts clearly following the same direction.

'I *think* so,' she said, after a pause – for the sensation of his breath tickling her neck had distracted her for a moment – 'though I would not like to promise anything.'

'Ominous.'

They began turning with their fellow couples. Lady Morton had joined the set, embraced by a distinguished older gentleman, and so too had Lady Phoebe, impossibly cheerful as she twirled about in the arms of Mr Brandon. Not for the first time that evening, Lydia was stunned by her resilience.

'She would have done it, wouldn't she?' Lydia marvelled. 'Left everything she has ever known to be free.'

She did not see Ashford nod, but she felt the movement of it, against her curls. 'It makes one feel rather cowardly in comparison.'

She leant back a little, to better look at him. His expression was reflective. 'Does it?'

'For so long I have thought of dutifulness as strength, but tonight . . . If I were in Phoebe's shoes, I could not have done it. I am too bound by rules, by custom.'

'You need not be, if you do not wish it,' she said fiercely. 'It is not too late.'

'Is it not?' he said. 'I do not know what I would be, without it. What would be left?'

'Oh, balderdash!'

'Forgive me,' Ashford said. 'I was trying to convey my feelings, but I should have known that you—'

'There is so much more to you than some antiquarian title,' she interrupted, indignant on his behalf. 'It could be the least interesting thing about you, if you would only step out of your own way.'

'You think so, do you?'

'You have a sharp tongue,' she said, 'and a temper which you hide. But you are kinder than you let on, too. You exercise so much caution, to be thought well of by Society, but when the moment came you did the right thing. Even though, strictly, it was "wrong".'

He drew them to a stop, as the music wound to a close.

'You think so?' he said, again, in a very different voice.

'I know so,' she said. 'I know you,' she added, more softly, as the violins played their final aching note.

Suddenly, in that moment it seemed the most natural thing in the world to take another step forward and turn her face towards him, and he appeared to agree for he was stepping forward too, his hands coming up to touch her face and—

The sound of applause had him leaping back from her, as if burnt. Lydia jumped too.

'My God,' he said. 'My apologies. Forgot where we were – good God, we almost . . .'

'D-do not apologize,' she stammered. 'We were not thinking. I-it happens.'

Ashford gave a minute shake of his head. 'Not to me.'

He looked unnerved by the lapse in control.

'Well, it is as I told you: not thinking suits you. You ought to try it more.'

'I'm not sure I agree with you.' His eyes were flickering and darting about the room as if to check the moment had indeed gone unnoticed.

'Why does that not surprise me?' She smiled up at him, and after a beat he returned it, agitation easing, at last.

'Come, they are making up the next set,' he said, offering her his arm. 'And even you will not convince me to dance *thrice* in a row.'

She acquiesced without argument. 'Shall we go somewhere? Away from all this?'

They had to speak again, just as honestly as they had last night – only this time, perhaps there might be a very different outcome. For so much had changed, had it not? Last night, he had told her there was no chance of his ever being able to love her, but he had reached for her, just now, hadn't he? Had looked at her, just now, as if his sentiments had undergone the very same change hers had. And even if he seemed more alarmed than pleased by it, surely, they had *both* felt it, this time?

Ashford nodded wordless agreement, but his smile had faded again. Some of Lydia's certainty lapsed with it, but she steeled herself. She could not spend another moment in confusion. She had to be brave, had to ask him, had to *know*, even if the answer was not the one she wished.

They made their way across the dance floor, in silence, passing the gentleman in the emerald domino again. He took a step into their path, smiling.

Lydia felt Ashford angle as though to move past and had to bite back a smile – when had his haughtiness become endearing?

'Good evening, sir, I am afraid we are already bound for—'

'What's this?' the gentleman said jocularly. 'No time for me, Ashford?'

Ashford stopped abruptly in his tracks.

'Father?!' Ashford said, blank with shock. Lydia took in a sharp breath. In all the excitement she had quite forgotten the imminent arrival of the duke.

His Grace gave a delighted chuckle, unravelling the strings of his mask to reveal a beaming face that much resembled Ashford's.

'But – but – when did you arrive?' Ashford said. 'I did not hear you announced? Phoebe did not say . . .'

'It's a masquerade, my boy,' the duke reminded him. 'If one was announced, then what, pray, would be the point?' He reached out to clasp Ashford's shoulder. 'Are you not pleased to see me?'

With visible effort, Ashford recovered some – but far from all – of his composure. 'Yes, of course, I am.'

The duke turned his beam onto Lydia. 'Now, I need not ask who *you* are. Miss Hanworth, I presume?'

'Your Grace. I am – I am so pleased to meet you.' Lydia dipped into a hasty curtsey – was it deep enough? Too deep? Why had she not prepared for this?

She stole a glance at Ashford. Was that the correct thing to say? Oh, how she *wished* they had had a chance to speak before this moment.

'No, no, it is I who am delighted!' the duke said. 'To meet the woman who has turned Ashford's head at last.'

'Oh how – how wonderful.' Again, she looked to Ashford for guidance, but he did not speak and his face was quite blank.

'I heartily approve this match,' the duke said, clapping Ashford again upon the shoulder. 'You have chosen very well.'

Lydia's eyes widened. She had not known exactly what she had been expecting, in Ashford's father, but such open amicability was not quite it.

'I am . . . so pleased you think so,' Ashford said, though no pleasure was evident in his expression. 'Is Lady Phoebe aware of your arrival?'

'I have been looking for her,' the duke said, shaking his head. 'It took me an age to spot even you – for a while, it was as if you had all disappeared entirely. Ah, she must be the one in red – Phoebe!'

He waved Lady Phoebe down from across the room, and she hastened over, face wreathed in smiles.

'Uncle!' she said. 'How dare you sneak in so! You are incorrigible.'

He laughed, not at all offended, and Lydia could not help but smile with him. His warmth was rather irresistible – to all but Ashford, apparently, for the open joy he had displayed on the dance floor had quite vanished from his face, which was now as even and opaque as a frozen lake. Lydia's brow wrinkled.

The duke did not appear to have noticed, patting his niece's arm. 'What a party, my love! You have outdone yourself.'

'I am so thrilled you are here – there are so many people I wish you to meet.'

'Ashford,' Lydia said in a very low voice. 'Ashford, what should I – how should we—?'

But he did not appear to hear her, and Lydia did not even quite know what question she wished to ask. Oh, how she wished they had spoken before.

'Yes, yes,' His Grace continued with Lady Phoebe. 'I am particularly intrigued by this explorer character of yours.'

Lady Phoebe pouted. 'Oh, I must disappoint you. It is the strangest thing. I left him with Colonel Lynton for the merest moment and the next time I saw him, he declared he was leaving! Urgent business. I am so terribly sorry.'

It seemed Reeves had been quite right about von Prett – for if the captain's history was as he claimed it to be, what reason would he have to flee the company of his old colonel?

'Not to worry, not to worry in the least!' His Grace said. 'The more important task is this announcement. How might we best achieve such a thing?'

Oh, lord! Lydia widened her eyes meaningfully at Ashford. He must ask his father to delay. They could not countenance any of this, before they had spoken.

'Announcing the engagement, you mean?' Ashford said calmly, reaching into the pocket for his snuffbox. Lydia fought a scowl. Could he truly not muster the smallest bit of urgency?

'I am not sure . . .' she began, throwing a pleading glance in Lady Phoebe's direction.

Lady Phoebe leapt to assist. 'Perhaps we should wait a little while?'

'Oh, the poor souls have tarried long enough,' the duke overrode her rather ruthlessly. 'It is my fault, for requesting such secrecy. I must confess,' he said, leaning in and speaking in confiding tones, 'I did so on the fear that Ashford might have tricked me into approving a marriage of convenience.'

Lady Phoebe let out a tinkling laugh. Lydia felt her expression became fixed.

'Did you?' Ashford said, taking a pinch of snuff calmly up to his nostril.

Lydia blinked. In that moment, he suddenly far more resembled the arrogant stranger who had proposed to her with such maddening calm, than the man she had come to know these past ten days. Why had the presence of his father altered him so?

'I mean no disrespect, my dear.' The duke availed himself of Lydia's hand and gave it a smacking kiss. 'A parent's prerogative – and of course, now I know there is nothing to worry about. I saw it at once!'

'Saw what?' Ashford asked, a frown marring the neutrality of his expression.

'Why, love, of course!' the duke said. 'Come, there is no need to balk. I have been watching you two waltz together and one cannot perform love such as that.'

Lydia's breath caught. Dear lord. It was the matter she herself had been intending to raise, but – not in such a way as this before they could themselves even touch upon it. And yet . . . To hear that someone else thought it, too . . .

'No,' came Ashford's voice from beside her. Lydia turned her head, very slowly, to look at him.

'Exactly!' the duke said.

But Lydia did not think Ashford was agreeing with the statement. His face was no longer calm, but wooden, his eyes glassy. Lydia felt her stomach drop.

'The way you looked at one another . . .' The duke sighed mistily. 'It reminded me of how your mother and I used to do so.'

Ashford's face blanched.

'The announcement, then!' the duke clapped his hands together again.

'No,' Ashford said, more emphatic this time. The vice around Lydia's heart clenched further.

'Ashford?' She reached out to tug his sleeve. If they could just speak, just the two of them, for a moment, she might draw him back from whatever precipice he was suddenly standing on – but he would not look at her.

'Feeling shy, Ashford?' the duke teased. 'You needn't be – everyone loves a love story; it will go down a storm, I promise.'

'No,' Ashford said, louder. 'No, I – Father, you mustn't.'

That caught the duke's attention. 'What, my boy? Whyever not?'

'I cannot,' Ashford said.

'Cannot what, dear boy?'

'Ashford,' Lydia urged. 'Will you please just . . .'

'I cannot deceive you a moment longer,' Ashford said, stepping back from Lydia, pulling his arm away. 'This whole thing is a sham, Father, a performance. I did intend to trick you into approving the match.'

The duke frowned. 'What on earth do you mean?'

'Perhaps we ought to move our conversation to a more private location?' Lady Phoebe said, ushering them further away from the dance floor.

But Ashford was not listening. His face was set, grim, as he turned towards Lydia for the first time since the duke had arrived.

'I cannot marry you,' Ashford said.

Lydia flinched backwards from him.

'I am terminating the engagement.'

Lydia felt each word as a separate blow. Her mouth dropped open, but no words came.

'I need air,' Ashford said, unable to look her in the eye. 'I need to get this wretched mask off.'

He turned sharply on his heel and made directly for the doorway.

'Miss Hanworth,' Lady Phoebe began, but Lydia did not wait to hear what empty reassurance she might offer her. Picking up her skirts, she gave chase.

He had only made it into the hallway before she caught up, darting in front of him, so that he was forced to stop.

'Ashford!' she said, finding herself suddenly full of words. 'You cannot just – just do such a thing as that and not explain!'

'What is there to explain?' he said, trying to move around her. 'Is this not what you wanted?'

'Yes, originally, but . . .'

'Then you win,' he said, spreading his arms.

She stared at him. His face was clear, closed. It was the same person with whom she had just danced with, minutes before, but he looked so different now.

'It is not about winning for me,' she said. 'Not for a while now. And I do not think it has been for you either. Surely you can see it?'

'What I see is that we have been making each other miserable. It is time to stop.'

'But I thought . . .' she faltered.

One had to be very brave, it seemed, to voice such thoughts aloud. So much had happened between them, so much shared, but very little of it out loud. Maybe she had been wrong. Maybe it had only existed in her mind.

But she could not retreat back from it now. She would regret it forever if she did.

'There were moments where it seemed as if we felt something for one another,' she began, sick with mortification to say such words, while he stared at her, so unfeelingly. 'That somehow these hellish and bizarre days of us both trying to end this – maybe was us beginning something.'

Ashford did not speak.

'When we kissed . . .' she began.

He hushed her, almost violently, looking frantically around the empty hallway. 'You ought not to speak of that. We should never have done it.'

'You said just hours ago,' she said, 'that you did not regret it.'

'I was wrong. *It* was wrong.'

'How can you say that?' she said – implored. 'You must have felt it. It cannot have been just me.'

He looked down and away.

'I cannot give you what you want.'

'That is not what I asked!'

'That is all that matters,' he said. 'You said you did not want the trappings of title and duty and service. You said you wanted romance and courtship and love. That is not what I can give you.'

'Why not?'

'What does it matter the reasons?' he said. 'I cannot give you what you want. That should be enough of an answer for you. I cannot change who I am because you would wish it otherwise. You might not like it—'

'I *do* like it,' she said. 'That is the issue. When you are not being a crushingly dense prig, I like it a great deal. And for a moment I thought—'

She broke off, a sob in her throat.

'I suppose it does not matter,' she said, through a constricted throat. 'You have made the decision for both of us.'

They stared at each other for another long, long moment – the longest one of her life, perhaps, as she willed him to say anything, *anything* else.

'Yes,' he said. 'I suppose I have.'

From the end of the hall, there was the unmistakeable sound of the grandfather clock striking midnight.

It was the tenth day. And she had lost him.

30

Wednesday – The last day

No one else was there to bear witness to their parting the next morning, for after the festivities and dramas of the night previous, Hawkscroft was quiet. No one had seemed in any particular hurry to rise, and Pip, Lydia and Jane would certainly not have woken by such an hour, if it were not for the fact they were returning to London that very morning. After the events of the previous night, Lydia did not wish to linger for even an hour longer than needed.

Outside, on the front steps, Ashford was waiting for them. For a moment, Lydia's treacherous heart leapt with hope – had he come to say he had made a mistake? Admit he had been wrong? But as soon as she saw his expression, neutral and distant, she knew he had not.

'I came to say goodbye,' he said. 'Lady Phoebe is still resting.'
'At last,' Lydia said.
Ashford nodded.
'Goodbye, then,' he said. 'I hope you have enjoyed your visit.'

Lydia gave a small, incredulous shake of her head. After all they had shared, such formality was ridiculous.

'Oh yes, marvellous,' she said sarcastically. 'Do keep us in mind for the next one.'

Ashford's expression remained perfectly benign. 'My family owes yours a great debt of thanks, for your aid last night,' he continued, so very formal.

He looked to Pip. 'I underestimated you,' Ashford said. 'I am sorry.'

'That's all right,' Pip said, cheerfully. 'Fact is, people often do.'

A screech on the driveway had them turning to see the hired chaise draw in. It was the same one they had arrived in, looking, if possible, even more garish than it had before. Ashford did not appear to notice.

He extended a hand to Pip, who shook it firmly before leaping directly into the carriage, Jane – carrying Lydia's reticule – following behind.

Ashford turned to Lydia. He opened his mouth, closed it, then held out a billet.

'This should explain matters satisfactorily,' he said. 'For your aunt and uncle.'

She took it from him, noticing instantly its thickness. There were several sheets enclosed, at least.

'They seem to have received a great deal more explanation than I did,' she noted.

Ashford bowed, but did not answer. 'Farewell, Miss Hanworth. It has been . . .'

'A pleasure?' she suggested.

The smallest of smiles twisted his lips for a moment.

'Something along those lines.'

When the carriage began to move, the urge to look back was almost overwhelming, but she forced herself to resist it, setting her jaw and staring determinedly ahead.

Jane reached out to touch Lydia upon the arm.

'It will be all right,' she said softly. 'At least you are free now.'

'Yes,' Lydia agreed. 'Yes, how – how marvellous.'

For he had achieved her goal, yes, but . . . it did not feel anything close to what she had thought it would.

Nothing about him had been what she had thought. He might have given her what she had wanted – but instead it felt as though something had been taken from her.

'I wish we had never come here,' Lydia said, as they drew out of Hawkscroft's gates. 'I wish none of this had happened.'

A sob rose in her throat, and she squashed it ruthlessly down.

'Bound to feel blue-devilled,' Pip encouraged. 'Feel better in a bit, I should think.'

Lydia let out a strangled laugh. She hoped he was right. She did not think she could carry this feeling with her for long, for it felt a physical weight within her – from which there could be no distraction.

There were more blows in store, that day. Ashford's billet was read by Uncle Edmund as soon as they arrived at Berkley Square, and though Lydia was given to understand it excused her entirely, it was not enough. She was still to be sent to Aunt Mildred.

The majority of her schemes – the social gaffes, the singing – had not, in fact, reached her aunt and uncle (the benefit of the slower summer months meaning that gossip did not travel as fast or as far as it might usually), but most unfortunately Aunt Agatha's cousin, Miss Slater, *had* spotted Lydia leaving the inn where she had changed into her puce travelling address on that very first day.

Thus, though Ashford's letter had been reportedly extremely apologetic, claiming all the blame for himself, the travelling dress was sufficient for Aunt Agatha and Uncle Edmund to announce their intention to remove to Brighton for the rest of the summer – so as, they declared, to wait out the resulting scandal, when it came – and banish Lydia to the north and Aunt Mildred.

Lydia did not protest, watching her baggage piled onto the chaise. There was a certain inevitability about it, truly, that after all she had done to hold onto her agency, all of the fight and effort and perseverance, it simply amounted to the same conclusion in the end.

In all of it, there was only one consolation to be had.

'A good thing I pack lightly, isn't it,' Pip said, sauntering up to the carriage, quizzing glass around his neck, and a small suitcase swinging in his hands. 'Not much room left.'

'You aren't – you aren't coming, too?'

'Course I am,' he said. 'Pretty shabby of me, if I didn't.'

'Pip . . .' Lydia swallowed around a lump in her throat. 'It is so kind of you. But truly – I shall be all right by myself.'

She could not allow him to make such a sacrifice for her. She could not.

'Fact is,' Pip said, 'wherever you are, I am too. Stands to reason.'

Lydia had yet to shed a tear over any of the events over the past ten days, feeling that to do so would be to open herself fully to the whirl of emotion inside of her. But now she could not help the tears springing to her eyes.

'What about Mr Simmons? You have been away so long already.'

'Yes, well . . .' Pip hesitated. 'Thing is, we need to lay low for a while, anyway. After he gave his assistance with Mr Villars, there have been some mutterings . . .'

'Nothing serious!' Pip added hastily, seeing the look upon Lydia's face, 'more about undue influence than anything else – but better to be safe than sorry and all that rot.'

'You cannot see each other?'

He shook his head. 'Not for a while.

'Can you write?'

'*I* cannot,' Pip said. 'Miss Phillippa Higglepiff, however . . .'

He gave a theatrical waggle of his eyebrows, an obvious attempt to amuse her that would, ordinarily, have worked – but Lydia was not easily amused, these days.

'I am sorry,' she said heavily.

'It is not ideal,' he said, 'but all is not dark. Simmons intends to visit family in Harrogate later in the summer . . . and by then, things will be easier.'

He looked down to Lydia. 'For both of us,' he added.

Lydia threw her arms round his waist, more relieved than she could say that she would not have to do this alone. She had a chance, now, to make the best of whatever came next.

At the very least, the company might offer some respite from the relentless return of her thoughts, over and over again, to the front steps of Hawkscroft, and the cold morning light on Ashford's face.

31

Ashford spent a long while watching after her carriage. He had forgotten quite how abhorrent it was. The *stripes*, dear lord. Garish yellow clashing so violently against the sickening green. Where had she sourced such a vehicle? Visions of Lydia – of Miss *Hanworth*, he corrected himself forcibly – brandishing a paint brush, swam irrepressibly to mind, and he might have laughed, had he not felt so very hollow.

He stood there until the freshness of the morning air began to warm upon his face. Only then did he turn his back upon the empty drive, to make his way back inside. The entrance hall was already thick with activity, maids bustling with brooms and feather dusters, while the gardener's boy dismantled the vast floral arrangement at the base of the stairs.

By the end of the day, Hawkscroft would be set entirely to rights. All evidence of last night's festivities and dramatics swept and brushed and polished away, and everything back to normal.

Ashford could only wish that setting his own self to rights could be achieved so swiftly.

'Such efficiency,' Ashford noted, as he passed Reeves in the corridor, supervising with a critical eye.

'Thank you, my lord.'

'Are you . . . well?' Ashford asked, pausing his feet for a moment. 'Last night's events were rather unsettling.'

He, at least, had been able to retreat to his bedchambers after the . . . after everything with Miss Hanworth – the household staff would not have been granted that luxury.

'Indeed,' Reeves agreed crisply – and for a moment, Ashford thought this was all he would elicit from the butler. But then, more to himself than to Ashford, he murmured: 'The future, however, does look a little brighter now.'

'For her ladyship,' he added hastily. 'Who is taking breakfast in her parlour.'

Reeves caught Ashford's eye, meaningfully.

'I shall join her, I think,' Ashford said.

'Very good, my lord.'

No one looking at Lady Phoebe, that morning, would suspect her of undergoing such distress as she had the night previous, for she was characteristically arranged in the highest kick of fashion, in a white morning dress of finest jaconet muslin finished at the bottom by a double flounce of pointed lace. She, much like her house, recovered quickly – or appeared to, anyway.

She extended a hand towards him. 'Sit with me?'

There were rolls, preserves and crockery on the table sufficient for two, as if she had been expecting him, though there was no maid waiting upon her. He was struck, suddenly, by how rare it was to find his cousin alone.

'How are you?' he said, taking the seat opposite her.

'Oh, just wonderful,' she said, reaching for the coffee pot. 'Not staring into the abyss of the unknown in the *least*.'

Her tone was ever cheerful, but her hand, as she poured coffee, shook slightly.

'At least you may be relieved it is all over,' Ashford told her quietly.

Phoebe leant back into her chair with a tired sigh. 'I am not sure relief is the correct word. If anything, I feel more unsettled than before.'

She sighed again.

'I have spent so long building my life and world around him, you see,' she said, almost apologetically. 'Worrying over his every expression, anticipating his every feeling, trying to keep him from anger. It made me feel frantic, *feverish*, half-mad at times, but . . . it was my life.'

Not for the first time in the past few hours, Ashford found himself wishing that the confrontation with Sir Waldo *had* turned violent. However badly he would have fared against Sir Waldo's bulk, at least he could have had the satisfaction of landing a few blows upon his person. He could only hope that the crossing to Mauritius was as perilous as reported – and pray for stormy weather.

Ashford reached out to touch his cousin's hand.

'Everything will be well,' he promised.

The corners of Phoebe's mouth wobbled. She pulled away from him to take a hasty sip of coffee.

'It is strange, is all,' she said, with more of her usual briskness, 'to have everything so different all at once. I'm sure I shall be settled again presently.'

'Of course you will,' he said. 'I will remain here a while, while you find your feet.'

She surveyed him over the rim of the teacup.

'How charitable,' she said, as if this were a bad thing. 'Does such altruism have anything to do with Miss Hanworth's departure this morning? Running away from your problems, are you, cousin?'

'I am not running away,' Ashford said, trying to keep the irritation from his voice. She has been through a great deal, he reminded himself. Now is not the time for squabbling. 'And everything with Miss Hanworth is resolved.'

Lady Phoebe took a bite of muffin and hummed consideringly.

'I saw you, last night, you know. You looked as though you were having the time of your life before your father arrived. What occurred to overset you?'

'I realized the selfishness of my actions,' he said. 'The immorality of deceiving him. I had to be honest.'

'I do not pretend,' Lady Phoebe said slowly, 'to understand exactly what has gone on between you two. But I do not know how jilting a young lady, whatever the circumstances, can be an honourable act.'

Ashford tried not to wince. He would tell Phoebe the full story as soon as he could bear to – for now, he would have to accept such judgement, however ill it sat.

'Sometimes the right thing is the wrong thing,' he quoted softly, looking down to his hands. 'I have behaved abominably, but she will be happy to be rid of me. She did not wish to marry me, you see.'

Phoebe gave a little harrumph. 'I agree that you behaved abominably, but I do not think she will be happy to be rid of you. She did not look so, last night.'

The memory of Miss Hanworth's shocked face swam across his mind and he winced.

'I should never have asked her,' he said – as much reminder to himself as it was justification to Phoebe. 'We are entirely unsuited. I can only thank goodness I realized it before it was too late.'

Lady Phoebe set down her knife with an ominous clink. 'Ashford, I can just about forgive you for deceiving me, these past ten days, but I do find it mortifying that you continue to deceive yourself.'

Ashford bridled. 'What are you talking about?'

'When Miss Hanworth first arrived,' Lady Phoebe said, fixing him with a steely eye. 'I thought her the most appalling choice imaginable. I could not believe you had fallen in love with such a person – and even now, knowing the truth of everything that has occurred, I still believe she is deplorably unsuited to the role of viscountess, let alone duchess.'

'I agree—' Ashford tried to intervene, but Phoebe raised a hand.

'However, I do think there is something between you,' she said. 'You have been more yourself, this week, sniping and snarling and spilling wine upon each other, than I have known you to be for years – and *that* is the future I wish for you.'

Ashford did not want to hear this – *could not* hear this.

'I am content with the future I have chosen,' he said brusquely.

'Are you?'

'*Yes.*' Perhaps he had expected to feel more relief, watching Lydia – Miss Hanworth – be driven away from him, but some agitation was to be expected, surely? It had been a strange few days, after all.

'It is done,' he told her. 'I have made my decision.'

'You can unmake it!' she said eagerly. 'Ride after her *ventre a terre* and tell her you were wrong.'

'*Ventre a terre?*'

'As fast as the wind, throwing caution to the – well, you know.'

The image was absurd. 'No.'

'Why not?'

'Oh, for God's sake, Phoebe! Will you not leave it be?'

'No!' Phoebe smacked a hand down on the table, shaking all the crockery. 'One *must* seize happiness, Ashford. It is a rare enough thing, and you are in danger of letting it slip you by.'

'Rest assured I am *very* happy!' Ashford snapped. There was silence for a moment. Then, a tiny giggle escaped Lady Phoebe's lips.

'I'm so sorry,' she said at once, pressing a hand to her mouth. 'I am not laughing at you, I promise.'

'You *wretch*.'

But Ashford could not prevent an answering smile, however begrudging.

'I just want you to be happy,' Phoebe entreated, reaching across to press his hand. 'Come, will you take a turn with me?'

He rose, following her through the parlour, out of the doors, and onto the gardens. There, in a perfect mirror of the tour they had made on the day of his arrival, they made a complete circuit of the gardens. By unspoken agreement they left the serious matters untouched, speaking only of unimportant this and inconsequential that, but even so, the distance between them felt vastly smaller.

'You know,' Lady Phoebe said, as they began to reapproach

Hawkscroft from the rear, 'I never liked this house. It is not very friendly, is it.'

'I do not think anyone would describe it such,' Ashford agreed. He took a sidelong glance at her. 'You could leave, you know.'

'Yes, I think I will,' she said. 'Though where or what I would do, I cannot think.'

'Wherever or whatever you wanted,' he said easily. 'What did you think you would do in Paris with . . . my mother?'

'I did not much consider it,' she admitted. It was her turn to steal a glance at his profile. 'Your mother promised she would organize everything.'

Ashford felt a prickle of tension run upon his spine. 'How kind of her,' he said pleasantly. Then, less pleasantly: 'I suppose she has a great deal of time on her hands, with no duties or responsibilities to attend to.'

'She asks after you,' Lady Phoebe said, 'in every letter we exchange.'

'She might ask me herself,' Ashford muttered, though he knew this was unfair. For years after she had left, he would receive a billet from Paris each month. He had not been able to open a single one. He didn't know what he was worried about finding inside, but he could not face it, somehow – a weakness he despised and yet . . . Eventually, she had ceased writing, and that had been even worse.

'It is not too late,' Lady Phoebe said gently, and he turned his head to find her still looking at him, 'to mend those fences.'

Wasn't it? These were old wounds. Before this week, he had thought them safely healed, and yet now they felt so very close to the surface. He did not like it. Better to close that chapter, put it in in the same box as Miss Hanworth and never consider each one again.

He could not say that to Phoebe, of course. 'I shall think on it.'

'Liar,' Phoebe accused him softly. She shook his arm a little. 'We must do better, you know. Speak with one another honestly – as we used to, before everything became so muddled.'

Her face was serious as she blinked up at him.

'I should like that,' Ashford said, adding, after a beat of hesitation, 'If you do not wish me to remain with you here, I . . .'

'I shall always be glad of your company,' Lady Phoebe said, squeezing his arm again. 'Though I'd rather *not* be used as an excuse to bury your head in the sand.'

'Let us not begin that again,' Ashford said imploringly. 'There are other things we must consider: papers that we need Waldo to sign so that you may live independently, the bankruptcy to avert—'

'Dacre has already left to meet Waldo and sort the papers,' Lady Phoebe interrupted. 'I have written to Christie's to arrange the sale of the necklace – that should go some way to paying off Mr Villar's demands.'

'Oh? Well . . . good.' He ought not have been startled by her efficiency – this was Phoebe after all – though he might have wished she had discussed the matter with him, first.

'There are no duties for you to fulfil,' Lady Phoebe said, as if guessing at the direction of his thoughts. 'Goodness knows you have enough of your own – and your father's – to deal with. I would not for the world add to them.'

Ashford was somewhat startled. 'It is no burden. I wish to help.'

'I know you do.' She patted his arm. 'But I am capable of managing my affairs, so you may *only* stay if you wish it.'

Ashford frowned. This was not what he had expected. He had imagined himself being put to immediate work, and though he had more than enough of his own business matters to solve – there being the small matter of the crumbling duchy still pending – this sudden lack of direction sat uncomfortably.

Lady Phoebe nudged his arm softly. 'Your father is here.'

They were almost at the house, now, and yes, there was His Grace on the terrace, holding up a hand in greeting. Without any conscious effort, Ashford felt his expression rearrange itself into neutrality.

'Good morning!' the duke called cheerily – though it was by now noon. 'May I borrow my son from you, Phoebe?'

'Of course, Uncle,' she said, slipping her arm from Ashford's. She tripped over to the duke's side and gave him a kiss on the cheek before disappearing into the house.

'Excellent girl,' the duke said, looking after her fondly. 'Join me for a spot of breakfast, will you? I have asked Reeves to set us up with a private room.'

'I've already supped,' Ashford said, hearing the reserve in his own voice. He always sounded so, in his father's company. It was the only means by which he could maintain civility.

'Perhaps we might request Miss Hanworth's presence as well,' his father continued, ignoring Ashford's tone. 'I have a notion I might be able to clear up this little misunderstanding.'

'She's gone,' Ashford said. 'Some hours ago.'

The duke looked so aghast that Ashford found himself irritated. What right did he have to such an expression, when Ashford himself was managing such calm?

'But I had desired most urgently to resolve matters between you,' the duke said, crestfallen.

'Not so urgently as to rise before eleven,' Ashford muttered.

'Ashford,' the duke chided. 'You know my views: rest is a man's most crucial tool.'

It was certainly one the duke used liberally.

'Perhaps we might speak after you have breakfasted,' Ashford said, 'for there are a few matters of business we ought to discuss. Did you read Ellery's correspondence regarding the Liston estate? He said he would write to you.'

'My boy,' the duke chided. 'That is not important right now. I care about *you*.'

I did not think such affection common, in your set, Miss Hanworth had said to him, two nights earlier, and she had said it as if he should think himself fortunate. But in truth, Ashford would prefer that his father act a little more befitting to his station. It did not help anyone for him to behave more as a country squire than a duke – and least of all Ashford.

'It is important, actually,' Ashford said. 'Very, in fact – if we do not act now—'

'You are using business matters as a mask,' the duke said, 'but you need not be afraid to *feel*, Ashford. Come, unburden yourself.'

'There is nothing to unburden.' In contrast to His Grace's warmth, Ashford's tone was almost comical in its *froideur*.

'Now, now, I do not think that true. Hmm?'

A few choice expletives sprang to Ashford's lips. Rather than utter them, he turned and stalked down towards the end of the terrace.

After a beat, the duke followed. 'Would you like to explain what occurred, last night?'

Ashford pressed his hands against the cool, stone parapet that separated the terrace from the gardens, looking out across Hawkscroft's rolling lawns. Calm, he reminded himself, calm.

'I regret all the events that led to my behaviour yesterday,' he said, without turning around.

'I should hope so!' the duke said, and from behind Ashford he heard chair legs scraping, and the sound of the his father seating himself. 'Such dishonour, Ashford.'

He made a little *tut tut* sound with his tongue. The embers of Ashford's temper reignited in one great rush, and he wheeled about, glaring at him.

'You pushed me there!' he accused, before he could stop himself. 'What did you think the effect of your decree would be?'

They ought to remove to a private room to discuss such matters, but in that moment, Ashford did not care.

'I thought it would nudge you into forming a genuine attachment,' the duke said. 'And I was correct!'

'No, you were not,' Ashford insisted. 'I told you, last night – I never felt anything for Miss Hanworth. It was all a ploy.'

The duke chuffed out a knowing laugh that made Ashford want to yell in frustration. 'It did not seem a ploy, to me. I have not seen you laugh in such a way for years.'

Dear lord, why was everyone so obsessed with his laughter? It was just laughing! It did not *mean* anything.

'Perhaps there will be more time for laughing,' he snapped, 'once I can be certain we are not on the point of ruin.'

'Such dramatics,' the duke tutted. 'We are not going to be ruined!'

'If you had read Ellery's letter!'

'Men of business, it's their job to find problems,' his father said. 'It's our job to ignore them!'

He chuckled. Ashford did not.

'I care a great deal more about you,' the duke went on, 'than silly financial matters.'

'These are not frivolous issues, Father. We need drains, and money to build them, or we will have to begin selling land!'

'We'll solve all that.' The duke gave a dismissive wave of his hand that had Ashford seeing red.

'Who is we, Father?' Ashford said derisively. 'You? Do you intend to do so, all the way from Scotland?'

The smile fell from the duke's face.

'One must take time for oneself,' the duke said, with great dignity. 'If I might pass on one piece of wisdom, Ashford, it is that.'

'Yes, you have always made time for yourself,' Ashford said savagely. 'Sauntering up to Scotland, resting in Bath, as if you have anything to rest *from*, spending days in bed after Mother—'

He broke off. Even now, he could not say it.

'You were incapacitated!' he rallied after a pause. 'For months you could not do anything. My uncles had to solve everything, for you. I had to—'

His voice cracked and he turned away to collect himself, staring across Hawkscroft's grounds. In the distance, two gardener's boys were hauling a gigantic potted palm in the direction of the greenhouse, and he fixed his eyes upon them until they disappeared from view.

'I will not apologize for my heartbreak,' the duke said after a long pause, adding, in defensive mutter: 'At the time you said you *wanted* to take on more duties.'

Ashford let out a humourless laugh. 'I was ten and six.'

He had become the duke that day, in all the ways that mattered. To be cut so shockingly adrift, the gilded softness of childhood abruptly rendered into grey – it had been terrifying. With his father unable to explain this awful new world, he had had to look to his uncles, with their rigid Ancaster propriety, for guidance. Their intervention had been blessed relief, at the time. For however nauseating it had felt, in those early days, to act as if the duchess had passed away – as if that were a better, more reasonable loss – it had shown Ashford a way forward. Had proven that, with calm and reason, one could carve order out of chaos – indeed, with the proper prioritization of rationality over sentiment, one could easily ensure that such hurt never occur again.

It was a system that had worked very well until approximately ten days prior.

'You were always so strong,' His Grace said, but he had not truly listened. After all that guff about Ashford unburdening himself, he did not wish to hear it when it was unpleasant.

The gardener's boys had reappeared, sans potted palm, and were trotting back towards the house. One of them tried to trip the other and – thinking themselves unobserved – they fell into a laughing scrap.

'I was a child,' Ashford said, and he could hear the wobble in his voice as if it belonged to someone else. 'I did not know what else to do . . .'

He cleared his throat. And then again.

Out of the corner of his eye, Ashford saw the duke reach out, arm hovering in mid-air for a moment, before he returned it to his side.

'My boy,' he said, 'I did not – I did not know.'

More recriminations sprang unbidden to Ashford's lips, as if they were all, now, begging for release. For *how* could his father not know, not have suspected, not have thought for a moment of what Ashford might need at ten and six? How, indeed was 'not knowing' a worthy excuse – had it not been his duty to find out?

Ashford pressed his hands against the parapet again, harder this time, watching his hands turn white from the pressure – forcing the words down as he did. If he began uttering them, he did not know if he would be able to stop. He did not know why, suddenly, he was so furious. He had thought this long buried.

When over a minute had passed in silence, the duke at last broke it.

'Armouring yourself against affection,' he said quietly, 'will not serve you, you know.'

Ashford huffed a sigh and raised his eyes heavenward. 'What do you mean?' He directed the question at the sky. It was very blue and cloudless. It was going to be a glorious day. 'I have not done so.'

'My boy,' the duke said again, and this time he did place a hand on Ashford's shoulder, gently turned him back around. 'I think that is exactly what you have done, by sending that poor girl away.'

Ashford moved so that he might feel the parapet against his back. Suddenly, the effort of holding himself upright felt exhausting.

'It was not real, Father. None of it.'

'I think you know very well that it is real,' the duke said quietly. 'And that scares you.'

Ashford looked away. He wished he might deny it fully, but . . . That moment, when his father had called it love, and Ashford had looked at her . . . He *had* felt fear. A fear so potent he had felt ill with it. Nauseous. If that was love, he wanted no part of it.

'Can you blame me?' he said, looking down to his feet. 'After what happened to you? After Mother . . .'

He let the thought linger in the air, unfinished. He and his father did not speak of his mother – ever.

'I'm sorry,' he said now, voice rough. 'I know you do not like to speak of what – what truly happened.'

His father heaved a long, slow sigh.

'It is . . . easier, sometimes,' he admitted, 'to bear that version of events. It helps me to hold onto the good – rather than have my memories poisoned. I know you think it weakness.'

'I—' Ashford tried to force a denial past his lips but found he could not.

'It *was* quite an unimaginable pain,' he reflected quietly. 'But I do not think I would do anything differently, if I had the chance.'

'What?' Ashford said, jerking his head up. 'Of course you would!'

'No, I would not. I might have – handled it better, I suppose, for you. But the years before were quite glorious, you know. We did love each other rather fiercely, back then. Perhaps you have forgotten, what she was like.'

'I have not.' He had tried to, very hard. But those golden memories were not so easily squashed.

'And she gave me you,' the duke said. 'And, you know, I'm quite fond of you when you are not being so very disagreeable.'

Ashford tried to smile.

'It was all worth it,' His Grace said gently. 'Even though it hurt terribly.'

'It was?'

'I promise. Avoiding the possibility of hurt does not make you safer. It only results in a life half-lived.'

Ashford looked out onto Hawkscroft's rolling lawns, digesting this.

'I,' the duke took in a deep breath, 'I shall learn about these drains, so I might lift some of this burden from you. Not next week, of course, for I have the races – and after that, Alvaney is joining me for some fishing, but then, perhaps in August, I shall seek out this, this Ellery fellow and see what can be done!'

'That is not . . .' Ashford began. He took in a deep calming breath. A step in the right direction, however inadequate, was still a step.

The duke extended a hand, and Ashford reached out to clasp it.

'Goodness, I am half-starved,' His Grace said. 'I would try to persuade you to take a second breakfast with me – but perhaps you wish to depart directly?'

Ashford raised his brows, pretending ignorance. 'Depart?'

His father cuffed him gently across his head. 'Come, now. You know exactly what I mean.'

Ashford sighed. For the dozenth time this week, he felt utterly at sea. What was the right thing to do now? He knew what he *wanted* to do, but what he wanted felt nonsensically rash. Childish, even. What was he going to do, ride *ventre a terre* after her? After everything he had done and said?

'Perhaps we might ride out,' His Grace suggested, eyes close on Ashford's face, 'so that you might think it all through.'

Ashford nodded. A ride, at this moment, was exactly what he needed. Some space to consider, to attain some distance from the whole affair, to evaluate the situation through with some *rationality* and think how—

He was interrupted by a quiet, familiar voice, speaking up from a very different corner of his mind.

Not thinking suits you. You ought to try it more.

Ashford let out another, longer sigh. 'I believe,' he began slowly, 'the time for thinking might indeed have passed.'

He took a step backwards, away from the parapet, then another.

'Bid Lady Phoebe farewell on my behalf, will you?' he asked his father. 'I must make haste.'

32

Saturday – Ten days later

'I do not intend us to remain late,' Aunt Mildred said, as their carriage turned into the gates of Malton Hall. 'I have little appetite for speaking this evening, and even less for listening.'

'Understood,' Lydia said, by now unfazed by this frankness. Aunt Mildred neither had a large social tolerance or any qualms about admitting this which bore no relation to her manners, which were – to Lydia's initial surprise – rather elegant.

A great deal had been surprising, about Aunt Mildred. Their journey northward had been long and hard. Already a distance of several days, they had been waylaid further by repairs, when two separate wheels – on two separate occasions – had fallen foul of potholes, and so it was four days later that Lydia and Pip found themselves arriving in Marnsley, where Aunt Mildred had her home.

From the reports delivered to them by Aunt Agatha and Uncle Edmund, Lydia had assumed this would be a mud and straw structure, and the locale so boring as to make dishwater seem a lively conversationalist. On their winding route through the village, however, it was quickly apparent that both these assumptions had been erroneous. Marnsley's pace was slower than London – hardly difficult – but it did not seem sleepy in the least.

Barely half an hour's drive from Harrogate and its thriving local assemblies, Marnsley boasted an energetic local population alongside beautiful scenery, and startled to attention twice a day with the noisy arrival of the stagecoach, unpacking all manner of travellers at the local inn for refreshment and board.

Aunt Mildred was waiting for them when the carriage drew up outside her home, a pretty Tudor cottage. Aunt Mildred, however, looked just as dour as her depiction, short and angular, she was dressed in a sombre dress of grey bombasine – as if in mourning for a close relative – with a cap of starched cambric drawn tightly beneath her chin. Nothing in her greeting assuaged this first impression of gloomy respectability.

'I hear you are in disgrace,' she said as they approached, without so much as a 'good afternoon'.

'Yes,' she said, too tired to put up any kind of defence. 'Uncle Edmund and Aunt Agatha have condemned me utterly.'

'Well . . .' Aunt Mildred considered them for a long moment. 'I suppose that is as good a character reference as any.'

Her expression warmed, her eyes began to twinkle, and as she followed her aunt inside, Lydia relaxed minutely. The cottage was just as charming within as it had appeared outside: light and elegant and possessing all the modern conveniences. Aunt Mildred's housekeeper showed them to bedchambers which, if smaller than the rooms to which they were used in

Berkley Square, were pleasant, comfortable and dressed with fresh flowers. It was not nearly so dire as they had been led to believe – and nor, indeed, was their aunt.

'Do you know why they have sent me to you?' Lydia plucked up the courage to ask, over the dinner table that evening.

'My sister explained it in rather hysterical terms in a missive that arrived just before you did,' Aunt Mildred said crisply. 'Jilted, dishonouring the family name, etc – is that about the sum of it?'

'It is,' Lydia said. 'I hope it will not make your life . . . difficult, if the news travels.'

Even if the exact details of Lydia's behaviour, and the nature of her relationship with Ashford, were kept as secret as they had all promised, there were other means through which gossip might begin to rise. She did not think there had been any who overheard when Ashford had jilted her, but she could not be certain. Who was to say a discerning eavesdropper might not put some names and references together?

Aunt Mildred fixed her with a beady eye. 'We shall not be troubled.'

'But—'

Her aunt overrode her. 'My standing is good here, and I wager my friends are a trifle stronger than the cads and charlatans who populate the capital.'

Her voice was crisp, not intended to be reassuring, and yet that was the effect.

'Aunt Agatha would have had us believe you are an ogre,' she marvelled.

'Slanderous,' Pip confirmed. 'A crime, you know.'

'A good thing too,' Mildred said with a pleased nod. 'Being unmarried, one is asked endless inconvenient favours. One must cultivate a little reputation, or else one's life can be entirely ruined by having your niece and nephew foisted upon one with no notice.'

Lydia and Pip exchanged uncertain glances.

'Just an example,' Aunt Mildred added, mouth ticking up at the corners, and they laughed – mostly out of relief, but still, it felt good to do so. Lydia had not, since Hawkscroft.

'Twice a week, I visit Harrogate to partake of the waters,' Aunt Mildred informed them. 'Once a week, I attend a public assembly in the evening, and there are occasional card parties and events closer to home – next week Mrs Lindell is to host a waltzing party.'

'How wonderful,' Lydia said, cast down once more, the mention of dancing recalling the last person with whom she had waltzed – and suddenly she was forcing back tears.

Oh, she was *certainly* going to be a popular dancing partner here, if she burst into sobs every time the music began.

This pessimism was shortly proved false. Though the prospect of their first assembly here, barely a day after they had arrived, had incited within her breast a veritable dread, she had forced herself to attend nonetheless. She was not foolish enough to believe remaining at home would alleviate her wretchedness. Her instincts led her correctly, for nothing could be more cheering than an evening at Harrogate Assembly rooms. While the entertainment ran in a very similar fashion to its London counterparts, it was noticeably friendlier and livelier. Under the guidance of Aunt Mildred – who gave none of the commands and judgement Lydia was used to receiving from Aunt Agatha – they were introduced to a succession of new acquaintances, all of whom seemed very pleased to meet them. Even when Pip expressed a far too close interest in the recent elopement of the Squire's son – wondering loudly if murder had been entirely ruled out – it did not seem to dampen the company's enthusiasm. By the flurry of invitations arriving by the next post, their first outing into local society had been a consummate success.

'You shall not be bored,' Aunt Mildred had observed, looking through the invitations over breakfast.

'I cannot accept all these invitations,' Pip said, making enthusiastic work of a boiled egg. 'Fact is, I have a *case*.'

'I can,' Lydia said rather grimly.

Distraction was to be her best medicine, now. Over the last ten days, which had been the busiest social whirl Lydia had ever encountered, it seemed to be working. There was something undeniably soothing about being around persons who did not know her, who could have no idea of anything she was feeling. It made it easier for her to pretend there wasn't anything *to* feel. To pretend everything was just as it should be, to pretend she hadn't been entirely undone by an engagement of merely ten days.

During the few blissful moments where her entire attention was taken up by conversation or dancing or riding, she pretended so well that she almost convinced herself.

By the night of Mrs Lindell's waltzing-ball, a sen'night later, Lydia was feeling . . . tentatively well. Not in the same way as before, no. It was akin to that teapot in Lady Phoebe's drawing room, the one Reeves had pointed out on their tour, run through the middle with a fissure they had mended with gold. One could not go back, after going through something such as Lydia had. One was different after, perhaps even better, in a way.

If Lydia thought about it fully, was it not a good thing she and Ashford had been parted? Whatever her . . . feelings . . . for him, their life together would be awful. She would not be here, jostling along the road in a carriage with Aunt Mildred and Pip, looking forward to an evening spent with people who actually seemed to like her – *her*, and not her fortune. No, she would surely be at some sort of highly stuffy event riddled with just the sort of tremendously dull persons she most detested – and that would just be the beginning. It would have been a lifetime of such things.

Yes, she could only thank goodness she had escaped in time. It had been a near thing, too, for there had been a moment where she had truly thought – but no. Whatever stirrings of sentiment she had felt were not real, they were merely brought on because truly, isolation in so gloomy a place as Hawkscroft would cause *anyone* to turn a little odd. She was better off, without him, and he would be better off with whichever puffed-up piece of lace he ended up choosing, too. Lydia wished him the best, she truly did, and she reminded herself of this as frequently as she could – in the hope that, one day soon, she might truly actually believe it.

The carriage was slowing. Outside the window, Malton Hall was coming into view.

Pip straightened in his seat and gave them each a very serious look. 'Recollect, if I give the signal, we must leave at once.'

'Very well,' Aunt Mildred said, as placidly unbothered by this as she had been by all of Pip's eccentricities. 'Though perhaps you might wait to discover the Scene of the Crime until I have visited the gardens.'

Malton was the most considerable house for many miles around, and though it did not stand in a park, it had extensive gardens which boasted – Mrs Lindell having a keen interest in botany – a variety of notable plants.

'Her gardener has installed a new Oleander since my last visit – imported from Spain which is very—'

'Poisonous,' Pip breathed ecstatically. He had been in exceptionally high spirits all day – ever since a letter from Mr Simmons had confirmed an earlier-than-expected arrival to Harrogate in only a fortnight's time.

'I was going to say "noteworthy",' Aunt Mildred said, but Pip did not heed her, predictably bolting for the gardens just as soon as the footman had taken his hat, leaving Aunt Mildred and Lydia to seek out their hostess.

The opening set of dances having already begun, Mrs Lindell was no longer at the entrance to the ballroom, having migrated deeper into the room. It took them a little while to weave their way through the throng of persons – Mrs Lindell had invited genteel families for thirty miles around and all had accepted – but no sooner had they reached her side than Mrs Lindell seized Aunt Mildred by the arm, and drew her in close.

'You ought to have told me!' she said in low, urgent greeting.

Lydia turned questioning eyes to Aunt Mildred. Having only met Mrs Lindell once before, she did not know if this was normal behaviour.

Aunt Mildred did not seem unsettled by the strange greeting. 'To what do you refer, Mrs Lindell?'

'The most extraordinary thing – I was utterly undone,' Mrs Lindell went on excitedly. 'Why did you not tell me?'

Lydia's interest waned. Mrs Lindell was a committed gossip and Aunt Mildred a negligent one – there could be any number of things she had seen fit to withhold. Over the top of her coiffured head, Lydia could already spot several young persons of her acquaintances that she wished to speak to – and how marvellous was that? She had made more friends in this past fortnight than in two whole years in London.

'Tell you of what?'

'Of your niece's *acquaintance* with the Marquis!'

As though drawn by a thread, Lydia turned slowly back around to Mrs Lindell. Next to her, Aunt Mildred had stiffened minutely.

So here it was. Gossip *had* spread, just when Lydia had begun to feel at ease, to lower her guard. She searched Mrs Lindell's face, trying to ascertain what, exactly, she might have heard. It could not be the full story, for she did not appear appalled, but then, her love for the aristocracy was well-known. Perhaps Lydia having been jilted by so high a personage had only elevated her in Mrs Lindell's eyes but there was no guarantee it would do so for others.

'I did not consider it of particular interest,' Aunt Mildred said guardedly. 'May I ask who, pray, informed you?'

Mrs Lindell let out a delighted trill of laughter.

'You do not know?' she asked. 'He told me, himself. Look, here he is, now!'

33

For a moment, Lydia was certain of being in some sort of strange dream. For so incongruous was the idea of Ashford, here, in Marnsley, that she could not believe her eyes. But there he was in the doorway. Lydia's heart began to quicken.

'He called on us this afternoon,' Mrs Lindell said, speaking very quickly through a beaming smile. 'To inquire after Rose Cottage – it is for let. I could hardly believe it, but he was most amicable. He tarried with us for an hour, chatting about the village – asking after you specifically, Miss Hanworth! And there was I, not knowing you shared a friendship! I invited him tonight, of course I did, but I had no real expectation of his . . . I shall go and greet him!'

As she bustled off, Lydia's eyes were still glued to Ashford's figure. He passed through the threshold of the ballroom, unhurried, though his eyes were scanning the room hungrily. People turned to regard him as he passed, with a little curiosity, but not as much as there would be as soon as word spread as to his identity. At the moment, he simply garnered the same excitement any handsome stranger must inspire.

Lydia wondered if she was going to be sick.

'It is rather warm in here,' Aunt Mildred observed, slipping her hand through Lydia's elbow. 'Let us take escape to the terrace where I believe they are serving lemonade.'

Ripping her eyes away from Ashford – now greeting Mrs Lindell with a smile – Lydia followed Aunt Mildred, only just managing to keep her pace to a sedate walk and not a mad dash. Mrs Lindell had set up a refreshment table on the terrace – though as the dance floor was so well populated, they were almost the only people making use of it.

Lydia accepted a goblet of iced lemonade and took an unladylike draught. The sudden tartness on her tongue had her eyes watering, and she jolted back to herself with a start.

Aunt Mildred said nothing but fixed her beady eye upon her.

'It appears,' she said, 'that perhaps my sister did not apprise me of the *entire* story.'

'I . . .'

Lydia could not think what to say, how to begin to explain. What was he *doing* here?

But Aunt Mildred's gaze was looking over her shoulder now. 'Brace yourself,' she warned.

For there was Mrs Lindell, veritably skipping towards them with a wide smile, and Ashford behind her, putting up a hand to shield his eyes from the setting sun. He looked quite irritatingly well, bathed in golden light akin to one of the Renaissance paintings in Hawkscroft's gallery, and how dare he, really? Come here, to disrupt her life in such a way when she was only just beginning to like it, looking such a way?

It was appalling behaviour.

'There we are!' Mrs Lindell said. 'I was worried you had disappeared. May I present to you Lord Ashford, Miss Hanworth?'

Ashford bowed before Aunt Mildred. 'A pleasure to make your acquaintance. I have heard a great deal about you.'

Aunt Mildred looked him over in that hard-eyed way she had, as if she were sucking out your soul with the force of her gaze. Ashford bore it with only a flicker of nervousness.

'Of course I do not need to introduce you to Miss Lydia, do I?'

Ashford bowed again. Lydia did not curtsey. She had found herself, suddenly and abruptly, awash with more rage than she would have believed her body possible of containing.

'What are *you* doing *here*?' she demanded.

'Miss Lydia!' Mrs Lindell breathed.

Ashford rose from his bow and smiled. 'As you may tell, Miss Lydia and I are old friends.'

'No, we are not!' Lydia snapped.

'Close acquaintances?' he suggested.

'No!'

Ashford paused, appearing to consider. 'Reluctant enemies?'

Aunt Mildred gave a soft snort of laughter. Mrs Lindell looked ready to swoon. Lydia only glared.

'Well,' Mrs Lindell said faintly, 'I believe they are about to call the next set so I shall . . .'

She backed away slowly.

'Perhaps I might have this next dance?' Ashford held out a hand towards Lydia with an encouraging smile.

'I'm afraid my dance card is quite full!'

Ashford looked her over. 'You do not have a dance card.'

'*That's* how full it is!'

Aunt Mildred raised her eyes to the heavens. 'Lydia, my dear, Lord Ashford wishes to speak privately with you.'

Lydia cast her a look of betrayal. Was she on his side, now? 'His wish is not reciprocated.'

Having spent the better part of a fortnight desperate to see him, she now very much found that she wanted nothing more than to never see him again.

'Now, now,' Aunt Mildred chided. 'Lydia, dear, perhaps you might gift Lord Ashford with a few moments of your time. He has travelled such a long way.'

Lydia scowled. From the corner of her eye, she saw Ashford reach into his pocket.

'If you take out your snuffbox now,' Lydia said, 'I shall scream.'

Ashford withdrew his hands, holding them up, supplicating.

'Why don't you show him the gardens?' Aunt Agatha said. 'You might locate your brother, while you are there.'

Lydia's hands clenched.

'I can leave now, if you truly do not wish to see me,' Ashford said softly.

She did not want that, either. 'Oh, very well.'

She stormed past him, ignoring his proffered arm, and made for the flight of stone steps that led down to the gardens.

It was not dark – it would not be, for several more hours, country balls taking place so much earlier than those in the city, and with the summer equinox still ahead of them – but still, Mrs Lindell had placed lamps all along the walkways, and there was the faint sound of music. Clearly, she expected people to take a turn of the gardens, and yet as they walked, Lydia did not see a single one.

They walked in silence for several moments, a yard of distance between their shoulders, Lydia's eyes trained resolutely forward.

'You do not seem pleased to see me,' Ashford observed.

'How *astute* you are.'

A brief silence.

'Your aunt does not seem . . . quite as monstrous as you described.'

Lydia decided she would ignore such conversational sallies. She would not be drawn into a trifling exchange of commonplaces, as if they were friends, until he had explained himself.

'Lady Phoebe sends her best regards,' he tried next.

Alas, fury and curiosity were not mutually exclusive emotions. 'How is she?'

'As well as can be,' he said. 'Keeping herself characteristically busy: selling the diamonds, the house. Dacre is helping.'

'He is still at Hawkscroft?'

'He intends to remain until a seller is secured,' Ashford said. 'At which point, he will return to his own country seat – with Reeves.'

Her eyes sprang, unbidden, to his. 'Lady Phoebe has permitted it?'

Ashford nodded, smiling. 'He goes with her blessing. If the house sells, she is unlikely to need both a housekeeper *and* a butler – and, as luck would have it, Dacre had a vacancy.'

'Fortuitous timing, indeed,' Lydia said, unable to prevent herself from smiling any longer. There was one happy ending, at least.

They had reached a fork in the garden's path and Ashford paused. 'Which way do you . . .?'

Lydia veered left at random, leading them away from the rose garden and towards the entrance to the hedge maze. With the light quickly fading, to be alone in such a place – even with Aunt Mildred's permission – was not quite the thing, but at that moment Lydia did not particularly care and Ashford followed her agreeably enough. Perhaps, if she got very cross with him, she would leave him within.

'How did you know where to find me?'

'I visited your aunt and uncle, in Berkley Square,' Ashford said.

Lydia narrowed her eyes. 'They are not in Berkley Square.'

'As I found out,' Ashford said pleasantly. 'It took a little while to track down their Brighton lodgings, which accounts – in part – for my delay.'

She turned to look at him, startled.

'Careful,' Ashford warned, nodding to where a branch had fallen across the path.

She thanked him distractedly. He had gone all the way to *Brighton*? 'Was it . . . an enjoyable reunion?'

'Not particularly,' he said. 'They were not very impressed with me – nor I with them.'

A thousand questions sprang to Lydia's tongue – most inconvenient, given her recent vow of icy reticence. But as they made another turn, following by instinct the sound of bubbling water which surely heralded some kind of fountain at the maze's centre, Ashford spoke.

'I wish to apologize. I thought my letter would have prevented your banishment.'

It was a good beginning, but Lydia was not feeling charitable. 'You cannot be so surprised, you are so often wrong.'

For the first time, Ashford's patience slipped.

'Am I to be continually insulted in this conversation?' There was a slight bite in his voice. 'Or are you able to speak civilly?'

Lydia fired up at once. 'What did you expect? How dare you be so presumptuous – so presumptuous as to presume to—'

'Presume my presumption?' Ashford suggested.

They had turned the last corner, reaching the maze's heart. At its centre stood a decorative fountain, with a vast half-moon tastefully illuminated at its centre. Magnificent in size and depth, it was said to be modelled, as Mrs Lindell frequently boasted, on the Fountain of Neptune, though neither Lydia nor Ashford spared it more than a cursory glance.

'I own I was not expecting quite so fierce a reception.'

Lydia whirled on him with a furious glare.

'How could you not?' she demanded. 'You rejected me, you sent me away, and now, when I am finally feeling easy again, here you are like some deluded scent hound – for what?'

'I told you, to apologize and to—'

'You might have *written* the same lacklustre apology,' she interrupted, 'not—'

Ashford raised his voice to override her. 'I did not think a letter would have felt quite as romantic a gesture!'

This took some of the wind out of her sails.

'R-romantic?' she faltered. Then, valiantly rallying the last of her ire: 'Attending Mrs Lindell's waltzing-ball is not exactly a Herculean task.'

Lydia did not know why she was still being so abrasive, only that she could not stop and it was tethering her to normalcy.

'Actually, it *was*.' Ashford took a step towards her. 'First, I rode to London – *ventre a terre* I might add – then to Brighton. Then, once I had extracted your location from them, I made my way here – a journey of two days in any case, had my wheel spoke not broken twenty miles outside of York.' He took another step forward. 'Then, a wrong turning took us to the *other* Marnsley – did you know there were two? – where I was looked upon as some lecherous villain, trawling the village for young ladies. A lowering experience, I assure you.' Another step. Lydia had to tilt her head back to hold his gaze. 'So yes, I should think that constitutes arduous.'

Lydia swallowed. 'All for what?' Her voice was hoarse. 'To tell me you are sorry?'

Ashford took in a deep, deep breath.

'Yes. But also to tell you: it was not just you. You were not making it up.'

He spoke carefully and deliberately, as if he had rehearsed what he intended to say ahead of coming.

'I did not plan for all this, you know,' he said. 'And – as you have pointed out – I do enjoy making plans. But you . . . you just crashed into my well-ordered life, ridiculous and dramatic and shameless and brilliant.'

He shook his head, a disbelieving smile crossing his face. 'When I thought I hated you – I could cope with that. But the moment I realized I did not . . . I panicked.'

Lydia was silent. She had no sharp words left.

'I ran away,' he said. 'But I do not wish to run, anymore.'

'What does that mean?'

Ashford swallowed. 'I suppose – well, this is my first visit to Marnsley, but what I have seen, thus far, is very nice.'

'Truly?' She would have thought it far too provincial for him.

'I have rented a delightful cottage,' Ashford said primly, 'and intend, indeed, to remain for the summer.'

'But . . . why?' She had to hear him say it. If she allowed herself to feel hope now, she would be crushed.

'So that I might see you. Might call upon you for morning visits. Invite you out for drives. Perhaps even escort you to the local assemblies,' he said gently. 'If you will save me a dance, next time.'

Lydia stared at him wordlessly.

'Dancing, courting, flirting,' he said softly, 'that is what I want.'

They were the same words she had used, in the library. Lydia let them sink in. For the long moment, the only sound was the gurgling from the fountain.

Ashford's eyes moved uncertainly across her face 'Do you . . . have any thoughts on that?'

'I'm thinking,' she said.

'Are you . . . ?'

She held up a hand. 'Still thinking. Do not rush me.'

'I'm not rushing you,' he said. 'But we are in somewhat of a secluded spot – we can't stay out here all night or people will talk. If you do not feel the same way . . .'

'It is not that.' Lydia shook her head, trying to understand her own reaction. ' It is not lack of feeling but . . .'

He waited.

'You have made a fool of me,' she told him. 'Many times, now.'

'As have you, of me,' he pointed out.

'Oh, not enough, not nearly enough,' she said. 'You have made decisions for me, again and again, proposed and jilted me with nary an explanation either time—' She cut herself off. 'Oh, this is old ground now!'

'You cannot help if you still feel it,' he said quietly. His lips quirked into a smile. 'Would that there were a fetid tarn here, for me prove my devotion.'

Lydia cocked her head to the side, attention arrested. What an interesting thought!

Ashford narrowed his eyes. 'What are you . . .?'

'We have a fountain.' She pointed. Ashford followed the direction of her finger.

'It was a jest,' he said. 'Not a serious suggestion.'

'It was your best idea yet,' she disagreed.

She sidestepped him to approach the fountain, pleased to find it just as large and deep as it looked from a distance.

'I am not going into the fountain,' Ashford told her very firmly. 'Not in my evening dress. Not at Mrs Lindell's waltzing-ball. Everyone will think me deranged.'

Lydia threw a challenging look his way. Then, maintaining eye contact, she slid off her left glove. He watched her with narrowed eyes. She eyeballed the fountain, taking aim – realization crossed his face.

He surged forward, hand outstretched. 'Don't!'

Too late. The glove landed with a soft splash, in the centre of the fountain.

'Oh no,' she said. 'What a predicament.'

He glared at her, then at the glove, then back at Lydia again.

'I could leave it in there,' he threatened.

'You could,' she said. 'Although, it is not how I should go about proving my trustworthiness.'

Ashford eyed the glove again. 'I suppose it belongs to a dead relative, too?'

'My great-aunt's cousin,' Lydia agreed promptly. 'We were very close.'

Ashford snorted. He took a tentative step forward, examining the fountain's floor with a great deal of misgiving. 'And this would constitute enough of an apology for you?'

'It would help my thinking,' she said. 'Perhaps even tip the scales in your favour.'

'You don't wish to give any firmer reassurance than that?'

'No,' she pronounced with great relish.

Ashford heaved a sigh. 'Very well.'

He leant down to the laces of his shoes.

'On,' Lydia stipulated.

He glared at her.

'These cost —'

'Shoes on.'

Ashford straightened slowly. 'I am not sure you should be allowed to have this much power.'

Approaching the fountain, he took a readying breath, and swung one leg over, immediately grimacing.

'How is the temperature?' she asked sympathetically.

'Chilly,' he said, teeth gritted.

Lydia was enjoying herself immensely. 'Oh dear. One would think the water would be warmed by the sunshine.'

'It has not been.'

He swung the other leg in. The water came to thigh height, and though it was clearer than the tarn, Lydia could see the bottom was slick with algae and moss.

Ashford took a step, wobbled precariously once – the bottom of his shoes did not seem to have much grip – then twice, but held his balance.

'You are getting rather good at this,' Lydia praised.

'Not a skill I imagine using again,' he muttered, letting go of the side.

Pausing for only a moment longer, he sloshed across the fountain and seized the glove 'There! Are you happy now?'

He held it triumphantly aloft. It was over far too quickly. Why, he was barely splashed. It had none of the satisfaction of the tarn experience, none at all.

Lydia withdrew the other glove.

Ashford glared. 'No. You are being—'

It sailed past him through the air.

'Ridiculous,' he finished. 'I am not getting it.'

'You have to,' she said imperiously.

'I refuse.'

'You *asked* me how you might prove yourself.'

'Which I have done,' he said. 'It does not mean I will allow myself to be run roughshod over. This is my line.'

He sloshed resolutely to the side.

'You cannot leave it there!'

'You should have thought of that before,' he retorted.

'Then I will get it,' she said. 'If you are too craven.'

She strode toward the fountain, nose in the air.

'Don't be ridiculous,' he said. 'You cannot.'

'I can do whatever I like – you do not tell me what I can and cannot do.'

There was the small matter of how she would actually get *in* – her skirts did not exactly allow for free movement, and she could not exactly lift them, for wouldn't that be the exact moment someone caught them and she was branded a harlot?

She whisked around the edge of the fountain, trying to get herself as close as she could, then – gathering her skirts firmly around her – placed one leg on the lip of the edge. If she held on here, she might reach out her hand . . .

'You cannot,' Ashford said, half in and half out of the fountain, reaching out his arm to try and prevent her.

She batted it away. 'This is your doing!'

'It is *not*,' he said, struggling to place his foot back in and splashing over to her once more. 'Get out! I shall retrieve the glove!'

But she was already placing her hand down and boosting herself upwards.

'You lunatic – get *out*,' he said, seizing her arm and trying to push her back over the edge.

'Remove your hands from my person!' she insisted, pushing him away, and he pulled her back and then his foot slipped and she teetered; he grabbed her arm and she his shoulder, and suddenly it was only each other preventing them from falling in.

'Don't . . . move,' he instructed, through a mouthful of her curls. 'We cannot fall into this fountain. Neither of our reputations could withstand it!'

She could not disagree. Last summer, gossip had reigned for two weeks about a woman who had dampened her skirts, just lightly, to more obviously outline her legs. What they would say about her, if she appeared inside utterly drenched, she did not like to think.

'You lunatic,' he muttered.

'Do not be rude to me,' she instructed. 'I could very easily push you in.'

'I would take you in with me,' he vowed.

For a moment, she was tempted. 'It might be worth it,' she mused, looking up at him.

'Oh, *please* do not!' And suddenly they were both choking back laughter.

'How you terrify me,' he said, grinning.

Their faces were very close together.

'You terrify me,' he said again, in quite a different voice.

Carefully, she slid one arm away from where it was clutching his shoulder.

He hastily pulled her closer as she teetered. 'What are you—'

'Don't move,' she whispered, reaching up to take his face in her hands. They were both trembling, she noticed, as she drew him closer still. He met her upturned face halfway, his lips touching hers with a carefulness that lasted one gentle instant – but by the next, without quite knowing how it had happened, her hands were in his hair and both his were clutching her waist, and – *goodness*, it felt so very different to the kiss they had shared in Waldo's study. There was less shock and more purpose, and without any person to interrupt them it could go on and on, and if they broke apart it was only to breathe and—

It took them almost falling a second time to break apart.

'We must get to dry land,' Ashford insisted, 'before anyone finds us.'

Their exit was not elegant – a lurching, graceless process that twice almost resulted in total submersion – and they were still laughing as they made their way through the maze again.

'We have been gone scandalously long,' Ashford mused, peering at the sky. 'Will your aunt suspect I have ruined you?'

'More likely that I have murdered you.'

He threw her a laughing glance. 'You would surely not risk such a thing, with Mr Hanworth on hand to catch you?'

Smiling, Lydia captured his hand in her own and tried to pull him towards her again. He resisted.

'Lydia . . .'

'No one is here.'

'We are too close to the house . . . one must consider your reputation.'

'Must one?' she cajoled.

'It is a matter of *honour*—'

'Oh, please do not start speaking of your honour again, it has got us into enough difficulty already.'

'What difficulty?' Ashford began to laugh again. 'Dear lord, can we not cease arguing for a minute? Even now?'

She shook her head, smile fading. He was not wrong. 'We are astonishingly ill-suited, aren't we?'

He tilted his head this side and that, not looking as if he particularly cared.

'This may well be a disaster,' she told him.

'I know,' he said, and she liked that he did not try to dispute it.

'I – I still do not know if I want the rest of it,' she said. 'Lady Ashford – the duchess – I do not know.'

'Neither do I,' he admitted.

'Does that not concern you?' she said, biting her lip. 'Ought we not be more certain about it all?'

'I am certain about *you*,' Ashford said. 'The rest . . . I do not know. Perhaps for now, we might just consider tonight?'

Lydia liked the sound of that. 'And then . . .?'

'Tomorrow,' he said promptly.

Lydia began to smile again. 'And then the day after, I suppose?'

'And then together we work out the rest, just the same as that.'

Finally, a proposal she wished to accept.

'Together,' she agreed.

Acknowledgements

Many thanks, as ever, go to my exceptional editors, Martha Ashby and Julia McDowell. They leapt into this book back when it was a document of only loosely related words and, with such kindness and humour, helped me chisel out a novel from the chaos. Thank you also to Maddy, Rachel and everyone at the MM Agency, for all your support and enthusiasm.

Handing in the manuscript is where (broadly) my work ends, but for the rest of the team, the hard work is only beginning, so big thanks must go to Lynne Drew, Jennifer Lambert, Katelyn Wood, Belinda Toor, Sian Richefond, Philippa Cotton and Sophie Waeland, for everything they and everyone at HarperCollins do to get this book out of my laptop and onto shelves.

As I write this, I am thousands of miles away from all (bar one) of the most important people in my life, and nothing else could more clarify quite how important you truly are to me. So please accept my thanks for the following services provided over the 1.5 years it took to write this book: for discussing the plot when I needed it, for not discussing it when I needed that, for persistently recommending my books to everybody you meet, and for putting up with my matted hair on deadline week (no time!!). Thank you for listening to 8-minute-long voice notes and sending your own, for admiring my dog pictures and supporting me through my kombucha phase. Thank you for our cold swim mornings, long afternoon chats about writing (so much better than actually writing anything), and for Swiftaggedon. Thank you for driving me places even though technically I am licensed to do this, for enduring all my obsessions, and for helping me repaint my room. You're the best.

Lastly and in fact, mostly, to any reader who has managed to get to this bit: thank you to YOU for reading it! Come and say hello if you have a moment, I would so love to hear from you.

If you enjoyed *How to Lose a Lord in Ten Days*, turn the page for an extract from Sophie Irwin's *Sunday Times* bestselling novel, *A Lady's Guide to Fortune-Hunting* . . .

Available now

1

Netley Cottage, Biddington, Dorsetshire, 1818

'You're *not* going to marry me?' Miss Talbot repeated, disbelievingly.

'Afraid not,' Mr Charles Linfield replied, his expression set in a kind of bracingly apologetic grimace – the sort one might wear when confessing you could no longer attend a friend's birthday party, rather than ending a two-year engagement.

Kitty stared at him, uncomprehending. Katherine Talbot – Kitty to her family and closest acquaintances – was not much used to incomprehension. In fact, she was well known amongst her family and Biddington at large for her quick mind and talent for practical problem-solving. Yet in this moment, Kitty felt quite at a loss. She and Charles were to be married. She had known it for years – and it was now not to be? What should one say, what should one feel, in the face of such news? Everything was changed. And yet Charles still *looked* the same, dressed in clothes she had seen him in a thousand times before, with that dishevelled style only the wealthy could get away with: an intricately embroidered waistcoat that was badly misbuttoned, a garishly bright cravat that had been mangled rather than tied. He ought at least, Kitty thought, staring at that awful cravat with a rising sense of indignation, to have dressed for the occasion.

Some of this ire must have seeped through to her expression, because all at once Charles swapped his maddening air of apologetic condescension for that of a sulky schoolboy.

'Oh, you needn't look at me like that,' he snapped. 'It isn't as if we were ever *officially* promised to one another.'

'Officially promised to one another?' Kitty's spirit returned to her in full force, and she discovered, in fact, that she felt quite furious. The irredeemable cad. 'We've been speaking of marriage for the past two years. We were only delayed this long because of my mother's death and my father's sickness! You *promised* me – you promised me so many things.'

'Just the talk of children,' he protested, before adding mulishly, 'and besides, it isn't as if I could call things off when your father was on death's door. Wouldn't have been at all the thing.'

'Oh, and I suppose now that he's dead – not a month in the ground – you could finally jilt me?' she said wrathfully. 'Is that really so much more "the thing"?'

He ran a hand through his hair, his eyes flicking to the door.

'Listen, there's no point us discussing it when you're like this.' He affected the tone of a severely tried man holding onto his patience. 'Perhaps I should go.'

'Go? You can't possibly drop news such as this, and not explain yourself. I saw you just last week and we were discussing marrying in May – not three months away.'

'Perhaps I should have just written a letter,' he said to himself, still staring longingly at the door. 'Mary said this was the best way to do it, but I think a letter would have been simpler. I can't think properly with you shrieking at me.'

Kitty cast aside her many irritations and, with the instincts of a true hunter, fixed only on the salient information.

'Mary?' she said sharply. 'Mary Spencer? What, exactly, does Miss Spencer have to do with this? I had not realised she had returned to Biddington.'

'Ah, yes, yes, well, she is, that is,' Mr Linfield stammered, beads of sweat appearing on his brow. 'My mother invited her to stay with us, for a time. It being so good for my sisters to make other female acquaintances.'

'And you spoke to Miss Spencer about bringing our engagement to an end?'

'Ah, yes, well she was so sympathetic to the situation – to *both* our situations – and I must say it was good to be able . . . to speak to someone about it.'

Silence, for a moment. And then, almost casually, 'Mr Linfield, do you mean to propose to Miss Spencer?'

'No! Well, that is to say – we already . . . So, I thought best to – to come here . . .'

'I see,' Kitty said – and she did. 'Well, I suppose I must commend you upon your confidence, Mr Linfield. It is quite the feat to propose to one woman whilst already being engaged to another. Bravo, indeed.'

'This is exactly what you always do!' Mr Linfield complained, mustering some courage at last. 'You twist everything around until one doesn't know which way is up. Have you thought perhaps that I wanted to spare your feelings? That I didn't want to have to tell you the truth – that if I want to make a career for myself in politics, I can hardly do it married to someone like *you*.'

His derisive tone shocked her. 'And what exactly is that supposed to mean?' she demanded.

He spread his arms, as if inviting her to look around. Kitty did not. She knew what she would see, for she had stood in this room every day of her life: the worn chaises huddled by the fireplace for warmth, the once elegant rug on the hearth now moth-eaten and shabby, shelves where there had once been books now standing empty.

'We may live in the same town, but we're from different *worlds*.' He waved his hands about again. 'I'm the son of the squire! And Mama and Miss Spencer helped me to see that I cannot afford to make a *mésalliance* if I am to make a name for myself.'

Kitty had never been so aware of the sound of her heartbeat, pounding a drum loudly in her ears. A *mésalliance*, was she?

'Mr Linfield,' she said, softly but with bite. 'Let there be no lies between us. You had no issue with our engagement until you encountered the pretty Miss Spencer again. A squire's son, you say! This is not the sort of ungentlemanly conduct I would have expected your family to condone. Perhaps I ought to be pleased that you have proven yourself to be so utterly dishonourable before it was too late.'

She landed each blow with the precision and force of Gentleman Jackson, and Charles – Mr Linfield forever, now – staggered backwards from her.

'How could you say such a thing?' he asked, aghast, 'It is not *ungentlemanly*. You're becoming quite hysterical.' Mr Linfield was sweating thickly now, twisting uncomfortably. 'I do want us to remain great friends, you have to understand Kit—'

'*Miss Talbot*,' she corrected with frigid politeness. A shriek of rage was howling through her body, but she contained it, gesturing sharply to the door with a wave of her hand. 'You'll forgive me if I ask you to see yourself out, Mr Linfield.'

After a quick bob of a bow, he fled eagerly from her, without looking back.

Kitty stood motionless for a moment, holding her breath as if to prevent this disaster from unfolding any further. Then she walked to the window, where the morning sun was streaming in, leant her forehead against the glass, and exhaled slowly. From this window, one had an uninterrupted view of the garden: the daffodils just beginning to flower, the vegetable patch, still thick with weeds, and the loose chickens picking their way through, looking for grubs. Life outside continued on, and yet on her side of the glass, everything was utterly ruined.

They were alone. Completely and utterly alone now, with no one to turn to. Mama and Papa were gone, and in this hour of most grievous need, where more than ever she wished to ask for their advice, she could not. There was simply no one left to whom she could turn. Panic was rising within her. What was she to do now?

She might have stayed in this position for several hours, were she not interrupted by her youngest sister, ten-year-old Jane, who barged in only a few minutes later with the self-importance of a royal messenger.

'Kitty, *where* is Cecily's book?' she demanded.

'It was in the kitchen yesterday,' Kitty answered without looking away from the garden. They ought to weed the artichoke bed this afternoon, it would need planting before long. Distantly, she heard Jane call to Cecily to pass on her words.

'She's looked there,' came the reply.

'Well, look again.' Kitty dismissed her impatiently with a flap of a hand.

The door opened and closed with a bang. 'She says it's not there and if you've sold it, she'll be very upset because it was a gift from the vicar.'

'Oh, for goodness' sake,' Kitty snapped, 'you may tell Cecily that I can't look for her silly vicar book, because I have just been jilted and need a few moments' reprieve, if that is not too much to ask!'

No sooner had Jane relayed this unusual message to Cecily, than the full household – all of Kitty's four sisters and Bramble the dog – descended upon the parlour, instantly filling the space with noise.

'Kitty, what is this about Mr Linfield jilting you? Has he really?'

'I never liked him, he used to pat me on the head as if I were a child.'

'My book is *not* in the kitchen.'

Kitty told them as briefly as she could what had happened, with her head still resting on the glass. There was silence after this, as Kitty's sisters stared uncertainly at each other. After a few moments, Jane – having grown bored – wandered over to the creaking pianoforte and broke the silence by bashing out a jolly tune. Jane had never received music lessons, but what she lacked in talent she made up for in both fervour and volume.

'How awful,' Beatrice – at nineteen years, Kitty's closest sister in both age and temperament – said at last, appalled. 'Oh, Kitty dear, I am sorry. You must be heartbroken.'

Kitty turned her head sharply. 'Heartbroken? Beatrice, that is quite beside the point. Without my marrying Mr Linfield, we are all ruined. Papa and Mama may have left us the house, but they also left an astonishing amount of debt. I was depending on the Linfield wealth to save us.'

'You were marrying Mr Linfield for his *fortune*?' Cecily asked, a judgemental note in her voice. The intellectual of the family at eighteen years of age, Cecily was felt by her sisters to have a rather over-developed sense of morality.

'Well, it was certainly not for his integrity or gentlemanly honour,' Kitty said bitterly. 'I just wish I'd had the sense to wrap it up sooner. We should not have pushed back the wedding when Mama died, I knew that a long engagement was asking for trouble. To think that Papa thought it would look unseemly!'

'How bad is it, Kitty?' Beatrice asked. Kitty stared silently at her for a few moments. How could she tell them? How could she explain all that was about to happen?

'It is . . . serious,' Kitty said carefully. 'Papa re-mortgaged the house to some quite disreputable people. The sales I made – our books, the silverware, some of Mama's jewels – were enough to keep them at bay for a while, but on the first of June they will return. Not four months away. And if we do not have enough money, or proof that we can start paying them, then . . .'

'. . . We will have to leave? But this is our home.' Harriet's lip wobbled. As second youngest, she yet remained more sensitive than Jane, who had at least stopped playing to sit quietly on the stool, watching.

Kitty did not have the heart to tell them that it would be worse than just leaving. That the sale of Netley Cottage would barely cover their debts, with nothing left after to support them. With nowhere to go and no obvious means of income, the future would be a dark place. They would have no choice but to split up, of course. She and Beatrice might find some employment in Salisbury, or one of the larger towns nearby, perhaps as housemaids – or lady's maids if they were truly lucky. Cecily – well, Kitty could not imagine Cecily being willing or able to work for anyone – but with her education she might try a school. Harriet – oh, Harriet was so young – would have to do the same. Somewhere that would provide room and board. And Jane . . . Mrs Palmer in the town, singularly mean-spirited though she was, had always had a sort of fondness for Jane. She might be persuaded to take her in until she was old enough to find employment, too.

Kitty imagined them all, her sisters, separated and cast to the wind. Would they ever be together again, as they were now? And what if it was far worse than this already-bleak scenario? Visions of each of them, alone, hungry and despairing, flashed before her eyes. Kitty had not yet wept a tear over Mr Linfield – he was not worth her tears – but now her throat ached painfully. They had already lost so much. It had been Kitty who had had to explain to them that Mama was not going to get better. Kitty who had broken the news of Papa's passing. How was she now to explain that the worst was still to come? She could not find the words. Kitty was not their mother, who could pull reassurances from the air like magic, nor their father, who could always say things would be all right with a confidence that made you believe him. No, Kitty was the family's problem solver – but this was far too great an obstacle for her to overcome with will alone. She wished desperately that there was someone who might carry this burden with her, a heavy load for the tender age of twenty, but there was not. Her sisters' faces stared up at her, so sure even now that she would be able to fix everything. As she always had.

As she always *would*.

The time for despair had passed. She would not – could not – be defeated so easily. She swallowed down her tears and set her shoulders.

'We have more than four months until the first of June,' Kitty said firmly, moving away from the window. 'That is just enough time, I believe, for us to achieve something quite extraordinary. In a town such as Biddington, I was able to ensnare a rich fiancé. Though he turned out to be a weasel, there is no reason to believe the exercise cannot be repeated, simply enough.'

'I do not think any other rich men live nearby,' Beatrice pointed out.

'Just so!' her sister replied cheerfully, eyes unnaturally bright. 'Which is why I must travel to more fruitful ground. Beatrice, consider yourself in charge – for I shall be leaving for London.'